I0691871

The *Devil's*
CARETAKER

Also by G.M.S. Altman

Fiction

Hoodie

Dippel's Oil

ൟൟ

Non-Fiction

Beethoven: a Man of His Word

Fatal Links: The Curious Deaths of Beethoven and the Two Napoleons

The *Devil's*
CARETAKER

a novel

Book One in the Story
of David Fouraker

G.M.S. Altman

Helenenthal Books

This is a work of fiction. Names, characters, places and incidents are products of the author's imagination or are used fictitiously. Any resemblance to actual events, locales or persons, living or dead, is entirely coincidental.

THE DEVIL'S CARETAKER © 2010 by GMS Altman. All rights reserved. Printed in the United States of America. No part of this book may be used or reproduced in any manner whatsoever without the written permission of the publisher except in cases of brief quotations embodied in critical articles and reviews. For more information, address inquiries to Helenenthal Books, 4191 Bradfordville Road, Tallahassee, FL 32309-6401. The author may be contacted via email at GMSAltman@gmail.com.

FIRST EDITION

10 9 8 7 6 5 4 3 2 1

ISBN-10: 1-888-071-10-9
ISBN-13: 978-1-888-071-10-8

With Special Thanks...
to Book Designer Extraordinaire and Technical Wizard, Greg Coad, for his help and expertise.

For my son, Eric,
with Love and Thanks
for teaching me how a
young man thinks.

Casa de Almas
Wakulla County, Florida
July 21_____

They left me my eyes.

I'm not sure why, but I have a guess. Maybe the answer's obvious to you: there's something they want me to see. Something really bad, I imagine, because where would be the fun in showing me anything else, like something *good*? And they do like their fun. They're regular laugh-riots, they are. Of course, you could only appreciate their humor if you took comedic pleasure from "Saw" or some other gore-flick.

The time I have left now (which may not be much at all) is spent in contemplation — erratic though my thought processes may be at this point — and one of my favorite topics is why they do what they do. And I know right now you don't have a clue as to who *They* are, but you will. Trust me on this one. You will. If I get the time to tell you, that is. All I can say right now is that they're really really bad things. But you probably already guessed that much, right?

This *contemplation* business, of course, also means they've left me my brain, which makes perfect sense if you think about it. What good are eyes to see with if they can't process what they're seeing? Gotta have the old gray matter for that. Besides, what fun would I be if I no longer had a mind that allowed me to feel? I'd be about as entertaining as a worn-out mop, I imagine.

So, leaving me my brain was also part of their plan. See, I've come to the conclusion that one reason they do what they do is because they enjoy cruel jokes. I can feel them snickering over my predicament.

Only goodness laughs out loud. Evil snickers.

Now if they'd left me a hand to write with I could have recorded that gleaming bit of insight. Too late for that, though. Hand all gone. So long. Bye bye. Knowing them as I do (and I *do* know them somewhat whether they like it or not—that's what leaving me a functioning brain will do) even if they'd left me a hand they would have deprived me of paper, a pencil, maybe even my opposable thumb. I guess they didn't think of that little cruelty. I hope they can read my mind and are saying, "Aw shit!" right about now. Ha ha, missed opportunity there, guys. Joke's on you this time.

I don't seem to have functioning eye lids so it's a wonder my eyeballs haven't shriveled up like two little prunes by now. It must be part of their power to control little things like that. Don't ask me how. No insights on that one, no matter how much I contemplate.

I don't know the why of my eyes yet, either. What do they want me to see?

I suspect they want to flex some muscle, impress me with their ability to draw in more victims. They want me to watch while they do to others what they did to me.

Is that it, guys? Need some more ego-strokes? Need to preen your feathers in front of the mirrors of my eyes?

No, wait!

It's so quiet out here that I didn't realize what else they'd left me.

My ears. Or at lest a vestige of an ear. Didn't do so well in biology when I was in high school so not sure what exactly they left. The cochlea, is that a part? Hammer and anvil? Ear drum, for sure. Doesn't matter. What does matter is that I hear something.

Think now, use the brain they left you. What's that *sound*?

It's a rumble, like distant thunder, but I know it isn't that. It's too steady, too continuous. Thunder comes and goes. This just comes and comes and comes.

Not too close yet, but it sounds big. Something with an engine, yes. Nothing natural. Mechanical. Definitely a motor. Too much bass in it to be a car or even a pickup truck.

Okay, so use your brain and contemplate.

My brain still has its memories, and one of the last of those was of me going on a rampage.

What was I swinging, an axe?

Yes. An axe.

Big old *mother* of an axe. Not a hand axe, but one of those mean jobbies like Phil Bunyan would've swung. The kind that brought down trees, chop, chop. Just like that.

I remember going crazy with that axe, at least until all my energy drained out of me like bath water out of a tub. *Slurk*—swirled right on down the old drain hole.

My bad. Should've hit and run, but didn't.

Okay, stop. Too late for thoughts like that. Blame is useless now. No time for shoulda, woulda, coulda.

How much damage did I do with that mother of an axe? Enough? Now that I couldn't remember. How much was enough, anyway? I'd done other damage, too, as I remembered, set off some bombs, some big mothers, too. Boom boom, blasted the hell out of the house (no pun intended). The house around me was pretty much in shambles. I did that. Me. I could feel good about that, at least.

But if they have the power to keep lidless eyeballs from becoming prunes, can they repair damage like what I did?

Dunno.

Time will tell, though. Time will tell.

Okay, so where was I? That's the trouble with contemplation: the old brain cells tend to meander. Oh, yeah, that sound. Get back to that heavy equipment heading my way.

For moving or demolition, that is the question.

Not to be or not to be, my fine Danish friend. Not this time. MOVE or DEMOLISH, that is the question.

Did they leave me my eyes so I could see destruction heading my way? My ears so that I'd hear it long before it arrived and thus prolong my suffering? Maybe. I can almost hear them snickering.

Did they think this would be the ultimate joke?

Maybe yes, maybe no. I think *yes*.

Can they hear me? Hear my thoughts?

I think yes on that one, too. Oh, I hope so.

Because I want them to hear me laugh out loud. (Only in my head, my thoughts, of course. Mouth, lips, vocal cords, gone, I think, at least not usable—adios, so-long, bye bye.) Jokes on you this time, guys. Definitely on you.

Me, afraid of the demolition crew?

Hell, they're my salvation! Saviors in hard hats. Bring it on! Swing that wrecking ball! Bite down with the crane's jaws! Ram with the bulldozer! Hallelujah, Jesus, Lord Almighty and all that! Yeah!

Of course, if the equipment was here to move the wreckage and not destroy it completely, then the joke *will* be on me, won't it? All that ranting and raving and rampaging for nothing. I would've have pitted my puny self against *Them*, dared to try to thwart their quest, gone on the ultimate ego trip—all for naught. That's still possible, I suppose.

At least I can say I tried.

Can't take that away from me, guys. No matter what. I may have only won a small victory, but I consider it a triumph, anyway, considering what I was up against. Wish now you'd left me a thumb and a nose. I would've put them to good use this very moment. I surely would have.

How long before the machinery gets here? Before I know? No telling. Minutes, maybe. Not too long to wait, but it feels like an eternity.

I'll know before too long, I guess.

Moving or demolition?

Please God—if there is a God, and if that God can still hear the prayer of the wretch I've become—make it demolition.

Destruction.

Please.

Wakulla County, Florida
Four Months Earlier
March 9_____

It was just a stupid little mistake.

You wouldn't think that things like that, that seem so inconsequential at the time, could have far-reaching effects, but they do. Your whole life can change course and go belly up because of one little mistake, one misstep, one wrong turn, one little slip, one tiny cosmic hiccup. Make a wrong choice, a bad decision, and it will come back to bite you. Hard. Then you look back and think, if only — If only I'd done that instead of this, been less hasty, chosen door number two instead of one or three, been more wise, taken time to think. Ah, but by then it's too late for do-overs. It's always too late. You know what they say about hindsight being 20/20. It's a bitch to admit it, but it's true.

At the time I made my stupid little mistake it seemed like the consequences wouldn't be more than a pain in the ass. An inconvenience. Not a life-altering event. They never seem that important when they happen, those mistakes, do they? Why don't we have more forethought and less hindsight? Was that God's little mistake? Who knows? All we do know is that we don't and that's a bitch, too.

My little mistake was not helping one of my best buds, Stanley Meldon, celebrate his 21st birthday, but it is related to that.

No one has called Stanley Meldon anything but Whippet as long as I can remember and I've known old Whip since middle school. Everything about him was sharp and lanky, from legs and knees to arms and elbows, all thin and jutting, to a nose like a pointer and a narrow, intense face. (I'm pretty thin myself—maybe two steps away from scrawny—but I'm freakin' Mr. Universe compared to Stanley Meldon. It's a wonder some dog hasn't tried to bury him.) He reminded us all of a greyhound, only back in middle school, before he had his major growth spurt that would shoot him up into the stratosphere and make basketball coaches in six counties salivate, he was a small greyhound.

The brainiac of our group, Parker Rodriguez, said a small greyhound was really a whippet, and don't you know we grabbed onto that ball and ran with it! Just like that, Stanley Meldon was no more; Whippet was born.

(Parker, of course, never had a nickname because brainy kids almost never got them and I never heard anyone ever call him Park, either. When I got older, I sometimes wondered whether kids like Parker ever felt bad about that—as if no one ever liked them well enough to give them a stupid nickname.)

People liked me, though. Real name, David Fouraker. Only no one has called me David since I was twelve—with the exception of my girlfriend, Theresa, who will resort to my legal name in a pique of ire, as the saying goes. All my friends call me Fresco, in homage to that carbonated soda, Fresca, which has been my non-alcoholic drink of choice for as long as I can remember. Don't ask me why I developed a penchant for what amounts to bubbly grapefruit juice. As a kid, I guess I thought it was just weird enough, just edgy enough to make me seem cool without having to do something truly radical. I wanted to be different, just like everyone else, yet I wasn't into weed (which just makes you stupid and if you don't believe that you probably smoke too much of it), or having an extra eyeball tattooed on my forehead, or anything *really* weird.

Anyway, I had been right — drinking Fresca when everyone else was into Pepsi or Coke or whatever was just weird enough. In my later high school years I also discovered that Fresca was the perfect mixer for rum, vodka and gin, so if you've got a can of Fresca in your hand, you're basically a party waiting to happen no matter what your host has stocked in his bar. (Unless he's pals with Captain Morgan and his spiced rum. With that you gotta go with a Coke. Trust me on that one.)

Whippet and I both graduated from Columbia High in Lake City, and then decided to spend another four years in college because we figured that the academic life beat the job market or the military by a country mile. Whip actually was determined to become an English teacher which for a time I tried to discourage mainly because I thought his physique would get him into trouble with his students. Stick one of those little wiggy things on his head, I thought, and you've got Ichabod Crane incarnate. But as I got to thinking about it — especially remembering most of my classmates—I realized that most kids probably have never even heard of Washington Irving or Sleepy Hollow unless they were major Johnny Depp fans and that Whip would probably be safe in his role as teacher. (I, in case you're wondering, am a closet reader. I do not let that be widely known because in my crowd reading for pleasure is definitely uncool. But I do enjoy a good read, that's a fact.)

As for me, I was clueless as to what I wanted to do career-wise. I had enough trouble planning my next weekend let alone the rest of my life. When I absolutely had to declare a major, I chose PSYCHOLOGY—mainly because most of the professors were a little nutty themselves and the classes (especially in abnormal psychology—boy, are there loads of crazy people out there!) were a helluva lot more interesting than, say, business. You want to compare the study of accounting practices to cases like the woman who believed there were Nazi soldiers armed with alligators hiding in her oak trees? Puh-leese.

As to choice of schools, that was a no-brainer. At the time, Florida State University was proclaimed the party school in the country. Whip and I sent off our applications the day after the media broke that story. I mean, if you're an 18-year-old guy with no real commitment to getting an education, where else would you go? (Naturally we made up bullshit for our parents, like how it was only 100 or so miles away from home and how we would qualify for instate tuition, and how it had impressive degree programs and all that crap. Parents do not want to send their kids to a bona fide party school, although most probably do anyway, in the end.) Like I said, going to FSU was a no-brainer.

Of course, by the time we were accepted and began to attend classes there, the horrified administration at FSU had already taken steps to crack down on the students' partying habits in order to "restore the university's academic image." Hell, the Party School image was a hit with me and Whip and probably 20,000 other students there, and why you would want to give up a coveted title like that is beyond me to this day. I guess that's something only those with years and years of practice being adults can really understand.

All was not lost, though. Whip and I ended up on a dorm floor with an RA (resident assistant who is supposed to enforce the rules but if you're lucky he won't even know what the rules are) who never took his job too seriously. For one thing, he never even sniffed my cans of Fresca—I have to give him credit for that—even when it was obvious that my grapefruits had done quite a bit of fermenting since I popped the tab. Across the hall from Whip and me we had good old Parker, also from our alma mater Columbia High, although he was still uncool enough to have to be assigned a roommate. Parker attained marginal coolness by virtue of being paired with a very cool roommate, Joseph Moultrie, a black dude and pre-med student from Tampa who could spin rap lyrics sweet enough to make Lil Wayne weep, I kid you not. (Roll call would make his name Moultrie, Joseph which led easily to him becoming Mojo.)

The four of us became pretty tight, although we sometimes included four other guys on our wing: two bully boys there on a football scholarship, Tom Wicke (who we called Wicky Persnicky, but not to his face), and D'Ante Jefferson (aka DJ, nothing ingenious about that one). Neither were dummies, exactly, but then again neither was exceptionally bright, either. However, on a campus, in a city, in a county, hell in a state that bleeds team colors, what really matters is what happens on a field of grass, not in a field of study. The other two, Johnny Chang and Gabe LaCroix, were bright enough but their real talent was when it came to the par-tay.

(Don't believe everything you hear about how Orientals are so committed to education. Johnny's family had been in the US since the California gold rush and that particular ethic had been pretty well bred out of his genes by now.)

Chang and LaCroix came up from Wakulla County down on the coast, some thirty miles south of the university. Gabe's Uncle Pete owned a fish camp down there on the Sopchoppy River that emptied into the Ochlocknee and finally into the bay. We were often invited down to the fish camp to partake of some good old southern hospitality. Pete LaForge didn't think much of the legal drinking age—"If you're old enough to spill yer blood in Iraq, you oughta be old enough to spill yer beer in a bar."—and if he'd ever been elected to office during one of the dozen times or so that he ran, he probably would've lobbied to lower the age to 16 (only because he probably didn't think anyone would go for lowering it to 12). Uncle Pete, who we of the under-age crowd thought was the coolest dude on the planet, would bring in a kegger or two and invite all his old best friends: Captain Morgan, Jack

Daniels, even Old Granddad and a couple of Wild Turkeys, and we'd have one helluva a par-tay. The fish camp smelled like the Devil himself had taken a dump there, but if you hung around with the old boys long enough, after a while you either didn't notice it any more or didn't care.

Needless to say, Uncle Pete was the main reason we cultivated a friendship with the Chang-LaCroix duo, one we maintained up through our junior year. Was that also a small mistake on my part? Maybe yes, maybe no, but I'm leaning toward yes. Had I let that friendship lapse, I would not have been at the fish camp on the night of March 10 and then (maybe) I wouldn't have made the other stupid little mistake that ended up having such dire consequences.

Uncle Pete's Fish Camp
March 10_____

Okay, so I was getting to my little mistake with the huge consequences that went down on Whippet's 21st, his official License to Drink Legally Day. What better place to celebrate, Gabe LaCroix said to us, than the place where we'd spent so many happy hours in illegal drunken stupors courtesy of Uncle Pete? Oh, yeah, I'd neglected to mention that Uncle Pete had named his fish camp "The Waterin Hole" which was one of those inside jokes that everyone seems to know. Although you certainly could get whatever you needed for a day on the water—boat rental, ice, bait, tackle, whatever—you also could get water that was more often 75 proof than not. Fire water, you might say. Gabe hinted around that Uncle Pete might be sorely offended if he were to be excluded from these momentous festivities and the last thing you wanted to do, drunk or sober, was to get on Pete's bad side. (He had a reputation around Wakulla County as being one bad mother, and though we mostly saw his more jovial side it wasn't hard to believe that he could be a hard ass when he wanted to be.) Of course we would celebrate Whippet's coming of age at the fish camp! Perish the thought that we might go to Hooter's instead! Why even *consider* tits and ass over fish guts and the devil's farts? The Waterin Hole was the only place for this par-tay.

So anyway, by late Saturday afternoon we were all down at the Waterin Hole gearing up for one high-octane celebration. I had driven my white Chevy Silverado with Mojo in shotgun and Whippet, our guest of honor, sprawled in the back. (Parker declined our invitation—no surprise there.) The bully boys were in Wicky's dark green Ram and the Chang-LaCroix duo was in Johnny's low-riding red Honda with the spoiler, pimped out with a bunch of Chinese hieroglyphs and dragons and other shit all over it. I figure that was an Asian thing, making up your rod like that. (Mostly if you're young, male, and living in the south, you're gonna be driving a truck, but street rods will get by—anything else and your peers are going to be riding your ass about what a queer mother you are for having such a lame ride.)

Although Johnny and one of the bully boys weren't legal yet, I had turned 21 in February and Mojo and LaCroix some time before that. So instead of relying on Uncle Pete's largesse this time, we showed up at the fish camp with a 25-gallon keg from Mike's Beer Barn and a few cases of good old hooch. Uncle Pete was so surprised, I swear for a minute I thought he was going to flat out cry, but the moment of sentiment passed quickly as we all got down to some serious drinking, where the idea is to get to the point where you either throw up or pass out. (I can tell you that it's better, though less pleasant, to do the former because death becomes less of a risk, but most of the time you're too far gone to think about options.) Usually our par-tays would include the female element but when one of your own reaches that momentous 21 mark, womanly distractions are neither wanted nor needed. Like I said, we had some serious drinking to do. It was a male bonding thing, ladies not invited. They would've just told us we were disgusting and made us feel guilty later on and who needs that? It's a guy's idea of fun that girls just don't understand: the need to chug-a-lug, to burp, barf or fart with abandon, to make stupid unfunny jokes and laugh ourselves sick over them and possibly puke on our shoes.

Of course, if Theresa had been there, she might have prevented me from making my stupid little mistake. On the other hand, in my state of mind, I might have blown her off. We'll never know, will we, so no sense playing the what-if or shoulda woulda coulda game, is there?

Around ten p.m. we realized that we'd brought tons of booze but nothing to eat and the Waterin Hole only stocked snacks—inconsequential for a bunch of ravenous young guys—or bait—which none of us were yet drunk enough to consider. At that point, Whippet, none too steady on his feet, shoved a wad of crumpled bills into my hand. "That's money," he said as if he were imparting some major state secret. He stabbed at my fist holding the cash with his finger as if he wasn't sure I could find my hand without his help.

"Yeah. I recognize it," I told him. "What's it for?"

"Sus—susten—" He burped up some beer gas. "—nance. Food!"

"Why do *I* have to make a food run?"

"'Cause yer the soberest one."

"Am not."

"Are, too." He leaned forward until we were nose to nose. "Yer eyes arn even — glazzy."

Of course, Whip was so blitzed he probably wouldn't have noticed if my eyes had turned into marbles. I decided not to argue with him. Can't argue with a drunk. I know that first-hand. Besides, it seemed from a quick survey of the room that only Whippet and me were still standing and I didn't give old Whip more than a few more turns around the room before he was going down. "Thurs a Popeye's jus down the road. Woan take but ten minutes. Get a bucket. Or two." He held up three fingers. "Whatever."

I remembered seeing the Popeye's Fried Chicken place on our way in. I figured, what the hell, it's just a mile down the road. Besides, my stomach was rumbling pretty good and I wasn't keen on hitting the bait buckets.

Fifteen minutes later I was pulling out of Popeye's parking lot with a jumbo bucket of their 16-piece extra-crispy chicken and a bag of biscuits on the front seat putting out waves of the most delicious fumes outside of Hershey, Pennsylvania. I wanted to just tear into that bucket and scarf down that greasy breaded chicken like nobody's business, but I exercised restraint — just vowed to get back to the Waterin Hole in record time.

Between the alcohol and the chicken fumes, it's no wonder that my judgment was a tad off. Sure, I saw the headlights coming down the road, but they didn't seem that close, and the vehicle didn't seem to be going very fast, either. In fact, it seemed to my impaired brain that he was going about as fast as a turtle through molasses and hell if I wanted to wait for some slow-ass country driver (who was probably some 90-year-old farmer used to driving nothing faster than a hay wagon) to go by when the air inside my truck was thick with chicken and my stomach was turning flip-flops.

And there was my stupid little mistake.

I pulled out and the vehicle turned out to be a lot closer or going a lot faster than I'd thought because I heard its tires squeal as he hit his brakes to avoid hitting me. I lowered my window and waggled my fingers in what I hoped would seem like a conciliatory gesture, saying "My bad!" to no one in particular, not realizing (I guess) that he couldn't hear my apology (heartfelt though it was, I assure you).

An instant later came the most dreaded sight ever to appear in a driver's rear view mirror.

Red and blue flashing lights.

Of all the cars that might have come down that rinky-dink road outside of Sopchoppy, the one that I chose to cut off had to belong to a Wakulla County sheriff's deputy.

I muttered a few expletives-not-deleted as I pulled over on the shoulder and waited. I breathed into my cupped hand and sniffed. Though I didn't smell alcohol, that didn't mean anything. All I could smell at that point was my chicken which would have to stay hot a little while longer.

At that moment I contemplated what just about every driver who has ever been pulled over by cop contemplates: my options. Play dumb? Flat out lie? I knew that going on the offense with a member of a rural posse would get me nowhere, and only a chick can cry and get away with it. I decided to go for dumb. Of course, by then my heart had both alcohol and adrenalin pumping through it and it was like it had grown fists that were hammering against my ribcage.

I rolled down my window the rest of the way as a middle-aged deputy sauntered up to my truck in a dark uniform—green, blue, too dark to tell and besides the headlights of his cruiser were making him mostly into a silhouette—and a hat that made him look like one of the Royal Canadian Mounties. I watched him approach in my side-view mirror. They all have that same sort of weary saunter, don't they, a gait that says, damn, another law-breaker, another fool out to ruin my night by making me put my coffee in the cup holder, my donut on the dashboard and get out of my cozy car just to write one of these blasted tickets which will just mean more paperwork. It's a gait that says *I'm pissed off and you're gonna pay for it.*

I tried to give the deputy my goofiest, most embarrassed and bewildered aw-shucks sort of grin as he leaned down to talk to me. It was night so he wasn't wearing one of those weird mirrored sunglasses that cops of legend wear. I could see his eyes clear enough in the glare of the headlights behind us, and as soon as he leaned down, I saw them squint and his face sort of pucker as if he'd taken in a bad smell. I figured it wasn't the chicken. "Is there a problem, sir?" I asked politely, trying not to breathe while I spoke. Could he smell more than Fresca on my breath, on my clothes? Who knew?

"Bit reckless there, son," he remarked in a drawl that put his birthplace farther north in the deep south (I know that sounds weird, but from Florida with its abundance of northern retirees, you really have to head north to get back to the real south)—somewhere around Alabama, maybe.

I pointed to my Popeye's stash on my seat. "Sorry, sir. Didn't want the chicken to get cold, you know?" I was going to add And I didn't know you were going so fast but managed to make my mouth shut up before I could seriously incriminate myself.

He looked over at the box of chicken and nodded. "Been drinking, have you, son?"

Dumb and goofy didn't seem to be getting me anywhere. I decided to lie in the most earnest way I knew how, although doing so made the sweat pop out on my forehead and on the back of my neck. I was glad it was probably too dark for him to see how slick my face had gotten. "No, sir, sure haven't. Just ran out to get some food for—" and I almost said something stupid like "the little woman" when my brain briefly hitched into gear and I said instead, "—me and my friends—" and then my brain stalled completely, and I added for no good reason, "staying over at Pete LaCroix's Waterin Hole."

He nodded again and I just knew immediately that had been a mistake. Never never never offer up information. He didn't need to know I knew Pete LaCroix. Pete LaCroix wasn't the sort you'd want as a damned character witness. Not a man who most folks in Wakulla County knew thought it would be okay to have Jack Daniels on the menu at Sopchoppy Elementary School.

The deputy went through the usual routine—asking for my license and proof of insurance and registration—and I actually started to hope that he might just let me take my chicken and biscuits and go on my merry way.

It's possible that alcohol and chicken fumes make you delusional.

Wakulla County Detention Center
March 11_____

If you ever want to know the definition of surreal, get yourself pulled over in the middle of the night on a DUI. My whole evening turned out to be one big Salvador Dali nightmare and if my wrist watch had melted, I wouldn't have even been surprised. Maybe if I had been a lot drunker than I was, I wouldn't have felt so freaked out about being slapped into handcuffs (as if I were some bank robber or something), read my rights, and shoved into the back of the cruiser where there isn't enough leg room for a munchkin. One minute I was having fun with my buddies at the Waterin Hole and the next I was sitting in a holding cell contemplating my fate, not to mention missing the end of one helluva par-tay.

It must have been a slow night in Wakulla County because there was only one other guy in the cell with me and he was snoring like a boar with a sinus condition. I lay on my bunk and tried to get some sleep, but my brain was squirming like one of Uncle Pete's worm buckets. No one could rescue me until morning, and insomnia made for one helluva long night. I stared up at the ceiling, counting the holes in the acoustical tiles—which was easy to do, given that they never turn out the lights—and wished I had a couple of giant gin and Frescas to help me sleep.

My first thought when I realized I would be given the opportunity to make a phone call was to reach out to one of my good buddies at the Waterin Hole. It reminded me of a saying that went A good friend will bail you out of jail; a great friend will be sitting in jail with you saying, *Wasn't that a helluva a night?* At the moment, all I hoped for was at least one good friend. However, I soon quashed the notion of calling Whippet or Mojo, or one of the bully boys. No one at the Waterin Hole would be sober enough to even remember who I was, let alone be able to negotiate posting bond. Besides, we'd already shot all our wads on alcohol (and Popeye's chicken which was by now slowly rotting on the front seat of my Chevy as it sat in the impound lot). What I needed was someone with cash. Someone with plastic.

Who else has something like that except...your parents?

Now I didn't want to call my parents, especially to tell them I'd been arrested and was facing DUI charges, but I couldn't very well sit in the Wakulla County Detention Center until my hearing came up, so I swallowed my apprehensions and made the call as soon as a deputy escorted me to a telephone. The phone was on a desk used by a guard assigned to watch us dangerous felons; the sergeant at that desk asked me for the number. Obviously I was too untrustworthy to be allowed near the push buttons.

He dialed and handed me the receiver. As I listened to the phone ringing on the other end, I started silently repeating my mantra: "Pick up, Mom. Pick up, Mom."

Of course it was my Dad who answered the phone. It doesn't matter if your mother answers the phone ninety-nine percent of the time, if you're calling to tell your parents about a stupid mistake you've made, your dad is going to be the one who answers your call.

I tried to make my voice sound as cheery as possible, although every parent knows that if their kid calls late at night—and by now it was close to midnight—they're not going to hear that the kid just made the dean's list.

"What's going on, Dave?" my dad asked. Dad never calls me Fresco; he believes *Dave* has a good masculine sound to it, and that his son needs all the help in that department that he can get. In the background, I could hear my mother. I wondered if I'd woken them up. I pictured her there in bed, hand clasped to her chest as if she were trying to ward off a heart attack.

"Is that David? What's wrong? Is he all right? What's happened?"

Mothers always assume the worst. That's because phone calls almost always herald the worst especially when you have children. I heard my dad gently shush her.

"I've had a little mishap, Dad," I said, hoping he still could hear me with his attention momentarily diverted to my mother.

"Did you have an accident?"

"David had an accident? Oh my god, is he all right?" My mother again with another assumption. Never mind that I was on the phone, she believed I was probably on the phone in traction, in a body cast, with someone else holding the receiver because I'd been rendered a quadriplegic.

"No, Dad, listen. The truck is fine, I'm fine. It's just that I'm....in jail."

"What?"

"What is it, Phil? What?" My poor mother. I bet she wished at that moment that she had answered the phone. I'd put money on it that tomorrow she moves the phone to her side of the bed.

"What are you in jail for, Dave?"

"David's in jail? Oh my god, what happened? What did he do?"

I could only imagine what they were thinking. My bet would have been on *drug bust*. I don't know why. I never have done drugs. But I was in college, so they probably figured it was just a matter of time. "I was down here at Gabe's uncle's place in Wakulla County, celebrating with the guys. It's Whip's—Stanley's—birthday. Twenty-*first* birthday," I added, wanting him to know we had been doing something marginally legal. "I went for a food run and accidentally cut off a cop, a sheriff's deputy, and he pulled me over, smelled alcohol on me...."

"And he charged you with a DUI?"

"Yeah. Not that I had been drinking that much...." I decided to put in, just so he'd know I hadn't exactly been drinking and driving, or at least not dead drunk and driving. I took a deep breath because I had gotten to the point of my call, the part where I had to ask for money.

For *bail* money. In the past I'd begged my parents numerous times for cash, but I could always justify my need somehow, even if the thing I wanted was sort of frivolous. Asking for bail money is different. Nothing you can say can justify the need for bail money. I might as well be asking them to take out a stack of one-hundred dollar bills and use it to light the barbecue grill.

The best thing about parents is the fact that, unless you have a totally crappy relationship, they almost always will help you out when you get yourself into what my mother would call a situation. Have an accident? They'll be at the hospital at 2 a.m. and wait with you five hours until someone treats you. Fail a class? They'll get you a tutor. Get a girl pregnant? They'll help you work it out.

End up in jail? They'll bail you out.

Of course if your situation was the result of your doing something stupid there will be a price to pay for that help. It will usually come in the form of guilt.

The fact that my parents arrived in Wakulla County, in the town of Crawfordville, when the bail bondsman first opened his doors—which meant they had left Lake City before dawn—was the first installment. They had foregone sleep on a Saturday to spare me another minute in jail. The fact that two such respectable people who have never had more than a parking ticket—and that back somewhere in the 1960s when they allowed a meter to run out—had to come to a prison to get their son meant they were willing to swallow their pride to save me.

"Your bail was five hundred dollars," my dad told me as we left the detention center, me a free man and stone cold sober at last.

"I'll pay you back," I promised.

"Damned straight. Also we're going to get the truck out of impound, but there'll be a fee," he said.

"I'll pay you back for that, too."

"I know," he said. I wished he shown me the least little bit of respect for owning up to my mistake, made the slightest mention that he was proud of me for stepping up to the plate and acknowledging my responsibility, but maybe that would have been too much to expect from a parent who has just gotten up at the crack of dawn, driven almost two hundred miles, and spent a week's salary on your stupid mistake.

"There will be court costs and fines," he added.

"On my tab," I mumbled under my breath.

"And God knows what else," Dad added with a weary sigh designed to be gut-wrenching and guilt-instilling.

Funny how you never think consequences are going to be quite as bad as they end up being. Even though I had incurred a lot of unnecessary expenses, I did have a part-time job. I figured I could handle the fines and then I could have my parents paid off by Christmas at the latest. Then would come the new year and the whole mess would be behind me, just another bump in the road of life, something I could laugh at years from now, or even tell my children and grandchildren about with a hardy har-har.

Silly me.

Oh, I knew that handling a DUI charge wasn't going to be as easy as paying off a parking ticket. I knew I couldn't just go to the sheriff's office, write them a check and be done with it. The officer who released me into my parents' custody had already apprised me that a DUI meant a court appearance.

I just didn't anticipate something from an episode of *Boston Legal*.

From the start I wasn't thinking *trial*. The officer said *hearing*. That didn't sound so bad. What I thought was, the judge would call me up and ask me for a plea. I'd offer up my *nolo contendre*—no contest—and he would sternly lecture me for a few minutes on the dangers of drinking and driving, how lucky I had been not to have harmed, maimed or killed someone or myself, how I had put my poor parents through an emotional and financial hardship, and then I would pay my fine and that would be the end of it.

Silly me.

What no one knew at that point—not even the officers of the court who had handled thousands of DUI cases over the years—was how the consequences of my particular DUI were going to be the start of a downward spiral, that my entire life was going to go into a major tailspin, and that me and my stupid mistake were going to drag a lot of people I cared about down into the very bowels of hell.

Wakulla County Courthouse
April 19_____

Phil Fouraker was a man with a plan. For as long as I could remember, my father has never been without one. Whatever the situation, circumstance or crisis, he could be counted on to have some way of dealing with it. After I called my parents to tell them about my stupid mistake, I imagine my Dad spent the rest of the night, lying flat on his back, contemplating the way the streetlight came through the window and threw patterns onto the ceiling, and making a series of contingency plans. Neither of my parents had any experience in dealing with the law but not knowing what to expect from their son's legal misstep would not stop Phil Fouraker from already planning what to do about it.

The hearing, which took place roughly a month after my stupid mistake, turned out to be quite the eye-opening experience. Not only did the wheels of justice not turn slowly—as the saying went—but they mowed you down in the street and left tracks up one side and down the other.

In the interim between my bail-out and the hearing, my folks had gotten my truck and driven it back to Lake

City—but not until the mandatory 10-day impoundment was up and then also not until the impound fees were paid. Another entry on my tab, cha-*ching*. My driver's license, the officer at the detention center had told us, would most surely be suspended for a while, but while I still had the right to drive until the hearing, my father deemed me unworthy of having a vehicle given that I obviously had no respect for the law. Hard to argue with that sort of logic after you've been stupid enough to garner a DUI, so I just didn't. En route to Lake City and home, my parents dropped me off at the campus, on the doorstep of my dorm, and told me they'd pick me up for the hearing. Fortunately I already owned a bicycle, a nice little mountain bike made by Giant with 24 speeds and great suspension that I used to zip across campus. Invariably you get classes back-to-back that are at opposite ends of the campus—which is some 450 freakin' acres—and they expect you to run this mini-marathon in the scant fifteen minutes they give you between classes. I found that feat to be possible only on a bicycle. The gears are nice (hell, a necessity) for the hills; otherwise Tallahassee is mur-der on a rider. For all other transportation, I had friends with wheels, so my life didn't change appreciably except maybe for having less alone-time with Theresa unless I bummed a ride with her.

The day of the hearing I made sure I spiffed up, hoping to make a good impression on the judge, and prepared to take my hand-slap with a good share of contriteness and humility. I practiced my sorrowful, pained expression until I looked as repentant as a sinner on Judgment Day. The truth was, I was sorry—sorry I had done such a stupid thing, even sorrier that I'd been caught doing such a stupid thing.

The Wakulla County Courthouse as it now stands has been around since 1948, but it looks newer. From the front—as seen by people coming down U.S. Highway 319—(aka Crawfordville Highway by virtue of it running through—you guessed it—Crawfordville, the main town— maybe the only real town—in the county.) it's an imposing, blindingly white block of a building, almost a fortress. In reality it's a U shape that's discernable only from the back where you have the public entrance. The courthouse itself actually sits on Ochlocknee Street running parallel to 319, between High Drive and Arran Road. My hearing was at nine in the morning; my parents picked me up at seven. Even though it was only roughly a 45-minute drive to Crawfordville from Tallahassee, my father always believes in being early. That is always a part of his plan. He and Mom stayed overnight at a Motel 6 the night before because Phil Fouraker also plans not to have to get up in the middle of the night just to make sure his wayward son gets to his hearing on time.

"Shouldn't we have gotten a lawyer?" I asked from the back seat of my father's very sensible and perfectly maintained Volvo as we pulled into the parking lot across the street from the courthouse. Those were the only words I dared speak to my parents beyond the cursory Good mornings we exchanged when I got into the car. Dad turned around and fixed me with a baleful eye.

"People hire attorneys when they're innocent," he said, which of course was not true. Probably more guilty people than innocent ones hired lawyers to prove they didn't do what they did, but I wasn't going to argue with him at that point. "You want me to spend fifteen hundred, maybe two thousand dollars to get some lawyer to stand up there and admit you're guilty?"

"No, sir," I said.

"'Cause you *are* guilty, isn't that right?"

"Yes, sir," I said, sorry I had brought up the idea at all. "It's just that we don't know the procedure and I thought...."

"The procedure will be that the judge will hand down a punishment. A punishment you deserve, whatever it is. And that's all you need to know about that."

At that point, though, I was still quite the optimist. I mean, how bad could my punishment be when the court system was having to deal with real criminals: drug dealers, thieves, rapists, murderers. The prisons were jammed full of these low-lifes. It wasn't like I'd hurt anyone or caused any property damage. I didn't think I deserved a really bad punishment.

It soon became obvious to me that the court system and I did not see eye-to-eye on such matters.

The first thing the assistant district attorney did when we got into the court room (2A, criminal traffic offenses) was hand me my plea bargain.

"A plea bargain!" I whispered frantically to my parents. "Plea bargain? Isn't that what they offer criminals?"

Phil Fouraker, he of the steely eye, replied, "So what's your point?"

I gawped at the sheet—typed, in quadruplicate—and at all the penalties that had been ticked off. My

offense had "only" been a first degree misdemeanor—
which was their way of saying that they were cutting me
some slack this time—so my punishment would "only"
include the following:

Driver's license suspended for six months. Check. I
figured that much. Still allowed to ride a bike, though.

Twelve hours of DUI school. I was already in
school. Not so bad.

Two hundred hours of community service in lieu of
six months jail time. I gulped and tried to do the math.
Two hundred hours, divided by eight—no, make that four.
I couldn't see doing community service forty hours a
week. That was fifty days. I felt a little better with that.
Fifty days. Less than two months. Bye-bye summer
vacation, but better than jail time. Next.

Six months probation. I had no idea what that
meant. It didn't sound good, but maybe it wasn't as bad as
I thought. Better, at least, than parole. Probation also had
an early termination clause which meant that if I finished
all the other stipulations of my plea bargain, I could get off
probation before my six months were up.

My BAC—which I learned stood for Blood Alcohol
Content—had registered a scant .09, barely .01 over the
legal limit. I suppose that's why they were willing to go so
easy on me.

The courtroom was jam-packed with criminal
traffic offenders. Who would've thought? There were so
many DUI cases called up, it was a wonder anyone in
Wakulla County drove sober. And then there were the
"driving with a suspended license" cases. Lots of those,
too. A zillion drunken, unlicensed drivers out there on the

roads. It was enough to make you want to let them keep your driver's license and take the bus the rest of your life.

The rest of my hearing remains a blur. I do remember hearing my name called. I remember having to stand up before the judge—an African-American version of my father—and hear the charges read against me by the assistant DA. I recall giving my plea—*nolo contendre*, as planned—and agreeing to accept the plea bargain offered to me. Yes, I waived my right to a trial by jury. Yes, I understood what this meant. Yes, yes, and yes, just let me out of here. Let me go and get a MacDonald's for lunch and pretend my life can still be normal after this. Free me from lawyers and prosecutors and courtrooms and stern-faced judges and even parents. Take me back to my dorm room, to Mojo and Whippet and the bully boys where for a while I can pretend none of this ever happened.

Not so fast.

On the way home, my father was silent for about ten minutes, which was about how long it probably took him to come up with Phil Fouraker's *Plan for Dealing with the Consequences of DUI.*

"The semester'll be over soon," he said. "Since your sentence has to be served in Wakulla County, I suggest you plan to get a place there soon as school's out." My father said the word sentence as if he were speaking to a man who had committed a double homicide and fed his victims into a wood-chipper.

"Okay," I said, in no mood to argue.

"Have to get yourself a job—that's a condition of probation," he reminded me.

After the hearing, I'd had my first brief encounter with the probation office housed in a wing of the second floor of the courthouse. I would have a formal meeting later, but basically I was required to get a job, meet with my PO once a month and pay $50 each visit for the service—for that kind of money, I figured I should also get a monthly massage and a haircut—do my community service in a timely manner, and not get into any more trouble.

"Don't know what kind of work's available here, but I'm sure you'll find something if you beat the bushes hard enough."

I was already a part-time employee at a Papa John's Pizza in Tallahassee, but you can't deliver pizzas on a bicycle unless you have the speed of Lance Armstrong. Guess I could kiss that job so-long, farewell, bye-bye. I wouldn't get a comparable job in Wakulla County for the same reason, but I did have a good job history and I figured my supervisor at PJ's would write me a recommendation.

At that point I shut down. I'd had enough of listening to Phil Fouraker's plan for my summer vacation in the justice system. I had no idea what it would be like to live in Wakulla County after spending three years in the hub-bub of campus life—and Tallahassee is no little podunk town any more, either. In all the time I'd spent at Uncle Pete's fishcamp, I'd never encountered a mall, a Cineplex, or a stadium in Wakulla County. If there was a social life there, I guessed it centered around the annual wild duck viewing at the St. Mark's Lighthouse, the Swine Show, the Wakulla Chivaree and Pioneer Breakfast and the

Sopchoppy Worm-Grunting Festival. I figured out of all that there would be one thing I could look forward to.
Culture shock.

Uncle Pete's Fishcamp
(aka The Waterin Hole)
May 19_____

"Why don't you just stay at the fishcamp?" Gabe
shouted from the back seat of Mojo's Jeep Cherokee. He
was yelling because Mojo had taken the top off and the
wind was whipping us pretty hard, blowing our words
away as soon as they left our mouths. It felt good, though,
the wind. What was better than a warm day and a cool
wind, especially when it was beating against you some 50
miles an hour. Sweat never stood a chance.

I turned toward Gabe from the front seat. "Thanks,
but I have to do my community service at Wakulla
Springs." The Springs were part of a large state park in the
area famous for being the setting of The Creature from the
Black Lagoon, various Tarzan movies and Airport '77—the
one where the plane took a nosedive under the alleged
Atlantic Ocean but which was really the crystal clear water
of the Springs. "It's too far to bike from Sopchoppy to the
Springs," I hollered at him, but not quite as loudly as he
had had to since the wind was carrying my words to him
in the back seat. Secretly I was grateful my probation

officer had agreed that I could do my service at the Springs as it gave me a damned good excuse not to stay at the Waterin Hole. I knew Uncle Pete would put me up—there were a few small cabins there that he rented out—but I didn't feel comfortable spending a lot of quality time with Pete LaCroix. It was one thing to be there with a group of your buds around you, but I wasn't sure I wanted to go mono-a-mono with the guy. I didn't want to hurt Gabe's feelings, and I sure as hell didn't want to hurt Uncle Pete's, so I was glad for the legitimate out.

"Can't beat the rent, though. Uncle Pete would make you a good deal."

"I know," I yelled back, "and I appreciate the offer, but if I have to bike all that way, I'll be too tired to do my community service and my PO is sort of hard-assed about that sort of thing. I can tell she doesn't do excuses."

Getting a place to stay down in Wakulla County was my first order of business, so on the weekend before finals started the four of us—me, Gabe, Mojo and Whippet—piled into Mojo's Jeep and headed south to find me some digs for the summer. I was a little bummed about it, because I wasn't sure what sort of employment I could find and I didn't think rent would be cheap. I sure as hell didn't want to spend the hot summer months holed up in some fleabag motel vying for my bed with mosquitoes, field rats, and—god forbid—Florida palmetto bugs (called roaches in this neck of the woods—not those small brown true roaches, but big, black flying critters with hairy legs, right out of a low-budget horror movie).

We pulled in at the fishcamp late morning. Gabe had already called his Uncle Pete so he was expecting us.

He had customers when we arrived, two old guys who wanted to rent a boat for the day. They had their own gear, we heard them say, but hauling a boat at their age was getting to be too much, and they wanted to put in at the camp. Lots of people did that, just for the convenience. Uncle Pete had several rowboats and a few canoes tied up at the dock—easy in, easy out. He acknowledged us with a raised hand, lifted a finger to let us know he'd be just a minute, then went back to taking the two fishermen's ID and deposit.

It was funny how once you were in the fishcamp's area for a while you no longer noticed the smell, even if you were stone-cold sober. The stink hit you smack in the face when you first walked in, but a few minutes later, it just went away, as if there were no such thing as stagnant water or fish guts. Uncle Pete turned his elderly customers over to a young high-school jock he employed to get them launched and then came over to us.

"Don't want to bunk with me this summer, eh, Fresco," he said jovially, poking me in the shoulder with one calloused finger.

"Not that I don't want to...." I began, feeling inexplicably guilty.

He waved off my explanation. "Nah, don't worry about it. I get it. The law stuck you out at the Springs—doing what? Picking up trash?" I nodded. "Yeah, I figured. Trash, mowing, whatever. Free labor. Don't let 'em tell you slavery's no longer legal. Anyway, I know you can't take that two-wheeler that far."

"I appreciate the offer, though," I said again and Uncle Pete gave me a grin and slapped my shoulder.

"I might have a lead for you, though," he said. "Lemme get the guy's card. He brought it by yesterday." Pete went behind the counter and rummaged around for a minute before coming up with a white business card. "I've been askin' around for you, you know? Just puttin' it out there that a friend of mine needed a place to stay this summer and that it hadda be sorta near the Springs. So yesterday this guy comes out to the fishcamp and gives me his card and said you should get in touch with him. Maybe he can fix you up with somethin'."

"He drove all the way out here just to offer me a place to stay?" I said, incredulous. Pete handed me the card and I looked at it. It was simple, just black letters on a white card. .

Pete shrugged "Not like he had to go to the far side of the moon."

"No, but…." I couldn't put my finger on it; it just seemed weird. But then again, I'd heard that Uncle Pete was connected, and maybe he was better connected than I even imagined. With who or what, I didn't know, and frankly didn't want to know. He was known for being something of a mover-and-shaker and maybe he did a little moving and shaking for me. Maybe yes, maybe no, but I was thinking yes. Why?…well, I couldn't answer that one either, and didn't really want to think why. Maybe he was doing Gabe a favor. Favorite nephew and all. "Did you know this guy?"

"Never saw him before in my life," Pete told me. "A real stranger in these parts, though."

"What makes you say that?"

"You call him. Meet him. You'll see." And that's all that Pete would say about that. I guess he liked being a Man of Mystery once in a while. Like it added to his persona or something.

I looked over at Mojo who, in my opinion, was the most sensible one of our group. (I hope that someone in pre-med has some sense, though you never know.)

Mojo shrugged. "Can't hurt just to call," he said.

I looked at the small white card I held in my hand. In this day and age when flashy advertisement that screamed Look at me!! was the name of the game, the business card Uncle Pete had handed me was strangely plain.

Eblis Realty
Property Rentals
Reasonable Rates
Harold Eblis, Owner
(850) 555-4355

"Phone's over on the wall if you wanna call him," Uncle Pete said. It was a pay phone. God forbid he'd let me place a call on his business phone. I nodded and dug a quarter out of my pocket. My call was picked up on the second ring. I had been expecting a silky-voiced receptionist who I could picture young, blond, and built like a brick shithouse. My expectations were not met.

"Speak to me," said a resonant baritone.

For a moment I couldn't do as he asked, so surprised was I by the way the phone was answered. But then I collected myself. "Is this Mr. Eeblis? Harold Eeblis?"

"It's *Eb*-lis and this is he speaking. How may I help you?"

"Eblis Realty?"

"Are you in the market to buy or rent?" The voice was not unpleasant, but it was cool, unemotional, clipped. As if my call had interrupted something important. As if I'd been a bother, nothing more than a pain in the neck.

"Rent."

"I'm not sure whether I have anything available at the moment."

This threw me for a loop and for another moment I was silent. "Oh? Because you gave a card to Mr. LaCroix at the Waterin Hole in Sopchoppy, so I thought...."

"Ah yes!" The voice suddenly warmed. "What I had in mind was not precisely a rental, though you may consider it that. You are calling so may I assume you're interested? Would you like to see the place?"

"Uh, sure. Is it an apartment?"

"A house, actually."

I was momentarily floored. "A house," I repeated and saw my companions' eyes widen at that. "Uh, I'm not sure I could afford...."

Eblis cut me off. "But we haven't even talked price, and my card does say my rates are reasonable, did you not see that?"

"Yes," I said slowly, though I knew from experience that what I thought was reasonable and what most people considered affordable were often two different things.

"It so happens that I'm not too far from you at this very moment. I could pick you up in, say, an hour?"

"I have three friends with me," I said. For some reason, I was reluctant to go anywhere with this guy alone. He had a soothing, kind voice, but in this day and age you couldn't be too careful. If I went off with this guy and he killed me with an axe, my parents would never forgive me.

"Not a problem," Eblis said gregariously. "I have plenty of room. You can get their opinion. Perhaps that will help you make up your mind."

"In an hour then," I said, and hung up.

Back when I was a teenager I dated a girl whose name now escapes me who was nuts about a movie about Dracula starring Frank Langella as the Count. It had come out some seven years before either of us had been born, but she was absolutely ga-ga over it (or should I say him), and so to please her (and possibly get lucky) I rented it from Movie Gallery one Saturday night. I didn't even think they'd have it but there it was, in their classics section. I remember that the back of the DVD box talked a little about why the handsome Langella had been cast as the bad guy in what was essentially a horror film. ("It's so romantic," Miss Whatever-her-name gushed at me when I reminded her it was about a vampire who killed people by sucking out their blood. Women. Go figure.) Anyway, the DVD box: Evil in the world, director John Badham wrote, hardly ever came at you in the guise of ugliness. If it did, it would repel us. Instead, evil came to us in what appeared beautiful so that we were easily drawn to it. It was charming, seductive, even erotic. It approached us not with fangs but with soft lips, not with claws but a beckoning hand, not as a bald, skeletal *nosferatu* but as a handsome, elegant nobleman.

If I'd only remembered that sooner. There was that damned 20/20 hindsight again. A poor memory will get you in trouble every time.

An hour later we all went outside to the Waterin Hole's parking lot to wait for Mr. Eblis. Exactly an hour after my phone call, he arrived. We'd all been half-heartedly shuffling around in the gravel lot, but when we heard the crunch of tires, we all looked up at the same time.

He didn't even have to get out of the car. We knew it was him.

The car that pulled into the fishcamp's lot was a late model silver Mercedes S550, with a V-8 engine that purred so quietly you didn't even think it was running. It practically slithered into the lot, like it was a living thing. Mojo whistled softly beside me and I knew the others were gawking at it as hard as I was. It easily went for a hundred grand (base price), and we knew from its sparkling silver skin and pristine custom rims shining the way only chrome in the sunlight can, that that baby was fully loaded. Just looking at Eblis's car we could see why Uncle Pete called him a "stranger in these parts." You didn't see a car like that in Sopchoppy just any old day.

I wish to God I never had seen it at all.

Bethel, Florida (Unincorporated)
May 19_____

The first thing we saw was a gray boot made out of some sort of skin, lizard or snake. The gravel crunched as Mr. Eblis got out of the Mercedes, hauling himself out of the driver's seat. He wasn't really a big man, or a fat man, but he looked imposing when he rose up over the car door. Above the boots was a pair of jeans. Not work worn— almost brand new, clear blue and crisp. Over a barrel chest he wore a cream colored Guayabera shirt, two stripes of fine embroidery down each side. It fit. He looked Latin American or maybe Cuban. What kind of name was Eblis? Hispanic? Middle-eastern?

His broad hawkish face was deeply tanned, and his dark hair, silvered at the temples and probably a shade too long for a dude his age—I figured him to be in his fifties, maybe sixty—was combed straight back from a high forehead. He had on thick gold rings, a heavy chain bracelet, a watch that might not have been a Rolex but was damned close if not. He grinned at us over the open car door and raised a hand in greeting. I half-heartedly waved back. Mr. Eblis shut the Mercedes' door and came over to us, looking more like he'd just stepped out of the Godfather's vacation home on Miami Beach than out of a car in the parking lot of Uncle Pete's fishcamp.

"So which one of you fine fellows called me?" he asked, pushing a pair of Oakley sunglasses onto the top of his head.

"That would be me," I said. "Dave Fouraker." I extended my hand.

"But friends call him Fresco," Mojo put in.

"Well, I hope one day you'll count me among them," Mr. Eblis said amiably, grasping my outstretched hand. I almost pulled away—and for no good reason, really. My mild distaste at his touch surprised me. Yet his hand was—I don't know—too warm, too soft, too....something. But I shook it anyway and tried to smile. I made introductions all around and was surprised to see that same sort of wave of faint revulsion pass over my friends' faces as Eblis shook their hands. It was like being slapped with a dead eel. No, that was a crappy analogy, seeing as how his hand was warm—it was more like shaking hands with someone who had just hocked a huge loogie into his palm. This is just a real estate agent, you idiot, I told myself. Not a damned thing weird or gross about him. In fact, his grooming was pretty damned impeccable.

"Gentlemen, shall we go?" he asked, ushering us to his Mercedes. "Room for everyone."

Mojo, Whippet and Gabe piled into the back, leaving me to ride shotgun. I'd rather have been in the back with them, but I was going to be the renter, so how could I not sit up front? I saw Mojo's face in the side view mirror and knew what he was thinking. This was one helluva fine car. The entire interior was dove-gray leather and there was fiber optic ambient lighting under the trim panels. It had a built-in phone with keypad, GPS, shift buttons on the steering wheel, and a rear-window sunshade. Most of us don't even dream cars this nice.

"The real estate business must be really booming," Mojo remarked and Eblis grinned at him in the rear view mirror.

"Not too shabby," he said.

I saw the guys in the back exchange glances as Eblis started the car. You barely heard the engine inside, either. We might as well have been floating on a cushion of air.

"So this place you have for rent, it's close to the Springs?" I asked.

"It is indeed. A scant two miles, maybe a little less. Not too far from Crawfordville, either, if that's a factor."

"My transportation right now is a bicycle, which is why I'm asking," I told him, feeling a little embarrassed admitting that to a guy who drove a car worth more than my parents' annual salary.

"Good exercise," he said, smiling. He pulled onto US 319, passed through Crawfordville about 10 minutes later, and a short time after that turned off on Bloxham Cutoff. "Now if you keep on going on this road, you'll come onto 61, then take a right and you're practically at the Springs. Lots of roads converge here, Spring Creek Highway, Old Shell Point Road—not that any of those places on the coast are easy to get to on a bicycle from here, but you might want to have friends visit, isn't that so?" He turned and glanced at my friends in the back.

"Where is *here*, exactly?"

"Welcome to Bethel, Florida, boys. Bethel Unincorporated, actually. The folks who live here consider it a town, but that's sort of pushing it, I think. Of course, there are a few businesses around. Down there at the intersection there's a small grocery store and gas station, a hardware store — lot of farms around here — a diner. Might be some others. They come and go. But that's about it. There was a church, but it burned down some years ago and there wasn't enough of a congregation to rebuild it."

"How many people live here?" I asked.

"Hard to tell. Fifty maybe. They come and go, too. Here we are." Eblis pulled the Mercedes onto a hard-packed dirt driveway between two larger paved roads. Bakersfield Drive, I read on one. I couldn't see the sign on the other. About twenty-five yards ahead we could see a small clearing and in its center a medium-sized wood frame house, pale yellow with white trim, shutters and front door. As we got closer, I could see a nice porch four steps up with white railings and two white rockers sitting on it. Eblis stopped the car in front and we got out. There was a grassy patch around the house — what sort of passed for a yard — but that soon gave way to a thick stand of pine: longleafs, slash pines, some loblollies and lots of underbrush.

"How come it's up on pilings?" Gabe asked, pointing to the lattice skirting that all but hid the concrete blocks on which the house sat.

"Solid wood floors," Eblis told us. "Needs the ventilation in this climate, you know."

"It looks like an awfully nice house to be set out here in the middle of nowhere," Mojo said.

"The owner likes seclusion."

"But not so much that he wants to live here."

"Oh, he lives here off an on, but he's a businessman and has to be away sometimes half a year at a time— travels all over the world, Europe, Asia. Likes to come here and unwind."

"So he rents it out while he's away?" I asked.

"Not a rental exactly. See, I take care of it for him, only I need to be away for a few months so I asked him if it would be all right if I had someone house-sit, so to speak. That's where you come in, young man," he grinned at me. "Shall we take a look?"

I nodded and my friends and I followed Mr. Eblis up to the porch and waited while he unlocked the front door. I noticed a plaque on the wall decorated with hearts and flowers in a sort of European design. It said Casa de Almas. I pointed to it.

"What's that mean?"

Eblis glanced at the plaque. "The House with Soul," he translated.

"Why is it called that?"

Eblis shrugged his beefy shoulders. "Why does anyone name a house?"

"Is the owner Hispanic or something?"

"I never asked." Eblis pushed the front door open and allowed us to enter ahead of him. Windows on all sides of the front room allowed light to come in at almost any hour of the day. The living room looked comfortable with big, overstuffed chairs and sofa, tables, a few lamps, a

TV, but surprisingly ordinary—certainly nothing special like you'd expect some millionaire businessman who regularly jet-setted around Europe and Asia to have. In fact, the furniture, while it looked nice enough, was sort of mismatched. The colors were slightly off and the pieces were not new, as if they'd been found at Goodwill or some other thrift store. Shabby chic, was that what they called it? The ceiling was high—a good sixteen feet at the uppermost point. That's because an open staircase went up the right side to a sort of mezzanine that overlooked the living area.

"Back to the left's the kitchen—all modern appliances—and there's a dinette in there, no formal dining room. On the right are two bedrooms and a full bath, back door down the hall. Screened-in porch out back."

"And upstairs?"

Eblis grinned again. "Everyone loves that loft."

"Everyone?"

"The owner's guests that he's had here from time to time. Not a recluse, you know, even though he likes his privacy. Anyway, you can use it for whatever you want. There's a sofa that folds out into a bed, second TV, library, desk and computer—dial-up, I'm afraid. No DSL or cable out here. Same with the TV."

"No satellite dish?" asked Whippet.

"The owner isn't really into television," Eblis replied. "But you can get all the networks on the 'ears. And there's a DVD player and VCR attached so you can always watch movies."

"So what's the rent on this place?" I asked.

"Oh, I told you, it's not a rental. Like I said, I take care of the place. Just need someone to fill in for me a while." Eblis looked at me with his dark eyes. "Someone like you, maybe, Fresco?" When I didn't answer immediately, he added. "It's a good deal for someone like you."

"Someone like me?"

"Someone needing a place to stay, close to the Springs," he said. "You pay no rent, just utilities and phone. Mow the grass—not much to that—keep the place clean. Not hard. You can even have your friends come stay with you from time to time if you want. As long as you don't overdo it, have a party if you want. So what do you say?"

I glanced at the guys. They were all staring at me with round eyes that said they would have me committed as a total nutcase if I didn't snatch this plum that had dropped into my lap.

"When can I move in?" I asked.

Mr. Eblis grinned.

Downtown Bethel, Florida
May 26_____

"You gonna be okay out here?" Mojo asked as he took my last bag into my summer place. That's how I was trying to think of the house in Bethel—my summer home-away-from-home.

"Why wouldn't I be okay?" I asked, taking my bike off the rack on the back of Mojo's Jeep.

"Pretty secluded out here," he shrugged.

"When was the last time you heard of a serial killer in Wakulla County?"

Mojo gave me a funny look, like he didn't even want to think such thoughts. I grinned at him.

"Don't freak on me, man," I told him. "No one will even know I'm here. Can't kill you if they can't find you."

"That's not that funny, Fresco." He forced a smile, though. "But I guess you're also not nice enough to be a murder victim. No one would have anything good to say about you. The media would hate it."

"Yeah, I'd make a lousy story. Everyone the TV news guys interviewed would just say, 'He was a real son-of-a-bitch. Hell, we're glad he got whacked.' Right?"

Mojo grinned and pointed a finger at me. "When you're right, you're right."

"You want to grab some chow before you head back?"

"Oh, hell, yes. For sure let's check out the downtown area. I bet they have real jumpin' Saturday nights in Bethel. Didn't Eblis say something about a diner?"

"And if we go now maybe I can put in an application at the gas station or something. I need a job, like yesterday. I have some cash saved up, but I've got a $50 probation fee coming up and my old man is going to start dunning me for the bail money any day now."

"I could bring you some candles. Then you can keep your electric bill low."

"Very funny, Mo," I told him as I climbed back into his Jeep.

We didn't really have to take a car to get to the booming downtown area of Bethel—it was all of three minutes down the road. (But what if you have to make a quick get-away? I have no idea what made that pop into my mind! Anyway, we took the Jeep so that Mojo could fill up his tank before he headed back to Tallahassee. My treat, of course.) The gas station was a Chevron and had a small garage attached to it. We stopped there first and I filled up Mojo's Jeep. When I went in to pay (the tanks were old and didn't accept cards) the guy behind the cash register, a small guy with sandy hair and a cheesy moustache, told me they weren't hiring unless I was a mechanic. Their regular guy, Marvin, was a whiz with motors and always had more cars than he could handle since people came all the way from Sopchoppy to get their cars fixed by Mr. Mechanic. Regretfully I had to admit I wasn't mechanically inclined. Mojo and I then stopped at the small grocery store about ten yards from the gas station to pick up some staples for me and make another job inquiry.

There was an old-fashioned bell over the door that tinkled when we opened it. A middle-aged woman in shorts and a tee-shirt was paying for groceries but the woman at the cash register flashed us a quick smile. There was a frozen food case along the left wall, four aisles of dry goods, and a refrigerated section in the back. Not a super Wal-Mart but adequate. I was used to eating on campus where there was fast food galore so I was stymied by what I actually needed to prepare meals. Mojo snagged a little shopping cart while I grabbed things off the shelves. I threw in a jar of peanut butter, loaf of bread, coffee, a box of Nutrasweet and a pint of half-and-half as well as three six-packs of Mountain Dew—they didn't have any Fresca which I found a real affront to my senses, but Mojo said he would bring me a supply next time he came down to see me. I bought a box of Cinnamon Toast Crunch cereal, a half-gallon of milk, and a stack of TV dinners and micro-wavable pizzas from their small freezer section. There weren't a lot of choices, but I didn't care. What I had in my basket was pretty much breakfast, lunch and dinner. Next time one of the guys came to see me I'd ask them to drive me to Crawfordville to one of the larger grocery stores there if I decided there was something I just couldn't live without. We heard the front door's bell tinkle. Mrs. Shorts-and-Tee must have left with her stuff.

"No cookies, no doughnuts, no Twinkies?" Mojo asked.

"If I'm going to be hauling my ass around on a bicycle, I better make sure it stays a small ass," I told him.

The older woman—sixtyish or so—behind the counter smiled at us as we unloaded the basket and began checking me out. While she rang up my groceries and I put the cold stuff into a cooler I'd borrowed from Uncle Pete, I again asked about a job.

"My husband and I pretty much take care of things ourselves," she said almost apologetically as if she really, really wanted to offer me a job—nice young man that I seemed to be—but she just couldn't, not with the economy the way it was.

"That's okay," I said, trying not to sound too discouraged. I could get a job in Crawfordville, maybe, but Bethel was closer and so much more convenient and right now I didn't want my life any more complicated than it already was. "Maybe I'll check back later in case you change your mind."

"Are you new to town?" she asked. "You have family around here?"

"No, I'm just here for the summer. I'm going to be doing some—" I hesitated. I didn't like using the term *community service* because I knew that term screamed convicted felon and any whiff of a criminal past would kill my chances of a job deader than a doornail. "—volunteer work out at Wakulla Springs."

She smiled again. She reminded me of my grandmother with her typical short gray Granny-curls, wire-rim glasses, blue eyes, her face lightly powdered and rouged as if she hadn't changed her makeup style in fifty years. "That's nice. Are you staying at the Lodge?"

The Lodge was at the Springs. It had been built back in the '30s by a wealthy railroad bigwig by the name of Ed Ball. It sported wrought iron, a giant marble fireplace, imported ceramic tile, and huge beams under the ceiling that were hand-painted with Native American folk designs and animals. It was still a hotel, some 80 years later, and had a huge restaurant attached to it. Corporate folks from Tallahassee often held company retreats there for their employees because you had a place to sleep and eat but you would be completely undisturbed. However, with the rooms going for some hundred dollars a pop, I couldn't imagine why Mrs. Grocer would think a young guy like me could afford to stay there.

"No, ma'am," I said. "I'm taking care of a place just down the road. House-sitting, you could say, but I only get board. I need a job to pay for my food, utilities, and all."

"A place down the road?" she frowned as if she couldn't imagine where I meant.

"Just past Bakersfield Drive," I told her. I had seen the other street sign by then. "Between Bakersfield and Ferrell."

"You mean the former Barnes house?" She was still frowning, and now she looked really troubled and was starting to creep me out.

"I—I don't know. I guess so. The regular caretaker hired me while he's away." Mrs. Grocer's eyes had gotten sort of vacant and the look never left her face, as if she had just gone somewhere far, far away and wasn't coming back any time soon. "Is there something wrong with the house?" I asked.

She looked at me then as if she had forgotten I was there buying groceries and all of a sudden remembered she had a customer. "What? Oh, oh no, there's nothing wrong with it. Land, no. It's just that Mrs. Barnes—well, she just left. Went missing, I mean. Never found out what happened to her. Sweet woman, Mrs. Barnes. Always had a kind word." She pressed her hand against her wrinkled throat and inclined her head toward me, lowering her voice as she did so, as if she were imparting some deep secret. "There was talk, just talk, mind you—" Then she stopped, frowned again. "Oh, I shouldn't be gossiping. Land sake, if Hubert could hear me now!" She began to hurriedly bag my remaining groceries.

"We love gossip," Mojo said. "And I don't see anyone else here."

She gave a small smile. "Hubert's my husband. He's always telling me I gossip too much." Then she sighed. "I suppose he's right." But you could just tell she wanted to gossip something awful. She looked around and then said quickly, "There was talk that Mr. Barnes had something to do with Mrs. Barnes's disappearance only they never could prove anything. There wasn't any—what you'd call evidence."

"You mean, they never found a body," Mojo said.

She nodded. "They never found her at all. So there was just a lot of speculation. He wasn't arrested or anything. Don't know what became of him. He was quite the businessman in the area. Owned Wakulla Wood. Why, I bet half the buildings in this area were built with wood from his company. Gave the business over to someone else, I think." She waved her hand impatiently. "Oh, there I go, just gossiping again. Silly old woman, Hubert would say. Don't know enough to keep my mouth shut. None of that is either here nor there to two young men like yourselves."

I thanked her, Mojo and I picked up my bags of groceries and my cooler, and went back to his Jeep. He started making noises like something out of a sci-fi movie, one of those eerie wooo-ooos that you usually hear in the cheesiest films out of Hollywood.

"What?"

"Casa de Almas could have been the site of a murder," he said dramatically.

"Well, just leave it to you to make me feel right at home there, Mo. Thanks a lot."

He grinned as we walked across the street to the diner called **ALICE'S EATS**. The burly man behind the counter had close-cropped gray hair and a stubble on his cheeks to match. He was jowly as a bloodhound and had good-sized duffle bags under eyes that watched us from under droopy lids. All-in-all, he looked sort of half melted. A younger dark-haired fellow manned the grill behind him. A few of the other diners looked up as we entered but we were obviously of no interest to them and they quickly went back to their meals. There were six booths in cracking red vinyl—three of which were occupied—four tables with similar red vinyl coverings—and six stools in front of the counter. The tables were empty but two of the stools at opposite ends of the counter had men—one middle-aged, one young — sitting on them. And lo-and-behold, an honest-to-goodness juke box in the corner though at the moment it was silent.

"Told you this would be the Saturday night hot-spot," Mojo whispered to me as he and I took a table. Mr. Burly brought us some menus—typed, Xeroxed sheets in plastic page protectors and waited while we read them which fortunately didn't take too long. **ALICE** might **EAT** but she didn't eat a big variety of stuff. We both ordered cheese burgers and fries. He didn't seem the sort to ask about Fresca so we both ordered Cokes.

"Pepsis do you?" he asked.

"Fine," Mojo said.

"Pepsi and a job," I said surprising myself with my impulsiveness, but what the hell. I needed work and at this point I wasn't beyond being a little pushy.

Mr. Burly eyed me for a minute. "You too good to bus tables? Load the dishwasher? Wash tables, windows, floors?"

"No sir, not too good to do it, but I'd be good *at* it." (I thought that was a pretty good response, myself.)

"You have any experience?"

What sort of experience you needed to do grunt work I didn't know, but I decided to be humble. "I worked at Papa John's Pizza back in Tallahassee. I'm a student there. At FSU, I mean, not Papa John's."

"What are you doing in Bethel?"

"Taking care of the Barnes' house," I told him taking my cue from Mrs. Grocer. "And doing some volunteer work at Wakulla Springs. Need a paying job to eat, pay utilities. Not a lot. Minimum wage will do."

Mr. Burly's eyes narrowed in his fleshy face. "The Barnes' house?"

"The one between Farrell and —"

"I know where it is. Just surprised is all. Didn't know anyone was living there."

"I'm just the caretaker for the summer."

He nodded. Then he stuck out his beefy hand. "I'm Carl. I own this place."

"Who's Alice?" Mojo asked.

Carl gave him a wry smile. "I'm Alice, now. Alice was my wife."

Mojo had the good sense to shut up after that.

"I'll be getting you those cheeseburgers. When can you start?"

"How about tomorrow morning?"

"Tomorrow's Sunday. We're closed on Sunday."

"Oh, yeah. Lost track of the time. How about Monday?"

He nodded again. "Come in around 10."

As Carl took our order back to the fry cook, Mojo looked at me and gave me two thumbs up. I grinned. "Never hurts to ask," I told him.

"Do you suppose Mrs. Carl disappeared like Mrs. Barnes?" he asked. "Hell, Fresco, you might be living in a town with its very own serial killer."

Mojo really knew how to make a guy feel at home.

Casa de Almas (Day One)

May 26, later on_____

I stood on the front porch with my arm raised in a wave until Mojo pulled out of my driveway onto Bloxham Cutoff and his red tail lights disappeared from view. And so there I was. Alone. In the woods. True, the town—what there was of it—wasn't so far away, but being surrounded by the thick pines and scrub bushes, I felt like I had been left on the far side of the moon. With Mojo there, the isolation wasn't quite so apparent. As soon as he drove off, it collapsed on me like a heavy wet blanket. I thought that if I kept myself busy the time would go by quickly, so I went inside and began to unpack and settle in. I decided to store my clothes and gear in the first bedroom but for some reason it didn't appeal to me as a place to sleep. After I hung up my shirts and pants and stowed my other things—undershirts, boxers—in an empty dresser drawer, I grabbed a chilled Mountain Dew and went upstairs. There were windows on three sides of the loft, too, but unlike the downstairs which had been painted in a cheery pale yellow, the loft was paneled in a medium cherry—probably pine made to look like cherry—what did I know about wood?—but you get my drift. The sun was getting lower but it was still high enough so that I didn't need to use one of the three lamps—a tall floor model by a recliner, one on the desk, and another next to the sofa bed. The natural lighting in the place might help my utility bill. Any little savings in electricity, you know.

In between the windows were bookshelves crammed with volumes. I took a look at them hoping to find some decent reading material—and it was decent—books by Twain, Kipling, Maugham, and many others—but the books themselves were mostly "designer" jobs. Like special editions that places like Readers' Digest put out. Collectors' editions, they called them. Handsomely bound, but virtually brand new, as if they'd been bought more for the way they looked than for their content. I took one down, half expecting the inside to be blank—a dummy book instead of a book for dummies—but no, there was text. The binding crackled the way a brand new book will when it's been opened for the first time. Why would anyone bother buying books they never intended to read? Such were the quirks of the rich, I suppose. Books as décor. Who would've thought?

The computer was a late-model Dell with a flat screen monitor—no expense spared there, and it was too bad it was hooked only to dial-up. The TV was a flat screen as well—unlike the weightier model in the living room—with a DVD/VCR combo attached. Obviously the owner spent most of his time up here among the creature comforts and I can't say I blamed him. It was a cozy nook, all right. There was even a small fridge—I made a note to stock it when Mojo brought me my stash of Fresca.

I paced around the room, suddenly feeling twitchy, as if the walls were putting out low levels of static. Whose bright idea had it been to come up on a Saturday? Oh, yeah.

Mine.

I wanted time to "settle in," to maybe find a job (check, at least I did that), get supplies (double check), get oriented.

Oriented to what?

Maybe I would have missed out on getting the busboy job at **ALICE'S EATS** (or maybe not) but I wouldn't have had so much damned time on my hands if I'd come up on Sunday. Not only did I still have Saturday night, I had all of Sunday to deal with. Was David "Fresco" Fouraker actually looking forward to going to work? I pulled out my cell phone.

NO SIGNAL.

That figured.

I saw an old-fashioned telephone on the desk. Not a cordless, but one that had a springy wire connecting the receiver to the base. Who wanted a phone like that any more? The rich guy who owned the place seemed more and more eccentric by the minute. I picked up the receiver knowing all I was going to hear was dead air, but no, surprise! there was a dial tone. Now, who to call?

The answer: no one.

Everyone I knew was finished with finals and would either be leaving campus tonight or first thing in the morning—either way they wouldn't want to drive all the way to Wakulla County just to hold my hand. Wicky Persnicky and DJ, the two bully boys, along with Johnny

Chang, had already left to go home. Gabe eventually would be working at Uncle Pete's fishcamp, but I knew he was taking a week's break in Jacksonville with his parents. Mojo and Whippet were staying in town for the summer but likewise were going for a brief visit home. Ditto my girlfriend, Therese. That left Parker Rodriguez. Did I really want Parker to come keep me company? Hell, no.

I put down the receiver and told myself to stop being such a damned baby.

I glanced at my watch. Mojo had only been gone an hour and I was already going stir crazy. What was wrong with just chilling? Just sitting around in my underwear, drinking Mountain Dews, scarfing down one of those frozen pizzas I'd bought and watching some network TV?

Now that sounded like a plan.

A bit more invigorated now that I knew I would be actually doing something, I went downstairs to check out the rest of the house (it being a little too early for dinner at the moment).

The back porch was screened with ceiling fans and another set of rockers. I picked one and sat down. There wasn't much to see out the back door—beyond a small back yard there was just more pine, more scrub bushes. The back of the house faced west, so maybe the owner was into sunsets. At any rate, it was pleasant out there. We weren't in the throes of summer yet, when the heat will take your breath away and the humidity will make you feel like you're drowning.

I closed my eyes. Just for a minute, you understand.

I woke with a start, realizing immediately that I'd dozed off and not just for a minute or two. Hours. I looked at my watch. Incredibly, I'd sat down when it was still too early for dinner and now it was nearly seven. The sun had just slipped below the horizon so that while the sky wasn't black, the light had faded dramatically. I suddenly became aware of tiny creatures that had ventured out with the coming of dusk. Out beyond the screen there must have been a thousand fireflies. I remembered camping with my folks when I was a kid, spending weekends on the Suwannee River or in the Apalachicola Forest. Even one or two fireflies are damned amazing, but out there in the middle of the woods, they came out in droves, making you feel like you'd just taken a plunge into the middle of the Milky Way. And this evening was like that, with those yellow-green flashes popping everywhere. I sat there a few minutes feeling a sense of awe—communing with nature, you might say. Taking some time to be one with the earth.

But then I let a bad thought creep into my mind.

It was getting dark. Had I locked the front door? What about the windows?

What was the likelihood of a serial killer strolling down Bloxham Cutoff, coming across my little house—my little *secluded* house—seeing it was inhabited and that— how convenient!—the doors were all unlocked? Might as well throw a welcome mat out there and hand him a bludgeon to kill me with.

I don't know why but I felt a sudden twinge of panic. Maybe it was just being out there in the woods, alone, but I jumped out of my rocker (*off* my rocker — that's a good one!) and almost ran to the front door.

Of course it was unlocked.

I threw the deadbolt, then wondered if that had been a good move. What if the killer was already in the house? (*the killer*. Hoo boy. Already there was a *killer*.) I'd be like one of those morons in a slasher film who can never get the door unlocked in time before the killer comes up behind them and cuts them to ribbons. I left it locked anyway.

There was now almost no light coming in through the windows. I went to the nearest lamp and switched it on, but only felt marginally better. It was still damned gloomy all of a sudden. And there was all this heavy blackness pressing against the windows.

Had I locked the back door when I came inside?

I didn't think so.

"Stupid, stupid, stupid!" I yelled at myself as I ran down the hall to the back door and threw that dead bolt. So now I was locked in. Hopefully alone.

At that moment I glanced to the right and saw the black rectangle that was the window over the kitchen sink. I realized that all the blinds in the house were open and I imagined eyes on the outside, belonging to god-knew-what, watching me.

When did I ever get so damned paranoid?

I ran back to the living room — can't say I didn't get my quota of exercise today — and began closing the blinds as fast as I could and turning on the remaining lamps. The hell with the electric bill. I imagined the meter's dials spinning around wildly, clocking money by the fistful, but I didn't care.

I stood still for a minute and listened. Listened hard.

Nothing. But not hearing anything didn't make me feel better. (They could be hiding.)

"There's no *they*!" I scolded myself.

I went to the first bedroom, flipped on the overhead light switch and closed those window's blinds. In the second bedroom I didn't bother with the light, only closed the blinds and then closed the door (but not before checking the closet). Then to the kitchen. There were windows that faced the porch and then there was that other one over the sink. I remembered a movie where a woman washed dishes while the killer outside watched her.

Now why did my memory have to dredge that up?

I shut all the blinds and turned on more lights. I thought I would finally feel secure but I didn't. There was a radio in the kitchen and I turned it on—at that point, I didn't care what it picked up, I needed noise. The first thing to come up on the dial was a country station, WTNT, and that's where I left it.

Leaning back against the counter, I was aware that my heart was racing like I'd just finished the Boston Marathon. (Well, I had run a marathon of sorts, back and forth between doors!) My blood was probably ninety percent adrenalin.

"Get a grip," I told myself, the sound of my voice seeming hollow and weird in that empty house.

The music helped some, and when the DJ came on, that was even better. Nothing like the sound of a human voice to make you feel like you weren't out in the middle of the woods, totally isolated, with hungry eyes watching you through the windows.

"Okay, so let's make some dinner."

So now I was talking to myself. One day on my own and already crazy enough to talk to myself.

But as long as I was talking to myself I decided to give myself a pep talk. All I needed was some time to get used to things. That's all.

The quiet, the surroundings—hell, it was enough to make anyone a little squirrelly. I was used to the sound of feet in the hall, voices talking, yelling, musical notes of all sorts bumping into each other, doors slamming. Sure, that was the problem: it was just too damned quiet around here. It just took some getting used to, is all. Give me a few days, hell, a week, and I would be loving my little place in the woods.

I nuked a frozen pizza in the microwave, grabbed another can of Dew, and sat down at the table to eat—which I did in record time because that was also weird: eating alone. Finally finished, I grabbed a second can of Dew and decided I would head upstairs to the loft.

(You'll be trapped up there.)

"Shut up!" I said aloud. There's something supremely stupid about scaring yourself shitless over nothing. Reluctantly I clicked off the radio and the silence crashed down on me threatening to send me into another full-blown panic. Despite that, I managed to stay in control, though I wasted no time flying up the stairs, turning off lights in my wake. Immediately I flipped on the TV. I got four channels with the rabbit ears. Three of them had shows dealing with law enforcement. How about that for a Saturday schedule? NBC had a series, *Law and Order*, FOX had *Cops*, and CBS had *Crimetime Saturday*. Only ABC was showing a movie—one of the Harry Potters. I kept it there and settled down in the recliner with my Dew. My third Dew. In no time I would have to go to the bathroom. Downstairs. Why hadn't I thought of that before drinking all that liquid?

I watched ten minutes of the movie and then started feeling twitchy again. I'd never been plagued with panic attacks before and I couldn't explain my sudden and unwarranted feeling of anxiety. Yet here I was, heart pounding, breath short, my palms suddenly cold and clammy.

Even though I was on the second floor and it was unlikely that prying eyes could watch me all the way up here, I still felt uneasy about having the blinds open. Putting my Dew down on the table next to the recliner, I got up and started closing them. When I got to the windows on the left, I stopped, my hands on the draw cord.

For no good reason, I broke out in a sweat.

No, not for no good reason. For damned *good* reason.

I closed the blinds but not all the way. I wanted to be able to see out.

I wasn't alone after all. (They're out there. Just like you thought.)

In the distance I could see a yellow-orange flickering and it took a minute for my adrenalin-soaked brain to realize what I was seeing.

It was a fire. A campfire. Someone was way out there in the woods, sitting by a fire.

But this was private property, wasn't it? Anyone who'd be camping out there would be trespassing, right?

So who was out there?

The Camp in the Woods
May 27_____

I woke with a start. Mostly I was surprised that I had slept at all. But here it was, morning. Sunlight. Each set of blinds had a golden halo I had never before been so glad to see the sunrise.

After seeing the campfire in the woods, I had turned off the TV. There was no concentrating on wizards and magic spells when I had what seemed to be a real menace just outside my window. I laid down on the sofa, not even bothering to turn it into a bed because I was sure I would never fall asleep, and listened to the sound of my heart pounding in my ears. I considered running back downstairs and looking for a weapon—though I honestly hadn't seen anything down there more lethal than a spatula, or maybe a butter knife—but I was reluctant to leave the loft for the vast unknown down there, in the dark. I toyed with leaving the lights on upstairs, and was torn with indecision. If I left them on, would I be able to see danger coming sooner? Or would the danger just be able to see me better? If I turned the light off, could he strike me a lethal blow before I even saw it coming? Could he see in the dark? All that these thoughts did was make more and more adrenalin flood my system until I thought I might just save the stalker a lot of trouble and die of a heart attack.

(Why do you think he's a stalker?)

He's just a camper. Just some homeless guy living out in the woods. Doesn't mean he's dangerous. Not like he's been prowling around the house watching me.

(As far as you know.)

I knew it wasn't good to jump to conclusions — it didn't do me any good at all — but I couldn't help it. I was damned jumpy and for no damned good reason except that I was.

So all I did was lie there and listen. Listen *hard*. For any creak, any groan, a footstep, the squeak of a stair step, the squeal of door hinges. Must have laid there for an hour, listening. All I could hear was the beat beat beat of my heart.

And then I must have fallen asleep in spite of myself, in spite of being scared shitless for no good reason. The adrenalin had drained away and I had crashed. Must have fallen asleep because all of a sudden I became aware of more light being in the room than could have been cast by the desk lamp. (I had decided I wanted to see the lethal blow coming; at least that way maybe I had a chance.)

I think I was also a little surprised that I was still alive.

I got up and peeked out through the blinds but in the morning light no campfire was visible — no smoke from smoldering embers, either. I saw no movement at all. I wasn't sure if that should be a comfort or not. What if he was standing beside the front door, just lying in wait for me?

(Who the hell is *he*?)

He is no one, a figment of my squirrely imagination, a complete fabrication by an overactive, over-tired brain.

At that moment I knew I wanted to be away from the house, just for a few hours, just to calm myself and convince myself that my behavior last night had been totally nuts. I ran downstairs, peed (and by then I really *really* needed that!), took a quick shower, (Didn't you ever see *Psycho*?) pushed thoughts of scary guys in old lady drag brandishing butcher knives out of my mind, changed into clean jeans and a tee-shirt, and went into the kitchen to grab breakfast. The bright, cheery, unscary kitchen! I made myself a quick peanut butter sandwich and washed it down with a glass of milk, eating standing up because I was still too much on edge to sit down.

My breakfast sandwich sat in my stomach like a stone because now I had to get out of the house. And what if he was pressed up against the wall just outside? I went to the front door, slowly, quietly unlocked the deadbolt, then taking a deep breath, I flung open the door and ran out on the porch, down the steps and into the front yard. If anyone had been laying in wait for me, he would've been hard-pressed to catch me. I whirled around, but the only thing on the porch was my bicycle. My heart was racing again, but as soon as I saw nothing amiss, it began to slow. I was glad that there were no neighbors to see me flying out the front door like I was being chased by a swarm of banshees. After I caught my breath — and after I acknowledged to myself that I was a complete moron — I went back to the front porch and closed and locked the door.

I was going to get onto my bicycle and pedal into town, really I was. But before I could get my butt on the seat, I remembered the campfire and my curiosity overcame my good sense. I made the decision to check out my mysterious neighbor.

Not that I was going to walk over there bold as brass and introduce myself.

My plan was to do what any sensible person would do.

I was going to sneak up on him.

I pulled my socks over the bottoms of my jeans — there's ticks and chiggers in the woods and the last thing I wanted to do was tease one of those nasty critters out of my skin — and started off in the direction of the campfire. I wasn't meant to be a hunter; I made enough noise to wake up roadkill, but I hoped my neighbor would just think I was a coon or possum or something

(A 160-pound coon, now that would be something to see!)

and not pay any attention. I guessed from the size of the fire that the campsite was about a hundred yards out, so when I looked back toward the house and saw its dwindling size I figured I must be getting close. I slowed down and actually tried to be quiet. I watched my feet and avoided twigs. Every now and then I heard one snap, and then I would freeze and listen. Not hearing anyone coming toward me —

(Killers in the woods are always ninja-trained not to make a sound, you know.)

--I would start up again. All of a sudden something bright green—unnaturally green—caught my eye. It was the top of a tent. I slowed down even further, and then something else caught my eye. A big, hulking black thing over to my right. I squinted at it but couldn't tell what it was. Of course if it had been a Florida black bear, it probably was close enough to have killed me, but it wasn't moving (was it?) I didn't even think it was alive. (Was it?)

I decided I had to know what it was. I didn't want to know, but I had to know. You know how that is, right? You're about to burn up with curiosity and yet you're afraid to find out?

(Curiosity killed the cat, you know.)

It didn't look dangerous. It didn't even look alive. In fact, it didn't look like much of anything except this big black thing.

As I approached it, the black thing took on the shape of something vaguely familiar and by the time I was right up to it, I realized what it was. It wasn't entirely black, either. Small pieces of its original fabric were still intact. Something floral.

It was a chair.

And someone had burned the hell out of it.

Not just scorched it the way you might if you fell asleep with a cigarette or if you spontaneously combusted, burning away the seat and back and only leaving behind your feet in a pair of shoes. This thing, this chair, was incinerated, like someone had doused it with gasoline and then thrown a match.

There was also something about it that niggled at my mind, like I should have recognized it for what it really was only I couldn't.

Why would someone drag a chair out into the woods and set fire to it? I'd never heard of such a thing. A sacrificial chicken, goat, maybe even a virgin, but a chair? Who worshipped the Great Upholsterer in the Sky?

Looking at it started to make me feel uneasy, like some little worm had gnawed its way into my spine and was wiggling its way up and down my back. I began to get the feeling that it was more than just a chair. It was almost like it was

(alive)

No, no, that was stupid. It was just a piece of furniture, just the burned up hulk of a chair.

Abruptly I pushed the puzzle of the chair to the back of my mind and turned my attention back to the campsite. Carefully I creeped a little closer, then flattened behind a tree and took a peep. The campsite seemed to be deserted for the moment, although the camper could have been sleeping in the tent.

The tent itself was a nice one, not the sort of shabby thing fished out of the trash that you would expect to find a homeless person using. And it was big. Probably slept eight adults, easy. There were zippered windows, an overhanging flap that formed a sort of porch, and a screened door. A tall man wouldn't have to stoop to stand up in the middle of it. About six feet in front of the doorway was a brick-lined pit with the ashes and partially burned logs of what had likely been last night's campfire. A spit had been rigged over the pit and a cast iron kettle hung from it. Next to the tent stood what looked to be a cistern, brimming with water.

I thought about calling out, yelling *Hel-loooo* or maybe *Hey, neighbor!* all bright and chipper and non-threatening, but the words stuck in my throat. I didn't think I was quite ready to meet this mystery man with the burned up chair and fancy tent.

At that moment the worm in my spine wriggled and an inexplicable feeling of panic struck me. I felt watched. Like maybe the man from the tent had heard me coming, taken off into the woods and even this very minute was out there, watching me. I felt eyes behind me. Or maybe that wasn't a chair at all. Maybe it was something else, something in disguise. I felt my heart starting to pound again. I froze. I didn't want to turn around because then it would know I knew it wasn't a chair. It wasn't a chair, it was this big black thing and it was coming up behind me and any minute now it was going to rise up, giant maw gaping and full of wicked teeth and

(eat you!)

A scream caught in my throat like a badly chewed hunk of steak and I took off toward my right, bounding blindly like a rabbit in a panic, crashing through the underbrush with the scrub bushes grabbing at my jeans and tee-shirt, scraping my bare arms as I pushed them wildly out of the way. After a few seconds of running madly through the woods, I stopped, winded, and whirled around.

I could see the burned out chair, sitting right where I'd seen it.

I could see the green tent, pitched right where I'd seen it.

I felt like a complete idiot.

I had no idea what had spooked me, but obviously my imagination was working overtime.

When my panic subsided, I began to tromp back to the house, not caring whether I made noise or not. Whoever was living at the campsite, he probably was not at home, and whether he was or not no longer mattered to me. I didn't care who he was. I didn't even want to know. What I wanted was to be away, far, far away from the campsite. Why he or someone else had burned that chair was none of my business. In fact, none of this was my business. If he was trespassing, that was his problem, or the property owner's, or the sheriff's department's problem, but not mine.

I decided to get my bicycle after all and take a ride around the area, clear my head. My intention was to ride until I was too tired to pedal a single yard further, tired enough so that I could fall asleep and not hear noises and not imagine boogeymen in floral upholstery, and not have a single dream, good, bad or otherwise.

But when I got back to the house I saw a car I didn't recognize sitting out front, as if waiting for me.

Tressels' Grocery Store
May 27_____

The only thing that startled me more than seeing a car I didn't recognize sitting on what passed for a driveway in front of my rental house was seeing who got out of that car. He wasn't the last person in the world I expected to see, but he was damned close to it.

"Parker?"

The blond head that rose above the vehicle's door as he got out of the car turned toward me and grinned. "Surprised to see me, Fresco?"

"Uh, yeah, you could say that. What are you doing here?"

He grinned wider. "Can't a guy visit a pal in exile?"

I couldn't immediately answer him because the gleaming car was burning holes in my retinas. It was a brand new Dodge Charger Daytona RT in Top Banana yellow, zero to a hundred in nothing flat with black honeycomb grill and black racing stripes. "Whose car is this?"

"It's mine. Like it?"

"Well, yeah, who wouldn't? Where'd you get it?"

"You going to invite me in to see your digs?"

"Uh, sure, yeah." I led the way up the porch and unlocked the front door, then stepped back and let Parker precede me. He pushed his sunglasses onto the top of his head, looked around and began nodding appreciatively.

From his name, you'd expect Parker Rodriquez to be dark with black hair and eyes and olive skin, but as I understood it, only his father was Hispanic—Mexican, maybe, possibly Puerto Rican. Parker's mother was Norwegian or something and Parker had a truckload of her genes. Pale blond hair cut very short and spiked in front, blue eyes with blond eyelashes barely visible, acne-plagued fair skin that would've burned in no time had he been inclined to spend any time out in the sun. But Parker Rodriguez was your typical geek, preferring to spend time with his computer or books rather than venture outdoors.

"Nice," he proclaimed. "Really nice. You really lucked out, didn't you?"

"That I did." The silence that followed was awkward as hell so I decided to play the accommodating host. "You want something to drink? I don't have much, just some Mountain Dew and ice water."

"A Dew will do," Parker said. I don't think he'd stopped grinning since he pulled into the driveway though what made him such a happy camper was beyond me. If I didn't know him better, I'd say he was stoned, but Parker wouldn't have done weed or any other drug even on a dare. Not even for a thousand bucks. (I would've done it for a hundred, myself. But it seemed from the car that Parker's folks had big bucks; money probably wouldn't have been much of an incentive for him to do anything.)

"You got it." I headed for the kitchen and Parker followed me. I took two Dews out of the fridge and handed one to my guest who popped the tab and swigged. "Don't get me wrong here, Parker," I began, "I'm glad for the company—Sundays are sort of the pits here—but what are you doing here? I mean, it's not like we're...I mean...."

"We're not pals," Parker finished.

"Yeah, well, we do know each other, but it's not like me and Mojo or Whippet. I'd expect one of them to drive all the way down here to see me, but...."

"But I'm a surprise."

I fidgeted with my can of soda, popped the tab and drank before answering. It was what you'd call a delay tactic. "Well, yeah. a good surprise, mind you," I said finally, "but...."

He waved my protest away with a pink-skinned hand. "It's okay, I understand what you're saying." Parker became serious for the first time. "We're not best buds so why'd I bother to come see you, right? Well, I know what it's like to be alone." He shrugged. "So shoot me for being a nice guy, but I just wanted to know you were doing okay, that's all. Figured we were in a similar boat for once."

I nodded. "I do appreciate the visit."

"How about we head on down to Spring Creek and grab a good lunch? Give you a chance to check out my wheels."

"I'd like to do that, Parker, but I'm afraid my budget is pretty tight right now and Spring Creek isn't exactly on par with McDonald's."

"My treat."

"Oh, no, I couldn't let you do that."

"Hey, I'd like to. Come on, it's just lunch. You won't be indebted to me for the rest of your life. You can always reciprocate some time....if you want."

I didn't really want to say yes. Despite how deadly dull my Sunday threatened to be, I knew spending any length of time with Parker was bound to be the ultimate in awkward. I barely knew him. What would we talk about? I also didn't want to give him the false impression that one afternoon was going to make us tight as two ticks. That would've been really unfair to him and would've also made me feel guilty as hell. On the other hand, he was looking at me with such need, such hope, that I didn't have the heart to turn him down flat, so against my better judgment, I nodded. "Yeah, sure, what the hell. Spring Creek it is."

"Great! It's a little early though. You got any errands you need to run? I wouldn't mind driving you around some. Heck, in that car, it'd be a pleasure."

"Well, I could stand to go back to the grocery store down the street. I'm going through Dew like nobody's business."

"Let's go."

We went back outside and I locked up while Parker used a little electronic gizmo to unlock his car. The inside of the Charger had that new-car smell that can send guys over the moon with ecstasy. The seats were gray leather striped with that same Top Banana yellow, and the interior trim and body panels were also the color of sunshine. I rubbed the butter-soft leather seat cover. "You never said where you got this car."

"It was a gift."

"Your parents sure are generous."

Parker grinned. "Well, you know how it is when you're an only child."

I wished I did! *I* was an only child but it would never occur to Phil Fouraker to give *me* a present like that. "The grocery store's just ahead on the right," I told him. A minute later Parker pulled his stunning yellow car into one of the few spaces in front of the store. There was one other vehicle in the lot, a nondescript white pickup. I hadn't noticed before, but the sign over the front door said **TRESSELS' KOUNTRY STORE.** (Why did people always have to spell C words with Ks? What was up with that? Was that supposed to be kute?)

The same woman from yesterday—who I now suspected was Mrs. Tressel—was behind the counter. She smiled when she recognized me. "Back so soon?" Then her face drew a cloud over it. "I'm afraid I still don't have a job for you."

"Oh, that's okay. The diner needed a busboy."

"That's wonderful! You'll like working for Carl. He's a nice man." She sighed. "Poor man."

"Martha," said a man's voice from the interior of the store and his tone was one of warning. An elderly man popped his head up from where he'd been stocking the shelves. Looking at him, it seemed there was something to the theory that people who were together a long time tended to look like each other. Even without telling me, I would've guessed that the man was related to the woman behind the counter. He wore similar glasses and his gray hair was curly, much like his wife's, only shorter and a tad higher on the forehead.

"Land sake, Hubert," Martha said impatiently, and I remembered that she had said her husband was named Hubert and didn't like her gossiping.

"I think Carl mentioned something about losing his wife, Alice," I said, hoping to prompt the couple into giving me the low-down on the Alice behind the Eats.

"He lost her all right," Hubert snorted.

Martha frowned in her husband's direction. "Now who's gossiping?"

Now they had me curious as hell. "Is there something I shouldn't talk about around Carl?" I asked, hoping that using a tone of sensitivity might get them to tell me why Carl was such a poor man. "I thought maybe his wife had passed away."

Martha glanced over at Hubert and though the elderly man was scowling at her, she just frowned back. "No, she's just fine and dandy, as far as we know. Just up and ran off one day."

"Didn't just run off," Hubert put in, and I suspected he liked gossiping as much as Martha but wouldn't have admitted it in a million years. "Not by herself, any way."

"He's such an old poop," Martha said. "Always complaining about me spreading gossip and all, and there he goes, flapping his gums to the first person to ask about Alice."

"In the case of Alice," Hubert Tressel said, coming over to the counter with a box so that he could load the "teaser shelves" — the place were store owners usually put gum and candy and other things people tended to buy on impulse—"it's not gossip if the story's true. And the truth is, Alice Quint run off with an insurance salesman."

"Adjuster," Martha corrected. "Alice had a minor accident, just one of those fender-benders as they call them, and they had to have a man from their insurance company come out and take a look."

"And he took a look at her, and before you know it, the adjuster's gone and so is Alice Quint. Never mind that she had a husband and children. Took off," Hubert snapped gnarled fingers, "just like that."

"When was that?" I asked.

Martha thought a minute. "Land, it's been quite a few years now. Carl Junior's got to be, what would you say, Hubert? Twenty?"

"Almost twenty-one."

"He was about sixteen when his mother left. Five years ago. Land sakes, has it been that long?"

"Time flies when you're having fun," Parker grinned.

I gave him a quick frown. "I bet that was really hard on Carl," I said.

"Oh, it was," Martha nodded. "Like to have broke his poor old heart."

"So she didn't disappear like Mrs. Barnes, then," I added. "I mean, at least he knows where she is, sort of. Not like Mr. Barnes. He doesn't know if his wife is alive or dead."

"She's alive, if you ask me," Hubert said, opening a box of Sweet Tarts and putting them on the shelf by the cash register.

"Now, Hubert," began Martha.

"Don't now Hubert me. You know well as I do that Nettie Barnes more'n likely took off with that floozy she called a friend, that Flo McIntyre. Just like Thelma and Louise. You ever see that movie?"

"Flo was not a floozy," Martha argued. She turned to Parker and me to explain. "Flo was a little flamboyant. Liked flashy clothes and all. Dyed her hair red and wore it piled up high on her head. Had a convertible," she added as if that was the epitome of recklessness. "Why she and Nettie Barnes hit it off, I don't know, but Nettie was just like that. She had all sorts of friends and maybe she felt a little sorry for Flo. Flo tended to put some people off. She was a real live wire."

"She was a floozy."

Martha just scowled and shook her head.

"So Mrs. Barnes didn't disappear all by herself," I said.

"Nope, the two of them disappeared together. Just like Thelma and Louise," Hubert said.

"Hush, now, you sound like a broken record with that Thelma and Louise business," Martha complained. "Don't mind him," she said to us. "There's nothing to prove that Flo and Nettie ran off at the same time." Hubert snorted. "What?" she said impatiently.

"Nettie's car was still in the drive and Flo's was plumb gone. They never did find it, or either of them. What does that tell you?"

"Don't you be bringing up that Thelma and Louise silliness again," Martha warned him. "Land sake, he probably thinks they drove off the edge of the Grand Canyon, just like in the movie," she muttered.

All of a sudden I remembered my mysterious camper with the big green tent. The Tressels seemed to be long-time residents of Bethel, and they seemed to know all the news in town, as well. They might be a good source of information. "Listen," I began, hoping I sounded casual, "I happened to notice that someone had a campsite near the Barnes' house."

Martha Tressel's eyes widened behind her wire-rim glasses. "A campsite?"

"Yes, ma'am, about a hundred yards from the house. I didn't see anyone out there, but they have a tent pitched. Any idea who it might be?"

Martha shook her head. "Not unless it's Mr. Barnes. That is his land."

"T.B. Barnes has a truckload of money," Hubert countered. "Can't imagine that he'd be living like a hermit out there. 'Course," the old man ran his hand through his thinning gray curls, "can't say we've seen much of T.B. since Nettie ran off."

"Disappeared," Martha corrected him. "If you're concerned, you could call the sheriff's department. I'm sure they'd check it out."

I smiled. "I'll think about it. I'm sure it's just someone passing through and I'd hate to get anyone in trouble." I knew all too well what it was like to run afoul of the law and I wouldn't wish that kind of hassle on another human being. Not even a boogeyman in a bright green tent. As long as he left me alone, I figured I could return the favor.

Alice's Eats
May 28_____

Desperation is a strange thing. Only the truly needy would have worked as hard as I did to persuade Parker to stay overnight with me. I just did not want to be alone, and would have been glad for the company of Sasquatch, that's how much I didn't want to be alone. After lunch at Spring Creek Restaurant—it's right on the water so the fish is so fresh it practically flops on your plate—Parker drove me around the Crawfordville area and damned if we didn't come across a Wal-Mart Supercenter. It would be a bit of a ride on a bike but definitely do-able if I absolutely needed to get there. (Got a couple of big fridge-packs of Fresca because they'd be a bear to haul back to the house on a bicycle.) I'm sorry to say that I treated my trip to Wal-Mart like it was an all-expenses paid vacation in Paris. A few days away from civilization and already I was craving something as mundane as a super-sized grocery store. Sad, really sad. Then, because I wanted to give Parker an incentive to hang around, we also stopped off at Lee's Liquors and I picked up an old friend: a fifth of Captain Morgan and some diet Coke. (We might get drunk, but at least we wouldn't end up as fat drunks.)

"I don't know," Parker said after we got back to the house and I'd had a chance to mix him a rum-and-coke. He looked at the glass like I was offering him hemlock.

"Come on, live on the wild side, why don't you?" I urged him.

"I won't be able to drive—as you should know."

That stung, but I let it slide. "So spend the night. I have plenty of room. You don't have to get back tonight, do you?"

"I was going to hit the road early to go see my folks before summer session started." (Leave it to Parker to go to school year-round.) But he must have seen that desperation for company in my face because he took pity on me and accepted the rum-and-coke. "I guess I could leave a little later than I figured," he said, and it was weird how relieved I was.

Parker sat down on the sofa and leaned back, propping his feet up on the coffee table while I fixed a drink for myself. "Never took you for being afraid to be by yourself."

"The house makes me a feel a little twitchy? You?"

He shook his head. "No. I think it's a great house. Quiet."

"A little too quiet," I told him. "I think that's it. It's too quiet and too isolated. I'm just not used to it."

"Well, I'm sure you'll be okay with it once you get a chance to settle in. You might want to invite some of your friends to spend some time with you."

"Offer them an all-expenses-paid vacation in beautiful downtown Crawfordville?"

Parker grinned. "Something like that." He raised his glass. "Best drinks in town."

That night I slept like a rock. I'm sure part of that was having Captain Morgan to keep my company, but I was also comforted knowing Parker was downstairs in the bedroom I'd left empty. (And no, it wasn't because the killer would reach him first and his screams would wake me up and give me a chance to escape. Well....maybe it was partly that.) Before we went off to our respective beds, I told him I had to be up early for work and if I was gone, he should just lock the door behind him when he left. I hoped he was sober enough to remember that, but if he wasn't there wasn't much in the house to steal, so no big deal.

The next morning I found Parker flat on his back in bed as if he hadn't moved an inch all night, snoring like a buzz saw. I knew he wasn't much of a drinker and I'd pretty well gotten him soused the night before so it wasn't too surprising that he was still sleeping it off by the time I left for my job at the diner. I wrote him a note thanking him for the visit (didn't want to burn any bridges there), and left him a bottle of aspirin with it. I grabbed my bike from the porch, ran it down the steps, and was about to pedal off when I stopped dead.

There was a man standing about twenty-five yards off in the middle of my driveway, just standing there, staring at the house and now that I was out there, at me. He was a tall, light-skinned black man in a long-sleeved plaid shirt, jeans and black boots, his hands jammed into his pants pockets. I stared back at him and then he slowly took a hand out of his pocket and raised it in a wave. Not a wave exactly. More like an Indian in an old Hollywood movie saying "How." Even though I was stunned to see him, I raised my own hand and waved in return at which point he nodded at my acknowledgement and stuck his hand back in his pocket.

I saw no weapon though why I had immediately thought he might have one, I don't know. I had never made assumptions like that about strangers before: thinking every one meant to do me harm. Like I told Parker, I was twitchy; no doubt that's why I was so damned paranoid all of a sudden. Slowly I walked my bike up to him and tried to smile.

"Morning," I said.

"Good morning," he said, and he had a resonant voice, not quite a dead ringer for the deeply melodic James Earl Jones, but close. As I neared him, I could see he was a lot older than I had first thought. His close-cropped hair was steely gray and there were deep lines etched on his face. He looked past me at the house and a look of loathing crossed his face before he turned his attention back to me. "You living here?"

"Just staying here for the summer."

"That your car?"

"Belongs to a friend of mine." I almost said, *Not that it's any of your business,* but for some reason, I didn't.

"Not a good place for a young man and his friends," the old man said. "We need to talk."

"We need to talk? You mean, you and me? About what?"

"This and that." He jerked his head over toward where I had seen the campsite. "I'm staying out there in the woods."

"I saw your campfire the other night."

"Then you know where I am. Come see me when you can. As soon as you can."

"I have to work today and I'm volunteering at the Springs tomorrow morning."

"Tomorrow afternoon, then," he said, as if he was sure I wouldn't refuse. And I didn't, only I didn't know why not. Who was this guy that he felt he could just come here and order me around? I felt annoyed but I didn't tell him to go screw himself or piss off or anything...and that was definitely not like me, either. Normally some stranger telling me—*telling* me—we had to talk would have made me dig in my heels. I didn't. And the funny thing was, I didn't even want to. I think some part of me—maybe a big part—wanted to know what he had to say. He looked at me and his dark eyes seemed to dig all the way down inside me, like he could see all the way to my bones. "Don't put it off now. It's important we talk."

He turned then and started to walk off, but then turned back. "Name's Trojan, by the way."

"Dave Fouraker. Friends call me Fresco."

He nodded and walked off down the driveway. I waited until he was gone before hopping onto my bike and taking off in the other direction, toward the diner.

The appearance of the black man in my driveway had rattled me, but I tried to put his visit out of my mind and concentrate on my new job. It wouldn't do to be hired and fired on the same day for being a slacker. Carl Quint introduced me to the fry cook as soon as I arrived at the diner. "This here's my son, Carl Junior. We call him Denny."

The younger version of Carl, a bloodhound puppy but not as gray or jowly, turned and gave me a little salute.

"Denny, huh? That makes sense," I said.

"Carl Dennis Quint, Jr.," he said. "I go by Denny 'cause it avoids confusion."

A middle-aged woman, so bland that a pan full of day-old dishwater would seem exciting by comparison, came out of the back tying on a pocketed apron as she did so. She had a pencil shoved into the mousy brown hair over her ear. "This here's Kathy Ingram. She does part-time waitressing on our slower days."

If ever there was a woman who didn't look like a Kathy it was Ms. Ingram. Yet when she smiled, it was like a ray of sunshine had suddenly hit her and her blue eyes — most definitely her best feature — were like they were lit from the inside.

"Our other waitress, Lorraine Franco, works Thursday through Saturday. I'll introduce y'all then."

"Rainey works the busier days on account of she's younger and got more stamina for keeping up with the folks," Kathy said, her voice cigarette-smoke husky.

"Nice to meet you," I smiled and Kathy gave me one of those such-a-nice-young-man smiles back, like middle-aged women tended to do to lanky, boyish college students who looked like maybe they were twelve.

A couple who looked fifty-ish was the diner's only customers at the moment. Carl introduced them as regulars, Russell and Rutha O'Brien. "The O'Briens own the Pine Run Ranch, sweetest 70 acres in Wakulla County. Rutha there's half Cherokee."

The pair turned toward me and smiled. Rutha O'Brien did look Native American, with dark, gray-streaked straight hair in a bob and almond eyes, though they were hazel rather than brown. The man looked like a leprechaun on steroids—a big guy, with the curly red hair of someone who'd just stepped off the boat from Ireland and a ruddy face, freckled from the sun.

"They raise mostly appaloosas but spend most of their time giving riding lessons," Carl told me.

"For children three to seven, mostly," Rutha said in a soft voice typical of people who worked with animals. They seemed to have a natural calm that the rest of us never quite manage to achieve. "Our Little Pardners program is very popular, especially in the summer."

"You ever decide slinging hash at his greasy spoon isn't your cup of tea, you come see us," Russ said. "We can always use someone young and strong to muck out the stables, and summer's our busiest time."

"I'll keep that in mind, thanks," I replied, though the thought of being ankle deep in horse shit didn't sound very appealing.

Carl slapped me on the shoulder. "We'll make nice with other customers later," he said. "Time for work."

I nodded and he started showing me my duties. I got a tour of the diner—which took all of ten minutes. My domain was the storeroom where the cleaning supplies were housed and the pantry. Part of my job was to refill the ketchup, mustard and sugar containers, the salt and pepper shakers and the napkin and straw holders. I was to wipe down the tables, chairs, booths and counter, wash the floors at closing, periodically do the windows, and, oh yes, clean the restrooms which, knowing what slobs most people were, was probably going to be a job worse than mucking out the stables at the Pine Run. Carl showed me how to load and run the dishwasher—important because the plates and silverware had to be sterilized; the health inspector checked and you never knew when he might drop by. He then showed me where to stow the cleaned dishes. "Any questions?" he asked.

"Yeah, but not exactly about the job."

"Shoot."

"You know an older black man who lives around here?"

"Son," Carl replied, clapping me on the shoulder. "This here's Wakulla County. We probably got a hundred old black men living around here."

"This one camps out in the woods near the Barnes' house."

Carl looked at me and I couldn't tell if he was just thinking or was trying to decide whether I was plain nuts. "No," he said finally, "can't say I know who that might be for sure, but damned if it don't sound like old man Barnes himself."

"The guy who built Wakulla Wood? The millionaire?"

"The same."

"Why would a millionaire live out in the woods?" I asked.

Carl shrugged. "Good question. Probably not him, then. Or maybe he's just gone eccentric. Rich folks do, you know. Listen, about the job," he said, reminding me with his tone what the really important thing was to talk about, "from now on, I'd like you to work Mondays, Fridays and Saturdays. Mid-week's sort of slow so we all pitch in and bus, but believe it or not we usually get busy on the weekend. Can you work until close?"

He must have seen me swallow. The idea of going back to the house in the dark on a bicycle creeped me out. "You mean, you mean until ten…at night?"

Kathy must have seen my face because she said, "Rainey's got a bike rack. I bet she wouldn't mind running you home after shift, and I could do the same on Monday as I've got a pickup and you could just throw your bike in the back."

I knew I was blushing because it seemed so damned pussy for a guy to worry about the dark. "I'm just down the road… I mean, it's just that I don't have a light on my bike and…."

"And the last thing we need is for our new busboy to end up as road kill," Carl said. "It's plenty dark out there—too dark for a guy on a bike. That's right nice of you, Kath."

"Yes, very nice, thanks," I said.

"That's what we'll do then."

"Hey, Kath," Carl said as an afterthought, "You have any idea where old man Barnes is these days?"

"Wakulla Wood Barnes?" she asked, then shook her head. "Haven't heard anything about him since his wife disappeared."

Carl looked at me and shrugged apologetically.

"Never mind," I said. "It's not important." And I had a feeling I'd find out about the black man in the woods soon enough.

Wakulla Springs Lodge
May 29_____

I got through Monday night at the house by
visiting with my old friend Captain Morgan. I know it
wasn't a good habit to get into, having the Captain around
so much, but I still felt uneasy about being in the house by
myself, especially late at night, and I needed a good night's
sleep before heading over to the Springs for my first day of
community service. Before hitting the hay up in the loft I
checked out the window and saw Trojan's campfire
blazing away. While it wasn't exactly a comfort to me, it
was good to finally have a name and a face instead of just a
mysterious camper in the forest, and also to know that he
seemed like a regular guy unlikely to hit me with an axe in
the middle of the night.

(What was that about how looks can be deceiving?)

No, I was not going to go down that road, not with
the Captain there with me.

Tuesday morning early I rode my bike the two
miles to the Springs. When I set up my community service
I'd been told to report to the office in the main lodge. The
stucco building — what you might call Spanish architecture

though what I know on the subject could fit on one page of a pocket-sized notebook—was nearly 80 years old and smack-dab in the middle of some 6000 acres. Over the years I'd spent at FSU, my buddies and I had spent many a late-spring or summer day here at the Springs. I don't know what the exact temperature of the freshwater springs is but I do know it's cold enough to freeze your balls solid. It does feel damned good on a blazing hot day, though.

I parked, walked to the front door—a big arched wooden jobbie with an outer screened door that looked like it belonged on a castle—set at the back of a U-shaped courtyard, and went into the coolness of the lodge. To the left is the restaurant—big arched windows along two sides—just opening for breakfast. Good smells wafted through the door, and my stomach was not inclined to ignore them. It gave a good rumble in protest as I turned right past the massive stone fireplace to the registration desk that served the hotel part of the lodge. A knot of tourists was milling around the combination gift shop and soda fountain or gawking at the glass case holding the body of "Old Joe," an eleven-foot alligator who'd been murdered by a poacher back in the mid-sixties. At the time a big manhunt had gone on, with everyone searching for the one who'd killed him, but the perp was never caught. I wondered if Wakulla County's finest had expended as much time looking for Nettie and Flo. A small window fronted the registration desk and a clerk looked up as I approached. I stated my business and he directed me down the hall around the corner to the office of Isaac "Ike" Flute, who could help me.

Ike Flute's secretary ushered me into his office right away which surprised me. I figured they might just keep a convicted felon like myself waiting god-knows how long. But Flute was nice enough, shaking my hand and telling me how glad he was to have me there. He was probably in his forties, dark hair creeping up his forehead so that you knew he'd be bald in ten years or so. He had on a plain white shirt, dark slacks, dark tie—looked a lot more like an accountant than someone who ran a historic landmark.

"Volunteers are our lifeblood," he told me, even though he knew I wasn't there because I wanted to be. "Your work will be very important," he added, which was nice enough of him, I guess. He could've treated me like crap and there wouldn't have been a damned thing I could've done about it. You gotta respect a guy like that.

"I'll do my best," I told him, and I meant it. Even though I probably could have thought of a thousand things I'd rather be doing that summer than working for next-to-nothing while busing tables and living in a house that gave me the night-creeps, I wasn't a slacker. My dad always told me that everything you do—and he did mean *everything*—reflected on you. A job well done here, even through community service, might serve me well some-time down the road.

Flute had his secretary page the head ranger, Zeke Nevins, and while we waited for him we engaged in some meaningless chit-chat about my life as a college student, what my ultimate plans were, how I was liking living in Wakulla County for the summer (really had to lie big-time about that!) where I was from—you know, the usual crap you banter around at cocktail parties. All the while I gave pleasant answers and smiled a pleasant smile so that most people would've probably thought I had been lobotomized in childhood.

Ranger Nevins arrived just as my face started to ache from smiling. He took off his tan hat—park rangers also look like Canadian Mounties. Can't quite figure why the style is so popular—shook my hand, told me how glad he was to have me volunteering there (whereupon I smiled with great humility), and told Flute he'd give me a tour of the place and explain my duties.

As we left through the back entrance (which went through the gift shop/soda fountain), Ranger Nevins engaged me in a little more in-depth conversation.

"Here for community service, is that right?" he asked, putting his hat back on as we went out into the sun. He had fair hair cut short and fair skin to match; I figured the broad-brimmed hat was his major defense against the ravages of the Florida sun. Nevins was thirty-something, well-built as if he'd once played football, with a broad amiable face and pug nose.

"I cut off a police officer by accident and I'd had a few beers," I confessed.

Nevins nodded. "DUI, huh?" He glanced at me and I know he saw my stricken face. Those are probably three of the worst letters there are, next to DOA and IOU. "It's okay. My brother had a DUI way back when he was seventeen. Put my parents through hell for a year, but he's doing fine now." He gave me a broad white smile. "Heck, probably better than me. Ranger's pay isn't gonna make me the next Donald Trump, but I don't care. Working outdoors and all—it's a good life, y'know?"

"I can imagine." And I could. The Springs are truly beautiful, trees draped with Spanish moss, squirrels scampering about, the water shimmering in the sun, silver mullets jumping—it was a regular Disneyworld without the lines of tourists.

To the right was a now-defunct snack shop and a red-brick bathhouse out of which came three co-eds in really small bikinis. I pretended not to look and Nevins knew I was pretending as I saw him glance at them and chuckle. "Every job has its perks," he told me making me smile genuinely for the first time that day. The maintenance shed was past the bathhouse and there was another ranger there, with a second one just pulling up in a green golf cart. Two other carts were in the shed, along with a garden tractor-mower, small trailer, and other equipment. My time sheet would be there, Nevins told me, and any ranger could sign it for me in case he wasn't around. Nevins then introduced me to Ranger Vickie and Ranger George ("The last names will just drive you crazy," he told me, "so we'll be informal, okay?") Like Ranger Zeke—I didn't have to deal with his last name, either— Vickie and George were both low-key and friendly, not at all what I had expected. Although Zeke would be my official supervisor, both the other rangers—and any others who came on duty, and I learned there were four others— might ask me to help them do some chore around the grounds. "For instance, there's a stand of Chinese tallow that's popped up just past the diving board area," Zeke told me. "It's an invasive plant and I could use your help in digging it up."

"No problem," I told him. And that wasn't a lie, either. I wasn't Mr. Muscles, but I was in pretty good shape and I could handle just about any job given to me. In fact, I figured that the more I had to do, the faster the time would go.

"Let's go tackle some tallow, then," Zeke said. He grabbed some shovels ("Gotta dig out the root 'cause they're persistent"), work gloves ("You'll blister good without them"), a cooler with bottled water, and a chain saw, put them in the back of the golf cart, and drove us way over to the edge of the springs to a clump of trees with waxy, bright green leaves just starting to put out its greenish-yellow and white spiky flowers. "*Triadica sebifer*," Zeke told me. "Chinese tallow. Also known as Florida aspen."

The leaves were dark on top, silvery green on the bottom, and the trees were covered in sprays of its delicate flowers. "They're awfully pretty trees," I said. "Are you sure we have to dig them up."

"They're pretty all right, but you know, bad things sometimes come hidden in a pretty disguise, isn't that so? Evil can come with a beautiful face." Zeke grinned at me. "Now don't I just sound like a regular preacher, though? Should have my own pulpit, you think?" I grinned back and nodded. "There are lots of toxic parts to these plants so keep your gloves on. When the leaves fall off and decay, they poison the ground for other vegetation, and from there, it'll just take over. If there's evil in a plant, it's in this one. Just kills anything that gets in its way. That's why the state's put it on the invasive list. We dig 'em up when we find them, but their seeds can go far and wide and they'll grow just about anywhere except the real shady spots."

There was something about what Zeke said that niggled at my brain, like it was something more important than just about a bunch of trees, like it was something I should remember or pay heed to.

But, of course, in a flash the moment was gone.

We unloaded the equipment, put on our gloves and set to work. Zeke showed me how to work the chain saw, but I figured I'd let him tackle the tallows first while I gathered up the limbs he lopped off. (Once you see the *Texas Chainsaw Massacre* things like that sort of give you the creeps.)

"You're not staying at the Lodge, I take it."

"No, sir. It'd be nice but...."

"But you'd have to be pretty darned rich to spend any length of time here," he finished. "Got a place in Crawfordville?"

"Bethel, actually. I'm house-sitting."

"That so? I've grabbed lunch now and then at the diner there."

"Alice's Eats," I smiled. "Busing tables there."

"Small world. That waitress—Kathy—still there?"

"She is."

"Like I said with the tallows, the insides and outsides of things don't always match. Now Kathy, she's plain as a bucket of mud, but inside, she's as pure and sweet a soul as you'd ever want to meet. Just the opposite of those tallows."

Zeke put on his safety goggles, revved the chain saw, and began mowing down the tallows, the noise cutting off any further chance for conversation. I had goggles on, too, as Zeke thought the sap might spray and he didn't want it getting into my eyes. Gloves on, I gathered up the branches and made them into a neat pile that we could retrieve later with the garden tractor and trailer. Once the tallows were leveled, Zeke took off his goggles and hat and mopped his face. "Damned if it isn't gonna be a scorcher today. More like summer than spring." He retrieved two bottles of cold water from the cooler and tossed me one. "Break time," he told me and we sat down under the shade of another tree — one I presumed we had saved from the attack of the killer tallows.

"You ever hear of people disappearing around here?" I asked.

"You mean, like cave divers? There're caves under the springs. Very dangerous."

"No, I mean like just people in the area." Before Zeke had a chance to form the opinion that I was nuts, I added, "The house I'm taking care of — I heard a woman lived there who disappeared not long ago. Her and her friend. You ever hear the names Barnes or McIntyre?"

Zeke thought a minute. "Oh, I do seem to recall that. Don't think they were ever found, dead or alive." He swigged his water. "Can't say I know much about the case, though."

"I was just curious, being in the house and all."

"Well, if you've a mind to, you can always go over to the office of The Wakulla Press. It's on the main drag, near the City Hall. It's not a big paper, but it covers all the local news, and I'm sure they have, what'cha call it, a morgue. Went to school with one of their reporters, Tracie McAdams. You can tell her I sent you, if you want."

"Thanks, I might just do that. Give me something to while away my time."

"And keep you out of trouble," Zeke grinned.

"That, too," I smiled back.

"Back to those tallows," he said, heaving himself up.

Trojan's Campsite

I worked five hours at the Springs before calling it quits. On my way home I stopped off at a little convenience store on the way back to the house where I picked up a Dew and a prepackaged tuna salad sandwich for lunch. (The tuna had been ground to glop and the bread was soggy, but at that point I would have eaten one of those damned tallows, I was so hungry.)

When I got to my drive I stopped on the road and peered down toward the house, half expecting the man who'd said his name was Trojan to be standing there once again, but he was gone as was Parker's car. For once I was relieved to be alone. I parked my bike up on the porch and went inside (Parker had remembered to lock up). On the bottom of my note Parker had written Thanks and See U, Park. I doubted if I could ever think of him as a Park no matter how many Top Banana Yellow cars his parents gave him.

I paced around in the house for a few minutes, trying to decide whether I should really go see what the black mystery man wanted. He hadn't seemed threatening, but then neither had Ted Bundy. After a while that old curiosity (the same one that killed cats) got to me. I almost had to know what he wanted, and I knew I was pacing just to put off the inevitable. I was going to go, anyone could see that.

(So what are you waiting for?)

I know this is going to sound totally nuts but I took out a piece of paper, scribbled a "note to be read upon my death" about where I was and with who, left it on the kitchen counter, and then I locked the front door and walked over toward the campsite. For once I did not try to be quiet. I didn't want to give him a reason to shoot me and then tell the police later, "Well, hell, I thought he was a panther sneaking up on me."

When I reached the bright green tent, (and that weird burned black lump of a chair—I would have to remember to ask him about that) Trojan was sitting out front in a bright blue camp chair, the kind that unfolds into a kind of butt sling and even has a place to put a soda. The fire was going and he had a chicken on the spit (at least I hope it was a chicken but for all I knew it could have been anything, even a swamp rat). Talk about heaven on a stick! My stomach rumbled even though it was full of Dew and tuna mush. There was a second camp chair next to the black man—still in his long-sleeved plaid shirt even though the temperature was now in the upper eighties—as if he had set it out just for me. Maybe he had. He had expected me to come and I hadn't disappointed. Somehow he must have known that I wouldn't.

"Come have a sit," he said to me by way of greeting. "You prefer Dave or Fresco?"

"Fresco."

"Been working hard, have you?"

I slipped into the camp chair next to him. "Cutting tallows."

"You have the air of a man who's put in a good day's work," he said.

"I should've showered first, I guess," I said and he smiled at that.

"You want a drink? Only have sodas though, none of that hard stuff."

"A soda would do me fine."

He nodded and retrieved a couple of icy RC colas from a cooler beside the tent. I hadn't seen an RC in years. We sipped in silence for a few minutes until I thought I'd just go nuts if one of us didn't say something. I figured it might as well be me. "You said we needed to talk. What about?"

"The house," he said at last.

"What about the house?"

Before he had a chance to answer, a gray and white cat came out from around the side of the tent and jumped into Trojan's lap. He settled there, then reached up with a paw and patted the old man's face, especially around his upper cheek that sported three thin pink lines, remnants of old scars that would never fade completely away. Trojan saw me looking at the cat and said, "This is my pal, Squint. He's what you call a marble tabby." I could see that the cat had swirls of white among the gray of his coat. His paws, face and chest were white, his nose was pink.

"How'd he get that name?"

"'Cause he's a bad ass cat, and a bad ass cat needs a bad ass name. Oh, I know he looks like a bunny rabbit, but he's as tough as they come. Saved my life, this cat."

I swear the cat looked at me as if make sure I accepted Trojan's explanation, and he did squint. He had narrower eyes than I'd ever seen on a cat before so that he seemed to peer intently at you. Made me a little uncomfortable, if you want to know the truth.

"How'd he do that?" I asked, taking a swig of my RC. "How'd he save your life?"

"Pulled me out of a very bad situation." He fingered those three thin pinkish white scars on his cheek and took a deep breath as if he was trying to buy some time and figure out where to go from there. "Got me out of that house before it was too late."

"You mean, the house I'm staying in?" I asked and Trojan nodded. "Was it on fire or something?"

"Nothing like that." But then he didn't say more about it. I figured it was my turn.

"Your last name wouldn't be Barnes, would it?"

"It would indeed."

"So you're Trojan Barnes? The same Barnes who owns Wakulla Wood? The millionaire?"

His lips pulled a bit as if he was going to smile and then decided it was nothing to smile about. "At your service," he said at last. "Only I don't own Wakulla Wood any more. My daughter, Tasha, and her husband took over the business from me. My heart's not in it any more, nor in making money."

"So you own the house I'm staying in? Because everyone calls it the Barnes House."

"Used to own it. Not any more."

"Who owns it now?"

He fixed me with eyes that were remarkably clear for a man his age. "The owner's a bad man, the worst," he said at last. "And it's a bad house,"

"Actually it's a really nice house."

"You mean, it *looks* like a nice house."

I frowned. "What's the difference?"

"Your not knowing the difference is what worries me." He scrutinized me a bit more and even the cat turned his squinty eyes on me. "Do you like staying in that house, young man?"

I felt a little uneasy with his question. "I get a little squirrelly, at night mostly. I'm not used to being alone, in the woods, in the dark. I mean, I live in a dorm at the university where there's always light and noise and all. I'm not used to the quiet."

"You really think you feel squirrelly, as you put it, over peace and quiet?"

"Well, yeah. Any time you're in an environment that's really different from what you're used to...."

"You really believe that?"

"Look, Mr. Barnes," I began, starting to feel a little irritated. "If you don't mind...."

"Call me Trojan, or T.B. Take your pick."

"T.B.?"

"Trojan Brand Barnes. That's my full name. Went by T.B. for years, when I was still heading up Wakulla Wood. Figured people wouldn't take me seriously if they knew my name was Trojan. But now," he shrugged. "Don't really care. Don't have to care."

"I can see where that could be a problem for a businessman, a name like the—uh—" I tried to think of the polite term for rubber, a pro-something, but he beat me to it.

"Like the condom," he said, nodding. "Exactly like the condom."

"You were named after a condom?" I asked, and he nodded. "Why?"

After a few minutes' reflection he said, "My mother had the sweetest black ass in all of Georgia."

I wasn't sure what to say to a statement like that, so I took another sip of RC. Finally, I managed to ask, "Who would tell you a thing like that?"

"My mother."

"Your mother told you she had a sweet—you know?"

"She was right proud of her ass. Used to rub it with a little oil to make it all shiny, like chocolate satin. The men really liked it that way."

I swallowed hard. "Are you saying your mother was a—(whore)—prostitute?" Yes, I was going to say *whore*, but somehow it seemed wrong to call someone's mother that unless he had seriously ticked you off and you wanted him to beat you to death.

"A lady of the evening," Trojan corrected me. "She was too high-class to be called anything else. Didn't take on just any client. Her johns were all rich men, white mostly. Funny how white men like that brown sugar." Trojan settled back in his chair and Squint nestled a little further down in his lap. "My mother made a lot of money with that sweet little ass of hers. Put me through college and gave me the seed money to start Wakulla Wood."

"So she named you Trojan because of her profession?"

"Not quite. See, she hadn't planned on having any babies as she knew life was hard and she thought it unfair to bring a child into a world like this. So she always insisted on her johns using protection, and birth control pills hadn't quite come on the scene yet. She would always ask, 'You got your Trojan on, sweet thing?' That's because that was the only brand she really trusted. And maybe she trusted her johns a bit too much, because sometimes rich people can be cheaper than anything. And one time a fellow broke faith with her. He used some cheap rubber and it broke and before you know it, she's got me in her belly. Well, she broke it off with him—I never knew him—but she wanted to make that a good lesson for both of us. From then on, she was the one bought the rubbers, always Trojans, and to me—as soon as I was able to understand—she said, 'I gave you your name so you'd always remember what happens when you don't do the upright thing. When you act cheap or lazy or lie, you cause hurt to others.' She loved me, but her life would've been easier without me, I know. Could've lived high on the hog without a child to raise."

"So your father was a white man?"

"So she said," Trojan said, giving me a look that seemed slightly amused. "But don't worry, I won't hold it against you."

"Did she leave her—profession—after you were born?"

"Not hardly. In fact, from then on she always took it in the back door—as she would say—because she didn't like looking in the faces of her johns anymore and they always liked looking at her ass anyway. So never mind how far along she was, her belly never got in the way and she was only out of commission for a few weeks after I was born. She was somewhere in her fifties before she retired that sweet black ass of hers. Moved to Florida on her own personal retirement fund. Passed on a few years back."

"Sorry."

Trojan nodded. "She was a good woman, my mother."

We had gotten off on one hell of a tangent, but as intriguing as Trojan's story had been, I hadn't forgotten why he had asked me to visit him: to talk about the house.

"Why did you say that the house is bad? How is it bad?" I took a deep breath. "Does it have to do with your wife?"

Trojan looked at me sharply. "What'd you hear about my Nettie?"

I immediately felt uncomfortable, like I'd just been called up to the witness chair in the courtroom of a hostile judge. "People in town told me she just disappeared one day. Some think she left with her friend, Flo McIntyre."

Trojan sighed and I could see tears pooling in his eyes. He didn't cry, but I could see he wanted to. Instead he took a drink from his can of RC.

"Linetta was as fine a woman as ever was," he said at last. "Police thought I had something to do with her disappearing. The husband is always the prime suspect, you know."

"I guess a lot of husbands wish their wives were gone, and vice versa," I said.

"Not me, and not her. I was with that woman forty-four years and I would've wished for forty-four more."

"What do you think happened to her? Did Flo McIntyre have something to do with it?"

"What do I think happened to her?" Trojan asked sharply, surprising me. "I don't think anything. I *know* what happened to her. I damned well wished I didn't."

"Did you tell the police?"

Trojan stared at me a moment as if I had just suggested to him that we go dive into a nest of ants. Then he gave a short laugh—not like a laugh when something's funny, but rather when something is so absurd that you can't do anything but laugh. I sat there and kept my mouth shut. Trojan seemed a bit off his rocker at that moment and if he was about to go bug-shit on me, I didn't want to make it worse. But then he seemed to settle down. "You can't tell the police something like that. Hell, I doubt I can even tell you."

"Why not?"

"Because they wouldn't believe me, and neither will you. I can tell. You are disinclined to believe anything I tell you."

"No, I'm not," I protested, irritated that he just assumed my mind was closed tighter than a rich man's fist.

He gave me the eye again. "You didn't believe me when I told you the house was bad."

"Bad in what way? You never said," I scowled, miffed that he wasn't even giving me a chance to show that I could keep an open mind about things.

"It destroys people," Trojan said. "It's evil. I may have built it, but evil took it over. Evil is in every plank and every board. You listen at night, listen hard. You'll hear them. The voices of the evil things." Trojan's eyes had suddenly gotten wild and were rolling in his head like they were made of glass. "They're in there, you hear me? It's no place for you or your friends." Trojan gripped my arm hard, startling the cat so that Squint jumped to the ground, startling me, too, and making me spill the rest of my RC. "You get out while you can, boy, before it takes your soul. Before it takes you, just like it did my Nettie."

I jumped out of the camp chair and backed away from him, a deranged old man with rolling eyes, like he was suddenly possessed.

"Leave that place while you have the chance!" he shouted at me, getting out of his own chair faster than I'd ever seen an old man move. He gripped both my arms with hands shockingly strong and shook me. "You listen to me, boy! You listen, now! It's the house of the devil!"

I pulled away from his grasp, backing up so fast that I nearly fell over, but then I caught my footing and turned and ran as if the devil was on my heels, ran like Ichabod Crane ran from the Headless Horseman, ran like I did that first day with the branches grabbing at me, scratching me all to pieces again. I could hear Trojan's voice yelling behind me, to stop, to wait, to listen. I did none of those. I ran until I was back at the house, wheezing as if my burning lungs would burst, slamming the door behind me and throwing the deadbolt. I ran to the window in the living room and peeped out between the blinds but I didn't see that Trojan had followed me. When my shot of adrenalin began to ebb, I started to shake and feel weak. It was a little early to be socializing with the Captain but I didn't care. I needed some company tonight and at the moment he was the best friend I had.

Casa de Almas (Day 4)
May 30_____

I was pleasantly surprised the next morning when I woke up and didn't have a hangover. The Captain and I had tied one on pretty tight last night but maybe I hadn't been as zoned as I thought I'd been. It was good to be clear-headed, particularly if I was going to have another day of chopping tallows. They could be anywhere, Zeke had said. Fresco Fouraker, Tallow Hunter. The only bad thing about being clear-headed was that I was a little concerned about whether Trojan would be outside lying in wait for me. The old campfire had burned again last night which meant he was still out there somewhere, and most likely crazier than a loon.

After I showered, dressed and had breakfast, I peeped out the living room windows but saw no one. I figured it was time to make my getaway.

Bad timing on my part.

I hadn't even gotten my bike off the porch when from around the corner of the house — likely in a blind spot I hadn't taken into account — came the tall dark form of

Trojan Barnes. My heart started doing some little skippety-doo-dahs in my chest and I stopped dead,

(Bad choice of words there.)

keeping the bike between me and him as if it would be any sort of defense against a nut job who outweighed me by at least fifty pounds. He looked up at me with a pained face.

"I'm sorry about the other day," he said to me.

"That's okay," I said, figuring that the best thing to do was to humor him. "I need to get to work." But having said that I made no move to leave and Trojan didn't get out of my way, either. So we just stood there, staring at each other. I saw him glance at the house and a look came over his face like he'd just taken a whiff of some really bad smell.

"We still need to talk," he said. "I let it get away from me yesterday. I think maybe that could've happened on purpose. I think they don't want me to tell, only I don't know how far their reach is."

"Who's they?"

Trojan winced as if he had suddenly been jabbed with a needle, then wet his lips. "You need to listen to me. I know you think I'm just a crazy old coot, and maybe you'd be half right, but I'm begging you to listen to me."

"Okay, but I've gotta go. I'll be late and I'm working at the Springs today." I moved the bike down the steps, but Trojan remained in my path. In fact, he deliberately moved so he'd be in my path. "I can't be late," I said again. "We'll talk later."

"Listen to me!" Trojan said sharply throwing out a hand to stop me from leaving, and I could see beads of sweat standing out on his dark forehead even though the sun hadn't warmed up the day that much yet. "The house is dangerous! To you, to anyone you bring into it. They'll come for you. Maybe not today, tomorrow or even next week, but—" He winced again and pressed his hand to his chest.

I felt a wave of alarm. "Hey, you okay, Trojan?"

" —they'll take you like—uh!" He grunted and then gave a little jerk as if he'd been kicked. " —like my Nettie, like they did Flo." He was gritting his teeth now, as if speaking against pain, and his eyes were rolling wildly in his head. "They won't just kill you. It'll be—worse than that. They—ah, Lord!" Trojan wrapped his arms around his chest and doubled over.

"Jesus Christ!" I threw down my bike. "Hey, man, what's wrong?" I grabbed the old man's bicep as he staggered, but just then Squint slipped through the bushes at the edge of the house's property and was at Trojan's side in a gray and white streak. He clawed his way up the old man's leg, clearing hurting Trojan who yelped as the sharp little claws found their way through the material of his jeans and dug into his flesh.

"Hey, get away there!" I shouted and waved my free hand to shoo the cat away. Squint was not easily deterred. He kept going, working his way up the old man's chest like he was climbing a tree. Trojan staggered away, pulling himself from my grasp and backing down the driveway, Squint the cat clinging to him, shrieking like a wildcat.

"God! Oh my god! Trojan! Hey!" I called out, but he waved me away. "I'll call 911!" I yelled after him.

"No! Leave it be! Just get out of the house while you still can! Please!"

Once halfway down my driveway, he seemed to recover a bit. He paused just long enough to cradle the cat in his left arm and then he jagged to the right, back into the woods, heading toward his campsite. After he disappeared in the scrub bushes, I realized I was shaking like a sapling in a good old Florida hurricane.

"What in god's name just happened here?" I said to no one in particular. The episode had spooked me enough to make me want to get out of there pronto. I hopped on my bike and pedaled as fast as I could toward the Springs. I was glad I had the haven of the park to go to. A little normalcy in the company of Ranger Zeke and pals was just what I needed right then.

❖❖❖

There was no tallow-cutting to be done at the moment so Zeke showed me how to operate the tractor-mower and set me loose on the extensive lawn around the Lodge. It was just the sort of diversion I needed. Of course, the trouble with diversions is that they never seem to last long enough. Before I knew it, one o'clock had rolled around and though I was tempted to hang around a few more hours, doing so wouldn't change a thing. I still had to go back to the house with Crazy Camper living next door.

Before leaving the Springs, I sat down under the trees at the front of the Lodge at one of the numerous picnic tables there. On the weekend, there wasn't a chance in hell of finding a table unless you were there at the crack of dawn, but this was midweek and only one of the tables was taken by a family of five. I had brought a peanut butter sandwich and a Fresca with me, hoping to avoid Tuna Glop on White as long as my PB held out.

As I sat there and gobbled my sandwich—all that exercise made me ravenously hungry—I couldn't get my mind off of Trojan or his cat. I'd never seen an animal behave utterly crazed like that before, nor seen a guy take the punishment like Trojan had. Almost as if he wanted it—and that was such a nutty thought, I began to wonder if Trojan's insanity might not be catching. The incident made me more curious

(it killed the cat, you know)

than I reasonably should have been. I knew I should just avoid Trojan from then on. I also knew I probably wouldn't. A moth is drawn to a flame, even though the flame usually incinerates the insect *zap!* in a few seconds flat. I liked to think I had more sense than a stupid bug, but the more I thought about Trojan, the more I wondered about him, the less sense I began to believe I had.

I got home a little before two. Plenty of daylight left. Plenty of time to run over to Trojan's camp, make sure the old guy was okay—or at least alive—and get back to the house before dark. So why did I just start pacing around the house, drinking a Fresca?

Was it because I couldn't believe I was actually thinking of going over there?

Was it because I knew I was going to go over there and was just trying to put it off?

Maybe yes, maybe no, but I think *yes.* I already knew I was going, and my tiger-in-a-cage routine was just my way of trying to stall, trying to avoid the inevitable.

I swallowed the last of the Fresca and headed out the door, tromping noisily through the woods towards Trojan's campsite.

Once again he didn't seem the least bit surprised to see me. He seemed to know that curiosity was going to kill this cat over and over and over again. Like before, he was sitting in his camp chair, his RC cola in the can pocket in the arm. He was wearing a baseball cap — Atlanta Braves, I noticed — to shade his eyes from the sun. I couldn't quite see his eyes but I knew he was looking at me. Looking through me.

"Hey, Troj," I said, keeping my tone light, as if we'd just run into each other at the bowling alley or something. "How you doing?"

"Fair to middlin', as they say," he replied. "Fair to middlin'."

At that, Squint the cat jumped into the old man's lap and curled up there. Trojan began to stroke the cat's gray and white fur, but except for giving Trojan's hand a brief nuzzle, the cat never took its squinty eyes off of me.

"You still have that cat around?" I asked. "For god's sake, Troj, the cat clawed the hell out of you. I almost thought he had gone rabid or something. There you were, having some sort of spell...."

"Don't you go raggin' on the cat, son," Trojan replied. His voice was soft and calm but there was an undercurrent to it, something that warned me not to go where I was thinking of going.

"He *clawed* you," I said again. Trojan was wearing his typical long-sleeved shirt and jeans, but I bet under his clothes his skin was raked with bloody welts. How could that not matter to him?

"He did what he had to do. I suspect old Squint is all that's standing between me and damnation."

I sighed. There was no arguing with a crazy person. "Okay, then. You mind if I sit a while?" Trojan motioned toward the empty camp chair beside him and I took it as an invitation. "I'm glad to see you're okay. You really had me going there. I should've called 911, you know."

"No need. I'm better now, but probably never will be really okay again. I could say I'm fine, but I know fine is never going to apply to me ever again."

"What happened yesterday? You have some sort of heart condition? Because, man, I was sure you were having some sort of heart attack." I wanted to know, mainly because I wanted to be prepared if it ever happened again and I really did have to call 911.

"Besides my old heart being broken clean in two since I lost my Linetta, there's nothing wrong with it. Last time I saw a doctor, he said I had the ticker of a thirty-year-old."

"So what happened?" I asked again.

Trojan regarded my question for a few minutes, as if he wasn't sure what to say. "You want an RC?"

"Sure, but I'd also like an answer to my question."

Trojan nodded. "Fair enough." He hoisted himself from the chair, got a cold soda from his cooler, and handed it to me. He looked down at me with grave eyes; I could see their shine through the shade of his cap's brim. "They don't want me telling you about the house," he said, taking his seat. "The problem is, I don't know how far their reach is. Could be safe here, but I don't know for sure. Could go all the way to California and not be safe for all I know. There's no telling."

I popped the tab on the RC cola and took a drink. "You keep talking about that mysterious *they*. Who are *they*, anyway?"

Trojan took another moment to look at his cat and old Squint peered up at him as if they had a little silent confab for a minute. Like they were reading each other's minds. Then Trojan screwed up his face as if bracing himself for a hit and said, "Demons."

When apparently no pain came on the heels of his pronouncement, Trojan's face relaxed a bit, though he didn't look less troubled. In fact, not suffering a pang seemed to bother him. He looked at Squint again and gave him a stroke, head to tail.

"Demons," I repeated. "You're saying there's a nest of demons in my house."

"That's about the long and short of it."

"You thought they were going to stop you from telling me that, but they didn't, am I right?"

Trojan gave me a weak smile. "You're smarter than you look, son," he said.

"Thanks a heap. So why not?" Sounded like I believed him, right? But at that point, I figured playing along was my best bet. Demons! House demons!

"Either I'm beyond their range or they just don't care because they know you're not going to believe me." His face dissolved in sadness. "I suspect the latter." When

I said nothing, he went on, "Let me ask you something. Why do you think that house makes you feel so damned twitchy?"

"Duh, because it's alone in the middle of nowhere, in the woods, in the dark?"

Trojan gave his head a slow shake. "It's them prowling around, biding their time. You feel them. I know you do."

"So what are they waiting for?"

"Now how the hell should I know? I can only guess. More victims, I suspect. And what's time to a demon? They got all the time in the damned universe. No clocks in eternity, son, and they've been around since the beginning of creation. They can afford to wait."

I took another sip of my RC. "You said victims. More victims. So am I to assume from that that these—demons—were responsible for the disappearance of your wife and her friend, Flo?" That sounded so nuts I was glad I was only having this conversation with a guy who was already bug-shit crazy.

"You may."

"Demons kidnapped Nettie and Flo?"

"So to speak. Would've gotten me, too, if it hadn't been for old Squint here. And I suspect they'll come and get you, too, unless you listen to me and get out of there while you can. Of course, I think they'll use you first before they do take you."

"Use me for what?"

Trojan eyed me fiercely. "Bait."

I finished my RC quickly, set down my can and got up as casually as I could. "Okay, then, Troj. Take it easy. Gonna go now. I'll think about what you told me."

"Did you hear what I said, boy?" Trojan was scowling and even old Squint seemed none too pleased with me. Neither one of them believed a word that came out of my mouth but at the moment, sincerity was not my strong suit.

"Yeah, I told you. I'll give it serious thought. Gotta run along now—" I said. I think maybe I even backed away. Figured it didn't hurt to keep an eye on him until I was at a safe distance. I thought I might be able to outrun him, but I'd heard that crazy people often have superhuman strength so I wasn't taking any chances. I gave him a calm wave and then hightailed it back to the house.

Bait.

So what the old man was saying was that I had the equivalent of a demonic fishcamp in my rental house. Now there was a comforting thought.

That night I listened for prowling demons. Listened hard. I didn't hear a thing. Of course, maybe keeping company with the Captain had something to do with that.

Alice's Eats

June 1_____

You know that old expression, *I done died and went to heaven*? That Friday it was truer for me than it had ever been before because that was the day I saw a real life angel. I don't know what her name was in heaven, but on earth it was Lorraine Franco and instead of wings and a halo she wore jeans and a pocketed apron.

I had spent Thursday at the Springs and then Friday was to be my second day on the job at the diner. Thursday had been remarkable in the fact that it had been unremarkable. Nothing weird or bizarre had happened— Trojan hadn't come over, ranting and raving with a crazed cat clinging to him, shrieking like a banshee. No demons had descended on me to kidnap me using Flo McIntyre's flashy convertible. No pieces of furniture had gone up in flames. The peace and quiet was almost unnerving.

Anyway, then came a new day, Friday. The first day of June. I liked marking the start of a new month because in some eight weeks from now I would be back home and all this would be behind me at last. And because the last day of May had been uneventful, I thought June first heralded a fresh new beginning of my time in Wakulla County.

And on top of that, June first was the day I met *her*.

Lorraine Franco. Part-time waitress at Alice's Eats. Petite, pert and plump with blond hair cut like a shag out of the sixties, only thick and cute framing her cherub's face. Big brown eyes, like a doe, and deep dimples in each cheek. She was

(adorable)

Yes, adorable. No other word fit her quite so well.

"Fresco Fouraker," I said, when Carl introduced us, and we shook hands. Hers was small, soft, warm and fit oh-so-well in mine.

"Fresco? Are you an artist?" She gave her cute (adorable) nose a little wrinkle. She had a sweet southern drawl that made me think of a very young Dolly Parton.

"Uh…no…why?"

"Because a fresco is usually a wall painting, you know, like on wet plaster?"

I was probably staring stupidly at her. I remember consciously closing my mouth. "It's just a nickname, like guys in college give each other. It's just what they do. And they call me Fresco because I like that grapefruit soda."

"That's what they do, huh?" she asked, and I wondered if she was thinking that that was probably the most ridiculous thing she'd ever heard.

"My real name's Dave. David," I offered, hoping it wasn't too late to change her impression of me.

"I like David," she said. "It means *beloved*. It's in the Bible."

"How do you know that?"

"I like looking up the meanings of names," she said.

"So what's your name mean?"

She gave her nose another (adorable) wrinkle. "'Fortunate in battle.' Don't that beat all for a girl's name?"

"Oh, a warrior woman," I said, feeling all I was doing was opening my mouth for the purpose of letting stupidity spill out of it. "I guess that means we have something in common. Uh, I mean, David was a warrior, too, right? King David."

"Yeah, David as in David and Goliath, though that David didn't look all that much like a warrior." She tilted her head. "You do look like a David, though. Sorta like Michaelangelo made him out to be."

(Like I should be naked? With a fig leaf? A little too much to hope for this early on, though I have to admit I already liked the way her mind worked.)

Suddenly I felt all blushy, like I was twelve and talking to a teacher on whom I had an enormous crush.

"You just work part-time?" I asked.

"Uh huh, 'cause Kath and I share a position. That's so Carl can afford to keep both of us on. And that's okay. The other days I work over to the hardware store across the street."

"The hardware store?"

"Uh huh, I know my way around tools if I say so myself. I'm an old farm girl."

"That's good. It's good for a girl to know tools, know how to use tools, I mean, equipment, uh, things like that." My tongue tied itself into a knot.

Lorraine gave me a bright smile and patted my chest. "You're awfully cute, there, David Fouraker," she said and I melted onto the floor.

Well, you know I didn't really *melt*, but you know what I mean. My insides had turned to liquid and it was all I could do to keep my mind on busing tables and loading the dishwasher. I couldn't keep from glancing at her. She kept up an easy banter with the customers, laughing, joking, smiling. And they were loving her with their eyes, their smiles, their voices. I felt pinpricks of jealousy seeing the ease with which they interacted with her—and the fact that they knew her well enough to talk with her so easily. What really killed me, though, was seeing how she seemed to love them. I wanted her to look at me like that.

(Oh, you got it bad for this girl already, David Fouraker. And you with a girlfriend, too, tsk, tsk.)

Yes, I know what you're thinking. I did say earlier on that I had a girlfriend. And I know I mustn't forget

(Theresa)

Yes, of course, Theresa! It's not like I forgot her name! It's just that I couldn't really think about Theresa when my mind, my eyes, my heart were so full of Lorraine Franco. Plump, pretty

(adorable)

adorable Lorraine.

So when break time came and she sat in a back booth with a cup of coffee I made a bold move. It wasn't that I wasn't shaking like mad inside, but I wasn't going to let anything like an adrenalin rush keep me from talking to this girl. I grabbed a cup of coffee myself and went over to her booth. I slapped a quarter down on the table. "Buy you that cup of coffee?" I asked, and I thought it was such a smooth move.

She gave me a smile that wrinkled that (adorable) nose of hers. "I'm not sure what century you're living in, David Fouraker, but coffee hasn't been a quarter since my grandma was in grade school, not even here in Wakulla County."

What was it about this girl that made me behave like such a raving idiot?

I sat down across from her. "I only had a quarter." I felt the blood in my face. "I wanted to come up with some cool line to sweep you off your feet, but in lieu of that, I decided to go for stupid."

"Well, I gotta give you points for originality," she grinned.

Okay, so even if I had been stupid, she was willing to forgive me for that. Maybe even find me adorable. But of course at that point—as usually happens when a guy meets a girl for whom he would cut off his right foot if only he could have her—my brain turned to mush and I couldn't think of another thing to say to her. Fortunately, she was easy around people and rescued me.

"Kath said you'd like a lift home after shift."

"If it's no trouble."

"No, no trouble at all. I have a two-bike rack on my car. I know I don't look much like it, but I'm a bike rider myself."

"Maybe we could ride together some time," I said. Okay, there, David, that wasn't too bad. It shows you were thinking. It showed her that you were listening to what she was saying.

"Yeah, uh huh, maybe we could." (Nose wrinkles, dimples pop, heart melts.) "Kath said you weren't but about two miles from here."

"That's right. I'm staying at the Barnes house."

She nodded. "I know where that is. I'm just a tad past that, on Rocky Bluff Trail off Quarry Spring Road. About a mile past the Barnes house."

"Glad I won't be putting you out."

"Not at all. Glad to do it. Well, back to work." She got up and I watched her adorable backside sashay

(Isn't that a great word? *Sashay*. And so right when it came to her backside.)

to the kitchen to leave her coffee cup by the dishwasher (for me to load). I sighed and picked up my own cup and headed for the kitchen. In a couple of hours I would be in the car. With her. Alone with her. I wished I lived fifty miles from the diner.

After loading the dishwasher, I went to the pantry to get ketchup and mustard and other stuff to refill the containers. I figured I'd get a jump-start on that job so that I wouldn't keep Lorraine waiting.

"Hey! Bus boy!" said a sharp male voice behind me, scaring me so badly I nearly spilled the box of straws I was holding. I whirled and saw the fry cook in his greasy, stained apron standing in the doorway, arms by his sides, clenching and unclenching his hands into fists. His face was all dark and mean—unlike the big loveable goof he'd seemed to be when I'd first met him—and he was looking at me like he wanted to put one of those fists into my face, though why he should be angry was beyond me.

"Hey, Denny, what'cha need?" I said lightly.

"I need you not to go messing with Rainey! She's my girl!"

I was so stunned by Denny's heated tone, that for a minute I couldn't answer. I might have contemplated messing around with Lorraine, but as far I could remember, I hadn't acted upon it. "We just had a cup of coffee—" I offered.

"A cup of coffee," he repeated, mocking me. "First it's coffee, then it's dinner, then it's messin' around."

"Wow, I didn't realize it was as easy as all that," I said. That was not the wisest thing I could have said, but diplomacy has never been my forte. I realized my mistake when I saw the blood start to turn Denny's already shadowed face purple.

"You sonuva—"

"Denny!"

I looked past the angry fry cook and saw my angel appear. She put her hand on Denny's arm. "What's going on here, Denny? What's wrong? Why are you yelling at David?"

"I don't like him messin' with you, Rainey," Denny pouted. His tone was more sullen now than angry and his face had lightened. It was amazing how her touch could do that, and so fast.

"Now Denny, you know you and I are just friends, and now David is another friend. To me and to you."

"Don't want no other friend but you, Rainey." Now he sounded like a sullen toddler.

"Oh, Lord," Lorraine sighed, and left me alone with the Hulk.

"You leave her alone, y'hear?" A lot of that dark blood that Lorraine had miraculously drained from the angry man's face suddenly flooded back and his eyes were hard.

"I told you, Denny. We were just having a cup of coffee. You know, break time."

"Well, don't get any ideas." Denny didn't seem quite as threatening as before, but I could tell that his anger was bubbling right below the surface and now that Lorraine the Hulk Tamer had gone, I was afraid he might erupt and smash me one. But that threat apparently wasn't enough to shut my mouth.

"Or what?"

"Or maybe I'll give you what for, is what." And with that he took two steps into the tiny room and shoved me against the shelves along the back wall. I heard the supplies rattle and a box fell off the top, nearly striking me.

"Denny!" Carl appeared in the door with Lorraine by his side. So she hadn't abandoned me after all; she had gone to get Denny's main handler. Carl grasped his son by the shoulder. "Go on back to your grill now, son," he said gently. "Lunch crowd's on its way and you already got yourself a customer."

"He was messin' with Rainey, Daddy," Denny said, little-kid sulky.

"Come on, Denny," Lorraine said, taking the fry cook's arm. "Let's go tackle that lunch crowd, what'd'ya say?

"I'll talk to Dave," Carl assured him.

I could only imagine what Carl was going to say, and on the top of my list was *You're fired!* But Carl surprised me.

"My son's a good boy but not the sharpest tool in the shed, if you get my drift. He's got quite a crush on Rainey. He got attached to her because she's always nice to him, and the way he is — a little slow, not much of a looker — well, kindness sometimes gets a little scarce."

"He got the wrong impression from me," Lorraine put in, reappearing at the door. "Denny's grilling a bunch of burgers," she said to Carl. "He's okay." She looked at me with those big brown doe eyes full of concern. "Are you?"

"Oh, yeah, no harm done," I said, though I wanted to claim major bodily injury just to garner a little of her tender loving care.

"Denny's wrong impression isn't your fault, Rainey," Carl said to her. "But if you don't mind, Dave, if you two could keep it real cool while you're at the diner — no coffee breaks and stuff like that — I'd appreciate it."

"Yeah, sure, no problem," I told him. "Whatever keeps the peace, Carl. I didn't mean to cause any trouble."

"You didn't. Thanks, Dave."

And Lorraine smiled at me, which was almost as good as her TLC.

Lorraine's Car
June 1 (evening) _____

For the next few hours I avoided Lorraine Franco like she was Typhoid Mary. I didn't even look at her (much as I wanted to). I wiped the tables, filled the containers, loaded the dishwasher, restocked the cabinets with dishes, the drawers with silverware. I kept my head down, my eyes averted, did my work and that was it. Every time I had to walk near the grill, though, I got a prickly feeling, and once when I dared a quick glance in Denny's direction, I saw his big jowly face scowling at me, his lips tight, his eyes screwed up into the points of two daggers. And once, when I passed close to him on my way to the kitchen with a plastic tub full of dishes, he moved toward me briefly and whispered, "You staying at the Barnes house, aren't cha. People disappear from the Barnes house." I pretended I didn't hear him, but both he and I knew I did. And before I got to the kitchen I had the feeling of worms crawling up and down my spine.

Just before ten, Carl flipped the closed sign in the door and told us we could go. I took off my apron and

hung it in the pantry and a minute later Lorraine did likewise.

"You think it's okay

(*Safe.* I was going to say *safe,* but thought that
sounded too much like something a total wuss would ask.)

for me to ride with you?" I asked.

"Denny's harmless," she told me, brushing off the
very idea that the fry cook might be a maniac with a flip of
her hand. "Besides, you can't ride that bike in the dark.
Someone'll run you over for sure."

As I walked back through the diner I saw Denny
scraping his grill, thankfully making him too busy to pay
me any attention. Carl shooed Lorraine and me out the
door.

I put my bike on her car's rack and tied it down,
then got into the passenger seat. Lorraine started the car
but didn't immediately put it into gear. "Listen, I'm sorry
about Denny going off on you like that. I probably
should've known better."

"Known better than to have coffee?" I asked,
incredulous.

"Coffee with you, with another man. In the diner
like that. I guess he thought I was rubbing that in his face
or something, and he took it out on you instead of me.
Honestly, I just want to be friends with Denny, that's how
it's always been in my mind, but I guess he took it the
wrong way. He doesn't seem to understand that we don't
have a relationship, but I don't want to hurt him. He's
really very sweet."

(Like a psychotic bulldog.)

"It's a dilemma, for sure." Lorraine put her car into drive and pulled onto the road. "You mind if we stop at the convenience store near the Springs? I'm out of milk for breakfast and it's the closest place that's open."

(Milk. She had *milk* for breakfast. How wholesome could anyone get?)

"I'm in no hurry to get home." What an understatement that was. "So let me ask you this," I said, surprising myself with how bold I was being, but as I recalled there was some saying that went *Faint heart ne'er won fair damsel* or some shit like that. "Hypothetically, if I were to ask you out, like for dinner or something, and you accepted, would I be taking it the wrong way?"

"No." (Smile. Dimples. Major heart palpitations on my part.)

"And if I were to ask you out, do you think it would be at the risk of having Denny beat me to death?" (Who was I kidding? If I asked her out and she accepted, Denny wouldn't have to beat me to death. I would just drop dead of pure joy.)

Lorraine smiled again and shook her head. "Denny's not dangerous."

"He sounded pretty dangerous to me."

A little frown appeared on her perfect brow. "Why? What did he say to you?"

"Just that people disappear from the Barnes house."

She gave a little laugh, clearly relieved. "Well, two people did disappear from the Barnes house."

"That didn't sound like a threat to you?"

"I told you, Denny's harmless. He's all talk, just trying to scare you."

I wanted to say that he did a damned good job of it, but I didn't want her to think I was a complete wuss. First I don't want to bike home in the dark, now I'm afraid of some big goof? Puh-*leese*.

She sighed. "I know I should've done more to discourage him, but I just wanted to be nice. He seemed so lonely. He's not the sort that girls go for, you know?"

"I'm not entirely sure what girls go for." (What kind of guy do *you* go for? That's what I wanted to ask, and I wanted her to say, Why, someone just like you.)

"The thing is, Denny's a good kid but he's a fry cook and won't ever be anything else. Oh, that sounded bad, I know. Snobby. But I don't mean that there's anything wrong with being a darned good fry cook. It's that he doesn't want anything else. He has no other ambition, and his idea of a good time is to watch TV with a bowl of popcorn and a cold beer."

"That doesn't sound so bad, depending on the person you're watching TV with."

"No, but he doesn't want to do anything different, or see different places, or do something worthwhile with his life, not even as a volunteer. He doesn't like to read unless it's a car magazine with lots of pictures, he doesn't want to learn anything new, or visit new places, he's not interested in history, and if Garth Brooks doesn't sing it, he doesn't want to hear it. I don't think I could stand having a life that narrow." She glanced at me and her look was dead serious. "You get what I mean?"

Dared I think that my opinion of her mattered to her? I nodded. Although my life had been a little bit too adventurous at the moment, I couldn't imagine being such in the monster rut that Denny seemed to have dug for himself.

"I know what you're thinking," she said flatly.

(I hope not. At the moment I'm thinking how much I'd like to see you naked.) "Uh, what am I thinking?"

"What is a waitress doing complaining about the ambitions of a fry cook? But I'm just waitressing to save up money for school. I don't want to be waitress my whole life. Not that there's anything wrong with being a waitress, either, but I just want something more. I want my life to matter somehow."

"And what do you want, Lorraine Franco?"

She gave me a sidelong glance as she pulled into the brightly lit parking lot of the Circle K convenience store. There were enough lights around that store to land a small plane. "You won't laugh?"

I placed a hand over my heart. "Never."

"I want to be a vet's assistant. I love animals and Sante Fe Community College—"

"Santa Fe, New Mexico?" I said.

Lorraine laughed. "No, Sante Fe in central Florida, near Gainesville. They just started a two-year course of study with the University of Florida's College of Veterinary Medicine."

"The University of Florida!" (To a student at U of F's biggest rival, those were very dirty words.) "You'd be better off in New Mexico!"

She gave me a puzzled look.

"Sorry. Only someone from Tallahassee would understand the depth of my horror. There's a saying up there that Friends don't let friends go to the U of F."

"You're funny, David," she said, though she gave me a dubious look. "Anyway, I'm just trying to save up enough money to go to school and get by with a part-time job until I graduate and then get a real job." She opened her door. "Back in a minute."

I watched her go (*sashay*. God those jeans were snug.) into the convenience store and continued to watch her as she went to the cooler, picked up a half-gallon of milk and went to the counter to pay for it. A minute later she got back into the car, putting the bottle of milk between us.

"Is there any reason why you're going for the vet assistant job instead of being a full-blown veterinarian?" I asked as if our conversation had never been interrupted.

She stuck her key in the ignition. "Well, as my Momma would say, I'm a little long in the tooth to be starting medical school now. I don't even have a bachelor's degree. I'd be over 30 before I even could get started."

"You can't be that old."

"Twenty-four—"

(An older woman. I always wondered what it would be like with an older woman. It? I've known her less than a full day and I'm already thinking about *it*? Hell…yeah.)

"—but there would be four years of college, then another four in medical school, an internship, a residency. That would be a long haul at this point. I'll be happy being a vet assistant." She stopped and looked at me. "What?"

I realized then that I had been staring at her. Staring at her mouth. "I love to listen to you talk. Your accent is — (adorable) cute."

"That's not from North Florida, you know," she said, though I'd already guessed that. "I was born in Eufaula, Alabama. You ever been?" I shook my head. "It's a pretty town. Historic. Not far from Providence Canyon. You should go some time."

"So how did you end up in Bethel?"

Lorraine started the car and backed it out of the parking lot. "My Momma's folks were from just outside Crawfordville. They left my parents sort of a farm. I live in Bethel because I wanted a little independence, but didn't want to be too far away. I have a little studio apartment over a garage."

"Sort of a farm?"

"A bee farm," she said.

"Bee farm? Your family raises bees? Those are — bugs."

"They're *important* bugs," she laughed. She seemed to do that a lot. "My parents' land sits up against a fellow who has an orange grove — well, oranges and lemons. Our bees pollinate his trees and end up making orange blossom honey from his flowers. We give him some of it, and he gives us all the OJ we could want. It's what you'd call the perfect symbiotic relationship. What?" She had caught me staring again. "You don't think a little old Alabama girl would know a big twenty-dollar word like that?"

"I'd never think that."

"Well, that's good because lots of folks do. I tell you, they hear a southern accent and right away they drop your IQ twenty points. Throw in the fact that I'm a waitress and a blond woman, to boot, and there goes another twenty or thirty points."

"I would never think that a blond waitress from Alabama was anything but amazing," I told her.

That made her laugh again, and the sound of her laughter was enough to keep me on the edge of bliss for about an hour.

Until sometime around midnight when the glass in one of my front windows shattered.

Alice's Eats
June 2_____

"You look like hell, son," Carl said to me the next morning when I showed up at the diner. He was just being kind, I know. Anyone else would have taken a gander at me and said I looked like a pile of warmed-over shit. That's what a lack of sleep will do to you.

The broken window at midnight had startled me awake, but it hadn't scared me as much as you would think. I was more angry than anything and I immediately called 911, hoping the vandal would hang around long enough to be picked up by the cops. No such luck, though. By the time the Wakulla County Sheriff's deputy showed up, Mr. Vandal was long gone. (And make no mistake. I felt very sure it was a *Mister* Vandal, probably with the first name of *Denny*. It was the sort of supremely stupid thing that someone like Denny would do—take out his frustration with me on a house that didn't even belong to me.)

The deputy and I stood on my porch at one in the morning while he took my statement—which was basically a series of I don't knows seeing as how I was in bed while Mr. Vandal was putting a rock through the front living room window. The deputy did retrieve the rock—just your generic, gray, run-of-the-mill rock, one of a million in the state of Florida—though why he bothered I don't know because he certainly wasn't going to dust it for prints and it's not like it came from someplace traceable. Finally he pronounced that the deed probably had been done by a bunch of kids who thought the house was empty and therefore a fun target until my lights came on and scared them off. He said he would be sure to file a report. For insurance purposes, of course, not for arresting the perpetrator.

As the deputy stood there finishing that report, I saw Trojan visible in the pulsing red and blue lights of the patrol car. He was standing at the edge of the house's property, just beyond the scrub bushes, and Squint was sitting by his side. The deputy followed my gaze.

"You know that gentleman?"

"He's my neighbor, Mr. Barnes. I don't expect that he'd seen anything."

"No, there are rarely witnesses to these sort of things," the deputy agreed. "I wouldn't worry too much. When kids do these sorts of things, it's usually on a lark and not something they're likely to repeat."

I nodded, thanked him for coming so quickly (even though he hadn't), and said good night. As the deputy left, Trojan sauntered over to me.

"You all right, son?"

"Just had some jerk put a rock through my front window," I told him indicating the ragged hole in the glass pane. "Don't suppose you saw who it was."

Trojan shook his head.

"Doesn't matter. I have a pretty good idea, only I can't prove it. I'll call Mr. Eblis in the morning. I guess they'll have to have someone come out and fix that window. I'll just tape it up until then."

Trojan gave the house a look of disgust. "The house'll take care of itself," he said.

"What does that mean?"

"Just wanted to make sure you were okay. Saw the lights and all and was afraid something bad had happened," he said, then turned with a wave and disappeared back into the bushes his crazy cat by his side.

I went back into the house, wondering if I should have told the deputy my suspicions, that it had been Denny Quint, fry cook, who had been so pissed off by me flirting with his so-called girlfriend that he had put the rock through my window. Maybe yes, maybe no, but I had decided *no* and I was sticking with it. I had no proof of his guilt, and any accusation I leveled against the big lout would probably have hurt his father more than the idiot son. I didn't think it would happen again—Denny probably just needed to blow off some steam—and until or unless it did happen again, I would spare Carl the embarrassment.

But after my sleep was so rudely interrupted, I had a hard time getting back to sleep. Dealing with morons like Denny Quint always pisses me off, and my annoyance kept me awake for hours. I lay there, periodically checking the digital clock next to the sofa-bed, watching the time pass (slowly) and worrying about how I was going to get through a full day of work. And a Saturday no less—the busiest day in the diner's week.

And that was why Carl pronounced me a refugee from hell the following morning when I dragged myself into **ALICE'S EATS** and started my shift.

"You been partying?" he asked.

"No one to party with. I iust didn't sleep well," I told him. "Occasional insomnia."

Carl nodded, although I caught a glimpse of Lorraine and from the look on her face I could tell she wasn't buying that story for a minute. "Okay, then," Carl said. "Just don't go falling asleep in the dishwasher."

I went to get my apron from the store room and Lorraine followed me there. My whole day perked up considerably just seeing that pert, adorable little figure standing there. "What really happened last night?" she asked.

The way she said it immediately depressed me, because her tone suggested that she thought I had had hordes of women over after she dropped me off and that we had had an orgy until dawn. I told her about the rock and my suspicions about Denny and her look changed to one of dismay. Dared I hope—concern?

"You didn't tell the police?"

"I didn't want to hurt Carl. Besides, I can't prove it was Denny."

She gave me one of her bright smiles. "You're sweet," she told me.

(Hey, break some more windows, Denny, you moron, and really cement things between me and "your girl.")

"Do you want me to talk to him?" she asked.

"No, I'll have a few choice words with him and then let it be."

And I did have choice words, believe me, I did. I was up half the night thinking about what I would say to the big jerk. Choosing just the right words. Oh, yes, they were choice, all right.

After I had bussed my first table of the day, I was going back to the kitchen with the plastic bin full of dishes when I took a moment to sidle up to the fry cook who at the moment was intent on flipping burgers on his gas grill for a party of six that had just come in. I put the bin down on the counter a moment and said under my breath, almost as if I were talking to myself, "I have some quirky friends back in Tallahassee. Some are football players, too. Big guys." Denny pretended I was invisible, but I knew that he knew I was there and that I was speaking to him — even if indirectly. "You know why these guys are so quirky? They all have the same pet peeve. Know what that is, a pet peeve?" Denny grunted but didn't answer me. "Anyway, they can't stand people who mess up other people's stuff. Vandals. You know, people who spray paint graffiti, and *break windows*. A person like that — a vandal — well, they would seriously fuck up someone like that. Yup, they're sure quirky that way." Denny didn't answer me, still pretended I wasn't even there, but he heard me all right, I know he did. I felt I'd said enough.

The fact that my guys back in Tallahassee wouldn't have given a flip about broken windows or the jerk who broke them wasn't important. For all Denny now knew, I had a bunch of freakin' Mafia people at my beck and call.

Maybe it would make him think twice about interrupting my sleep again.

Just then I heard a *THUNK* from the party of six and a woman's voice shriek, "Oh, Matthew!" and then Lorraine's (adorable) southern voice said, "David, we seem to have had a little spill—it's all right, ma'am. No harm done, just a little milk and you know what they say, no use cryin' over that, isn't that so?" I looked over at the party—a mother, father, grandmother and three children—and saw them starting to titter at that, embarrassed, but no longer mortified by their child's mishap. She had that way about her. Always knowing just the right thing to say. "We'll just get this cleaned up and get your little boy another milk, no trouble at all, right, David?" She met my eyes. "David, could you get a mop and bucket, please?"

I nodded. I swear that woman could make a person eat ground glass and like it. Matthew's mother, who moments ago had been angry and upset, was now smiling. That girl had such a way about her. I knew that first hand. Her way sure had an effect on me.

"Sure thing, Lorraine," I said, not caring whether Denny heard me talking to her or not. I went back into the storeroom, got a wheeled bucket and mop and some cloths, filled the huge pail with water from the big sink next to the dishwasher, and headed back into the dining area, rolling the bucket ahead of me.

You know how it is when really bad accidents happen, how time seems to slow way down, like everyone and everything goes into slow motion and every detail becomes magnified and etched into your brain because of that?

That's what happened as I went into the dining room and all hell broke loose.

As you go from the store room to the dining area, you pass by the cooking area: refrigerator, stove, cabinets and coffee urns and Denny's large gas grill. Then there's an aisle for the cook, server and cashier, and finally a counter for those customers who like their bar stools. As I went by, out of the corner of my eye I thought I saw Denny's grill flare, the light catching my attention and making me turn toward him at that very moment. I swear I saw what looked like an orange tongue of flame come out of the grill and lick the front of Denny's greasy apron.

With all that hamburger fat on the apron, Denny went up like a torch, giving out the most horrible scream of fear and pain I've ever heard a human muster, and beating wildly at his flaming torso as if he were trying to brush away a swarm of stinging insects.

That's where the slow motion kicked in. I was aware of Lorraine crying out in alarm, of Carl yelling in anguish as only a parent can when they see their child in grave danger, and of Matthew's mother who finally had something really bad to shriek about.

And there I was, probably the only thing that stood between Denny and a burning death.

At that moment I was running on pure instinct fueled by adrenalin because I knew that the rational part of my brain had shut off. I picked up my huge pail of water — something only minutes before I had huffed and puffed to lift down to the floor from the sink — and threw its contents in Denny's direction, dousing the flaming fry cook. Most of the fire instantly went out. I flung down the bucket and hurled myself at Denny, bringing him down hard on the floor. Not that he offered any resistance. He was writhing and smoldering and stunk of burning flesh — not a pleasant scent, I can tell you. It's sweet and sickening and will probably remain in my nose's memory for life. I remembered yelling, "Call 911!" and "Get wet towels!"

That was my first aid training kicking in, one of those courses you take in college just to get enough hours to graduate, one your friends tend to laugh at for it being a pussy class. Not something you ever believe in a million years that you're going to need. I bet old Denny wouldn't be laughing at me for taking that class.

Wouldn't be breaking any windows anytime soon, either.

Carl stood over us, eyes wide in terror, frozen, mouth gaping, anguished.

I heard Lorraine ask, "Ice?"

"No, that's too cold. Just cold wet towels. Hurry!"

The flames had singed off Denny's eyelashes and brows and his skin was a mass of ugly red rawness. I could see that the fire had literally melted what was left of Denny's clothes onto his skin. He was moaning pitifully and though moments before I had hated his guts, no one should have to suffer anything like this. Imagine burning your finger and how much that hurts, and then multiply that by a thousand, ten thousand.

Lorraine brought the sopping towels and together we covered Denny's burns.

"The ambulance is on the way," she told me and Carl, although he didn't seem to hear her. His eyes never left his tortured son. "Hang in there, Denny," she said to the stricken man.

"See if you can keep him quiet," I said to her. Denny was groaning loudly and squirming and I was afraid he would push off the wet towels and tear his mutilated flesh. Lorraine moved to Denny's head and pressed her hands on his shoulders—the one small part of him that wasn't burned—to keep him still. She leaned over and said something soothing to him. The big mutt started weeping, but occasionally he nodded his head in response to her, and he stopped writhing.

I slid down on my backside, completely spent, and leaned against the wall. There was not a drop of adrenalin left in my system to sustain me and if I had stood up, I would have fainted dead away.

The house took its revenge.

I have no idea where that thought came from, but when I thought it, it seemed almost plausible. Denny had pissed off the house and the house had gotten even.

I knew it was just because I was so emotionally and physically spent that I was even thinking a crazy thought like that.

On the other hand, that tongue of flame from the grill had ignited Denny's apron (licked him) for no apparent reason. It had seemed surreal, alive, like a fiendishly living thing. I didn't need to threaten Denny with being fucked up by my quirky, Mafia-like friends; it seemed the house could do serious fucking up all by itself.

But that was a stupid thing to think.

Wasn't it?

I moved out of the way for the paramedics, barely aware of their presence. I did hear Lorraine's voice (which I could probably could have heard through anything, even if I were drowning in a hundred feet of water). "You don't worry about a thing, now, Carl," she was saying. "You go on and be with Denny and we'll handle the diner."

Then, all of a sudden, there were sirens but those gradually faded as the ambulance headed toward the hospital. (Was there a hospital in Crawfordville? Probably not. They were no doubt bound for Tallahassee.) I felt Lorraine standing in front of me. I looked up and there was her pretty, plump (adorable) little figure, hands on her hips, smiling at me. "David Fouraker, if you aren't just a genuine hero!"

I waved away her pronouncement, but when I stood up, a knot of people in the diner applauded and I felt uncomfortable with the attention. Throw one bucket of water on a burning guy and suddenly you're Superman, champion of the people. But to see the look on Lorraine's face—well, god forgive me if I wasn't just a little glad for the fry cook's misfortune.

St. Marks Trail
June 3, 2007_____

"What's your hurry?" I called out to the speeding figure ahead of me, the plump, adorable little woman with legs strong as a kangaroo who could pump bicycle pedals like nobody's business. Lorraine immediately slowed and stopped, and was grinning at me when I pulled up next to her, huffing and puffing. "I thought this was going to be a leisurely little excursion."

"I like to feel the wind."

"I like to feel the wind, too, but I don't need a damned hurricane!"

Lorraine laughed. "There are some benches just up ahead. We could take a break, since it looks like you need one."

We pedaled—slowly this time—about fifty yards further along the trail and stopped on the right where there were picnic tables and a water fountain. These were new amenities added to the St. Marks Trail—a pathway for bicycle riders, skaters, pedestrians and the occasional person on horseback—that had been created by paving over the old Tallahassee-St. Marks rail bed, a train route that was abandoned in the early 1980s. The little town of St. Marks sits on Apalachee Bay and is actually a very old and historic Gulf port despite the fact that less than 300 people live there now. An old wooden fort was built there by the Spanish back in the 1600s, and rebuilt several times, most recently as a stone structure called *San Marcos de Apalache* that still stands there and was used up through the Civil War. The trail originally started just north of Woodville, a community some ten miles south of Talla-hassee, and ran 16 miles down to the coast. Another five miles were added from the trail head going north so that it now extends to the Tallahassee city limit. I've biked the whole original 32 miles before, though I have to admit that one's butt is not the same for some days afterwards.

We'd had a rough Saturday what with our fry cook going up in flames. Carl called us a few hours later to tell us that Denny would make a full recovery eventually, but that he would be out of commission for a while. Without Carl and Denny, that left only Lorraine, Kathy and me to handle the busiest day at **ALICE'S EATS**. Lorraine took over like a first lieutenant whose commanding officer has just been shot to smithereens and needs to deal with being surrounded by enemy gunfire.

"Kathy can handle the grill and other cooking," she told me. "She has a passel of kids and so cooking for a bunch of customers isn't gonna faze her any." She handed me an order book and pencil. "I'll need you to help wait tables, David."

(Are you out of your mind?)

"Okay, sure, Lorraine, just tell me what to do."

"You don't have to know prices or anything like that. I'll wait tables when I can, but mostly I'll handle the cash register and ring up the tabs. All you gotta do is write down what people say they want." She looked at me earnestly. "I know you can do it, David. It's not that hard, honest."

I nodded. Even if I had never held a pencil in my life, I would have agreed. Now was not the time to wimp out in front of the girl of my dreams.

"You know the menu's pretty simple. Just gotta ask how they want their burgers cooked, or what sides they want, or drinks."

"I *have* eaten in restaurants before," I said.

Lorraine grinned. "And I bet you're a fine, big-tipping customer, too," she said. "You and I will just have to bus together as we can." And with that, our first customer since Denny became a candidate for the Olympic torch walked through the door for lunch.

Kathy was a tad leery of firing up the grill, but there were no flare-ups. It behaved itself as I already knew it would, even though I couldn't reassure Kathy of that without sounding nuts. The house isn't mad at you, Kathy, I could have said and she would have immediately called the nearest asylum. The idea even sounded crazy to me.

"Heard there was some excitement around here earlier," the man said as he settled into a booth and studied the menu. I had a feeling we would get a lot of that and braced myself to recount the drama as required.

I won't say it wasn't hectic, but it was also a challenge and the three of us worked together like that well-oiled machine you keep hearing about. By 9:30 that evening we were tired, but also very self-satisfied with how well we had managed to run **ALICE'S EATS**, short-handed as we were.

"Carl'll be proud of y'all," Lorraine told me and Kathy.

"Carl will be proud of all three of us," I replied, making her smile.

We fell into our usual routines for closing up, and when Lorraine finally flipped the sign to **CLOSED** we all sighed with relief.

"At least tomorrow's Sunday," Lorraine said to me as I loaded my bike on her car's rack. "We all need a break after today. And then Carl'll probably be back on Monday. I've got the hardware store otherwise I'd lend y'all a hand. Maybe I can pop in after we close."

"We'll be okay," I assured her. "You whipped us into shape."

I felt as if she wanted to say something else to me, but didn't know how to spit it out, so I just got into the passenger seat of the car and bided my time. When she pulled into my driveway, I could tell that she knew it was now or never time.

"We had quite a time today," she said. "Hard work."

"We did indeed."

"Sure glad it's Sunday tomorrow."

She was getting mighty close to making me start smiling. I didn't know exactly what she was trying to get at, but I had a feeling it involved me, her, and recreation.

"You have any plans tomorrow," she asked finally—but casually. I bet she'd had to practice that off-handed tone to get it sounding that laid-back.

"Well, first I was going to sit out on the back porch and watch the scrub bushes grow. Then if I really want to have some fun, I might do my laundry...."

"I thought maybe you and I could do something together," she said, and I also saw that she had turned an adorable shade of pink.

"Sure, two people can watch those old bushes, and do laundry...."

"Something fun!" she scolded me, but she was smiling so I knew she wasn't mad.

I grinned at her. "What did you have in mind?"

I suppose for a few minutes there I actually thought—because of the depth of her blush—that she meant something romantic, like a candlelit dinner, some drinks and dancing, followed by some very hot sex.

So here we were on Sunday, pedaling for all we were worth out on the St. Marks bicycle trail.

Don't get me wrong, I really would have watched the damned bushes grow, if it meant I could spend the time with her, it's just that I was a tad dismayed to see all that incredibly adorable blushing go to waste.

As it turned out we had a spectacular day. Sunny, not too hot or humid the way it would get when summer hit full force. We only did half the trail, a scant eight miles from the parking area to St. Marks, that to avoid having to drive most of the way back to Tallahassee to get started. We had two BLTs at the River Cantina. (The traditional stop-over, Posey's Oyster Bar — previously the hang-out with autographed one dollar bills stapled all over its walls in a sort of funky decor—had been all but blown away by a hurricane not long ago.) After lunch we made our way to the old fort and graveyard. At that point I made a bold move and took her hand, the main point being that she did not resist this move, and I relished the feel of that warm, soft hand in mine. Relished it a little too much, maybe, because it got me started thinking about how soft and warm the rest of her probably was, and I had to silently scold myself to enjoy the moment and not let my imagination start screwing things up. While reading the grave markers, though—a romantic spot if ever there was one—I took a second bold step, pulled her gently toward me and kissed her and she didn't resist that either, and damned if her lips also were soft and warm, just like I imagined!

I suppose, then, it isn't a big surprise for me to admit that I decided to see just how bold I could be. On our way back toward Crawfordville we stopped at Hammaknockers BBQ for two plates of their well-sauced baby back ribs. That was something else I grew to admire about Lorraine: she wasn't food fussy. She didn't go to a BBQ and order a salad with dressing on the side. She didn't mind getting sauce smeared on her face and fingers. It spoke of a kind of sensuousness that I hadn't seen in other women I'd dated

(like Theresa)

Believe me I hadn't thought about Theresa all day and I certainly didn't want to think about her now while I was sitting across the most adorable, BBQ-sauce-smeared girl on the east coast. Her name just popped into my mind because Theresa was food-fussy and therefore had a hard, athletic body that most guys would kill to know in the Biblical sense, and who, for some reason I could not fathom, had suddenly become very unattractive to me. I'd dated Theresa since my sophomore year, knew her very well in the Biblical sense, but right now I wanted her to be last thing to creep into my mind and that made me feel just a little guilty.

Scratch that. *A lot* guilty.

I literally shoved my thoughts of Theresa out of my mind and concentrated entirely on the (literally) saucy little wench sitting across from me.

Because I wasn't planning on my day (and night) with Lorraine ending any time soon, and as soon as we got back to my house, I thought I might see how far my bold moves might take me, and whether I still might get some part of my agenda fulfilled.

Need I say how encouraged I was when we arrived back at my place, I unloaded my bike, and I asked if she wanted to come in for a while — and she said *Yes*?

I was even more encouraged when she told me how much she liked the loft. Would she like it enough to spend some quality time there? I thought I would see. Nothing ventured, as they say....

I brought up a few cans of Diet Coke and handed one to her as she sat on the sofa upstairs. No, the Captain was not invited. Whatever happened between us, I did not want it to be under the influence.

We sat together. We sipped. I kissed her. She kissed me back. And not like the chaste kiss we'd shared back at *San Marcos de Apalache* but one that was long, lingering and oh-so-promising. She took off her tee-shirt (not at *my* behest, I might add, but because she wanted to) and I took off mine. Okay, so there was still a little matter of a bra, a minor detail at the moment.

No, I take that back. Her bra—her lacy pink bra—was not a little matter by any means. It overflowed with bounteous goodness, and the phrase, *My cup runneth over,* popped into my head. She saw me staring at her and that pretty blush reappeared.

"I know this probably seems silly, to wear something so—frilly—under these old clothes."

"Silly was the furthest adjective from my mind," I told her.

"It's just that I wear tee-shirts and jeans to both jobs—seems I live in old clothes like that, guy clothes, and I like feeling that underneath all that, I'm still a girl."

I couldn't take my eyes off her. "Oh, you're a girl, all right," I said, deepening her blush. "It's pretty," I added, "and the only way it would be prettier is if it was draped over the arm of my sofa." One thing David Fouraker isn't and that's subtle!

Did I mention that this girl was smart? She knew exactly what I meant and she didn't even pretend that she didn't. And she didn't seem to mind that I wanted to look at her breasts. I hope she was even a little bit flattered that I thought her pretty enough for me to want to look at.

When she reached behind her back I felt suddenly breathless. Boobs on a first date. I done died and went to heaven. Funny how I kept thinking that every time I was around her.

And then when she opened the hooks-and-eyes, and took off that frilly pink bra my first thought was that I had just won two Golden Globe awards, and only my desire not to appear a complete goofball kept me from saying something that stupid out loud.

I slid closer to her, I put my arms around her, I kissed her, and while I was kissing her I put my hand on her soft, warm breast.

Isn't memory a funny thing?

What came to mind as I was enjoying (fondling), okay, okay, *fondling* her breast, was my Grandma Merle. Merle was a bread baker and when I was little, she used to let me help. I remembered how much I enjoyed it when she'd take that big, soft, lump of dough that she had put in a warm oven to rise, and give it to me to knead. Lorraine's breast was like that, and it put part of my mind back in Grandma Merle's wonderful, fragrant kitchen with that deliciously soft dough.

Which is why I didn't immediately catch the change in Lorraine's behavior.

She had stopped kissing me back.

When I realized that, I let go of her and sat back. Her brown eyes were wide,

(Terrified. Terrified?)

her gaze darting around the loft, reminding me of a rabbit cornered by a pack of hounds.

"What's wrong, Lorraine?"

"I—I just got the—strangest—" Her breath was coming quickly, as if she were starting to panic. "Are we alone here?" Her voice had dropped to a whisper, like she was afraid she might be overheard.

"Yeah, of course we're alone."

"It's just that—" She wet her lips and kept looking around nervously. "Are the blinds closed? Completely? Because they look closed, but—"

"Yes, they're closed, and we're on the second floor and I have no neighbors." (To speak of.)

"Something is watching us," she said, her voice breathless, barely audible, and she moved her arm so that she was covering (hiding) her breasts.

(If not from me, who?)

"I feel like something's watching us," she whispered again.

"What? Some*thing*?" I was confused, I was frowning, and Lorraine took that entirely the wrong way.

Her brown eyes filled with tears. "I'm not a tease, really I'm not!"

"I know, it's just that—"

She moved away from me quickly, snatched up her tee-shirt and pulled it on, grabbed up her purse and stood, before I even had a chance to say anything else.

"Lorraine—"

"There's something—something—oh, I don't know! I can't stay here!" She ran down the stairs to the first floor. "I'm sorry, David! I'm so sorry!"

"Lorraine!" I flew down the stairs after her, but she had already flung open the front door. "Lorraine, wait!"

She was so rattled that I managed to catch up to her before she could get her car door open. I grabbed her arm and turned her toward me. She looked like someone

(Or some *thing*)

had just scared the bejesus out of her. "What's the matter? What happened?"

"I'm not a tease, David!" she said again, tearfully. "I swear I wanted to be with you. But that house. I just couldn't be in that house, be with you in that house. I just couldn't. Oh, I'm sorry!"

She looked at me with her tear-filled eyes and I knew what was in that look. It was a look that said, I'm never going to see him again. He's never going to call me again.

"It's okay," I told her, knowing she didn't believe me. "It was a good day. I enjoyed today, being with you."

She nodded, but there was no conviction in it.

"I'll call you. No, I'll come by the hardware store before I go to the diner, check out the tools, you know?" I said lightly, and then realized it was not the time for lightness. "To see you, Lorraine. I do want to see you again."

"Okay," she said, but there was no trust in her face. She didn't believe me and that hurt, but I can't say I blamed her. How many guys say *I'll call you* and never even think about calling? Lots. Too many. I wasn't one of those, but she didn't know that. Maybe she'd had a lot of guys say that to her. I couldn't imagine it, a guy doing that, not to her, but then there are a lot of jerks in this world and, unfortunately, most of those jerks are males. I leaned forward and gave her a sweet little kiss. She returned it, but it felt like goodbye. She got into her car and started the engine. I would just have to prove to her that I meant to see her again. I did mean it. I wasn't going to let a girl like this get away so easily. After her car's tail lights disappeared, I turned back toward the house. Something in that house had spooked her and I didn't get the impression that Lorraine was easily scared.

But what was it?

Casa de Almas (Day 14)
June 8_____

"You have company." Lorraine stopped her car halfway down my driveway.

"Not expected company," I told her. I did recognize the vehicles, though. It seemed the whole gang was here: Johnny Chang's red Honda with the spoiler, Mojo's black Ford truck, the bully boys' green Dodge.

"They're my friends from college. Want to come in? I'd like them to meet you."

Lorraine gave me a pained smile. "Some other time, all right, David? I'd like to meet your friends, but it's been a long week and I'm not feeling very sociable this minute."

"Frankly, neither am I, but they did drive all the way down here to see me." I leaned over and kissed her. "See you tomorrow?"

This time her smile was genuinely happy because she believed me. "You bet. Have a nice visit."

It had been a hard week, and I guess I should catch you up because right about now you're probably sitting there scratching your head.

Carl came back on Monday, but with Denny out, Kathy had to take over his fry cook duties permanently. Lorraine worked at the hardware store Mondays through Thursdays, but ended up coming over to the diner after the store closed to pick up the slack. I still had my community service at the Springs three days a week, but since I got off at one, I had lunch and then pedaled over to the diner to help out as well. It made for a helluva long day, but the upside of that was that I was too tired to lie awake listening for demons crawling around the house. As soon as I stretched out on the bed, I was gone. They could've recreated Woodstock and eaten my soul as an encore and I wouldn't have noticed. Carl promised he would find another fry cook to fill in as soon as possible and none of us would be sorry to see Denny's replacement even if he was a bigger lout than the younger Quint had been.

After the bad way Lorraine and I had parted the previous Sunday, I had been eager for Monday to come, just so that I could prove to her that I was not one of those jerks who dump a girl just because she pulls out of an intimate moment at the last minute. Besides, I felt something had been wrong and I was eager to find out what had spooked her.

Monday was not the time to do that, though. Before going to the diner, I stopped at the hardware store just for a quick visit—and to prove myself to her. She seemed genuinely surprised to see me.

"Are you okay?" I asked. "You seemed pretty freaked last night and I hope it wasn't anything I did. That I moved too fast or—"

"No," she interrupted. "No, of course it wasn't you. I just felt spooked. I don't know why."

"Well, to tell you the truth, the house does that to me sometimes, too. Especially when I first got there. I think it's because it's out in the woods—"

"— because our subconscious knows those two women disappeared from that house, maybe? It probably sets us up to be creeped out." She looked around. Her manager wasn't in eyeshot, but I could tell she didn't want to chance him catching us chit-chatting. "Can we talk about this later? I'm supposed to be working."

"And I'm supposed to be kissing you," I said, "but I have to get to the diner. Oh, what the hell." I leaned over and kissed her, quickly, but not too quickly.

Anyway, even though the week had been a bit brutal given the sheer number of hours we were putting in, I was a happy camper. Spending the extra hours with Lorraine, even if I wasn't really *with* her, but could only look at her, made me feel so happy it scared me a little. The idea that I might actually be

(in love.)

(Say it.)

I certainly liked her a great deal, but could you actually be

(in love)

have strong feelings like that for someone you've known for such a short time? Was there actually something to that

(love)

at first sight business?

Wow.

What I really, really had been looking forward to was Sunday, when Lorraine and I had planned to go over to the beach and look for crabs over at Mashes Sands. (She thought hermit crabs were the cutest things ever and liked to go there and play with them. What a girl, huh?) And then I was going to take her to dinner over at Angelo's in Panacea, a favorite seafood restaurant that had been rebuilt since a hurricane had taken it out a few years back. I was *not* prepared for an impromptu visit by the guys from Tallahassee, fond as I was of them.

I was really not ready for the surprise they brought with them.

Theresa popped through the group of guys, flung herself at me, and wrapped her legs around my waist, kissing me all over my face. You have no idea how grateful I was that Lorraine had begged off. The last thing I wanted her to see was

(my girlfriend)

Theresa Sorrenti, model beautiful, with masses of glossy dark brown hair, greeting me like I'd just come home from Iraq.

"What are you all doing here?" I asked when I could finally come up for air. I wondered if Therese noticed I hadn't been kissing her back, at least, not with any measure of enthusiasm.

"We missed you, fool," Mojo told me. "Her especially, can you tell?"

I put Theresa down, but she wrapped her arms around my bicep, hugging me so tightly I felt like she'd put on a tourniquet to stop my blood flow.

"You're getting buff, Fresco!" she said, squeezing my arm. For a minute I was put off by her calling me that. I'd actually gotten used to a girl calling me *David*, and I found I actually liked it.

"Hard physical labor on a chain gang will do that," I told her, making her laugh. "I'm glad to see all of you but I wished you'd called. I've been working overtime at the diner and I'm whipped."

The guys herded me into the house. "Well, then you're in desperate need of some R&R, I'd say, wouldn't you, guys?" Whippet asked. The gang all agreed, but they would agree to the need for R&R no matter what. They had hauled two large kegs and several coolers full of mixers along with enough alcohol to fuel a good-sized jet. They hadn't forgotten chips, salsa and other nibbles—you needed something solid to soak up all that booze. I had a gin and Fresca in my hand before I barely had time to get through my front door.

What was weird was my genuine lack of desire to get rip-roaring trashed. Oh, I drank my ginned Fresca with relish, and even had a second one, but in the old days (all of two weeks ago or so) I would already have been on my way to being seriously blitzed. The only two to notice my restraint were Mojo and Whippet. Mo leaned over to me at one point and grinned. "Sly dog," he said.

"Why?"

"Drink too much, and you go out of commission," Whippet said.

"And we *know* you're gonna want to be in commission tonight, what with Tessie here," Mo added.

"She's so hot, she practically set our truck on fire," Whippet grinned.

"Lucky sonuva bitch, in about an hour you're gonna have that hot woman all over you. If you need any help—"

"Yeah, don't forget who your friends are. Tessie can probably handle a threesome easy. No offense."

Whippet and Mojo were so busy yapping and teasing me about how I was going to get lucky, that they never noticed that I was one step away from flat out fainting. Given Theresa's strong libido and the fact that she was here, I should have known what was coming, but I must have been too tired to realize what this visit had really been about. The guys had made a mercy trip, bringing two dear horny friends together.

I put my drink down and didn't touch another drop of alcohol. I needed a clear head. Theresa, however, took my sudden abstinence entirely wrong. Never inhibited even when stone-cold sober, now that she was tipsy, all restraint flew right out the window. She got up from where she had been sitting on the floor, weaving a little and giggling, took my hand and said blithely, "You'll excuse us, boys? Fresco and I have some catching up to do."

Of course everyone hooted and teased and pelted us with all sorts of sexual innuendoes. In the old days I would have been grinning like an idiot. This time, I was like a man going to the gallows.

"We won't look!" Mojo called to us as we went up the stairs to the loft.

"We'll *try* not to look!" Whippet amended.

"We might *try* to look!" D'Ante, one of the bully boys snickered.

"Just a little peek!" Wicke Persnicky added. "And just at her!"

Theresa turned around just a moment, yanked up her tee-shirt to give the boys below a quick flash (making them all hoot and holler some more as if they were about to live out a vicarious fantasy through me), and then, laughing, she pulled me up the rest of the way.

By the time we reached the loft, Theresa was all over me like Tar Baby was all over Br'er Rabbit. She stopped kissing me only long enough to pull my tee-shirt off over my head and remove hers as well. "Let's get naked," she whispered. Lips locked, she put my hands on her breasts: firm, like two grapefruit halves. Definitely not soft, warm bread dough. And then I did something I had never done before.

I pushed her away from me.

Oh, I was gentle, but from the shock on her face you would've thought I'd hit her with a club. "What's wrong?" she asked.

I put my hands on my hips and tried not to look at her bare breasts. It was hard enough to know what to say without being confronted with those—something that had once been a great source of enjoyment—until Lorraine, that is. "Tessie, we need to talk."

You know what I hate about women? I hate that with just a few words—and it doesn't matter what words. I could've as easily have said, "Let's get ice cream."— women can read your tone, your body language, maybe even your mind. At any rate, I didn't need to say anything else. Theresa gaped at me, backed away until she found the sofa, and sat down heavily, behaving as if I'd just confessed that I'd murdered an entire family with an axe. She clamped her hands over her mouth and her eyes were huge with horror, so that I almost thought they would pop out of her head and roll away under the desk.

"Oh my god you're sleeping with somebody else!!" she shrieked. "Somebody from—*Wakulla County*!" The way she said that, it was like she thought I was sleeping with an Iraqi suicide bomber.

And all of a sudden it got really quiet down below. So we would have an audience through this, my confession of infidelity. Swell.

Okay, honestly, I think that infidelity was a bit harsh. First of all, all Lorraine and I had done up to that point was some good old fondling on my part. And second, it wasn't as if Theresa and I were married or engaged. The most we had was an *understanding*. But I always thought that that understanding would be null and void if either of us fell in love with other people. I didn't think Theresa was really in love with me. I always figured she just liked me a lot, like I liked her, and that she enjoyed me—like I enjoyed her, I admit it. Honestly, I didn't even think that at this moment—even confronted with the idea of another woman—that she really was reacting in horror because she was in love with me. Maybe it never occurred to her that I could enjoy another woman as much as I did her, and therefore could never want another woman. Until I met Lorraine, it hadn't really occurred to me, either, that I might want something more than a woman who offered me hot sex.

Oh my god.

That sounded frighteningly mature, didn't it?

(*And* that I might actually be — *in love.*)

"Tessie, it was never my intention to hurt you...." I began and all the while she was staring at me with those wide dark eyes. I think she was too shocked even to cry.

And then something fell off the arm of the sofa and caught her attention when it landed on the floor. In this moment of extreme emotional turmoil, I had forgotten all about it. Lorraine's pretty, lacy, pink bra.

I should have given it back to Lorraine, intended to give it back to her on Sunday, but in the meantime I just enjoyed having it around, remembering what she looked like in it. How she filled it to overflowing.

Remembering what she looked like *out* of it.

As soon as I realized what it was that Theresa had spied, I had tried to wish it away. But of course, that never works.

She picked it up. Took it in both hands. Held it up in front of her eyes. Ogled the sheer size of the cups.

"Oh — my — god — " she said slowly, staring at it. "You're dating a — a *cow!*"

And though that was an awful thing for Theresa to say, at that very moment it was the best thing she could have said. For me, anyway. All the guilt I'd been feeling up to that moment flew right out the window, replaced with a flare of anger. In two steps I was in front of her. I snatched the lacy bra from her fingers, furious that she should even handle something that belonged to my Lorraine.

(*My* Lorraine?)

(Yes, my Lorraine! No *maybe yes, maybe no* about it! *My Lorraine* who had big, beautiful, sexy breasts and most certainly was not a cow!)

"Don't say that!" I snapped. "You don't even know her! I didn't mean to fall in love with someone else!"

(What was that? The L word? David Fouraker used the L word?)

"It just happened. I didn't set out to hurt you. I'm sorry, Theresa. I'm really, really sorry — for hurting you, not for meeting Lorraine."

"Lorraine," she whispered as if hearing the sound of the other woman's name was something loathsome.

"These things happen," I said, lamely. Because even though these things *do* happen, it was obvious that these things had never before happened to hot, sexy Theresa Sorrenti. I didn't know what more to say, so I put the bra down on the desk and ran downstairs. All the guys were staring at me, all except one. That one was glaring at me. His sudden hostility surprised me until I realized what that was all about.

He was in love (or at least in lust) with Theresa Sorrenti.

"What did you do to her, you son of a bitch?" Johnny Chang spat at me. "You have a girl like that and yet you go cattin' around with some other woman?"

"Why don't you just go comfort her?" I said, too weary to even defend myself. I looked at Mojo and Whippet. "Don't leave, and don't let Tessie leave, okay. You've all been drinking. Don't get out on the road tonight." Johnny Chang was already halfway up the stairs to the loft. I felt sure that if you put a half naked woman and a man who cared about her together, there would be enough comfort spread around to make her forget a hundred David Fourakers.

"Where you goin'?" Mojo asked.

"Just out on the porch. I need some air."

I ended up sitting there for quite a while, until things inside the house wound down (which didn't take long given that there was nothing like a confession of infidelity to ruin a party), and things got quiet, signaling that everyone had gone off to bed. The bully boys in the beds in the front bedroom, Mojo and Whippet in the one in back, Johnny Chang no doubt upstairs in my bed, busy comforting my ex-girlfriend, Theresa. I felt badly about the way the whole thing had gone down, but not that it had happened. At least I no longer had to worry about Theresa. My entire focus could be on Lorraine. That was remarkably freeing. After a while I went inside and lay down on the sofa in the living room.

I thought the odd secretive little sounds I heard as I lay there in the dark were made by the bully boys snoring through their beer haze, or (more likely) Johnny and Theresa commiserating.

If I had recognized them for what they were, would it have made a difference?

Casa de Almas (Day 15)
June 9_____

When the sun rose I woke feeling surprisingly good. Amazing how not drinking yourself into oblivion the night before can make for a better morning. I showered, then retrieved some clothes from the closet in the bully boys' room, glad I hadn't kept my things up in the loft. Persnicky and DJ had pretty much single-handedly (or double-handedly, I guess would be more accurate) polished off the contents of one of the kegs and for all I knew, had been sharing the second one with the Captain and Old Granddad before they passed out in a drunken stupor. Of the gang, I knew they cared least about the drama unfolding in the loft of Casa de Almas. Girl-friends came and went with Tom Wicke and D'Ante Jefferson. A breakup was no big deal to them. Mojo and Whippet seemed to still be sleeping and for all I knew, Johnny was still comforting Theresa. Gabe had not come along to this par-tay, having had something to do over at Uncle Pete's fishcamp.

Dressed, I went into the kitchen to make myself breakfast. I still had plenty of time before I needed to be at the diner, although getting there early, leaving home before I had to confront Theresa and Johnny again, really appealed to me. I had just bitten into my toast smeared with peanut butter when Mojo and Whippet came into the kitchen.

"Coffee's made and on the counter," I told them. "Help yourself."

Neither one of them looked really bad, either, given that they hadn't had time to get completely trashed before the little melodrama started playing out. They each got a mug of coffee. "Any more of the PB around?" Mojo asked.

I pointed out where I had the jar stashed, as well as the bread for toast. When they had both made their breakfasts, they joined me at the table in the nook.

"What went down last night?" Whippet asked. "You really break it off with Tessie?"

"I did indeed."

Mojo whistled. I suppose when you're a young guy, it's hard to imagine willingly breaking off a relationship with a hot girl who had the libido index of a rabbit.

"How come? Does it have to do with this girl Lorraine?"

It didn't surprise me that everyone had been listening to the conversation. "I'm afraid so. At first I was pissed at you guys for bringing Tessie here, but at least it's over. I would've had to break it to her eventually."

"This Lorraine must be one hot tamale," Whippet said, taking a big bite of his PB sandwich. "Why'd Tess call her cow? Is she—like—" He hefted his hands in front of his chest.

"She is."

"And Tessie knew this how?"

"Let's just say Lorraine left some intimate apparel here by accident."

Mojo and Whippet exchanged smirks. "So she *is* really hot," Mojo proclaimed. "I mean you've know her what? Ten minutes? And she's already leaving her jug cups at your house?"

"She *is* hot, but she's a lot more than that."

Mojo whistled again, as if that concept was beyond belief.

"I didn't realize that Johnny was so hot for Tess," I said. "But that's good, I guess. At least she'll have him. He'll take care of her."

"He'll take care of her, all right," Mojo agreed. "In fact, she drove down with him, well, with him and Gabe. We spent the afternoon at the Waterin Hole, then we all left Gabe there and came here."

"You didn't call me," I said, deciding to scold them a bit.

"Nah, man, we wanted it to be a surprise," Whippet explained, mostly mumbling because he had a mouthful of PB and toast.

"It was that, for sure" I told them. "Listen, I need you two to do me a favor. I have to get to work soon. We're shorthanded at the diner so I can't be late. Will you get everyone up and on the road? I don't really want to confront Johnny and Theresa, if you know what I mean."

"Boy, you got that right!" Mojo agreed. "Johnny was pretty damned ticked off last night. I knew he had it bad for Tessie, but not that bad. But he should be thanking you, shouldn't he? I mean, he's getting what he wanted."

"I bet he got exactly what he wanted last night," Whippet sniggered, making me roll my eyes.

"We'll get them up and out," Mojo told me. "In fact, you think I should check in on the lovebirds? It's pretty quiet up there."

"They're probably exhausted," Whippet said, enjoying this conversation a little too much.

"We better start sobering them up if they're not already, you think?"

"Just as long as I don't have to deal with either one of them," I said with a shrug. "You can stay as long as you need to. I won't be back until late."

Whippet drained his coffee mug and stood up. "I'll just go take a little peek."

"What if they're nakers? What if *she's* nakers?" Mojo asked.

Whippet grinned and shrugged. "So much the better."

Mojo and I sat and munched and sipped and five minutes later Whippet came back. "They're gone."

Mo and I gaped at him. "What do you mean, gone?"

"What do you think gone means?" Whippet frowned. "Gone. Vamoosed."

"Did either of you hear them leave?" I asked.

"No, didn't you? You were in the living room."

"I didn't hear a thing. Maybe they left by the back door," I suggested.

"Why would they do that when their car was out front?" Whippet asked.

"Maybe they wanted to sneak out," Mojo said. "If I were them, that's what I would have done."

Immediately the three of us got up. Mo and I went to the front to look out the window for their car while Whippet went to the back to check the door. He joined us less than a minute later by the front window. "Back door's locked. Dead bolt, too."

"Johnny's car is gone," I said from the window.

"Front door's locked, too," Mojo said and then frowned. "And get this. The dead bolt is still thrown there, too."

"It is?"

"You can't lock that from the outside without a key, can you?"

"No, and I have the only key on my ring. In my pocket. What do you think they did, climb out the window?" I asked. Mojo shrugged. He started trying some of the windows downstairs, but they all appeared to be locked, too. Not just closed. Locked.

"Doesn't seem as if they went out any of the windows down here," Mojo said.

"Anyway, why would they do that?" Whippet asked. "I mean, wouldn't opening a window make more noise than just going out through a door? And if they wanted to avoid you, Fresco, why not go out the back door?"

"I have no idea, but they must have left if Johnny's car is gone." I looked up toward the loft. "I don't suppose they left a note."

"I didn't see one," Whippet said.

I decided to go up and check anyway, thinking maybe they had climbed out of a second floor window — but why would they do that? Were they *that* desperate to avoid me? Maybe yes, maybe no, but I'm thinking...well, I didn't know *what* to think at the moment. I ran up the stairs to the loft, with Mojo and Whippet behind me.

My sofa bed was a mess. Not only did Johnny console Theresa, it looked like he engaged her in Olympic sex. Even the mattress looked lumpier than usual and the bedcovers were wadded into bunches, including the sheets.

"Wow, I knew she was hot, but—" Whippet said.

"That bed looks like they could've grilled hot dogs up here," Mojo added.

"Something weirder than that," I told them and pointed at the floor.

Whippet reached down and picked up a pair of men's briefs. They were *very* brief and *very* red. "No kidding," he said. "Who would've thought Johnny wore stuff like this?"

"Red is a lucky color to the Chinese," Mojo said. "Guess it finally paid off for him."

"That's weird, but what's even weirder is that Johnny isn't in them," I said. "He's not in his jeans, his tee-shirt, and Theresa's not in any of her clothes. Not even her—" I bent and picked up a lacy bikini and held it up. "Not even these."

"So—right this minute there are two naked people driving toward Tallahassee in a red sports car?" Mojo asked.

"Did you all bring a change of clothes with you? Them, too?"

"Of course," Whippet said. "But we didn't get a chance to bring any of that in last night. We figured that could wait."

"So they could've just gotten clothes out of Johnny's car," Mojo said.

"Yeah, Mo, but they would have had to go out there butt naked. Why would they do that when they had clothes here?"

I checked all the windows in the loft, but every one of them was closed and locked. "They didn't climb out of any of these windows."

"Well, if they didn't leave by these windows and they didn't leave by any of the doors and windows downstairs, how *did* they leave?" Mojo asked. "And why they leave their clothes behind?"

"You don't have any secret passages in this house, do you, Fresco?"

"Not that I know of. It's not even that big a house. Not anywhere to hide."

"An attic?"

I shrugged and shook my head. "It's like they just disappeared." I sounded nonchalant but inside my guts were squirming like a barrel of toads.

"Beam me up, Scotty, but ditch the clothes?" Mojo frowned. "No one just disappears."

(Except maybe for Nettie and Flo.) I gave an involuntary shudder, and it must have been a humdinger because my two buds noticed.

"What's wrong, bro?" Mojo asked.

"As a matter of fact, two women did disappear from this house, a couple of years ago. At least, they were in this house right before they disappeared."

"Did they disappear butt naked?"

"Not that I know of, and I'm sure the local gossips wouldn't have left out that juicy little tidbit."

"Look," Mojo said, "we'll head back to Tally Town. I'm sure they're back on campus by now. Hell, Johnny's car is gone, and he wouldn't have left that behind. You know how he loves that thing. I bet they ditched their clothes on purpose, just to make us crazy. To make you crazy, Fresco. They probably *did* drive back nakers, just to bug you."

"And how did they get out of the house?"

"Probably swiped your key. Bet they locked the door and left it under the mat."

I shrugged. "Guess that's as good an explanation as any." (I didn't believe it, though, because my key was in my pocket, and I hadn't even been close to being blitzed last night. I would've felt someone reaching into my pocket, for god's sake!) "I gotta go. Call me when you get back to campus, will you?"

We said our goodbyes and I went downstairs. Maybe what I'd heard the night before had been Johnny and Theresa planning their escape. Maybe they had done just as Mojo suggested.

The only thing was, the noises I remembered from last night didn't sound like two people plotting their revenge against an unfaithful lover.

They didn't even sound like they came from something *human*.

And my key was not under the mat. It was still in my pocket where I'd put it the night before.

Alice's Eats....
June 9_____

"Phone call for you, Dave," Carl said. He let the receiver of the wall telephone dangle and went back to the cash register. It was just after the lunch hour and I was loading dishes like mad into the washer. I dried my hands on my apron as I went to grab the phone.

"They're not here, Fresco," Mojo said after I'd said hello. "Whip and I talked to Gabe and he hasn't seen Johnny since we dropped him at the fishcamp. The Changster's not back on campus, at least, we can't find him."

"Have you seen his car around?" It was a pretty unmistakable car. How many dragon-festooned red Hondas are there, especially outside of Chinatown?

"Not in any of the usual places he parks."

"What about the unusual places?"

"Hey, it's a big campus, bro!"

"I know. Have you talked to Sandy?" Sandy Wycliffe was Theresa's roommate at Murphree Hall.

"She hasn't seen Tessie, either. They're not in town, leastwise, not on campus. I guess we could wait and see if they show up for their classes on Monday."

"That's two whole days, Mo. I don't think we should wait that long. Damn," I said, more to myself than to Mojo. "Where could they be?"

"Maybe they eloped."

"Be serious, Mo. They practically just met."

"Yeah, but Johnny's been hot for Tessie for a while, according to Gabe."

"He has?" That was certainly news to me. I wondered if those feelings had been the least bit mutual.

"And it would be the ultimate pay-back."

"Getting even with me is a helluva reason to get married," I said.

"People have gotten married for stupider reasons than that," Mojo countered.

"Have you called their parents?"

"Dude! They'll freak."

"Mo, their kids are missing! You gotta call them, man. What about the police?"

"We can't get them involved until twenty-four hours have gone by. We'll call tonight."

"Okay, well, I'll be around. I'll check in, just in case you can't reach me. My cell doesn't work too well out here in the sticks."

I hung up and felt someone touch my arm. It was Lorraine, her face screwed up with concern. "What's the matter, David? Bad news from home?"

"Sort of. Think we can take a break?"

She nodded. With Denny still in the hospital, there was no need to live under Carl's gag order. We went out back behind the diner for some privacy.

"Two of my friends who came to see me the other day have gone missing," I told her. And as much as I didn't want to tell her the whole sordid story, including about Theresa and my breakup with her, I did. They don't call it spilling your guts for nothing, though I'd already decided I was going to fudge a bit. I wasn't about to tell her how hot and heavy it had been between Theresa and me and maybe I never would. The thing is, that part of our relationship wasn't all that important in the scheme of things. Usually sex is synonymous with commitment, but not in our case. As intimate as the two of us had been sexually, emotionally we had barely scratched the surface. Intimate really wasn't a good word for what we had. "My friends, Johnny and Theresa." I added, pressing my eyes tightly shut. For a minute I wanted to avoid seeing the expression on Lorraine's face when I said the name of another girl. "My... girlfriend... ex-girlfriend now." I opened my eyes and faced her. *Take it like a man*, my Dad would've said. At the moment, though, I felt more like a male *rat*. It might have been my imagination, but I could've sworn her eyes were about to bore a hole through me. She didn't look angry—I suppose that was a good thing—but she had an expression of... I don't know. Disappointment? I hoped it really wasn't that. Believe me, I can take mad better than I can handle someone else's regret, especially for knowing me. But the cat, as they say, had been let out of the bag, so I forged on. No way I could say, "Theresa? Did I say *Theresa*? Silly me! I meant *Terence!*""

"I meant to tell you about Theresa, Lorraine, I swear, only there never seemed to be a good time to do it. We dated two years, Theresa and I, only I never thought it would go anywhere. Like after we graduated. I thought we'd go our separate ways. I never thought it was a forever kind of thing between us." Not like us, I thought but didn't say out loud.

"And what did she think?" Lorraine asked softly.

I dared to take another look at her then. I wanted to keep my eyes anywhere but on her face, but I felt I owed her that sort of look-'em-straight-in-the-eyes sort of honesty. I wanted her to look in my eyes and see the truth there. "I honestly believed she felt the same way. I still think that. I'm not saying she wasn't upset when I told her about you, but I really think it was because she couldn't believe I'd ever find someone—better." I hoped then that she could read my face and see sincerity there. "I'm not handing you a line, Lorraine. I never thought I would never meet a girl like you."

"A girl like me?" Her brow creased. "What does that mean?"

"A girl who I think is really too good for me but who I want to like me anyway," I said, knowing that that probably sounded too corny for her to doubt it. "Honest to god, I would've told you about Theresa before—before things went too much farther with us. I'm sorry I didn't do it sooner. I should have told her about you, only I was here and she was there and I didn't want to do it over the phone."

"No, of course not," Lorraine said.

"Please tell me you don't hate me," I said, shocked at how desperate I sounded. The thought that she might now detest me and never forgive me stabbed at my very core. I never thought a human heart could hurt so much.

"Of course I don't hate you," she said slowly, but her forehead was still creased. "Still—it wasn't the nicest thing to do. Poor girl. It mustn't have been easy on her."

"I didn't mean for her to get hurt. And anyway, Johnny was—is—crazy about her. I'm sure Theresa won't stay upset too long."

"And you said they just left?"

"Yes, but we don't know how they left or when exactly. The doors and windows were locked. And they didn't take their clothes." I bet no matter how many times you relate something like that, it never sounds less bizarre. I sighed, feeling deeply weary. "I just wish I knew where they are. And…that they're okay."

Lorraine stroked my arm. I hadn't intentionally played the pity card, but she took up that hand anyway. That was just her nature, that sort of compassion and empathy for others. It was one of the reasons I

(loved)

liked her so much.

"I'm sure they'll turn up," she told me. "Are your friends looking for them?"

"Yeah."

"Police?"

"Not yet. Not enough time's gone by. Don't that beat all?"

She nodded. "You want to go out looking after work?"

I tried to smile at her. "I wouldn't know where to look that Mojo and Whippet haven't already looked. They watched out for Johnny's car all the way back to Tallahassee. I guess we'll just have to let the police handle it — eventually."

Lorraine nodded again and sighed. "We'd best get back to work before Carl comes looking for us." Her tone suggested that she had some thinking to do — mostly about us — and that made me feel even more despondent. I should've been upfront with her right away about Theresa, but damn, who wants to tell a girl about another girl especially one he's slept with? Repeatedly. Even if he had no intention of sleeping with Girl Number Two ever again. Why was I such an idiot? I swear if my leg had been long enough I would have tried to kick my own ass.

It was a miserable five hours before our shifts ended.

As soon as I got into the car, I turned to her. Didn't even give her a chance to start the engine. In fact, I stayed her hand as she was reaching for the ignition. I had to know where she stood on the issue of us.

"I didn't want to break up with Theresa over the telephone. I thought that would be a crappy, cowardly thing to do. Otherwise I would have told her it was over the day I met you. Even if you'd never given me the time of day. Because until I met you, I didn't realize how shallow my relationship with Theresa really was and always would be. You made me realize I wanted something more." Maybe that sounded stupid or cheesy, but I didn't care.

It was the truth.

Lorraine studied me for a few minutes, considering what I'd said, then she nodded. "I believe you, David. I don't think you're the sort to lead a girl on."

"And do you also believe that you're the only girl I want to be with? That I (*love you love you love you*) care about you more than any other girl I've ever known?"

She looked into my eyes then, like she was trying to read my soul, and any woman who will look at you that deeply and truly has to know when you're telling her the truth about being an upright sort of guy. And not just because she didn't like thinking she'd been a real idiot to show her boobs to a complete jerk. "I believe you," she said softly. "And I feel the same way."

And just like that, whoosh! the burden that had weighed me down for the whole damned day lifted from my shoulders. If only I knew where Johnny and Theresa were, all would be right with the world.

I couldn't know at that moment that the world wasn't likely to be right again, at least, not for a long time.

She pulled into my driveway but for a minute I couldn't force myself out of the car. I sat there, staring at the house, dreading having to be there, loathing the idea of sleeping in the bed where they had been—and not just sleeping, either. Commiserating. Lorraine gave me a puzzled look. "Sorry," I said. "I hate the idea of being in the same bed where they—"

"There other bedrooms and other beds downstairs, right?"

"There are," I nodded. "It's just that up in the loft I feel—safer. I'm— the house makes me feel—"

"Scared?"

The last thing I wanted to admit to Lorraine—well, second to last, the first being how many times I'd had sex with Theresa—was being afraid of this house, especially in the dark. "Yeah, it scares me. And that has got to be the stupidest, most pussy thing you've ever heard a guy say."

She shook her head, surprising me. At first I took that to mean that she'd known lots of pussy guys in her life, but I was wrong. "That's what I felt the other night, too. Scared. Not for any good reason, just because the house is....creepy. It looks like a nice house, but it isn't somehow. I can't explain it. It's only something you can feel."

"Twitchy. Squirrelly."

She nodded. "Something like that. Like I told you— and I wasn't making it up, honest.—I felt like something was watching us. Something not quite human. It was an awful feeling."

"My neighbor says the house is infested with demons." I said it nonchalantly, at least as off-handedly as one can mention demons.

Lorraine frowned. "I thought you said you didn't have any neighbors."

"I tell you I'm living with demons and you're concerned about my *neighbor*?"

"Who's your neighbor?" she asked, not to be put off.

"Trojan Barnes. He lives way out there in the woods. He's just barely a neighbor."

"Trojan Barnes, the wood magnate, the million-aire?" she said surprised, and I nodded. "What is he doing living out in the woods?"

"Former wood magnate, actually. He lives in a tent. Claims he doesn't ever want to live in a house again. This used to be his house, you know."

"Yes, I do know. Of course, I know."

"And as you said, it's the disappearances from this house of Nettie Barnes and her friend that's probably behind our feeling creeped out by the place. I've sort of gotten used to that, but now that the bed—*my* bed—" I couldn't say it, but she knew what I was talking about. Johnny had screwed Theresa in that bed and all the soap powder and bleach in the world was not going to wash those sheets, that mattress, well enough to suit me.

"Maybe a nice thick foam mattress pad and new sheets," she suggested. "We could go to Wal-Mart tomorrow."

"Sounds like a plan. But I guess it's the downstairs for me tonight."

"I do have another alternative," she said.

And that's how I ended up at

....Lorraine's Place....
Later June 9 to Early June10_____

    I'm not the sort of guy to kiss and tell so I'm not about to cover all the juicy details of my evening with Lorraine. Suffice it to say that it was the most spectacular night of my life, bar none. Yeah. That just about sums it up, all right.

    First I called Mojo to see if there'd been any word on Johnny and Theresa. There's hadn't been. He said he was going to go ahead and call their parents and then the cops too, unless the parents were going to handle it. I didn't give him Lorraine's phone number. The last thing I wanted was any interruptions or to have her involved in any of this. I did allow that he could call my cell phone if there was a real emergency, but I stressed the *real*, just so he'd know it had better be the same caliber as a nuclear accident.

    I'm a bit ashamed to admit that from the moment I took Lorraine in my arms and kissed her—really kissed her, I mean, not that namby-pamby stuff we'd been exchanging up until then—Johnny and Theresa were the furthest things from my mind. I didn't care if they were running all over Florida stark naked, rutting like two rabbits. All I cared about was having adorable Lorraine—in-the-all-together Lorraine—next to me in her very sensuous queen-sized love nest of a bed.

"The sheets are Egyptian cotton," she whispered to me. "One of my few indulgences." That, and lacy underwear, of course—pale blue this time. Top and bottom this time. Not that I spent any more time with them than I did their pink counterpart.

I think I murmured something about how nice and soft her sheets were, just to be nice, to be polite, but to tell the truth, I didn't notice. I could've been lying on burlap, hell, on a bed of juniper branches, for all I cared. The only soft thing I did care about was her.

I didn't think I would sleep, or would ever want to sleep, or even find sleep necessary ever again, but some time later, some hours later, when my body had had as much of her body as any human male can stand, I did drift off. When the sun finally woke me up and I saw her next to me, still sleeping, her perfect back turned toward me, her back with the silky pale skin and the plump pear of her bottom toward me, I didn't think I could ever, ever bear not to have her there every day for the rest of my life. I wanted to touch her so badly it was like an ache through my whole body, but it seemed selfish to wake her. Believe me, no one has ever wanted to be selfish more than I did at that moment! But I let her sleep, proving, I guess, that I actually did

(love her)

Yeah.

At that moment I heard the ringer of my cell phone go off, (playing the Shop Boyz hit *Party Like a Rockstar*, something I would definitely have to change to suit the newer, more mature me)

. It was early. Early phone calls are never good news.

Casa de Almas (Day 16)
June 10, later_____

Detective Bret Randall, Leon County Sheriff's Office. That's who the man on the phone introduced himself as. Then he asked me if I could meet him at the house in two hours. What was I going to say? No, sorry, going to the beach with my girlfriend? For sure that wouldn't fly.

Though I spoke quietly, as soon as I rang off I noticed that Lorraine was awake and sitting up (wrapped in her Egyptian cotton sheet, damn it) "Who was that? Any word on your friends?"

I shook my head. "One of the guys must have called the police, or their parents did. That was a detective. Wants to meet me in a few hours up at the house. Ask me some questions, I guess, though there's not much I can tell him."

"Time for breakfast and Wal-Mart?" she asked.

"I'd hoped for a nicer day with you than that—especially after such a wonderful night," I added and for god's sake I think I might even have been blushing. Nah, it was just that I was still heady over being with the girl of my dreams. Totally besotted. Completely blotto in love.

(And I wasn't even fudging on the L word, any-more, either!)

"There'll still be plenty of time for us to salvage the day, I'm sure," she said. She was all cute and tousled and looked perfectly (adorable). "In the meantime we could go do our part to stop global warming by conserving shower water."

"You mean not shower?"

Lorraine rolled her eyes. "No, silly," she grinned.

I could be so dense first thing in the morning.

We probably didn't conserve a whole lot of water, given that showering was so much damned fun we stayed in there twice as long as we would have separately, but we made up for the lost time by eating a hasty breakfast and then beelining over to Wal-Mart. I bought a thick foam mattress topper and new sheet set, and already felt better knowing that there would be a solid layer between me and the remnants of Johnny and Theresa. (If only I'd known at the time how truly ironic that thought was.)

Lorraine pulled her car into my driveway well before the two hours was up. "They sure outfit the cops in your county pretty darned good," she said.

"Why?" I confess I'd been paying attention to her and not to anything else.

"That detective is driving a Mercedes."

I looked towards the house and saw the sleek silver automobile sitting there. Inexplicably my heart rate went up a few notches even though I had no reason in the world to feel so nervous. "That's not the detective. That's my landlord."

"What do you think he wants?" she asked, pulling her car up next to Eblis's Mercedes so that the passenger door was adjacent to his driver's side.

"No idea," I said. "Maybe he just wants to make sure the window had been fixed." (And it had. I'd left a message on his voice mail and by the time I got home from work that day there was a brand new window in place. It had been such a perfect job the workmen hadn't even left dust behind.)

"He could have seen that for himself without waiting for you," she said, voicing my unspoken thought. He had *waited* for me. Heart rate clicked up another notch. Up close I could tell that he had the motor running. The glass was tinted but I could just make out his profile. He was just sitting there, staring at what? The house? No radio on, not listening to music, nothing. Just sitting there. Waiting. I got out of Lorraine's car and knocked gently on the glass of his window. Far from being startled, he slowly turned his head toward me, though there appeared to be almost no expression on his face. I raised my hand in greeting, but he did not wave back. After a moment, his door started to open and I stepped back so that he could get out.

He was in a pale blue Guayabera shirt this time, but he still wore the ostentatious gold rings, bracelets and chains, still had that slicked back dark hair silvered at the temples. The only difference was that his amiable good-old-boy expression on his tanned face had turned hard. The eyes that studied me were cold as black ice. I tried not to shiver under his gaze. "Where have you been?" he asked. His voice was soft, his tone flat, but there was an undercurrent of menace that puzzled me.

"Wal-Mart," I said.

"Before that," he said with a tinge of impatience. "Last night."

"At my girlfriend's house," I said. I wanted to add, Not that it's any of your damned business, but he wasn't the sort of guy (at least, not at this minute) who I thought it would be wise to say that to. It would be akin to telling a Mafia hitman to go screw himself with his own gun.

"You are not supposed to leave the house alone."

"It was just an overnight."

"It is in the contract."

"You mean in the lease agreement?" I didn't remember anything about a clause requiring me to spend each and every night at the house. But then Phil Fouraker always did say I wasn't very good at reading the fine print. "There's a stipulation that I have to be here all the time?"

"And you signed it. You agreed to it."

I didn't know what to say to that.

"What kind of a lease agreement is that?" Lorraine had by now gotten out of her car and came to stand next to me. "That's outrageous. I've never heard of such a thing."

Harry Eblis turned his strong, tanned face toward Lorraine and studied her until I felt her move closer to me, as if made uncomfortable under his gaze. His nostrils flared, almost as if he were

(sniffing her)

taking in her scent, and then he again looked her over carefully, tasting her with his glittering (lustful?) eyes. I could understand Lorraine being creeped out; I certainly was. Finally he turned back to me. "It is in *my* lease agreement," Eblis said. "I do not want the house to stand empty."

"It was just for one night," I said. "I had two of my friends go missing last night."

"I heard."

"You did? From who?"

"What does that have to do with your agreement with me?"

"Just before they disappeared they — they were in my bed in the loft and I didn't feel comfortable sleeping there. So — " I was reluctant to say her name. I didn't want to say *Lorraine* to his man. "So she invited me to spend the night with her."

Eblis grinned but there was no genuine amusement in it. "A hardship, I am sure."

I could tell by how hard Lorraine was squeezing my arm that Eblis was seriously upsetting her, but remarkably she kept on a poker face, as if she would be damned before she would let Harry Eblis know how much he was scaring her.

"You are more than welcome to have friends spend the night. There are plenty of beds. But you must not leave the house unattended again, or you will break the contract. I do not believe it would be in your best interest to do that."

I almost gaped at him. "Are you threatening me?"

"Breaking a contract can have serious consequences."

"Damn it, you *are* threatening me!" At that point I was both shocked by his nerve and angry as well. Who did he think he was, anyway?   I felt my blood rise into my face, making my cheeks burn with fury.

"He won't break it again," Lorraine said quickly, acting the coolest, the wisest of the two of us. She gave my arm a quick, urgent squeeze in an effort to shut me up. Fortunately I heeded her warning, otherwise I probably would have just opened my mouth again, definitely said the wrong thing, maybe even tried to deck him, and Eblis no doubt would have taken my face in his one meaty hand and crushed my skull like an egg.

But Eblis seemed not to hear her. His attention was drawn past us, back toward the woods. I didn't think it was possible for his face to harden further, for his eyes to grow colder, for the anger to become more apparent in his reddening face, but it did. I turned my head to see what he was looking at and Lorraine followed my gaze.

Trojan Barnes stood there, in his old plaid, long-sleeved shirt and jeans, arms at his sides, not the least bit menacing. Just an old man, standing there. And yet, to Eblis he must have seemed threatening. Squint crouched beside Trojan, his fur bristled like a porcupine, his eyes squintier than ever. I saw the cat draw back his mouth in a silent hiss, showing his sharp little feline teeth. He was no match at all for Eblis—and yet Eblis seemed wary of him. He was big enough that he could have reached out and crushed me, and yet he was afraid of a ten-pound cat? What was up with that?

"Leave the boy alone, Eblis," Trojan said. His voice was calm, but there was an unmistakably hard under-current to it.

"You would be wise to mind your own business, Barnes," Eblis said. "And keep that animal away from me." He glanced at me. "I have allergies."

"The boy is my business. This was my house."

"The operative word is *was*. It does not belong to you any longer. Thus it is of no concern to you."

"Maybe not, but it's sure a big concern to old Squint here. So why don't you just get back into that big fancy car of yours and be on your way now."

Eblis glared coldly at Trojan and the cat, made a face, then opened his car door. Before he slid his bulk behind the wheel he turned back to me. "Just remember the contract," he said. "You do not want to break a contract with me. Trust me on that."

Eblis slammed the Mercedes into reverse, spun around, and then threw it into **DRIVE**, spinning the back tires a moment and spraying Lorraine and me with dirt.

"Now there's a pleasant fellow," Lorraine said, brushing off her tee-shirt. "You sure burned his cookies." Squint ran over to her and she scooped him up. "Aren't you a sweet kitty," she said and the cat put his paw on her nose, his squinty eyes looking her over as if trying to make sure she was okay.

"Hey, Troj." I lifted my hand in greeting and the old man came over to us. "Sure seems to be some bad blood between the two of you. Did Eblis handle the sale of your house?"

"He did. You two all right?"

"I guess we were lucky you guys came along when you did. Trojan Barnes, meet Lorraine Franco. Lorraine, this is Trojan and Squint."

"He really doesn't like this cat," Lorraine said, "and I don't buy his *I have allergies* nonsense, do you?" She put Squint down and he ran back to Trojan.

"His kind never likes cats. That's because cats recognize them for what they are."

"What's his kind?" I asked, feeling dense. "What does that mean?" But as usual, Trojan didn't answer me. Funny how he did that. Ignored my questions like I hadn't even asked them.

"Did I hear you right?" he said instead, "You had some friends of yours go missing?"

"Last night," I nodded, and I told him about Johnny and Theresa and the little I knew about their disappearance. His face grew more and more pained, almost as if he had known them. "A detective is coming in a little while to ask me some questions."

"Doesn't matter. Won't ever find them," Trojan said sadly.

"We don't know that," I protested. "They've only just started to look for them and —"

Trojan held up a weary hand. "I'm sorry, son, but those friends of yours are gone. Just like my Nettie and her friend, Flo. Just like who knows how many others."

"You don't know that," I said again, starting to feel a little hot under the collar. "As soon as they find Johnny's car —"

"Doesn't matter if they find the car, son," Trojan said. "They didn't leave with the car."

"They must have!"

Trojan shook his head. "Didn't leave the house at all." He glanced at Casa de Almas with a look of loathing.

"They're still in there, somewhere, just like poor Flo, just like who knows who else. And they're never coming back."

"Just like your wife?" Lorraine asked.

Trojan looked at her with watery eyes. "No, ma'am, not like my Nettie. I got my Nettie out, all right, but it cost me. Cost me a part of my soul you could say. Don't know how God'll forgive me for exchanging her for the others."

"You found your wife?" I asked, confused. "Where is she, then?"

Trojan shook his head and turned to leave, Squint twisting around his legs as if to offer comfort. "Gone," he said. "My poor Nettie's gone for good."

Casa de Almas (Day 16)
June 10, Still Later_____

It was actually a relief to see the guy getting out of the dark blue Crown Victoria who looked so normal. Detective Bret Randall had ditched his suit jacket because of the heat, and his white shirt sleeves were rolled to the elbows. As he walked toward us, he loosened his tie. He was miles away from his home base; he could afford to be a little casual.

While we had some time before the arrival of Detective Randall, Lorraine helped me take the foam pad and new sheets up to the loft. I stared at the bed, still imprinted with Johnny and Theresa, and at the clothes they had left behind. "Maybe we'd better wait until the detective comes to change things out," Lorraine had suggested, so we stowed the stuff in the corner and went back downstairs. If it had been creepy up in the loft before, now it was *really* disturbing, what with all those remnants of my friends around. I hoped I would feel better about the place when things were put to rights but I sort of doubted it.

I got us both cold drinks from the refrigerator and we went out on the porch to drink them. Lorraine said the inside felt too claustrophobic and I couldn't disagree with that.

"What kind of lease agreement makes the tenant stay on the premises 24/7?" she asked as she sipped her soda and rocked slowly back and forth.

"I don't even remember that being in the contract, but then there's always that fine print thing."

"And your landlord!" she said. "He looks like he should be carrying an automatic rifle and a shovel in his trunk."

"A shovel?"

"For burying the bodies of his victims."

"Yeah, he definitely does have that Mafioso demeanor about him—especially today. Guess I'll be staying put until my time is up."

"When is that?"

"August 15th. I have to be back on campus by then. I have one semester before I graduate."

Lorraine didn't say anything and didn't look at me, but it was as if I could tell what she was thinking. This was just a fling and soon I would be gone and that would be that. That, however, was the last thing on my mind.

"You didn't ask, *and then what*?" I prompted.

A little frown creased her ever-adorable forehead. "Okay," she said slowly. "And then what?"

"And then I turn traitor and you and I move to Gainesville."

Lorraine looked at me sharply. "What? Move to Gainesville?" she asked.

"Isn't that where you said you wanted to go to school?" I leaned forward, resting my arms on my knees. I figured it made me look more intense so that she'd believe me. "You didn't think I would just let you go, did you? Just let what we have end?"

"Are you serious?" Her voice was small, as if maybe she was close to getting a little teary and didn't want to.

I leaned back again and started rocking. "I really like working at Wakulla Springs. That was sort of a shocker to me, because up until now, I didn't know what I was going to do for an actual living, and I'll have a degree in psychology which is just plain stupid."

"You wanted to be a psychiatrist? Or psychologist?"

"No, I just wanted to take interesting classes. No career goal in mind *at all*. How dumb can you get? But then, working there at the Springs, even as a grunt, well, damned if it isn't a great job. I like it, and shoot, there are tons of state parks around Gainesville. I bet I could become a park ranger. Maybe have to enroll in some law enforcement classes or something. I'll google it later and find out. My point is," and I looked at her then and saw her staring at me as if I'd suddenly sprouted horns, "I want us to be together and if we were to live together, we could both go to school and work part-time and make it—financially." I wet my lips because here came the hard part, the part I didn't think I'd get to right at this moment in my life, me being only twenty-one and all. "We could even get married." I'd said it fast and wasn't sure if she'd heard me, but I saw her eyes widen and knew she had. She looked back toward the driveway and took a sip of her soda before saying anything.

"It's a good plan," she said finally, still not looking at me, "but before anyone got married, someone would have to be asked, I think. *Proposed to,* I think the term is." She gave a little smile, not at me directly but I knew it was meant for me. "And a proposal probably should come from someone a person has known longer than a week."

"Yeah, I guess you're probably right," I agreed.

And at that moment the dark blue Crown Victoria came down my driveway and pulled to a stop behind Lorraine's car. The two of us went down the steps to meet him.

Bret Randall was tall, sandy blond, your basic all-American type. He stuck out his tanned hand as he approached and I shook it, then I introduced Lorraine. He took out a notepad. "Just have some questions for you," he said, "but do you think we could go inside? Hot as blue blazes out here."

I led the way into the living room and the three of us sat.

"Tell me about the night they disappeared," Randall said and I began with how the gang had surprised me Friday evening.

"The Sorrentis told me that you're their daughter's boyfriend." Randall looked at me with those guileless blue eyes that nevertheless had a way of peeling away your skin and taking a peek underneath. He could see that I had a girl here with me and I knew he was wondering about that.

"*Ex*-boyfriend," I corrected him.

"How ex?"

I hadn't figured on having to squirm quite so early in the session. "As of Friday evening."

"Your idea, hers, or mutual?"

"Mine."

"Uh huh, and how did she take that?"

"She wasn't happy, but it's not like we were in love or anything. I think she was just more surprised than anything. Tessie had — has — something of an ego." (Had he caught the fact that I'd put her in the past tense? Probably.)

Bret Randall's blue eyes slid over in Lorraine's direction and I knew exactly what that meant. He had just branded her as The Other Woman.

"Lorraine had nothing to do with this," I said. "I mean, she didn't ask me to break it off with Theresa. She didn't even know about Theresa. I've been seeing Lorraine since I got to Bethel and I just knew...." I looked over at her and she met my gaze. "I just knew she was *the one* and that it wouldn't be fair to string Theresa along. Like I said, she was surprised — "

"Just surprised?"

"Okay, maybe a little more than just surprised. It did come out of the blue. I wasn't expecting my friends — especially Theresa — to be here on Friday. I thought I'd have better opportunities to tell her. Anyway, she had Johnny."

"Was she seeing Johnny Chang?"

"No, she didn't even know that Johnny liked her, but I can tell you that he let his feelings be known in no uncertain terms Friday evening."

"And you know this how?"

"As I came down the stairs, he went up to her. And she never sent him back down."

"Was that the last time you saw the two of them?" Randall had been writing all this while in a pocket notebook, looking up only when he paused to ask a question.

"It was."

"And what time was that?"

"Around eleven, I guess. I went outside to get some air, to let things settle down. Then I came back in around midnight and went to sleep."

"And where was that?"

"Right here on the sofa. That's what's so weird about all this. No one saw Johnny and Theresa come downstairs, and I was here all night. I'm sure I would've heard them."

"Was there drinking?" Of course, that is always the question, isn't it? Were you too drunk not to have noticed?

"Yes, some, but I'd only had two drinks. The others had had a lot more, and that's why I asked Mo..." For a minute I had to stop and think what his real name was. "I mean Joe and Stan..."

"That would be Joseph Moultrie and Stanley Meldon?"

"Right—to make sure no one left. I didn't want them out there in a car, in that condition."

"Yes, I'm sure you know how badly that can go," Randall said. He had obviously done his homework and knew about my DUI. "So what time were you up the next morning?"

"Eight. I had to be at work at the diner by ten."

"And by then they were gone?"

"Uh huh. Whip—Stan—went upstairs to check on them and they weren't there."

"So you, Moultrie and Meldon had been otherwise occupied before you discovered they were missing?"

"Just having breakfast. Just there in the kitchen. It's not that big a house. We would've heard them come down the stairs—or if not, we certainly would've heard Johnny's car. He has a high-powered exhaust on that baby. Besides, when we checked, all the windows and doors were locked. And they hadn't taken my keys because I checked and they were still in my pocket. We can't figure out how they got out of the house."

"May I see the loft?"

"Yeah, sure, of course." The three of us got up and once again I played leader as we trooped up the stairs. Upstairs Randall stood still for a moment while his eyes moved all around the room.

"You disturb anything since they left?"

"No. I was going to change out the sheets and all, but Lorraine suggested I wait until you arrived."

"Don't watch *CSI: Miami* for nothing," she smiled, but Randall either got that a lot or was not easily amused.

"These their clothes?" The detective stooped to examine the pile left on the floor.

"Uh huh."

"Two sets of jeans, two tee-shirts, two underpants. No bra." He looked up at me.

My face suddenly felt hot and I almost wished I didn't have Lorraine there for moral support. "She wasn't wearing one," I told him. I kept my eyes on Randall. I didn't even want to know if Lorraine was looking at me or not.

"Really?" The detective watched me—watched me slowly incinerate actually.

"She wasn't in the habit of wearing one and when we came up here to the loft, she thought—" I had to lick my lips and it's a wonder my tongue didn't come back dusty. "—that we would have sex."

"So as soon as you got up here she took off her shirt."

"That's what happened."

"Didn't put it back on? Not even after you dropped your bombshell on her?"

"I don't think she was thinking about that at the moment. Anyway, she was used to being—(naked) She didn't have any hang-ups about her body."

"Pants off too?"

"She didn't get that far." By now, I could barely swallow. All the saliva in my glands had just dried up. "I guess she saved that part for Johnny." I don't know why I added that. It sounded spiteful, and maybe I wanted it to. I didn't want anything bad to happen to Theresa, but damn it, I broke up with her one minute and the next she had another guy in her bed. It was hard to feel too badly about a girl like that, someone who was so damned easy. Even if Johnny did take advantage of her heartache. And that didn't exactly make him Mr. Nice Guy, either, actually.

"I'd like to take these as evidence. If you'll go to the computer and type up an inventory list as I call out these things, then you can print two copies and we'll both sign them. You'll have a copy as a receipt for these things. I have evidence bags in my car. I want to take the sheets, too, so I'll need to know who the owner is."

"I don't know who he is, but I have the name of his agent."

"That'll be fine."

I went to the computer and booted it up. When the screen came on, I opened Microsoft Word and waited for Randall. By now he had put on a pair of latex gloves that he'd taken from his pocket. He carefully lifted the shirts, the briefs, the panties, then came to Johnny's jeans. Randall went through his pockets. Wallet with ID, cash ($24), change (53¢) and then something that made him pause. "You want to look at these?" he asked, making me turn from the monitor screen. Pinched between his thumb and forefinger was a red diamond-shaped key ring with a dragon on it. On it were several keys. "This one's a Honda key. Wasn't that the kind of car that Mr. Chang was driving?"

"He did drive a Honda," I said, frowning. "But that can't be his car key."

"It looks like his car key. Is this his key ring?"

"Yeah, it matched his car. Red, with a dragon on it. But it can't be his car key."

Couldn't be, but had to be.

"Could he have had two sets of keys?"

"Well, sure, but—"

"—But who carries their spare keys and their regular keys with them?" Lorraine asked. "Why would anyone do that?"

"But if Mr. Chang's keys are here, where's his car?"

Casa de Almas (Day 16)
Still June 10, Even Later_____

"Yeah, how *did* someone drive his car away without his keys?" I asked.

"How, indeed?" Bret Randall looked at me, through me, his eyes so intensely blue that I thought they might burn a hole in one side of me and come out the other. For a long minute that was all we did, stare at each other. Finally he folded his arms across his chest, taking an "at ease" stance.

"Where do you suppose the car is, David?" he asked. Not Mr. Fouraker. *David.*

I knew what he was doing, putting me into an inferior position, but I didn't quite have the balls to say, "Well, Bret, hell if I know." Instead I simply said the truth. "I have no idea," I told him.

Detective Randall hung his head a moment, as if he needed to collect his thoughts, but then he shook his head slightly, almost like he wanted to show his disappointment in my answer. When he looked up again, there were those blue eyes, as riveting as ever. "You said there were seven people here that night, including yourself?"

"That's right."

"And the other six were highly intoxicated?"

"Pretty much."

"But you put them in charge of watching Johnny and Theresa."

"Well, actually, Stan and Joe weren't highly intoxicated."

"When you came back into the house, was everyone asleep?"

"As far as I know."

"Sleeping it off, you might say," Randall said.

I wasn't sure where he was going with this and I started to feel a little nervous. Funny how cops have a way of doing that, even if you haven't done a damned thing wrong. I shrugged. "I guess."

"So they wouldn't be able to tell me what had happened after they went to sleep and you came back into the house."

I can be a little dense, I admit that. Phil Fouraker's only son isn't always really quick on the uptake. But all of a sudden it occurred to me what he was really asking. "Wait, are you saying you think I had something to do with Johnny and Theresa disappearing?"

Randall didn't answer immediately, but when he did, his voice was cool, flat. "In an investigation of this sort, we tend to look at several things besides hard evidence, those being motive, means and opportunity. And you, David, seem to have at least two of those three."

I could only stare at him. "I do?" I asked.

"Certainly motive."

"How do you figure? Why would I want to hurt Theresa? If anyone should have motive to hurt someone it would be her. She was mad at me, not the other way around."

"Maybe she didn't take it quite as easily as you've told me. Did she threaten to go to your new girlfriend, here?"

"And tell her what?"

Randall shrugged. "Something kinky, maybe."

"We didn't have anything kinky going on between us."

"Well, now, only you and Theresa would know that, isn't that so? And she's not in a position to say. As for Johnny, you said that he went up to comfort Theresa after you two spoke. But as a matter of fact, that comfort probably came in the form of sex, isn't that right?"

"Maybe. Yeah, probably. So?"

"So maybe that made you angry."

"Are you actually accusing me of killing Johnny and Theresa?"

"Motive and opportunity. That's all I'm saying."

"I could never be angry enough to actually murder someone! And anyway, I wasn't angry with Johnny. I was glad he could...."

"...be there to have sex with your girlfriend?"

"*Ex*-girlfriend! I didn't hurt either one of them. She needed somebody. Johnny was there for her. You could say he took her off my hands. I know that sounds bad, callous, but if he cared for her, that was fine with me. Really! It was fine with me!"

"But you have no one to vouch for you. You were essentially alone with Johnny and Theresa for quite a long time. Long enough to have gotten rid of both them and Johnny's car. The keys are here. *Someone* (meaning *me*, I know) could have used them to ditch the car and then put them back."

I didn't know what to say. I looked over at Lorraine and she was wide-eyed. But she shook her head in what I hoped was disbelief. "I didn't," I mouthed to her. And then, thankfully, she nodded, but her face was creased as if she didn't like where all this was headed. "I did not hurt Theresa and Johnny," I told Randall again, firmly, protesting as strongly as I could, as any innocent man would, or so I thought. "And damn it, how can you suggest that they're—dead—when you haven't even looked for them yet."

"Even you used the past-tense," he reminded me. "I'm going to leave you now," the detective said. "I trust you won't leave the county."

"I can't leave the county. You know that." It occurred to me that it was stupid for him to say that. Why even *bother* saying that? If I had been a murderer, why would I have been concerned about violating probation by leaving the county? Didn't only innocent people stay put? If I'd been guilty, I would have lit out of there like a jack rabbit on steroids.

"I'll be back tomorrow with a forensics team and some cadaver dogs."

"You're bringing dead dogs?"

"Specially trained dogs who can sniff out human remains. Please do not disturb the loft area. In fact, it would be best if you vacated the premises."

"I can't do that. It'll break my lease contract. There will be—consequences."

"I don't understand that."

"It's in my lease, I have to be here at night. I'm watching the premises for the owner. I'm what you call a house sitter. A caretaker. I can't leave. But I won't go up into the loft."

Before he left, the detective placed the clothing, wallet and keys, and bed linens into large plastic bags, sealed them, tagged them, then had me sign the inventory. He put several strips of that yellow **CRIME SCENE DO NOT CROSS** tape at the bottom of the stairs. "This doesn't come off easily," he warned me. "I'll know if you go through it."

"I won't touch it." My tone had gotten decidedly sullen. It was all I could do not to lose my temper. What was up with this guy, accusing me of murdering my friends? After Randall left, the adrenalin drained out of my body and I felt suddenly weak, shaken and scared. Could they convict me of a crime with just circumstantial evidence? What if they didn't find Theresa and Johnny alive?

"David." The sound of Lorraine's voice snapped me out of my dark thoughts. She touched my arm. "It'll be all right."

"You don't know that. Innocent people go to jail all the time. Do you think I need a lawyer?"

She shook her head. "Don't worry about that now."

"You mean I should wait until they arrest me."

"I mean, they won't arrest you. They'll find your friends and all this will go away."

I put my arms around her. "I wish I felt as confident as you about that." Johnny and Theresa had been gone so long now. Longer than if this was just a bad joke.

"Let's get on with our day. Let's just forget all this for a little while."

I didn't think there was anything on God's green earth that could make me stop thinking about Lorraine and how much I loved her, but I was wrong. Being faced with a possible murder charge has a way of pushing everything else out of your mind, even those things that are as wonderful as being with a girl like Lorraine. Only part of me went with her to Mashes Sands beach, only a small piece of me held her hand as we walked along the white sandy shore and waded in the shallow water, only a bit of me enjoyed watching her find the hermit crabs and let them walk on the palm of her hand, and when she turned to me and kissed me, only a little portion of my mind devoted itself to those kisses. Most of me was still standing in the living room of Casa de Almas while Detective Randall's eyes bored holes through me.

When the sun started to get low in the sky, I suggested we get something to eat. It was a diversion, I know. A reason not to go back to that house too soon. We drove to Spring Creek and the little restaurant there. Spring Creek is an old fishing community that has been virtually unchanged over last half century. It consists of three fish houses, about 50 residents, and one restaurant known for its seafood caught off the coast by the owner's family since the mid 70s. It was all wood paneling inside, dark enough to be cozy, with a mural of fishing boats along one wall. We lingered over a feast of shrimp and oysters and perfect hushpuppies, and a crisp salad served with their house dressing—served in glass fish-shaped bottles on each table.

But, as they say, all good things must come to an end. And there was only so much two people could eat.

"I'd ask you to stay with me...." she began as we drove back to Bethel.

"I know I can't."

"No, you can't. Goodness knows what that Eblis guy would do to you. He didn't seem like the sort you'd want to cross. Why does he want you there so badly, anyway?"

"No idea."

"Well, I've decided that I'll stay with you. If you want me to, I mean."

"No, Lorraine, you can't. I mean, I want you to, but you *shouldn't*. You know what that house does to you. It scares you. Hell, it scares me, too. Especially now."

"I'm staying, David," she told me.

The twin beds didn't lend themselves to great moments of romance, but I was too drained emotionally to care. We took the back bedroom, for no special reason except that it was nearest the back door and

(escape)

except maybe if we had that in mind, we should've stayed closer to the front door and Lorraine's car. She didn't bother to go home first—maybe she was afraid to leave me alone there and equally afraid to take me to her place for fear that I'd be too tempted to stay there, and thereby bring down the Wrath of Eblis upon me—so she opted to sleep in tee-shirt and panties. I kissed her, held her, touched her, and yet I couldn't get Bret Randall out of my mind. The possibility of a murder rap has a way of putting a serious damper on your love life. Lorraine didn't seem to mind. She hugged me tightly and we went to our respective beds and said good night.

Emotionally drained, I fell asleep almost immediately and was wakened just as fast by the sound of moaning. At first I was disoriented. I had never slept in that bedroom before, and it had none of the familiarity that the loft had gained over the past few weeks. For a moment I couldn't imagine where I was or who I was with, then gradually the realization that I was in the back bedroom with Lorraine in the bed next to me dawned on me. I heard her moan again. Not like she was in pain, though. More like something good was happening.

"Oh, David," I heard her whisper and there was a hint of a giggle in her voice. "Oh my god, David. You are soooo bad."

I almost said her name, but my confusion kept me silent. Was I dreaming? Was she really talking to me?

"Oh my, oh god, David," she said, just breathless at first, then she started to gasp. "That... oh...that...hurts a little... oh, David. Stop...I think you should..." And she moaned again only this time it was decidedly not good. "Oh my god! Stop, David, you're hurting me!"

"Lorraine?" My voice sounded too loud there in the pitch dark.

There was sudden silence. Then: "David?" Her voice first was confused, then alarmed. "David?" And then out-and-out scared to freakin' death. "DAVID!"

I sprang upright, groped frantically for the lamp I knew was on a table between our beds, and switched on the light. I looked over at Lorraine and as soon as the light came on, I saw her face and the horror there. Because seeing me sitting there in my bed she realized that it had not been me that had been with her.

Her hands were above her head, as if they had been pinned there, and her tee-shirt was pulled up over her breasts. The left nipple was red, inflamed, as if had been roughly pinched or worse, bitten.

"OH MY GOD!" she shrieked, sitting up and pulling down her tee-shirt as she did so. Immediately plunged into hysteria, she brushed frantically at her body as if trying to wipe off whatever she'd felt on her, like one might try to knock away a nasty swarm of beetles. "*OH MY GOD!*"

I flew out of bed and was next to her in an instant, gathering her up in my arms, subduing her wildly flailing arms. She was screaming and crying and squirming in my arms and it took all my strength to hold her. After a moment she calmed a bit, and I could rock her, stroke her hair, whisper comfort to her (in the form of *shh shh* which was probably stupid but it's the sort of thing that just comes out of you in a moment of distress) and be sure she would hear me. She wept against my shoulder and finally put her arms around my neck and held on for dear life.

"There was something—hot and wet—on me. Oh, god, something was *on* me. Sucking on me! Touching me, down, down *there*. Oh my god, David!"

I got up and pulled her with me. "We need to get out of here now!" I said. I went not to the back door but to the front, grabbing her keys off the dresser as I went by, Lorraine clinging to me and weeping hysterically. It wasn't easy to run and drag Lorraine but somehow I did, and we stumbled down the hall and through the front door and finally clambered down from the porch and got into the back seat of her car. I slammed the locks shut and then put my arms around her again, holding her close.

After a few minutes she wiped her face and sniffed. "I didn't mean to cry like that. I'm such a wimp."

"No, no you're not. God, Lorraine, what happened? What did you mean, that something—something—" I couldn't even bring myself to repeat it.

"I don't know! At first I thought it was you, you know, being—romantic. I wasn't dreaming," she insisted, but I already knew she hadn't been. I could tell that by her posture, by the terrified look in her eyes when she saw me not in her bed but in my bed across the room. "Something—pinned my hands and I felt my shirt being pulled up and then—" She shuddered. "My god, I'll never forget what that felt like!" She wiped her eyes again because even though she was determined not to cry, her eyes did fill with more tears. "It felt like a mouth. I thought it was your mouth. It was on me. You know?"

I nodded. I could guess what it was like and it made me feel sick. It made me sick and it hadn't even happened to me. But I was also a little amazed that I wasn't totally freaking out. I think the realization that Lorraine was depending on me to hold it together was keeping me from flying to pieces. I had to be strong for her, and by god, I believe I was actually capable of doing that.

"It touched me, stroked me. Oh, god, David, what *was* that?" She looked at me with eyes full of terror. "Are there really demons in that house?"

I didn't want to admit something that outrageous, that preposterous could be true. "I don't know. Maybe there's just something in the house that causes us to...."

"Hallucinate? You think I was hallucinating?"

I almost said yes, but I remembered how red her nipple had been and it seemed more preposterous to think she had done that to herself.

"No," I admitted. "Not really." I stroked her hair. "Lorraine, you need to go home. I don't want you to come to this house ever again, understand?"

"No, David, you can't be here alone!"

"I'll be all right," I told her, hoping I sounded more convincing than I felt. "Besides, I have to stay here, and not just because of Eblis and his threats, but because I have a feeling I need to be here to find out what happened to Johnny and Theresa."

"No," she shook her head, tears threatening again. "It's too dangerous for you to be here."

"I don't think whatever's in the house will hurt me. At least not yet."

"Why not? What makes you immune?"

"I'm not sure, but Trojan Barnes told me that I was here because I was bait. I didn't understand that then, but I think I do now. The house or something in the house wants to use me to—get to others. Like Johnny and Theresa. Like you." I touched her cheek. "I'm guessing it still wants me to be bait, only I'm not going to play that little game any more."

"What happens when they realize that you're not willing to be bait any more?"

"I don't know, but I don't think that'll be for a while yet. Anyway, I can't let it have you. You have to stay away, Lorraine. The driveway is as close as you can come. You have to promise me that."

"But I don't want to be alone tonight, David. I can still feel that—thing—and you can't leave. So what do we do?"

"We'll just stay here in the car until morning. I think we'll be safe here. I can run in quick, grab some pillows and blankets—"

"And then what?" she asked, nestling down next to me.

"And then I think we need to do some research. Can you get off from the hardware store on Tuesday afternoon? I'm going to need your help."

Here and There
June 11-13_____

"Not a very big building, it is?" Lorraine asked, peering at the white wooden frame newspaper office building through her front windshield. Over the front door in black gothic letters it read **WAKULLA PRESS. SINCE 1969**. She had picked me up after my stint at the Springs on Wednesday, as our plans to visit the office sooner had been thwarted by her boss at the hardware store who claimed he needed more notice to let her off. I'm sure there will be a big run at the Bethel Hardware Store any day now and god forbid if he doesn't have enough help on hand.

"Maybe it's bigger on the inside," I said and she rolled her eyes.

"That's a little too Twilight Zone for me to even consider."

"Our lives are in the Twilight Zone, in case you hadn't noticed."

"Oh, I noticed all right."

I stayed her before she could get out of the car. "You don't really have to get more involved in all this than you are already, you know."

She stared at me as if I had just metamorphosed into a large bug and was chewing on her car's upholstery. "Are you serious? How much more involved can I be after the other night? Besides," she told me, "no one messes with a country girl and gets away with it, especially an Alabama country girl."

I didn't think I could love her more, but I was wrong.

Of course I've gotten ahead of myself.

At dawn on that Monday after Lorraine and I had taken refuge in the backseat of her car, I ran into my little House of Horrors, grabbed up Lorraine's clothes and a change for myself, then scribbled a note for Detective Randall that I slapped onto the front door. It read:

**Door's open. I'm working
at the diner. D. Fouraker**

I wanted to add, **Have a Nice Day!** or **Make Yourself at Home!**, but I didn't think Randall would appreciate me being cutesy, so I just left it at that. And I did leave the house unlocked. If anyone wanted to go into that house and steal anything, more power to 'em. Lorraine and I then went to her place to shower and change, zipped into Crawfordville to a pancake house for a quick breakfast, then we headed to work. She had to be there when the hardware store opened at nine and my shift at the diner didn't start until ten, but I told her that was no problem. I sat in a back booth and scribbled notes that I hoped would somehow shape into a plan.

At two o'clock Detective Randall came into the diner with a Wakulla County Sheriff's Deputy. They took a booth and though they didn't summon me in words, I knew they wanted to talk. I didn't feel like sliding in next to either one of them, saying "Hey, boys, how's it goin'?" so I dragged a chair over from a table and sat on it backwards, sort of like you used to see in cheesy old Westerns when the marshal sidled up to a table full of poker-playing baddies.

"You finished searching the house?" I asked. "Can I move back into the loft?"

"We did and you can." That was all Bret Randall said. I was hoping he'd tell me what they found, if anything, but he didn't. Just sat there, nailing me with those blue eyes.

"So, did you find anything that's going to help you locate Theresa and Johnny?" I asked. Hell, I wanted to know, and sometimes the only way to find out is to ask.

Randall turned his eyes on the deputy. He had a name tag with **ADKINS** on it. "They luminoled the whole dang house," Deputy Adkins told me.

"So was there any blood?"

"How do you know about luminol?" Randall asked.

"Are you kidding? There are a bazillion cop shows on TV and they all use luminol. So?"

"Not a drop," Adkins told me.

"Well, that's good, isn't it?" I looked from one to the other but neither one's face registered anything.

"Maybe," Randall said finally.

"What about the dogs? They pick up any scent?" I was hoping they were dogs that could find more than dead bodies — like maybe live ones. I looked from one to the other for an answer.

"Nope," Adkins said finally.

"The dogs did pick up traces of them in the driveway, but the trail didn't go anywhere but inside the house," Randall added.

"Well, that's where they were. They went from Johnny's car to the house and then, I guess, back to the car."

"Without clothes and car key," Randall added, and gave me a pointed look, but what could I say to that? I knew it was bug-shit crazy that two naked people had hotwired the Mustang and taken off to god-knew-where. Finally the detective stood up and the deputy followed suit. I wasn't even sure why they'd bothered to come and see me. Maybe just to make me squirm one more time. Randall looked down at me. "We'll be in touch."

I had no doubt about that, although I didn't say anything, just nodded. Sometimes it's just best to keep your mouth shut. Even David Fouraker knows that, though he doesn't always follow that advice.

Lorraine got off work at six, but came back at ten to pick me up. "I hate taking you back to that place," she told me on the drive to the house. That's when she told me her sweetheart of a boss wouldn't let her off on Tuesday but grudgingly told her she could have Wednesday afternoon. "If you just took off back to Tallahassee, you think Eblis could drag you back here?"

"He wouldn't have to," I told her. "The law would do it for him. Not allowed to leave the county while I'm on probation, remember?"

She pulled into my driveway. "You call me if anything happens, you hear?"

"I will."

"I'm serious. Anything."

I kissed her good night and trudged up to the house. Her headlights stayed on me a long time, as if she couldn't bear to turn around and leave me there—which did feel good, I have to admit, that she cared so much, but on the other hand, I didn't want her hanging around the house too long. God only knew what kind of connection the house had made with her the other night. I turned on the porch and waved at her. Finally she turned the car around, and I watched until her tail lights disappeared. I no longer felt afraid to be out there in the woods in the dark. What was inside, after all, was so much worse.

I locked up and headed to the loft. First thing, I folded up the sofa bed. Even with the foam pad, there was no way I was sleeping on that thing. I put the sheets on the thick piece of soft rubber, deciding to sleep on the floor instead. I turned on the computer and after it booted, I logged onto the internet.

That's when I heard them.

Now rationally I could have chalked up the noises to field mice that had gotten into the walls, but there was nothing rational about this house. Besides, it didn't sound like mice. It actually sounded a lot more like some giant python, a slithering noise that sometimes changed into scrabbling but mostly reminded me of a large, sinuous (possibly *wet*) eel-like body moving in the walls. I tried to ignore it and probably would have succeeded, too if it hadn't been for the other noises.

The snickering.

It was faint, but that's what it was, all right. Like naughty children crouched in the corner, giggling about some misfortune they had caused some unsuspecting soul, giggling but trying not to giggle, giving little snorts into their hands cupped over their mouths—snickering. There wasn't any other word for it. It was just barely audible. I figured they were just being loud enough to make sure I heard them, knew they were there.

I got up and turned on the TV. I didn't care about the program, didn't even bother flipping around the channels—all four of them—or looking in the listings. All I wanted was noise to drown out those hideous little snickers. I could've put on the radio, but the light and movement from the TV screen was a distraction, too, and right then, that was exactly what I wanted. I went back to the computer and tried not to think about what might be watching me.

First I looked up **PARK RANGER REQUIREMENTS** in Google. The program looked doable: two years of training would make me official. I printed out the page for future reference. Well, that had been pretty innocuous— and lasted all of ten minutes. I went downstairs and brought back an old friend to keep me company. A quick shot of my pal Captain Morgan and I felt a little more mellow. A second one and I was almost relaxed. I poured a third into a partially drained can of diet Coke. Nothing like having old friends around in times of need.

I looked up **WAKULLA NEWS** and got their address.

I played a few hands of Spider Solitaire.

By now the old Captain had his arm firmly around my shoulders as I poured another shot. Just out of curiosity, I went back to Google and typed in a name.

EBLIS.

I wondered—although wondering was getting harder to do at the moment, given the fact that thinking wasn't one of the Captain's fortes—who he was, really. Real estate agent? Mafia hit man? I hit **RETURN.**

No kidding, there is weird shit on the internet, as anyone who has ever googled anything can tell you. The first thing that came up was some webpage in Arabic featuring a middle-eastern hip-hop rap artist (if, indeed, they have such music there), a guy name Eblis Hossain, about my age. Probably not related to Harry Eblis, Real Estate Agent.

The second entry told me that Eblis was a place name used in the video game Rune Escape. The graphics looked crappy. Probably some low-budget mindless game only a moron would play. Ho hum.

Eblis also seemed to be a popular name for rock bands working the genre of Black Metal. I'd never heard the term, myself. I'd heard heavy metal, but black? The first group was based in Austria and formed in 2003. Their album was called *Pesthausch* (translated as "Breath of Pestilence" on the webpage. Nice title, there.) The band members (Magog Eblis, Sir Curwen and the Beast) were pictured in black and white horror makeup (very much like Kiss, and not very original, in my opinion), brandishing wicked medieval weaponry. Magog had a familiar ring to it, but I couldn't remember right off where I'd heard it before. The second band was from Poland, formed in 1992 and disbanded since. I read over the list of band members, labels, albums. Nothing interesting there. But then I got to **ADDITIONAL NOTES** and the entry there made me sit up and go cold all at once, even with the Captain doing his best to keep me warm. It said

Eblis: another name for Satan.

My chest felt a little tight and my breath started coming a little faster, but I felt I was on a roll now, as much as maybe I wanted off this particular roller-coaster. I went back to Google and typed in **DEFINE EBLIS** and then read:

> **The renamed demon Azazel, after being**
> **ejected from Heaven. Also the principal**
> **evil spirit or devil of Islamic mythology.**

And then because my curiosity never seems to be satisfied, I went back to Google and typed in **DEFINE AZAZEL** even though my scalp was prickling and if my hair hadn't been too long to stand straight up, I would be a regular porcupine by now..

> **In the Bible, the evil spirit in the wilder-**
> **ness to whom a scapegoat was sent**
> **on the Day of Atonement.**

The picture that accompanied this entry was of a naked, horned man-beast, carrying a trident in one clawed hand and grasping the horns of a goat in the other. His face was twisted ugliness, bearded, menacing, his feet ending in talons. Not a dead ringer for Harry Eblis, but somehow striking a resemblance that went deeper than just the outer skin. I stared at the old woodcut.

What happened next was probably caused by having had too much to drink.

Probably, but I wouldn't swear to it.

The hideous face of the demon in the woodcut seemed to turn slightly, bringing its eyes to rest on me, to gaze directly into my own. I sat there, frozen to the spot, and watched, horrified, as the lips slowly peeled back over sharpened teeth and the thing on the screen seemed to grin at me. The prickling became an electric shock running up my spine into my scalp.

I got up so fast I knocked over the chair I'd been sitting on, falling over it and then scrabbling backwards like a frenzied crab, back and away from the image on the computer monitor. If my throat hadn't closed up, I'm sure I would've screamed bloody murder. I may have uttered some garbled cry of fear but I may have just yelled in my mind. For an instant I sat there, on the floor, looking up at the leering creature that seemed to get closer, to grow in size, as if it were on the other side of a window instead of a monitor and moving toward me, until that the monstrous, repulsive face filled the screen. Suddenly I found a burst of strength born of pure terror that allowed me to push myself up onto my knees. I scurried forward in frenzy, dove under the computer table and grasped the power cord in both hands. I yanked it from the wall socket, then I scrabbled back to my original position, panting like a marathon runner, afraid to look at the screen yet afraid not to.

It was blank.

Blessedly blank.

By now I was shaking and sweating and damned glad that I was already on the high side of being drunk as a skunk. Leaving the TV on and lights blazing, I crawled over to the makeshift bed of foam on the floor, got on top of it, and pulled the covers over my head.

＊＊＊

When I opened my eyes and it was daylight, I was amazed on two counts. One that I had survived the night and two that I had actually fallen asleep at all. I guess having the Captain as a houseguest wasn't such a bad thing after all. At first I thought I had dreamed the episode about Azazel/Eblis about to climb out of the computer screen, but when I sat up and looked over at the computer, I saw the plug lying on the carpet instead of being in the wall. Either I'd been sleepwalking or it had been real. I didn't care much for either possibility. I got up and turned off the light and the folks saying *Good Morning America* on TV.

Lorraine called at eight to say she was sorry if she was phoning too early but that she couldn't stand a moment longer not knowing if I was all right (of course that made me grin) and that she hoped I'd be ready to leave for the diner early. I allowed that I could be ready by the time she got there, which wasn't entirely true given that she made a beeline for my driveway immediately after hanging up and I was still pulling on my shoes when she drove up. I brought two PBs on toast and two cups of coffee out to her car where we had breakfast. (I sort of wondered if there was a clause in my contract about that, but figured Mr. Eblis would let me know if there was.)

"Is everything all right?" Lorraine asked me, peering closely at my face. I knew I looked like shit warmed over, but I'd already decided not to tell her a thing about my wonderful night of googling on the internet.

"I'm fine."

"You don't look fine."

"Well, I am. Anyway, not so terrible that it can't be fixed with a few Excedrin." I glanced over at her and smiled (mostly at her worried face which was sort of nice, having someone care that much). "I had company last night."

"Who?"

"My old friend, the Captain." I could tell she wasn't quite sure what I meant. "Captain Morgan? The rum?"

She nodded and sipped her coffee. "You got blitzed last night."

"And probably will every night between now and August, unless there's a clause in my contract against it."

"Can't say I blame you," she sighed.

❖❖❖

Tuesday night I wasted no time in tying on a good buzz with the Captain. I moved the computer downstairs, turned on the TV and watched mindless television programs from the floor until I passed out. All in all, that was a pretty good evening. Nothing like a little induced semi-coma to while away the hours.

On Wednesday Lorraine picked me up early to take me to the Springs. "I don't care about the hour," she had told me. "I can't sleep anyway, wondering how you are."

"You really do care," I smiled.

"You know I do," she said, and though I had made my comment lightly, she did not reply in kind. "I'll pick you up at one. Are we still on for the newspaper office?"

"We are," I told her.

And that's how we came to be sitting out in front of the white wooden building with the gothic **WAKULLA PRESS. SINCE 1969** emblazoned over the door, contemplating the Twilight Zone of our lives on Wednesday, June 13th.

The Wakulla Press
June 13_____

"Not a very big building, it is?" Lorraine asked, peering at the white wooden frame newspaper office building through her front windshield. (And I know I told you this part already but I was just refreshing your memory, is all.) Over the front door in black gothic letters it read **WAKULLA PRESS. SINCE 1969**. We got out of the car and went inside. At the receptionist's desk I asked if we could speak with Tracie McAdams, the old schoolmate of Ranger Zeke. The good thing about a small town is that you usually don't have to have an appointment to see people like that. Walk into *The Miami Herald* and I bet you have to give references in order to speak to a reporter and then get on a six-month waiting list for a turn. We were asked to take a seat in their miniscule lobby while the receptionist buzzed a back office.

A few minutes later Tracie McAdams, a short roly-poly sort of woman with a quick step and red curls, came down the hall. "How can I help you?" she asked brightly, sort of chirpy, like a chipmunk on high-potency vitamins.

I introduced myself and Lorraine and told her how Zeke had said that if we wanted to look at some back news items she might be able to help us out.

"What sort of articles are you looking for?"

"Local stuff," I replied stupidly. I hadn't considered what I was going to ask for. I didn't want to say that we were interested in Wakulla County crime because when you start poking into disappearances and murders, local people can get a little squirrelly — even reporters who sometimes cover stories like that — but we hadn't really decided what we would tell people about what sort of research we wanted to do.

She gave me a grin and a quick eye roll, "Well, this is a very local paper, you know. Not going to find a lot of world news in these pages. What kind of 'local stuff' specifically?"

"We're interested in some background on a Crawfordville business called Wakulla Wood," Lorraine said and I tried not to look surprised at her interruption. She was damned good at thinking on her feet.. "We're college students doing a paper for economics on successful small town businesses."

Man, she *was* good.

"Any particular years?"

"Recent," I said. "Anything published after, say, the year 2000."

"Oh, that's good," she said, leading us upstairs. "We keep our archives up here. So far, we've digitized most everything from 1989 to the present, but the older things are still on microfilm. The digitized documents are easier to search through, not to mention read." She pointed to a large door to our left. "That's where our press is. We do all our printing here. The archives is back here." She led us to the rear of the building and it actually was bigger on the inside, only because you couldn't see the full length of the building from the front. It was narrow and long, but appeared small from its entrance.

"The cabinets here," she pointed to small media drawers facing us, "have all the CDs of digitized material. Back there are the microfilm rolls and the reader, but you probably won't have to worry about those if you want recent material." There was a bank of four computers on a table in the middle of the room. One of the machines was labeled **FINDING AID**. "Use this one to do a search for your articles. You can search by title, reporter, date or keyword. It'll bring up a list along with a number. That's the CD number and you just have to check the drawers. It's pretty simple. You can use any of the other three computers to look at your material. They're all on a hub linked to that printer over there." She indicated a laser printer that sat to the left of the computers. "You can make copies of the articles if you want. We don't charge for what you print, but take it easy on that, okay? Paper doesn't grow on trees, you know," she said, then giggled making her roly-poly body jiggle. "Well, actually it does, silly me!" I told her we'd be careful not to take advantage.

After Tracie left us, ("Just leave the CDs on the table when you're through. We'll refile them," she said, waggling her fingers in a toodle-oo as she went) we sat down at the **FINDING AID** computer. "What are we looking for?" Lorraine asked me.

"I thought of two topics to start with. Trojan Barnes and missing persons."

She nodded. "Sounds like a plan."

In the keyword field, I typed **MISSING PERSONS**. I hoped that wasn't too narrow, but if I had typed in **MISSING**, we might get every cat and dog in the county who went on the lam since the turn of the millennium.

A list was generated and appeared on the screen. I scrolled to the end. There were 23 entries.

"You think more than twenty people went missing in Wakulla County?" Lorraine asked. "That doesn't even seem possible, not in a county this size. It would've made national news."

"Probably most of these are follow-up articles." I printed out the list, a scant three pages, and we took a closer look. In 1999 an article noted that a businessman had disappeared, and two years later another reported a missing couple, then a year after that, a woman, followed by Linetta Barnes and Florence McIntyre. We noted the CD numbers for the articles that first reported these disappearances and Lorraine pulled them. She brought them up on one of the other computers and we had four names.

Grantham Kincaid
Vernon and Sharlee Hutchinson
Martha Preston

There were also several articles about missing teenagers and one Alzheimer's patient, but later on, follow-ups noted that they all had been found. I crossed those off. That narrowed the list to—sixteen. Not a big purge.

"Let me start looking, David. At least maybe get some more names."

I handed her the list and went back to the keyword field where I typed in **BARNES, T** and pressed **ENTER**. A long list of articles came up and I whistled. "Our friend Trojan was a busy guy."

"I'd imagine most millionaires are," Lorraine said as she started pulling more CDs from the drawers. "Do we have to look at them all?"

"I think we can focus on the later ones. His wife went missing a few years ago, so let's guess 2005. How about 1998 to then?"

"That won't eliminate a lot of those entries."

"Maybe we can't eliminate them."

She sighed. "Then the sooner you print a list and get started, the more likely we'll be able to finish before the office closes."

Before I left the finding aid, I also typed in **WAKULLA WOOD**. There were ten entries—one page—and I printed that out as well.

Side by side we started looking at the articles on the CDs. The digitization wasn't perfect although it beat microfilm by a country mile, as they say. We still had to scroll through the issues to find the right pages. And both of us were aware that the clock was ticking. God only knew when Sweetheart Boss would be willing to let Lorraine off again, and though I could've ridden my bike over here to the newspaper, it was quite a pedaling job and the days were getting warmer all the time.

Lorraine abruptly moved to the finding aid computer. "What's up?" I asked.

"Just have an idea."

"I'm all ears."

"I think we need to find out something about the missing people. But isn't our unspoken theory that maybe they had some connection to Trojan Barnes?"

"Yeah, maybe. Or Harry Eblis."

She started typing on the keyboard. "I don't think so. Eblis seems more like a behind-the-scenes sort of guy, not one who would have any direct connection to disappearances." She hit the enter key and nodded.

"What did you ask it for?"

"I did a Boolean search on Kincaid and Barnes. See here? There're four entries." She wrote down the numbers of the CDs and then typed some more. "Now let's try Barnes and — what's another name?"

"Hutchinson."

She nodded, typed. "Bingo, three entries. And who's the other one?"

"Preston."

Lorraine typed, pressed **ENTER**. "Nada. Martha Preston has no connection to your friend, Trojan. Let's see what the other articles say, you think?" She got up, pulled the CDs related to the articles and put them into one of the other computers. After a few minutes she pointed at the screen. "Here's the first one, Kincaid and Barnes." The entry was a captioned photograph rather than an article. It showed a group of people — and I recognized Trojan as the second from the right even though he appeared much younger. The caption indicated that it had been taken at a national meeting of businessmen in the lumber business. "'Local businessman T.B. Barnes,'" Lorraine read, "'joins colleagues at the annual meeting of Lumbermen National in Raleigh, North Carolina.'" She pointed to a man with short light hair—gray or blond; we couldn't tell in the black and white photograph—and wire-rimmed glasses in a spiffy suit. "Here's Kincaid, over on the left."

"So they sort of knew of each other," I said. "Let's see what the other articles say."

Lorraine popped in another CD and scrolled through the pages. "Here. Short article." We scanned it together. It was titled **Wakulla Wood Contemplates Merger** and briefly reported on T.B. Barnes hosting Grantham Kincaid of Central Carolina Lumber while they talked about the possibility of merging their two companies. A third article titled **Carolina Businessman Missing** was dated four days later and related that one Grantham Kincaid, in town discussing a merger with T. B. Barnes, was reported missing by his family. The police invest-igation, the article said, was inconclusive at the moment but would be on-going. A last entry, dated two weeks later, gave an update on Kincaid's disappearance and how investigators had questioned T. B. Barnes but had turned up no new leads. There were no more articles on Kincaid, probably because at that point the case went as cold as a dead fish.

"Let's look at the Hutchinsons," Lorraine said, putting another CD into the drive. The first article was a "business brief" and merely reported that Vernon and Sharlee Hutchinson of Tallapoosa Timber in west central Georgia were hosting a meeting of the Southern Lumber

Association in Haralson County and that Wakulla County's very own T. B. Barnes was giving the keynote speech. The second entry was another photograph showing a grinning foursome posing together at the SLA meeting: T. B. and Linetta Barnes and Vernon and Sharlee Hutchinson, a light-skinned African-American man with a blond wife.

"Anything about the Hutchinsons disappearing?" I asked.

"They came up on your missing persons list, so I assume so. You must have that one."

I looked through the CDs I had pulled and retrieved the one with the Hutchinsons. The article was brief and on the back page, doing no more than noting that Haralson County police were investigating the disappearance of the Hutchinsons whose last known whereabouts had been around Crawfordville, Florida. It mentioned that they were friends of lumber magnate T. B. Barnes and his wife, Linetta. There apparently was no follow-up in the Wakulla paper since they weren't locals.

We'd spent an hour at the paper so far and we had less than two hours left before closing. "Let's find out more about our friend, Trojan Barnes," I suggested. Glancing through the three pages of articles relating to him, many of which went back into the microfilm years, it seemed like his business hit a turning point right around the mid-90s.

"He was small potatoes until 1992 and then all of a sudden, business took off for him. There are small ads relating to Wakulla Wood, but no real articles. Then, in 1992, the company was awarded a major contract in the Crawfordville revitalization program. The next year, another contract, this time for building condos on coastal property — we're talking million-dollar stuff here."

"So that's where he made his money," Lorraine said.

"So it would seem."

"Kind of funny that a small business would just take off like that, for no apparent reason. I wonder where he got the contacts to get those contracts."

"The county probably put the projects out for bid and he won."

"I guess," she shrugged. "But he must've been competing against some high-powered companies. What was his edge, do you think?"

"I dunno. Usually the 'edge' is knowing the right people."

Lorraine eyed me. "So who do you think he might have known?"

I gave a noncommittal shrug. I felt a little guilty not telling her about the encounter I'd had the other night with the monstrous thing on the computer but I didn't like her getting too close to the evil that that thing represented. If Harold Eblis had been Trojan's contact person— well, I really didn't want to think about what that meant.

There was just one article after another, reporting new contracts being awarded to Wakulla Wood. "And look here," I said, pointing to the screen, "T. B. Barnes Elected President of SLA. That's in 1995 and at the end of that year he was invited to join the board of directors for Lumbermen National."

"When did he retire?"

I scanned the list and down in 2004 there was an article entitled Local **Lumber Magnate Passes the Torch**. "Here," I pointed and popped the CD into the computer's drive. It was big news, right on the front page. There was a picture, too, showing Trojan and his daughter, Natasha Barnes Reynolds and her husband, Jefferson. Trojan was smiling but it looked like he'd had to force himself to do so. He looked about like he did now: like a man in perpetual pain.

"Where's the article on his wife's disappearance?" Lorraine asked, and I searched for it. Together we read on the screen the story of the mysterious vanishing of Linetta Brisbee Barnes and her friend, Florence McIntyre. Apparently the police hounded Trojan mercilessly but could never prove that he was involved in his wife's disappearance. No bodies were ever found, no blood was discovered in the house, grounds or in any vehicle, there had been no potential murder weapon and, most important, there was no apparent motive. Everyone interviewed insisted that T. B. adored his Nettie. And he stood to gain nothing from her death. From the subsequent articles, the authorities had been reluctant to pack this particular case off to the cold case archives and pursued Trojan a good year before finally deciding it was a hope-less case and giving up on it.

"What's the time frame on Linetta and the other people?" Lorraine asked.

"Short, within two years. Kincaid disappeared first, then the Hutchinsons, then Linetta and Flo."

"So what's next?" Lorraine asked.

"Now I guess we need to talk to the man, to Trojan."

"Good idea," she said, "but not without me."

Trojan's Campsite
June 14_____

"What *is* that thing?" Lorraine asked as the two of us emerged from the woods into the clearing and tromped up to Trojan's camp.

"A burned up chair," I told her.

"Who burned it and why?"

I shrugged. "No idea." I had some idea that Trojan had been the *who* who had burned it, but the *why* of the matter escaped me.

"It's from the house," she said. "See the upholstery? It matches the sofa."

I hadn't noticed that before, but that was what had been niggling at my brain since I first saw it. It *was* from the house. But why Trojan had taken one chair from the house and then set fire to it, I hadn't a clue. I said as much to Lorraine.

"That's weird."

"What isn't these days?" I asked. Trojan was not sitting outside in his camp chair, but there were lights coming from his tent. It was just after six and the sun was still up, but the thick stand of trees cast long dark shadows over the campsite. "Trojan? Hey, Troj?" I called. Obviously you can't knock on a door when the person you're visiting lives in a tent.

"Wow, this is quite some piece of camping equipment," Lorraine whispered to me. "It's huge!" A tag on the tent said it was a Eureka Econo-Condo and that about summed it up. I bet you could host a dinner party for twelve inside that baby.

"Come on in," Trojan's voice came from inside.

I opened the screened flap that served as a door and stepped in. Trojan was sitting in a camp chair by a small table. He looked over at us and raised his hand in greeting. The ceiling was over eight feet high so I had no need to stoop. An opaque flap at the far end partitioned off a second room but the one in the front was the size of a master bedroom. "Quite some digs you got here," I said. I introduced Lorraine as Trojan rose and took her hand, then, in a courtly gesture, lightly kissed it, making her smile.

"Two hundred ten square feet," he told us. "Living quarters here, bedroom in the back. Outside a small shower and composting toilet."

"How do you power the lights—and is that a TV?" Lorraine asked. "You must keep quite a supply of batteries."

"Solar panels out back," Trojan told us and shrugged. "When you have money, you can afford to camp in luxury. Extra chairs in the corner," he pointed. "Have a seat. Get you a drink?" Lorraine and I unfolded two other camp chairs and sat. The tent was very cozy and after staying in Casa de Almas, I could see why Trojan preferred this little nest. He handed us each an RC and then took his own chair. "I don't think this is a social call," he said. "Am I right?"

"We need to talk," I said. "And you need to give us some answers."

Trojan regarded me solemnly for a long moment, took a swallow of his soda, then nodded. "I guess I owe you that much. Didn't do such a good job trying to convince you to leave the house be."

"I'm not blaming you," I told him.

"Question number one," he said.

"Did Grantham Kincaid disappear from Casa de Almas?"

Trojan eyed me. "Don't beat around the bush, do you, son?" He sighed and drained his can of soda, then put the empty into a bucket. "You two been doing some research, have you?"

I nodded. "Over at the Wakulla Press."

"Can't prove it," he said at last, "but, yes, I'd be willing to bet the house is responsible for what happened to Grant."

"Tell us," Lorraine said softly. She leaned forward, her posture expectant.

"Grant was a long time friend," Trojan said. "We started in the business around the same time. Got to know each other when we were bidding against each other to cut a stand of trees in southwest Georgia. Funny thing is, we didn't fight about it, and that's mainly due to Grant's generosity. We were both hurting for a supply of trees and he could've put me out of business, but he wasn't like that. He was all for us small business guys sticking together.

"Grant probably could've won the bid on his own but he allowed that we could put in a better bid if we went in on it together. His company was in better financial condition at the time and he could've left me in the dust, but chose not to. Thought that was damned nice of him, and we became friends after that, looking out for each other. After all, we weren't really rivals. He—"

"Was in central Carolina," Lorraine finished. "As in Central Carolina Lumber."

Trojan nodded. "You two've been doing your homework. Yes, he and I were operating out of two different states, so there wasn't any competition there except for lumber sources. But by pooling our resources we were able to offer better bids and win more of them. Working cooperatively kept us both going. I guess that made Grant a smart man as well as a nice one."

"The newspaper said something about a merger," I added.

"Lord, that goes back a ways. Yes, we'd talked about it. In fact the weekend he—disappeared—he'd come down here to meet with me and see my operation and talk about it. In the end, we weren't all that sure a merger was in our best interest—interstate rules and all that—but it was a good excuse for a nice visit. Took him fishing. More like a canoe trip down the Sopchoppy, but we called it going fishing because that's what men do around these parts and hell, it sounded better than saying we were two coots sitting in a canoe watching the water weeds."

"You wouldn't have used the Waterin Hole fishcamp, would you?"

"Can't remember. Could've been. There's lots of little places like that down there, though." Trojan eyed me. "Why? Is that important?"

I shrugged. "Dunno. Just thought I'd ask. So you went fishing—"

"And I had him stay at the house with Linetta and me. We'd just finished building it a short time before and we were eager to show it off a little. Our little cabin in the woods." Trojan shook his head.

"Was it your association with Kincaid that caused the boom in your business?" I asked making Trojan look at me sharply. "I noticed that you were sort of small potatoes for a long time, and then all of a sudden you got all these high-powered contracts."

He shook his head. "No, Grant and I helped each other out, but he wasn't the reason for my upward turn." He looked at me as if to say *And I think you already know that.*

"So what—?" I began but before I could finish my question, Lorraine interrupted.

"What about the Hutchinsons?" she asked, and I'm sure she had been anticipating me, but as it was, she was wrong.

"What about them?" Trojan asked.

"I think you already know the question," I said, deciding to go with her train of thought.

Trojan heaved a breath and nodded. "Vern and Sharlee were also good friends of mine and Linetta's. Knew them for years. We'd visit them, they'd visit us. Vern and I met because at the time we got started there weren't many brothers in the lumber business. It was sort of a white-guy enterprise, if you know what I mean. We stuck together through the rough times, and Grant and I even cut him in on stock. There was plenty to go around. We didn't mind sharing the wealth. It made prosperity more enjoyable, knowing your friends were along for the ride. Leastwise, that's how Grant and I saw it."

"Were they at your house right before they disappeared?"

Trojan stared at me for a long minute and his eyes grew watery. He rubbed them and pinched the bridge of his nose before answering, although I already knew what he was going to say. Like Grant Kincaid, Casa de Almas had been the last stop the Hutchinson's made before oblivion.

"People go into the house but they don't come out, is that how it goes?" I asked.

"Something like that."

"Exactly what happens? Where do they go?"

Trojan seemed to wither in front of our eyes. He didn't get physically smaller, but it was as if his soul were shrinking. "I—can't." He covered his eyes, trying in vain to block out a memory, and shook his head.

Lorraine leaned forward and touched his knee. "I know it's hard, Mr. Barnes, but we need to know."

At last Trojan took his hand away from his pinched face. "I don't know where they go. They just go." He sounded so weary that when Lorraine and I exchanged glances we silently made the decision to drop our line of questions for the moment. When he spoke again, he surprised us. "Vern, Sharlee and Grant—they weren't the only ones, you know."

"There were other disappearances?" I asked.

He shook his head. "Not everyone disappears. I have a theory." Trojan took a deep breath, then got up to get another can of RC from his portable refrigerator. He popped the tab, then took a swig which he rolled around in his mouth a minute. Finally he turned to us. "Those three, they were wonderful people, good people. I think the house takes those outright. But then you get others who aren't quite on the up-and-up. Not really bad, but with a tendency to—fudge a bit, in business, in life. People who are on the edge of not being really legit." He looked at both of us, first at Lorraine, then at me, and sat back down in his camp chair. "There were three others that didn't make the papers. At least, not the Wakulla Press. That's because they weren't from around here, but you can check them out on the internet, I bet."

"Who were they?" Lorraine asked. "Lumber people?"

"Two, the other was an attorney. Orin Saylor owned Loxley Lumber in southern Alabama, just east of Mobile. Mike Thatcher was his lawyer. Saylor was interested in acquiring Wakulla Wood because he wanted some of the coastal projects I had. I invited the two of them to stay at the house so we could talk about it even—just to be nice, you understand. Giving up Wakulla Wood wasn't in my plan. I admit, they made a good offer, but I wasn't interested in selling."

"Did you part bad company?"

"No. I don't think Orin was happy about it, but there were no hard feelings as far as I knew. The other person to stay at the house was Jessamine Tilden. She and her husband, Elgin, were involved with a lumbering conglomerate in central Georgia called GreenGold Timber. In fact, although the two of them were listed as co-owners, it was Jessie who controlled everything. Mind you, these three—Orin, Mike and Jessie—weren't bad people, but they had ruthless tendencies. And I think—" Trojan hesitated, drew a breath. "—I think the house takes advantage of people like that."

"So what happened to them?" Lorraine asked.

"I suspect you'll have to get the full stories off the internet. I have no doubt they're there. I can only tell you what the rumor mill brought my way. Orin Saylor took up a new hobby—child pornography. Police found thousands of digital photos on his computer starring himself and a number of neighborhood kids. He was like everyone's favorite grandpa, you know? They obviously trusted him. Or maybe feared him. Leastwise no one talked for a good number of years. Mike Thatcher raped four young women and was caught in the act of raping number five. Like Orin, he's in prison somewhere, I believe. And Jessie, well, Jessie was a mite more colorful." Trojan took a swig of his RC while we waited. "Jessie divorced Elgin and with her settlement had some physical enhancements done."

"Like what?" I asked.

Lorraine elbowed me, hefted her breasts and rolled her eyes. "*Enhancements,*" she said emphatically. She looked at Trojan. "Right?"

Trojan nodded. "Decided she wanted to build GreenGold Timber into an empire. She might've taken up with others, but the two I heard about were Winston McNamara and J. Nelson Fogarty, two of the biggest timber men in Georgia. Older men, out of the ballpark as far as women went. Married with kids, grandkids, but missing their sex appeal something fierce, you know? Winston was fat, balding; Nelson not much better. Jessie didn't care. Seduced them. Made them believe they were hot stuff again. Gave them favors in exchange for stock in their companies. After a while, what with all her teasing and putting out, those poor old coots would've given her anything, I think, and damned well did. Before too long, Jessie had controlling interests in both their companies, then dropped them. Winston couldn't take the loss and humiliation and shot himself. Don't know what happened to Nelson, but I can tell you, both families were ruined right enough. What Jessie's doing now, I don't really know since I'm out of the business, but I suspect most lumber men are pretty leery of her by now. 'Course, now she probably owns the biggest conglomerate in the south, maybe on the entire east coast."

"And you're saying the house was responsible for that?"

"Only a theory, son. But it seems to me that the house takes good souls outright and takes corruptible ones and uses them to inflict misery on others. Attaches itself or part of itself, or one of the demons that lives there, and uses them, pushes them over the edge of what's right and wrong." Trojan shrugged. "Like I said, just a theory, based on what I know."

"And the good ones—there's no way to get them back?"

Trojan looked at me sadly. He knew what I was thinking, and that was rescue. How to rescue Johnny and Theresa from the house.

"It's not like the good ones are being held prisoner, son. It's not like that."

"What is it like, then?"

A terrible, pained expression drew over Trojan's face like a veil. Some memory was sickening him from the inside out. "You don't ever want to know that," he whispered finally, his voice harsh.

Squint suddenly appeared and jumped into the old man's lap. He kneaded Trojan's chest a few minutes until the man's agony subsided from his face and he was able to reach out and stroke the cat's gray and white marbled fur. Then Squint turned around to face us, sitting straight up in Trojan's lap like a statue of that Egyptian goddess, Bastet, and squinted at Lorraine and me. Not a warning exactly, but more like a forceful hint that it was time to back off.

Lorraine touched my arm. "We should go, David. Enough is enough."

I looked at the cat and marveled at how formidable he seemed, that little bit of feline fluff, guarding the man. Reluctantly I got to my feet. "Okay, Troj, we'll let it go for now. But there are still things I think you know that we'll need to know if we're going to beat this thing."

Trojan looked up at me his face still pained. "Haven't you been listening to anything I've said, son? You can't beat that house. The best you can hope for is to get through the lease and leave it behind. And pray it hasn't destroyed you between now and then."

"If I can't get Johnny and Theresa back," I told him, "I'm damned sure going to make certain it can't take any body else. We are going to beat it, one way or the other. You may not think that's possible, but maybe there's a way you just haven't thought of yet. I'm going to be back, Troj," I said. "And when I see you again, I want you to plan on telling me everything you know. 'Cause man, we're making ourselves a plan."

Casa de Almas (Day 20)
June 14, Later_____

I must've stood there, staring at the damned thing –
the Dell computer, I mean—for twenty minutes before I
finally decided to plug it in. I didn't like living in such a
state of paranoia, nor of suspecting the computer of
harboring evil demons that were hell-bent (ha ha) on
gobbling me up. A fear of inanimate objects sounds really,
really nuts, although I guess after what happened the
other night my anxiety is understandable. Of course, too
much partying with the Captain might have caused me to
just imagine that a demon was about to climb out of the
computer monitor but I didn't believe that, not really. I
knew what I saw. And I sure as hell didn't want to see it
again.

Still, I wanted to use the damned thing. And a
computer refuses to run without electricity no matter how
much you want it to. After a while I gave in, got down on
my hands and knees and plugged it in but trailed the cord
out from under the table so that I could stop anything
freaky that might happen with one good yank. Because I
had not taken the proper steps to shut it down (like *that*

was going to happen!) it took an inordinate amount of time to check itself out, declare itself undamaged by my rash move, and boot up. I started at the screen as if I expected it to turn into a mouth filled with four-inch fangs sharp enough to slice through sinew and bone like butter, but the pastoral wallpaper came up on the desktop and the icons popped up without incident. Only then did I dare sit down in front of it. I kept the cord close at hand, though, just in case.

The first thing I learned was that archived newspaper articles are not free, and I wasn't about to raise the balances on my credit card just to read about the dire consequences of staying at Casa de Almas. But I figured that the headlines, first paragraphs and sometimes accompanying photographs would give me enough material to understand what had happened to the house's hapless guests.

Jessamine Tilden. The photo that came up was not in conjunction with any crime she had committed, but rather with an important business conference in Atlanta that she recently hosted. The face that stared grimly from the electronic pages of the *Atlanta Constitution-Journal* couldn't have seduced a blind man. I figured that's what happens when evil gets hold of you. It eats you from the inside out until it distorts the skin and bone and muscle and makes you as ugly on the outside as you've become within. Within a few years, Jessie Tilden had changed from a sexually vibrant woman at whose feet men were stupidly willing to lay their empires and fortunes to a repulsive old hag, her surgically enhanced hooters notwithstanding.

Orin Saylor, once leader of a million-dollar corporation, was now locked up, though not in a jail cell as Trojan had thought, but in a psychiatric hospital, serving a life sentence for a thousand counts of child pornography and endangerment, still protesting his innocence. He apparently had no recollection of having collected all those naked photographs of himself with his young victims, and even when he was confronted with said photographs, he repeatedly denied that the leering old man in them could possibly be him. Whether he was lying or guilt had robbed him of his memory, no one seemed to know.

Michael Thatcher, attorney at law, seemed to have taken to his new and improved evil lifestyle with more relish than his former employer. Although convicted of raping four young women — and being sentenced to four consecutive life sentences for them — he bragged that there had actually been many more victims of his unbridled lust, some in their early teens who he had disgustingly described as "deliciously ripe."

All of these people left behind spouses — although in Jessie's case, it was an ex-spouse — and both Saylor and Thatcher had children and even grandchildren who were shocked and devastated by their patriarch's sudden turn to the dark side. Yeah, no kidding. Must be a real bummer to wake up one morning and find out that the guy who had been sleeping beside you for the last twenty or thirty years had been prowling the streets for victims he could sexually abuse, or that the guy who dandled his grandchildren on his knee probably would have rather been fondling them naked.

There were only two small notices about Jessie's victims: obituaries for Winston McNamara and J. Nelson Fogarty. (Those were freebies, probably thanks to pressure put on newspapers by genealogy groups.) The causes of their deaths weren't noted, of course, but Fogarty's age had been listed as 85 and it had occurred only recently. He probably had not taken his own life, as had McNamara, but his obit was still pretty grim. Everything was *former* this and *one-time* that and his survivor list was very small as if most of his family had distanced themselves from him.

Interesting though this research was, I hadn't learned anything new about Casa de Almas that might be used against it. The one thing it did do was make me wonder—

Was I a good person or a bad person?

I *tried* to be a good person, and I felt I always had good intentions, even when they went awry. (The road to hell is paved with good intentions, right? Was that the saying? Was it even true?) If I was inherently the sort who could be pushed over into the dark side, would Casa de Almas eventually make me go careening out into the world, raping and pillaging? Or if I was a good soul, would I one day soon be gobbled up by the forces in this house? Was one fate better or worse than another?

Better question: could either or both of these fates be avoided?

Ah, yes, that was the question. Maybe yes and maybe no but I was thinking—hell, I hadn't a clue! At this point, the answer was a definite *maybe*.

I got up from the computer (switching off the monitor, which might have been silly but it somehow made me breathe a little easier knowing it couldn't watch me) and picked up the three pages of articles on Trojan that I'd printed out at the Wakulla Press. I took them downstairs, got the bottle of Captain Morgan, a can of diet Coke, and a glass of ice and took them into the living room. My initial fear of being downstairs had subsided, probably because I knew nowhere in the house was safe, so what the hell did it matter where I was? I fixed myself a drink (heavy on the rum) which I knew would not be my last of the evening, and sat down on the sofa.

Funny how it looked plush but wasn't all that comfortable. In fact, it was downright lumpy. I took a heavy swig of my drink feeling that first slow burst of warmth that started in my stomach and then radiated down my legs, a pleasant feeling, one I normally would have savored, but now was eager to move beyond into full-fledged drunkenness. By the time I finished looking over the Barnes Papers I wanted to be three sheets to the wind with the Captain firmly at the helm.

A listing I hadn't really noticed before caught my attention.

BUSINESSMAN T.B. BARNES HOSPITALIZED WITH MYSTERIOUS INJURIES.

The item occurred right around the time that Linetta and Flo had gone missing. No, actually, from my list it appeared that Mrs. Barnes's disappearance was reported only a day after the one about Trojan's hospitalization.

Even with the Captain buzzing in my brain, I was intrigued. Hell, downright curious! I wondered if the Press bothered to put their archives on line and decided to check it out. Upstairs again, I logged into their site and lo! they had their digitized materials available for purchase. My curiosity was such that there was no pain in reaching for my credit card — besides a one-time print of an article was a scant five dollars. A little searching pulled it right out of the online archives and I hit **PRINT,** and since I was right there, with my credit card so very handy, I decided to get a copy of the initial report on Linetta Barnes's disappearance. At that point I put my credit card back into my wallet so as to avoid the temptation of printing articles with wild abandon. Anything I still wanted I was sure I could get simply by paying another visit to Tracie McAdams over at the paper. While I waited for the two articles to print, I turned off the monitor (Why I thought that was some sort of protection against the forces of evil, I don't know. It was akin to closing a window to keep out a force five tornado, I suppose, but it made me feel better.) Then I grabbed up the pages and went back downstairs where the Captain awaited my return. I took a hefty swig before starting to read.

The article on Trojan was briefer than I'd hoped. He'd been discovered in the front yard of his house (Casa de Almas, I assumed) by a passing motorist who had been stopped by the sight of a gray and white cat on the side of the road holding in his mouth a piece of a man's torn blue shirt covered in blood. The cat had darted in and out of the road in an apparent frenzy and one Horace Dent of Panacea, passing through after a visit with his sister, Rutha O'Brien of Pine Run Ranch (I recognized that name!), had been so shocked by the bizarre scene that he'd stopped his car. Following the cat—still dragging the shirt—down the dirt driveway, Mr. Dent had found Mr. Barnes face down, covered in blood, and unconscious. Mr. Barnes, in fact, had lost so much blood that at first the ER doctor had given him very small odds of recovery. What had caused the injuries, the paper reported, was unknown and under investigation as they had likely been inflicted by a person or persons unknown.

I wondered if this was what Trojan had meant when he said that Squint had saved his life.

But saved it from who—or what?

Damned but the sofa was uncomfortable. Even with me rapidly going over to the other side of sober it was a miserable excuse for furniture.

The story about Linetta Barnes's disappearance was also brief, the only interesting thing in it being speculation as to whether Mr. Barnes's injuries suffered around the same time were somehow related. I took this to mean that Mrs. Barnes—or maybe her friend Flo McIntyre—had been considered a suspect in the wounding of her husband.

They thought what? That she'd attacked him—her loving husband of more than 35 years—with a machete and then taken off with her old pal, Flo, just as old Hubert Tressel, grocery store owner, had suspected, like Thelma and Louise? Or that maybe Florence McIntyre—someone who obviously could not be trusted in those red dresses and flashy convertible, right?—had attacked Trojan all by herself and kidnapped Linetta Barnes? Without a good reason? Without ever asking for ransom? It was so bizarre that there was little wonder why this case went cold fast.

I leaned back in order to think about what I'd just read and what I should pursue with Trojan. He must know who had attacked him and why. He didn't implicate Flo or Nettie so who had it been?

(Or *what*?)

I hated it when my mind took me in directions I didn't want to go.

And the sofa was damned uncomfortable. Enough so to be annoying. I sat up and touched the back. There was a lump there, something hard. What the hell could that be? I ran my finger over it. It felt like a piece of wood, a curved piece of wood with ridges. Who put chunks of wood into upholstery?

Curious (and why was I always curious? Didn't I ever learn that nothing good *ever* comes from being too curious?) I went to the kitchen for a knife. Yes, I was planning to cut through the upholstery of the sofa. Why should I care what happened to Eblis's furniture? Let him and his mysterious boss sue me.

I felt for the hard chunk, located it, and plunged the knife into the fabric, drawing it to the left and making about a five inch slit. I threw the knife down onto the sofa and dug my fingers into the hole I'd made. What the hell was that?

I pulled it out and stared at it.

It took about three seconds for my mind to register what my eyes were seeing.

I threw the thing down on the sofa as if it's temperature had suddenly shot up to 300 degrees and burned my fingers clean off.

Oh my god oh my god oh my god oh my god.

First I walked around in a circle.

Then I started pacing back and forth.

I stopped only long enough to steal a quick glance at the thing I'd retrieved from the sofa cushion. Just to be sure it was really, really there. I didn't want it to be there.

But it was.

Oh my god oh my god oh my god oh my god

I circled. I paced. Then I stopped long enough to once again make sure I had seen what I thought I had seen.

Holy Jesus mother of God!

At that moment I wished I had cozied up to the Captain a lot more than I had. I saw the bottle. I took a swig. A gulp. Another gulp.

I was still shaking like a yellow pine in a hurricane.

After a few minutes, the Captain's magic brew began to work on my nerves and I could finally stand still for longer than two seconds. I took a few deep breaths. Now was not the time to fall apart.

If anyone had the right to go to pieces, though, it surely was me.

How many people find a piece of a human jawbone with five white teeth still embedded in it in their sofa?

That was what it was. I'd looked at it enough to know that it wasn't some person's partial. Not a misplaced set of dentures. These were real teeth in real bone.

A little calmer after my initial shock — though not by much — my thoughts turned to the question: what to do with it?

(Call the police.)

Yeah, right. I don't know why the cadaver dogs didn't find this particular relic. (Maybe *They* had a way of masking it or something. Maybe those things infesting the house had only just left it for me to find.) But I was already a primary suspect in the disappearance of my friends as far as Detective Bret Randall was concerned. You can't just hand over human remains and think they'll thank you for taking the trouble.

Human remains.

Human. Remains.

Isn't that a creepy term? I had never thought about how very creepy that term was until just now.

So what should I do with these human remains?

First thing right off was to get them — it — off the sofa. Not that I would ever ever *ever* sit on that sofa again, of course, but I couldn't just leave those teeth lying there. I went into the kitchen and rummaged around, at last coming up with a small stack of brown sandwich bags probably left over from when Mrs. Barnes did the grocery shopping and would pack Mr. Barnes a nice little lunch to take to the office with him. I tried to put Mrs. Barnes out of my mind because for all I knew it was part of Mrs. Barnes that was lying on my sofa.

I could not bring myself to touch it again. I opened the bag and maneuvered the edge under the piece of bone, wiggling and jostling, sort of the way I used to see my mother pick up an ugly dead roach from the floor. Finally enough of the bone was in the bag that I could lift it and let it fall inside. It did so with a soft smack

(like bone on paper)

that was mildly repulsive. I quickly folded over the top, as if I half expected it to jump out of the bag, gnashing its five remaining teeth, trying to take a bite out of me even though there was no upper jaw for it to partner with.

(The most it could do would be to scrape—)

No, I couldn't think about stupid things like that right now. I had to dispose of

(the remains)

the *bag* and it didn't feel right just tossing it in the trash. After all, at one time it had been human, or part of a human, and that seemed disrespectful.

Not to mention the fact that I would then have to get rid of the trash and the damned dumpster was down by the road. No way was I going to walk all the way out there in the dark to dump the trash.

Carefully I laid the bag on the coffee table so as not to

(disturb it)

let it make any more noise and I went back into the kitchen, quickly finding what I was looking for. A small plastic lidded bowl, the kind you keep

(leftovers in).

Yeah, whatever. That would certainly be an interesting twist for a hostess at a Tupperware party, wouldn't it? Imagine the things you can keep in here! Leftover veggies, last night's stew, part of your husband, Bob.

I quickly went back to the living room, picked up the bag and stuffed it into the plastic container, snapping on the

(keep fresh)

lid. Try to sniff *that* out, you cadaver dogs! Then I took it to the back bedroom, the one I would never use, never go into ever again. I put it in the closet, way up on the shelf, closed the closet door, closed the bedroom door. Did I finally feel safe, relieved?

Hell, no.

I would have to get a lot drunker than I was at the moment to get over this major dental work.

I grabbed up the Captain and downed a few more gulps, then picked up the phone before I even comprehended what I was doing. It was only when she answered that I realized how automatic my reaching out to her had become.

"David? What's wrong?"

The alarm in her voice made me feel very, very guilty for pulling her into this and at the same time, very, very glad that I had.

"Nothing. I'm sorry. I shouldn't have called. It's late. I wanted to hear your voice and and... and I just dialed without thinking and...and I'm okay, I'm just calling to say I'm okay I'm just drunk that's all and... and I'm going to bed now so I'll see you tomorrow okay?"

When I stopped to breathe, her worried voice came back into my ear. "David! What's going on? What's happened? Something bad's happened!" She sounded close to tears and I felt guilty and happy all over again—that was the Captain's thinking, I'm sure. Only someone who had been palling around with the Captain would have major regrets and be blissfully joyful all at the same time. I guess that's what they call being in high spirits.

"It's the house, isn't it? What's happened? What's it done now?

The thing was, she *cared*.

"No no no nothing I'm okay really I've just been drinking, got a little freaked out but I'll tell you all about it tomorrow okay, just go back to sleep or whatever you were doing and I'll see you tomorrow, okay I love you."

"I love you, too," she said, but her voice sounded sad in its sincerity.

Still, I would take an *I love you* any which way it came. I just hoped that no good bye would come with it.

The Waterin Hole
June 17_____

     Drinking and working was a hell of a way to spend your days (and nights) but for the next two days, that's all I did. I was at **Alice's Eats** before ten in the morning and stayed past ten at night. Twelve hours of bussing followed by another hour of getting as drunk as possible. Sometimes I thought most of my salary was going toward keeping the Captain as my roommate.

     The next morning after my find in the sofa Lorraine came by early just to make sure I was still alive and sane. She and I walked over to Trojan's camp before heading to the diner but though we called out numerous times, we failed to rouse him. Squint sat in one of the mesh windows on a cushioned box that seemed had been made just for him and stared at us.

     "I'm going in," I told her. "I know it's trespassing, but if he's in trouble and I didn't check, I'd never forgive myself."

     "I'm right behind you," she said.

     But Trojan wasn't at home. His bed had been made, breakfast dishes had been washed and left to dry in a plastic bin by the makeshift sink. Squint stood up and stretched, arching his back and yawning, when we came in, but did not seem alarmed.

"Where do you think he went?" Lorraine asked.

"Better question, *how* did he go? I haven't seen so much as a bicycle around here."

Lorraine just shrugged. I rummaged for a piece of paper and pencil in a small desk up against the wall and also found a paperclip in the top drawer. I quickly scribbled a note in all caps to emphasize its importance:

CAME TO SEE YOU. WE NEED TO TALK.
I NEED ANSWERS, OKAY? PLEASE!
DAVID

I paper-clipped it to the front flap of his tent and then Lorraine and I tromped back to her car.

I hadn't wanted to tell Lorraine about my grisly find in the sofa but keeping things from her wasn't the way a true relationship was supposed to work. I figured she could handle it, and I was right. Although she sat for a moment with her fingers pressed against her lips—to keep from crying out or throwing up, I don't know—finally she just nodded with a grim look on her face. "I really, really hate you being there, David. Who knows what's next, what it'll do to you?"

"I think maybe they still want to use me as bait, though," I told her.

"There's a comfort."

"But I'm very *poor* bait. No fish. I'm the worm that will chase away the fish."

Lorraine said nothing, probably wondering (like I was) what Eblis and his employer would do once they realized that I was being poor bait *on purpose*. We both knew that that could mean they might just take me and call it a day, but neither one of us wanted to say that out loud. We all believe that if we don't say something, it won't come true. It's stupid, but we all do it.

"Where are we going today?" she asked instead.

"Could we head over to Uncle Pete's fishcamp? Troj mentioned taking his friend to a fishcamp in Sopchoppy and maybe it's a long shot that they went to the Waterin Hole, but I want to ask. Then we could take a canoe out, if you want."

"I think I'm too tired to even move an oar," she said. "I'm not getting much sleep these days." She eyed me pointedly. "Too many weird late-night phone calls."

"I'm sorry."

"I just wish you'd tell me what was really going on instead of letting my imagination run wild."

"You think what you're imagining is worse than what really happened?"

I know she was thinking about the teeth in the jawbone and shook her head. "I suppose not. I still want to know, though."

"And do what about it?"

"Nothing. Just know. Just be there for you."

What a girl! I felt like the luckiest guy on earth, even though we were trying to conduct a romance under the worst possible conditions. If we survived this, I was convinced we'd be married long enough to celebrate our diamond anniversary.

⇥❙❙❦

I was glad to see Gabe working at the fishcamp for the summer. A familiar face far away from Casa de Almas was like a balm on my soul. He raised a hand when he saw me get out of Lorraine's car. After I introduced him to her he leaned over toward me with a sort of wolfish leer and said in low voice, "Nice!" I ignored him.

"Uncle Pete around?"

"Working in the store. Hey, if Lorraine has a friend, we could double some time," Gabe suggested. "Have one of our famous par-tays at that fancy house you've rented."

"No!" Lorraine and I said in unison making Gabe's eyes bug out in surprise. I quickly added, "My landlord doesn't want any parties going on there. But we could still hang out somewhere else some time," I suggested, fearing I might have offended my friend with my vehement rejection of his offer to have a good time. "Gonna go talk to Uncle Pete a minute, okay? We'll catch up later. *Okay?*" I stared at him hard, trying to read whether I'd totally scared him off or pissed him off or what.

"Yeah, okay, sure."

I took his arm for emphasis. "We really okay, amigo?"

"Yeah, absolutely. Landlords can be a bitch, can't they?"

"You have no idea."

"Okay, then. We can always hang out here."

"That's a plan," I grinned hoping I didn't look like I was snarling, but Gabe grinned back. A par-tay here, a par-tay there, location didn't matter.

"Gotta get a boat in the water for that couple over there," he said, nodding his head in the direction of a middle-aged couple in life-jackets and Australian Barmah bronco hats. The fact that you'd probably have to be under two and a half feet tall to drown in the Sopchoppy River did not keep them from erring on the side of caution. He waved me away and I waved back before taking Lorraine's hand as we walked to the bait shop.

"Well, look who's here!" Uncle Pete said from behind the counter. "Where you been, stranger? Thought you'd be a regular here at the fishcamp this summer."

"You're a little far away from my digs, Pete," I said. "Have to be near the Springs, you know. Community service. Not to mention being reduced to riding a bicycle."

"Hell, I could use one of you community service people here at the camp. Gabe's great but I gotta pay his ass to be here."

"I don't think they allow for community service in profit-making businesses," I said.

"Who says I make a profit?" he grinned.

I introduced Pete to Lorraine. He shook her hand but grinned at me. "Nice!" he said and I couldn't keep my eyes from rolling. "Be careful of that nephew of mine. He might try to steal her away. Couldn't blame him for that, either," Pete added looking her up and down. "So what brings you and the lady to the Waterin Hole?"

"I wanted to ask you something. You ever hear of T. B. Barnes, the guy who owned Wakulla Wood?"

"Oh, yeah, the guy with the big bucks whose wife went missing."

"That's him."

"What about him?"

"Do you remember a few years back having rented a boat to him and a friend of his?"

Pete folded his arms across this chest and tilted his head back as if that would focus his memory. "Can't say I recall him being here. Doesn't mean he didn't come here, but I could've had an assistant rent him a boat. Did he say he came here?"

"No, just a fishcamp in Sopchoppy."

"There are quite a lot of us out here."

"I know," I said, feeling a little disappointed, though what I hoped to learn from knowing Trojan had been here, I couldn't say. "Just thought I'd ask." Then something else occurred to me. "Listen, Pete, you remember when I first came here and said I needed to rent a place to stay?"

"Sure nudgin' the old memory cells today, ain't you, boy? Yeah, I remember. So?"

"You also remember that Harold Eblis guy?"

"The fellow in the fancy Mercedes," Pete nodded. "I never forget a car, and that one was a beaut."

"That's him. He left you his card and you gave it to me. Do you recall how he knew I needed a place to stay? I can't believe him coming here was just random."

"Oh, nah, it wasn't random. He said a friend of yours told him you might be needing a place for the summer."

"A friend of mine," I repeated. "Did he say who?"

"Nope. You got so many friends you can't figure it out?" Pete grinned.

"I guess not." And two less since the last time I was at the fishcamp. I thanked him and told him we'd get out of his hair. Lorraine and I walked back to the car.

"So can you figure who told Eblis about you needing a place for the summer?" she asked.

"It couldn't have been Mojo or Whippet because they would've told me and besides, they seemed as awed to see Eblis as I was. They for sure hadn't seen him before. Same with Gabe. Could've been Johnny or Theresa, or maybe the bully boys, though I doubt it."

"The who?"

"Two football players on our floor. D'Ante and Tom. I guess it could've been them. Funny they didn't mention it, though. It would've been more like them to brag about having gotten me set up in such nice digs." I sighed. "To which I do not want to go back too soon. Any ideas?"

"A nice afternoon at the Springs," Lorraine suggested.

"Oh, yeah, I don't see enough of that place."

"You never see it as a tourist," she reminded me.

And so that's how we spent our afternoon, doing all the touristy stuff that people from other parts of the country go there to do. Of course, I've played tourist there a few times, myself, but never with an adorable girl like Lorraine at my side. The glass bottom boats weren't running because the water was too dark — a shame because there is some cool junk down there in the Springs, left-over stuff from when Johnny Weissmuller swung through the trees as Tarzan, and when the Creature from the Black Lagoon arose to terrorize the locals, and when the movie airplane went underwater in 1977. Instead we took a ride on one of the jungle boats which is sort of a cheesy thing to do if you're a local—the tourists all ooh and ahh over the alligators that have practically been crawling around in your backyard your entire life. Moorhens and turtles and mullets that jump clean out of the water—the tourists are right there with their cameras, craning their necks to catch a glimpse of our exotic native wildlife. It's a hoot but Lorraine and I kept any snide comments to ourselves, enjoying the breeze that came off the water, holding hands, and just enjoying the peace of the river and each other. After that we had a late lunch in the lodge's restaurant— huge windows overlooking the Springs, comfortable black swivel chairs, great food served on gold-edged china and white linen tablecloths.

"I have an early day tomorrow. Calvin wants to do the annual inventory and I need to be there two hours before opening."

"Calvin?"

"Sweetheart Boss," she told me.

"Jesus, that's practically dawn!"

"Seven in the a.m., but I can handle it. It's time and a half." She looked up at me from her plate with a pained expression. "What it means is that I need to get to bed early tonight." And that meant she had to drop me off early, at the house. Oh, I understood her meaning all too well and I also knew how much she hated having to do that.

"It's okay. I'm learning to live with my demons." And I chuckled at that but she wasn't amused. I reached across the table and took her hand. "Really, it's okay. It's not like I'm going to let you come in, or that I can come to your place anyway. Stop stressing over this. Look at the bright side. Maybe the house won't eat me. Maybe it'll just turn me into a raving lunatic."

"It wouldn't have far to push you," she said, then gave me a little smile that brought out those adorable dimples of hers.

After our early dinner we ambled around the grounds with me showing her all the exciting things I did at the Springs, like cutting and mulching and trimming, but there were mobs of people there hoping that the cold water of the springs would relieve the steadily rising temperatures, so we soon abandoned our stroll and went back to her car. A few minutes later she arrived at my driveway.

"You sure know people with fancy cars," she remarked as she pulled down the dirt drive. "My poor little heap is getting mighty intimidated."

I looked toward the house and there was that familiar Dodge Charger Daytona RT in Top Banana yellow. "That's Parker's car," I said. The vehicle fairly glowed in the lowering sun.

"Friend of yours?"

"Not really. He lives a few doors down from me in the dorm. He's more like a friend wannabe." I sighed. "Damn, I wonder what he wants." I turned to Lorraine. "It's okay, he's sort of our token geek. I'll get rid of him. No need for you to hang around. I'll see you tomorrow." I kissed her and got out of the car.

I started walking toward the Top Banana car and saw Parker get out from the driver's side, raising a hand in greeting. He had on a Ralph Lauren polo, Christian Dior khakis and a pair of sunglasses I could've sworn were Oakleys. Easily a five-hundred dollar outfit, and that didn't even count his shoes. His hair was longer, well styled, and he had managed somehow to get a tan to stick to his pale, bunny-pink skin. He grinned when he saw me.

Funny how we never know when we're walking into a nightmare.

Casa de Almas (Day 23)
June 17, Later_____

Okay, *nightmare* wasn't a very good way of putting it. In a nightmare you plunge immediately into a horrendous situation and the minute you reach the point where death is right there about to bite you on your butt, you wake up.

The point being, you were asleep and none of it was real.

The bad situation that I was walking into (but didn't know it at the time) wasn't going to be something I could wake up from and find it had all been nothing more than a bad dream. This bugaboo was reality, baby, and reality was a *bitch*.

This reality (though I didn't know it right then) was going to put me on the edge of a pit I couldn't even see the bottom of, where I was ankle deep in slimy mud that was slippery with algae, with my footing just about to give way. Some time soon, I was going to plunge down god only knew how far to a bottom where god only knew what waited for me. I know now that I had sensed (way back in the parts of my mind that we all try to ignore when they make us feel nuts) that my feet were just about ready to slip out from underneath me, sending me on that long, long slide into

(hell)

the unknown. At that moment, though, all of those feelings were being blocked by my conscious mind because, given that my visitor was Parker, super geek, super innocuous Parker, such ominous thoughts seemed supremely stupid. What could possibly be bad in a harmless visit by a friend-wannabe?

"So, Park, what's up?" I asked, trying to sound as if I were glad to see him as I walked over to his stunningly yellow car. He pushed his sunglasses onto the top of his head and grinned at me.

"Just came for a another visit, good buddy. Wanted to see how you were doing."

(Good buddy?)

"I'm doing fine, thanks for asking."

"Got time for a little R&R? I've got a six-pack sitting in a cooler in the back seat, all iced down and all. Can I come in for a while?"

Sure, Parker. Just come in and get a one-way ticket to nowhere. But sending him away after he'd driven all that way seemed the epitome of rudeness. "Why don't we just sit on the porch? The house is a little — you know — bachelor-pad messy at the moment."

"Lousy housekeeper, huh?" Parker grabbed the cooler and carried it up to the porch where he and I sat in the two rockers, while I hoped that this area was a safety zone and not another gateway to hell like the rest of the house.

"Let's just say Betty Crocker isn't going to hand me the Good Housekeeping Seal of Approval any time soon."

Parker took two Bud Lights out of the cooler, handed me one and popped the top on a second. "So, have you had many visitors while you've been here?"

"In the beginning, but not lately. Not much time for that," I told him, popping the tab and taking a swig. The beer was as icy cold good as he'd promised. If I hadn't been so antsy about getting over to see Trojan, I might have enjoyed the impromptu visit, even from Parker.

"Haven't had your friends here for one of your famous parties?"

"No, Parker, I told you. I've been working 'round the clock. And I'm sure they're busy, too."

"What about weekends?"

"I work Saturdays."

"And Sundays, too?"

I couldn't understand his line of questioning. What was it to him what my social life was like? "Then I see Lorraine."

Parker grinned over the rim of his beer. "Oh, the little blond who dropped you off. You didn't invite her over. I would've liked to have met her."

"Yeah, sorry. Another time. She has an early day tomorrow."

"You have her over on Sundays? Maybe a little sleep-over on Saturday night?"

"Saturdays are pretty tiring for both of us," I said, getting a little annoyed. I felt like adding *Not that it's any of your business*, but I bit it back. It seemed a mean thing to say to a man who had just driven an hour so he could hand you a refreshingly cold beer. "We try to get out and do something fun on Sundays."

"Seems to me there'd be a lot more fun in the bedroom," Parker said. "I bet she's pretty hot. I mean, knowing your taste in women and all."

I decided not to answer hoping he'd get the hint that I didn't appreciate the direction our conversation was heading.

"You need to let your hair down some, man," Parker said. "You know what they say about all work and no play. You don't want to get dull as dishwater, do you, Jack?"

"There'll be time enough for play once I get back to Tallahassee. Got to get this legal mess behind me, first."

"Just have some visitors some time. It's good for you to see your old buds."

"Yeah, maybe," I said.

"I mean it, Fresco," he said, more forcefully than I thought such encouragement should be. "You should have friends out." Parker's mouth was smiling but the humor stopped there. There was none in his eyes. In fact, the blue eyes that studied me were as cold as the cubes in his cooler and if it hadn't been so hot out there on the porch, I would have shivered.

I polished off the rest of my beer and put the can down on the porch floor. "Yeah, sure, Parker. You're right. I'll do that first chance I get." I clenched my hands between my knees as if to say *No more beers. Time to go.* I hoped he understood body language, but at first he just sat there, rocking slowly, so I added, "Look, I'm sorry to cut this visit short but my neighbor's not feeling so good and I want to go check on him before it gets dark. Sun's setting and it's no fun tramping through the woods in the dark."

Parker's good-old-boy cheerfulness seemed to have abandoned him. He finished his own beer and then crushed the can with his fist. It was such an unParkerlike thing to do, that it surprised me. The geek was giving me some tough-guy routine; what was up with that? He stood up so that he was looking down on me. That sort of superior-inferior position creeped me out somehow and I quickly got to my feet. "Thanks for coming to see me, man," I said. "And thanks for the cold one."

Parker nodded, taking his sunglasses from the top of his head and shading his eyes. "Okay, then," he said with a smile that seemed weirdly insincere. "Well, it was good to see you, Fresco. I'll check on you again sometime, maybe."

"That'd be great, Parker," I told him,

(Check on you?)

hoping I sounded truthful even though I was lying as blatantly as anyone ever has. If he never came to visit again, I would be thrilled beyond belief.

I didn't wait for him to drive away, but immediately went inside and found a flashlight, a nice high-powered halogen, then turned on the front and rear porch lights and headed toward Trojan's camp. Parker's bright yellow car was just pulling onto the road making me sigh with relief. He was such a weird bird.

I'd been thinking all sorts of bad thoughts while I tromped along the path that I'd by now worn between Casa de Almas and Trojan's campsite, so it was a great relief to see him sitting in his usual camp chair in front of a small fire over which he was roasting a small hen.

"Figured you'd be around sometime soon," he said as I arrived. He eyed me. "Got your note."

"I was worried about you. Didn't expect you to be gone."

"The groceries don't just appear on the table, son. My daughter takes me to the store once a week, or sometimes her husband if she's busy. A peach, my Tasha. Husband's a good guy, too."

"Chicken on the menu tonight?"

"Squab. You hungry?"

"No, thanks. I had an early dinner with Lorraine. Isn't that a pigeon?"

"I figure if they poop on us we have the right to eat them. So," he said, heaving himself out of his chair. "What did you want to talk about?"

"Well, for starters, how did the bad things—what you call the demons—get into your house in the first place? You built it, didn't you? What did you use? Tainted trees?"

"You know how you can make one stupid decision that can change your life?" he asked, then nodded in my direction. "'Course you do. That's how you ended up here in Bethel, isn't it?"

"Yeah, Troj. I know all about making stupid decisions."

"My business wasn't going so well. I was working my butt off and just barely managing to hang on. I didn't want to let it go. I don't give in easily, not even in the face of bad odds." He got up and went to the cooler for some sodas, talking to me over his shoulder. "One day I had a visitor, fellow who made himself out to be some sort of philanthropist. Liked to help out the little guy, the independent business, he said. I knew a lot of good people, so I guess I wasn't savvy enough to see a con when I met one. I still believed in people helping people, you know? Not that there's a good excuse for being that naïve. And do you know who that fellow was?"

"Let me guess. Harold Eblis."

Without asking Trojan handed me an RC, popping the tab on one for himself and raising it in a salute. "You got it. It seemed like a simple enough deal. He'd put me onto some lucrative contracts, pull a few strings, and all I had to do was promise to patronize other companies he worked with — use them, recommend them to my friends. Didn't seem like anything bad, not immoral or illegal, so I agreed."

"Other companies? Like furniture companies, maybe?"

"Furniture, appliances. Harmless stuff — or so I thought. Right away, business started booming."

"You got that big contract on the coast."

"That, and others after it. Money just rolling in. So when Nettie and I built our house I didn't think twice about buying all the furnishings from Eblis's people. He knew all sorts of contractors — painters, electricians. A walking conglomerate. But he also offered good prices. Reasonable. Why shouldn't I do business with him?"

"Yeah, why not? Who wouldn't?"

"Well, it was stupid. You know what they say about something that sounds too good to be true? But I was driven to be a success. My Momma didn't turn tricks and offer up her ass just for me to end up a failure." He looked at me pointedly. "Just so you know it wasn't just about the money."

"I understand, Troj. How soon after did Grant go missing?"

"Not long. At first I was real puzzled, like you with your friends. Didn't make sense that he would just up and leave like that, good friends that we were and all. And the fact that he didn't make it home.... But I didn't get the message until Vern and Sharlee...." He stopped, his face creased, the memory pinching him hard from the inside out. "I don't know what gave me a bad feeling about Eblis, except that he was always around, checking up on me, pushing me to make business contacts, to be hospitable, you know? Have them out to the house, wine and dine 'em. Eventually I began to suspect he might have something to do with my friends going missing. But it wasn't until—" He stopped again. The memory must have been really bad for it to put that much pain on the old man's face.

"Until what?" I prompted.

"Until it began to get to me. Make me like Orin and Mike and Jessamine," he said and the dark eyes that looked at me were hard. "Make me evil."

Trojan's Campsite
June 17—even later_____

He told me he was evil and then—nothing. Trojan sat there, his face stony with bad memories. But there was no way I was going to leave it at that.

"You gonna drop a bombshell on me like that and then clam up?" I complained to him. "No way, Jose! Uh-uh! There's no point in stopping now, Troj, and I really need to know what you know."

Squint seemed to recognize Trojan's distress and he jumped into the old man's lap, kneading him gently as if trying to soothe him. Trojan reached out his hand and began absently stroking the gray and white fur. "Why?"

"Why? We've got to do something about that hell house. Oh, don't give me that look! I know what you're thinking."

"Is that so?"

"Yeah, only it's not my goal to try to eradicate evil in the world. I just want to get rid of it in one small place on this earth—the place that took two of my friends. The place that stole your wife."

"You won't be able to do that." Trojan's voice was soft, defeated and I hated hearing that tone.

"Isn't there a saying that evil wins when good chooses to do nothing? Maybe I can't win, not completely, but damn it, Troj, someone's got to try to do *something*." I took a deep breath getting my anger under control. "So tell me the rest of it. Even if you think it's all for nothing and I'm just a dumb kid, tell me anyway."

"I don't think you're dumb, David. Maybe just a little naïve."

I frowned. "Whatever."

After a moment Trojan conceded with a nod and shrugged. "All right then. First off, I heard about Orin and Mike, and then I started having bad thoughts."

"Bad thoughts don't make a person evil. You're not evil," I told him.

"You want me to tell this or not?" Trojan asked, an irritable edge to his voice. I gestured that I would shut up and he could continue.

"I meant, not thoughts *about* bad things. About *doing* bad things. Cheating. In business. And... elsewhere. One night I told Nettie I had a late meeting over in Apalachicola and was going to stay over, that I'd find some little motel to spend the night. It was a lie, of course. Never lied to her before, but I did that night. Drove over to Panama City and picked up a prostitute, a sweet little black thing. Sweet looking, but hard. She was young, but she'd been at it a long time and it had made her hard. I would've done her too, only when I looked into her face, into her eyes, I saw my mother, saw Momma all those years ago offering herself up to any man who wanted her.

I remembered how she'd lived that life to give me a better one, and there I was, dishonoring her and my wife. In that moment, I felt sick. It—broke whatever spell or whatever was on me. Maybe only because I was so far from the house, that it couldn't maintain its control, I don't know. The point is, I didn't go through with it, and at that moment, I was determined that I'd take Nettie and we'd leave that house, maybe even the business."

"But you didn't."

"I couldn't," Trojan corrected me. "You know first hand how Eblis doesn't like his contracts broken. I got back to the house and as soon as I did, somehow he, or it, knew. It had gotten into me and it knew me. It was determined to punish me for even thinking I could defy it." He took a deep, shaky breath. "Nettie had been feeling lonely without me there."

"So she invited her friend, Flo, to spend the night," I finished for him

Trojan nodded.

"And they were gone by the time you got there?"

"If only, son," he answered softly. "If only." He stopped and didn't seem like he was inclined to go further for the moment so I decided to bring up the issue of my grisly little find. I told him about the jawbone and teeth in the sofa but he didn't even seem surprised.

"Anything you want to tell me about that?" I prompted.

"My guess is that it belongs to Flo. From that night when I got back from PC."

"And why is that?" I couldn't believe how calmly we were discussing human remains in my furniture. It's a scary thing when horror becomes such a part of your life that you can talk about it like some people discuss new recipes.

"'Cause I'm pretty sure Grant, Vern and Sharlee were in their beds when they were taken, and I know it can't be from my Nettie."

My eyes slid over to the burned chair and suddenly understood its significance. "Your wife was in the chair, not on the sofa, when she—" I said letting my voice trail off.

(When she what?)

Trojan nodded. "Why did Eblis let you take it? He doesn't grab me as the generous sort."

"I traded him the house for it."

"You swapped a house for a piece of furniture?"

Trojan gave me a steely look. "I swapped a house for my *wife's soul*," he said. "When I got it, I dragged it over here, away from the house, away from those things that had her, and I set fire to it, to set her free."

"And did you?"

Trojan nodded. "I felt her—her spirit—when she left it. Some things you just know. Especially when they're about people you love."

"So why didn't you just set fire to the whole house and set everyone free?"

"The house can't burn, son," Trojan replied with an edge of annoyance to his voice as if this was something I should've known. "You think creatures from hell are afraid of fire? Truth is," he added, "I tried burning it, but the fire went right out and the part that got charred just healed itself right up. You think you've seen it all and then—" He closed his eyes briefly and swallowed hard. "The house is like a living thing—you think a glazier came out and fixed that broken window? Think again, son— but the furniture's another matter. Way I figure it, they're really portals to the other side, a dark side, where the living are pulled through by the demons in the house."

"Like—mouths," I suggested.

Trojan shrugged and sipped his RC. "Only a theory, of course. No way to know for sure. Lord, when I saw the fire damage on the house reverse itself like that—" He shook his head and contemplated his soda.

"So what you're saying is that there's no way to destroy the house? Is that why you have such a defeatist attitude?"

"Defeatist?" Trojan snorted hotly. "You haven't tried going up against the forces in that house. They can and will hurt you, son. I'm just being a realist."

"So you're willing to believe that there's nothing that can be done," I snapped. "Just let it go on taking good people, corrupting others?"

Trojan saw the anger pouring off me and I suppose it softened him a little. "I'm not saying that, David," he said gently, "only I haven't figured out how to get rid of it. Maybe if you could do enough physical damage to it, not with fire, but—oh, I don't know. Only thing I do know is that I can't do it. The house'll kill me before it lets me close to it again. The few times I've come near it, it reached out to pinch me, just to give me a warning."

I remembered one such visit very clearly, the sudden pained look on his face, and Squint going crazy, clawing him like a wildcat. Trojan looked at me sadly.

"Here's something else you need to consider, son. I told you that while Nettie and I were living there, the house or what's in the house got inside me somehow. It changed me. And I think that if you spend any time in that house, especially on that furniture, it gets hold of you, chews on your soul so to speak, so that it can control you." He shrugged again. "That's what I think, anyway."

"It hasn't been controlling me," I told him.

"That you know of," he replied making me feel sort of queasy. "Every night you sleep in that house, though, son—."

"But I haven't been sleeping on the beds," I interrupted him. "I couldn't stand the thought of being in the same bed where Johnny and Theresa—you know—so I bought a thick foam pad from Wal-Mart and I've been sleeping on that."

Trojan raised his brows and nodded. "Well, then maybe you're safe. For a while. Until it finds out that you're trying to cross it, anyway."

"You're saying that I'm being protected from a hoard of demons thanks to Wal-Mart?"

"Kind of makes you think twice about condemning the big-box corporations, doesn't it? Wal-Mart: discount house and demon fighter. If it wasn't so damned shitting scary it'd be funny."

I then told Trojan about the article I'd read about his injuries. "Who did that to you?" I asked. "And is that how Squint saved your life?"

Trojan took the squab off the spit with an old oven mitt and put it on a plate. "Sure you don't want a bite? Sure is tasty done over an open fire."

"Well, maybe just a leg," I said, the smell making me ravenous even though dinner was only a few hours old in my stomach. Trojan obliged me, then broke the bird apart and tore off a piece of breast. "So you were going to tell me about those injuries of yours?"

"It isn't pretty."

"What about any of this is pretty, Troj?"

"You got a point there, son. Bugs are getting a little thick out here. What say we move this conversation indoors?"

I tossed the bones from the leg—which had been tastier than the fare at most five-star restaurants but unfortunately so small it was no more than an hors d'oeuvre—into a makeshift trash can and followed him into the tent. Our camp chairs were still set up from our talk the other day. Trojan took out a plate and pulled some pieces of the squab off for Squint who sniffed it like a regular little gourmet restaurant critic before partaking.

"The day I found Nettie—"

"What? Wait! You found Nettie? In the house? In the chair?"

There were tears standing in the old man's eyes and he swallowed hard. "You'll forgive me if I don't go into detail on that, son. Suffice it to say that one minute she was still there, sort of there, and then she was gone. At that point, because of how it happened, I was pretty damned crazed. Only like I said, the house had a hold on me, and it has a way of draining out your energy, your spirit, if you will. After a few minutes, I was so damned—tired. Weak with grief, I guess, that was part of it, but weakened by the house itself, too. I sat down on the sofa, just a minute, I thought. To collect my thoughts, my wits, to figure out what to do. And that was all it took. The sofa took hold of me, like my flesh and its fabric had started to fuse together, like I was glued to it, or more like melted into it."

I could feel my face twisting. "That must've—hurt."

"No, that's the thing. It didn't hurt at all. If it had, it might've roused me, but I was fading at that point, and I figured I was going to be joining my Nettie. Even in hell. Better to be in hell with the one you love than be in heaven without them, you know? And then—all of a sudden—there was Squint."

I turned to look at the cat who regarded Trojan for a moment when he heard his name before going back to his gourmet feast.

"Squint was a feral kitten. Don't know how he ended up here or where he came from. Maybe his momma birthed him out here in the woods and then got herself killed by a fox or possum or out on the road. Don't know, and I suppose it doesn't matter. He didn't want to come into the house, but Nettie had a soft spot for animals and she fed him and put out blankets for him when it would get cold, and many a day I'd go off to work and see him still curled up on the porch. I call him Old Squint but the fact is, he isn't but a few years old. He's got an old soul, though—that's what I think, anyway—to know what he knows."

"What does he know?"

"He knows about those demons, son. And he's not afraid of them. They're not so keen on him, either. You saw how Eblis acted around him."

"Like he was scared of him."

Trojan nodded. "Anyway, I was there in the house, on the sofa, my life about to be drained clean out of me, and then there was Squint."

"How did he save you?"

"Jumped into my lap like a wild beast. Didn't even appear to be a small cat, but some sort of fantastically huge beast of a feline. I know that was my imagination, or maybe I was just seeing his soul that day, larger than life. He was scratching and spitting, clawing my arms, legs, chest, and he got my face good." Trojan touched the three white scars on his cheek. "I don't know if you've ever been scratched by a cat, son, but they have claws that are so sharp that when they cut into your skin, they almost burn. He hurt me bad, real bad."

"And that was a good thing?"

"It was," Trojan nodded. "Because that pain shot enough adrenalin in my system to pull me right out of my stupor, to pull away from that sofa, gave me just enough energy just long enough to get through the door, to get away — from *Them*."

"The paper said your injuries were mysterious and that you lost a lot of blood. But that wasn't from the cat clawing you, was it?"

"It wasn't." At that point Trojan stood up and unbuttoned the cuffs of his shirt, then unfastened it down the front and slid it off his shoulders. He turned around so that I could see.

"Good God Almighty!" was all I managed to gasp.

Trojan's Campsite
June 17—well after dark_____

There are some things that are just so awful and so
shocking that they take away your ability to think, to
speak, except maybe to make some exclamation, utter
some expletive deleted and for me *Good God Almighty* was
about all I was able to say at the moment.

Trojan's back looked like it had been stitched together, a crazy patchwork quilt of skin and scars, like a
modern day Dr. Frankenstein had experimented on him.
When he figured I'd had my fill of looking at it, he put his
shirt back on and buttoned it, cuffs too.

"Jesus, Troj," I said.

"Back of my arms and legs, the old buttocks, every
part of me that was on that sofa is still in that sofa. I was in
the hospital for months, had more skin grafts done than I
can count, was practically an honorary member of the
Wakulla County Ladies' Sewing Circle. When Squint
clawed me I pulled away from the hold that house had on
me, only like I said, at that point I was damned well pretty
near melted, fused, glued onto that sofa, so there was no
pulling away without me l eaving a lot of me behind. It's

ugly as shit, I know, but now that Nettie's gone, there's no one around to have to look at it." He eyed me steadily. "I showed it to you just so you'll understand what you're up against. They fight hard and they fight mean and you damned well know they don't fight fair."

I didn't know what to say so I just nodded. Trojan put his hand on my shoulder. "I know you want to do something, son. But you've got your whole life ahead of you, and now that sweet girl, too—don't be too eager to throw it all away."

"What do you suggest I do? I can't leave."

"You can leave when the contract's up."

"Seven weeks from now. It didn't seem like a long stretch until now. If it doesn't corrupt me, it'll try to—absorb me. How do I fight against something like that?"

"Sounds to me like you're already doing it." Trojan thought for a minute, looked over at his cat who looked back at him with his green almond eyes. "Listen, son, Old Squint here won't go into that house, but if you were to camp out on the porch he might be willing to keep you company. Those demons—or whatever they are—wouldn't come around if he was there."

"What about you? Don't you need him to protect you?"

"Not out here. Long as I'm not near that house, I'm fine. Or as fine as an old scarred-up widower man can be who's seen way too much misery in his life. The house doesn't care about me. I was good bait for a while but it thinks it has better bait now."

"So if I stay out on the porch, I'm not really leaving, am I? But I'm not where they can get at me, is that right?

All I have to do is camp out for seven weeks and have no visitors, is that it?"

"That's the way I figure it," Trojan said.

By now it was pitch dark and I was glad I had taken the flashlight and had the presence of mind to turn on the porch lights as beacons to guide me back to hell house. Casa de Almas. Not house *with* soul, house *of* souls.

The whole way back I muttered to myself about the ridiculousness of the situation. Why I wasn't scared shitless at that moment, I don't know. Maybe there's only so much horror you can have thrown at you before things start getting absurd. You get immune. Sort of. Maybe you just get mad. Yeah, that's it. You get freakin' mad. You wish you could just get your hands on those soul-sucking, skin-melting, body-eating demon things and beat the shit out of them.

(Maybe that was all just a bunch of bullshit bravado, but I figured it would psych me up and help prepare me for surviving the next seven weeks, so I just kept those thoughts coming.)

I was still grumbling when I got to the house. One freakin' mistake. You go out for chicken with a few drinks under your belt and all of a sudden you've gotta be David Fouraker, Demon Fighter. Reduced to sleeping on a Wal-Mart foam mat on the freakin' porch, for God's sake! What if it rained? Sleeping on the porch in the rain! Probably can't even take a damned shower without worrying about going down the drain. Probably can't even take a leak without having some freak-ass son-of-a-bitch demon-thing reach out and grab my dick and pull me into the freakin' toilet! Like a bunch of "Komodo — or *commode* — dragons," ha ha.

I stomped up the stairs to the loft and pulled the foam pad down to the front porch. I'd considered sleeping on the back porch which was screened, but felt it might still be too enclosed. I felt safer on the front porch, even if the buggies might eat me alive. (Avoiding being eating by something seemed to be a damned impossibility at the moment!) I grabbed the fridge box of Mountain Dew, too, figuring since the cans of soda were only *in* the house and weren't part *of* the house they were probably safe to drink. There was no guarantee of that, of course, but if the demons could get into me through a can of soda, then they were already inside of me from breathing the freakin' air.

I sat down on the sheet-covered foam pad and for the hell of it I took out my cell phone and turned it on. Interestingly, it found a signal. Maybe the house itself interfered with transmission — no contact with the outside world, you know! — and I had never thought to try it outside. I had two missed messages, one from **FOURAKER, A** (my mother) and the other from **MOULTRIE, J** (Mojo). I planned to make the call back to my Mom a short one so I dialed her first.

"David, honey!" she exclaimed when she answered, no doubt seeing my name on her caller ID. "We've been so worried about you, we almost drove down to see if you were all right!" I knew that Mom was using the "royal we." Not that my Dad didn't care about me, but worry was something Mom was more likely to do. Dad could probably go six months without hearing from me before he got worried — and then maybe only because I hadn't made a payment on what I owed him to get my truck out of impound.

"Sorry, Mom. I've been busy working and doing community service. Haven't had much free time and I'm pretty tired when I do." It was a lame excuse and we both knew it. Who is ever too tired to make a phone call?

"You've had your phone turned off," she said with her tone mildly accusing. One thing you did not do to your mother is turn off your cell phone. Mothers look at that the same way they would tying a knot in the umbilical cord before their kid is born.

"I haven't been getting a very good signal out here."

"You don't have a house phone?"

"The land line is pretty quirky," I told her, avoiding having to add that the use of a telephone at Casa de Almas might cause a demon to enter your brain through your ear. Just then I saw two green eyes come out of the bushes and they made my heart pound-pound-pound until the animal came into the porch light and I saw that it was Squint. Without missing a beat he bounced up the stairs and settled in my lap, giving me a quick once-over as if to make sure I was all right. He squinted at me, then yawned as deeply as only a cat can and put his head down.

"Please indulge me and call once in a while, all right, David? Even if you think it's stupid, just call me."

"Okay, I will. But don't worry. I have a great neighbor."

"Does he have a telephone?"

"Not that I know of," I said, although Trojan probably did have a cell phone with which to call his daughter.

"What an odd county to live in," Mom sighed. "Didn't think there were such rural places left in Florida, at least, not where people actually lived."

"I'll be home soon," I reminded her. "Just seven more weeks." Seven more weeks of hell—but I didn't say that either. I stroked the dozing cat in my lap. It was true what they said about an animal being a calming influence. Especially when the hounds of hell were literally at your back.

"I'll give your love to Dad," she said as we rang off, not trusting me to send it without her prompting.

After pressing **END** I dialed Mojo. "Yo!" he said on the fourth ring.

"It's—um—Fresco." Using my old college nickname seemed so weird now, like I'd outgrown it a million years ago and just couldn't go back to using it and liking it.

"Hey, bro, how's it goin'? I was beginning to think you'd run off to join Johnny and Tessie."

"No word on them?"

"Not a peep. Doesn't look good, does it?"

"No," I admitted. I confess that when I saw he'd called, I had a glimmer of hope that maybe he was going to tell me they'd been found. I knew deep down that they would never be found, but that's what people do—hope. Even when it's stupid to do so. Even when they know better. "What've you and the guys been up to?"

"You know, working hard, playing hard. You?"

"Same here," I said, not saying *Fighting the forces of evil in my spare time*. I'd turned into some sort of Batman, Green Hornet, or whoever it was fought corruption in the comic books these days.

"Whip and I thought maybe we'd come see you this weekend or next."

Alarm shot through me. "No!" I said more forcefully than I'd wanted to, but there was no way I was going to let any of my friends come to this house. "I mean, I'm not free on the weekends. Not Saturdays anyway. I work all day Saturday. It's the busiest day at the diner."

"The diner in Bethel, population six, actually gets busy?" Mojo said dubiously. Who could blame him? You wouldn't think you could give food away in a town that small.

"The food is legendary in these parts. People come from miles around."

"Uh huh, sure. I have a feeling you just like reserving Saturday nights for your new shawty, what's her name? Lorraine?"

"That, too, but really—by Saturday night, I'm pretty well worn out. A real party pooper, major emphasis on the pooper."

"Okay, well, you know the fourth is coming up," Mojo said.

"The fourth?"

"Of July? You know? Independence Day, genius."

"Oh, yeah. Is it almost July already? Time flies."

"It falls in the middle of the week, which means we're gonna get off on the second, a Monday. A three-day weekend, bro. Whip and me could come see you—"

"The house is a mess!" I said quickly.

"Hell's bells, bro! All of a sudden you're a clone of Martha Stewart?" Mojo said and I could hear the irritation in his voice. I knew it was because I sounded like I didn't want him and Whip to come see me and nothing could be further from the truth. I desperately wanted to see my friends, but not here, not in this house. "Gabe said we could camp at the Waterin Hole. He's reserving a cabin for us. If we wouldn't be inconveniencing you."

"I'm sorry, Mo," I said and meant it. "I can't tell you how badly I want to hang with you guys. It's just that—things are bad around here. Ever since Johnny and Theresa—"

"The po-pos been giving you grief?"

"The police have been around, yeah. And I can't even stand to sleep in the damned house, myself."

"Then bunk at the fishcamp with us," Mojo offered.

"Yeah, maybe," I said, knowing I couldn't do that. I'd have to come up with yet another lie to tell him as to why not. "It'll be great to see you and Whip. I really miss you guys."

"We miss you, too, Fresco."

"Uh—David," I corrected him. "It's—David, now."

There was a moment of silence on Mojo's end, then I heard his deep chuckle. "Man, that shawty of yours is working your head, baby! David is it? Well, David—or might I be so bold as to call you Dave, there, bro?—we will see you on June 30th. That's a Saturday but you come on over after work, no excuses, and bring the gal—not that we can guarantee you much privacy. Maybe a few minutes, which might be all you need, I don't know."

"You're so bad, Mo," I said, smiling despite my dire predicament.

"You're one bad mother, too, *Dave*."

"You gotta be to live around here," I said. He probably wondered what the hell I meant by that, but maybe took it to mean the cops swarming all over the place. For all he knew, they had me under 24-hour surveillance. Which wouldn't have been far off, except it wasn't the police doing the surveying.

As I rung off with Mojo, I saw headlights swing into my driveway. "Oh, Lord, now what?" I sighed under my breath. I stood up, picking Squint up in my arms as I did so. A cat seemed a weird weapon against the forces of evil, but I felt safer holding him. Once again my poor heart was put through its paces until the car came into the light and I saw that it was Lorraine's.

"What are you doing here?" I said as she got out.

"That's a fine way to greet me," she scolded.

"You're not supposed to be here," I reminded her.

"I'm not supposed to be *in the house*," Lorraine corrected me. "Am I in the house? Well, am I?"

"You aren't."

She looked at the mattress on the porch. "Planning to camp out here?"

"Trojan agreed it would be a good idea."

"So do I. And here's a news flash for you. I'm staying with you." She held up her hand to stop me from protesting which, I admit, I was about to do. "No argument. I can't sleep worrying about you being here by yourself. If I have to sleep out here on the porch, at least it'll be better than lying there alone, wondering if the house had killed you yet. Lack of sleep is going to turn me in to the biggest bitch this side of the Mississippi and that'll probably lose me my job as the customers don't expect me to be bitchin' at them, you understand?"

"I'm glad for the company," I told her, and meant it. True, I was a little worried about how being close to the house would affect her—especially after the demons had touched her the way they had the other night—but staying there alone was getting to me, too. I needed her there, as much or more than she needed to be there.

"Looks like you already have some. Company, I mean."

"Yeah, but he's not much of a conversationalist," I said. "Trojan let him wander over here. As long as old Squint is around, I think we'll be safe."

"I think so, too," Lorraine said and she joined me on the porch where we both sat down on the foam mattress. "I've been thinking this out. We can sleep here—per your agreement—but we can shower, change and eat at my place before work. You might want to get some new clothes, though. You don't know if the stuff you have in the closets and drawers got—infected."

"You really know how to make a guy want to strip naked," I told her.

Lorraine smiled, dimpling her cheeks and making me wish I really was naked that very moment—her, too. "I'll remember that for a better time, but at the moment—"

"Right. You never know when you might have to make a fast getaway."

"And you wouldn't want to get caught butt naked in that old heap of mine."

What concerned me more was feeling that the things inside the house—and maybe out here on the porch, too—would get a perverse kick out of seeing us naked and maybe would have drawn some sort of energy out of our sex, like depraved little vampires sucking up our sexual energy and tittering over it. That vulnerable I did not intend to get, not even with adorable Lorraine right there next to me.

"It's so peaceful out here, you'd never think—" Lorraine began, but stopped when a strange sensation came up from the floor boards. It was like sitting on a nest of eels, our mattress a makeshift raft on top of a squirming sea. "What is that?"

"I don't know." I managed to stand up, taking Squint with me, though it was hard to stand on such a precarious floor and I felt myself reeling. I reached out one hand to steady myself with a porch post, but instead of hewn wood, it felt slippery and slimy and seemed to coil and writhe beneath my hand, a feeling so disgusting that I immediately snatched my hand back and wiped it against my jeans. Lorraine clung to me, partly to steady herself, but also, I'm sure, out of fear. The porch seemed to be alive, squirming like ropes of muscle beneath a wooden veneer.

"Oh my God, David!" she gasped. But just as we were about to make a dash for her car, the movement stopped, and the house settled down into its wooden frame once more. Lorraine and I felt as stunned by its stopping as we had moments ago when it had started. "What just happened here?" she asked.

"I can't be sure, but I suspect it could have been a warning or—"

"Or what?"

"Or an announcement," I said ruefully, for a few minutes later headlights pulled into my driveway and my heart, which was already skipping all over the place, began to bang around in my ribcage like an animal desperately wanting out. Before the car had pulled all the way up into the meager glow of the porch lights, I recognized it.

A silver Mercedes.

The way I figured it, there were several ways to play this scene, and the one I liked best was playing dumb. Acting the idiot was usually the best way to avoid major trouble. If I'd become belligerent with the cop who pulled me over for my DUI, I might be in jail this very minute— which, in retrospect, I realize would have been an improvement over my current situation; nevertheless, staying calm and acting stupid is usually the best course.

I raised my hand in greeting as the big man in the Guayabera shirt decked out with gold chains hauled his ass out of his fancy car. "Evenin' Mr. Eblis. What brings you out here on this fine June night?"

Oh, I was pretty sure I knew why he had come out there, and I was equally sure he knew I knew, but he decided to play along. Why, I don't know. Maybe evil likes to play games. In fact, I would almost bet on it.

"I told you I'd be around to check on you," he said amiably but with no warmth in his smile. There was so much evil in this man—this thing, this whatever he or it was — that it poured off him in waves. And then he saw

Squint. "No pets allowed in the house, you remember," he said.

"Well, doesn't seem as if this cat is in the house," I replied with as friendly a tone as I could muster. "Wasn't anything in the agreement, as I recall, that said animals weren't allowed on the porch." With that I handed Squint to Lorraine. If he could protect only one of us, I wanted it to be her. That was not a brave or selfless act, I want you to know. If anything happened to her, I couldn't live with it or without her. Handing her the cat was a matter of self-preservation, if you want to know the truth.

Eblis eyed the mattress. "Camping out, are you?"

"We were waiting for a meteor shower," I said. "Falling stars can be really spectacular. You should try watching them some time."

"Planning to sleep out here, are you?"

"Nothing in the agreement says we can't, is there?" I asked. Oh, my tone was damned smooth, but I think we both knew I should be up for an Oscar for this performance.

"Wouldn't the young lady be more comfortable inside?" he asked in his oily voice, giving new meaning to having ones gorge rise.

"Camping out is one of my favorite things, actually," Lorraine replied evenly. "And I'd hate to miss that meteor shower."

Eblis shrugged. "There is always the possibility that you might wish for some intimacy and the porch does not afford much privacy, does it now?"

"You're the only one here, Mr. Eblis," I replied mildly. "Once you leave, seems to me we'll have all the privacy we could want. Just her and me and the fireflies."

"Though we'll probably just nod off after watching the celestial show," Lorraine added. "Rough day at work, you know."

Eblis stared at us longer than was comfortable, his dark unctuous eyes roving from me to Lorraine to Squint and back again. Then he nodded and the gesture gave me the creeps. "Whatever's your pleasure," he said softly and then he smiled, sending an army of worms shivering down my spine. "Good night, now." He turned, got back into his Mercedes, and left us standing there.

The house had complained. He had come. He had seen what infraction we had committed. The idea of punishment about to be meted out was a stone in my gut.

"Do you think he'll retaliate for us sleeping out here?" Lorraine asked. Seems to me that was a rhetorical question if ever there was one.

The Waterin Hole
July 1_____

Here's something else I've learned about evil: it likes to play games, especially with your head. It likes to make you think you could actually win a game against it. That maybe you've found your way into the catbird seat. This is what they call being *lulled into a false euphoria*. Why I forgot Trojan's warning, that evil was hard and mean and above all never plays fair, I don't know, but somehow I just got full of myself. I thought I was clever, that I had outsmarted beings that have been playing this game since the beginning of time. Just sleep on the porch and keep everyone away. Did I really think it would be that simple? It's not easy to admit it when you've been an arrogant idiot, but that was me. And it would end up costing me. A lot.

So here's a lesson for you: thumb your nose at evil and when you're not looking it's going to come back and hit you with a grief so profound you'll think you've been whacked up the side of the head with a two-by-four. A grief so deep and so hard it's a toss-up whether anyone can ever get over it.

Unfortunately you never think about those things—those warnings people give you—until it's too late. Hindsight is a bitch.

But I've gotten ahead of myself, again. Bad habit of mine, I know. My bad. First, before all the really bad shit came raining down on me, there was the gang's Fourth of July at Uncle Pete's fishcamp and the almost two weeks leading up to it. (Okay, so it wasn't really going to be a Fourth of July celebration, but it was as close to it as the government would allow us to get. God forbid you get the long weekend. We'd really be celebrating the First of July—rather like a mid-year New Year's Day.)

Part of my complacency came from the fact that my nose-thumbing ploy against the Forces of Darkness worked pretty well for a while. Lorraine and I spent every night on the porch and the rest of our free time at her place. While having her beside me on the mattress was a temptation even Adam didn't have with Eve we didn't give in to our urges. The last thing you wanted to have happen was for a silver Mercedes to pull up at the house while you're lying on the porch stark nakers. The very next day after Eblis's visit we went to Wal-Mart so I could get a second pair of jeans, two pairs of shorts, a couple of polos for work (not the Ralph Lauren kind, the Sam Walton type), several tee-shirts (none of which promoted beer, marijuana or crazy sex—I guess I really was maturing), swim trunks (anticipating our big Fourth bash), socks, underwear and some toiletries. (It's not like you can exorcise your boxer shorts or shave cream and know for sure that they were demon-free.)

Anyway, my posse came on down to the Waterin Hole on the 30th, but it was Sunday before Lorraine and I headed over there—me in my new swim trunks and tee-shirt and she in a deep blue bathing suit with a cascade of flowers from one shoulder to her waist over which she wore a pair of cut-offs. Who would think raggy jeans could be so damned sexy? I'd already called Mojo back and told him that working a full day didn't lend itself to partying afterwards. (Yeah, I know that Friday nights the bars are always crowded with people taking advantage of end-of-the-work-week happy hours, but I've never been one of them. And now—well, you give me twelve hours of work—which is about what my Saturdays amounted to these days—and by closing time I just wanted to crash and burn.) Lorraine and I took our time heading over to Sop-choppy because I figured the guys had tanked up the night before and wouldn't be up too early and I really didn't want to sit around making chit-chat with Uncle Pete until they roused themselves. The two of us took our time showering and changing (lots of time) followed by a leisurely breakfast.

We got to the fishcamp just as Uncle Pete was firing up his Char-Griller Outlaw 1500, a big bad mother of a barbeque grill, and we figured the posse itself was just now rousing itself from alcohol-induced sleep. "Isn't that the same car that came by your place a few weeks back?" Lorraine asked me as we pulled into the parking lot.

There was no mistaking it: Parker's Top Banana yellow Daytona RT. "I wonder what the hell he's doing here."

"Isn't he a friend of yours?"

"He lives on my floor in my dorm but we're not friends. We're only acquaintances. Extremely casual acquaintances. He's too much of a dweeb for us to be friends."

"A dweeb owns that car?"

"It's an anomaly," I grinned. "I figure his parents bought it for him in an attempt to de-dweebify their son."

Lorraine parked her car net to Mojo's truck and as we got out we heard the sounds of splashing and laughing coming from the river. As we walked toward the sound, we saw that the commotion was coming from the bully boys and two young women frolicking in the water. There was a satiny chocolate brown girl in a yellow bikini I assumed was with D'Ante from the way she hung all over him, and a pale, copper headed gal in a blue bikini who I figured had paired up with Persnicky. (Though maybe they were interchangeable. With the bully boys, you never knew.)

We saw Whip, Mojo and Gabe kicked back under the roofed picnic area in a trio of striped lawn chairs, drinking beers and watching Uncle Pete get the burgers and dogs ready while the grill heated up. I raised a hand in greeting and the three of them lifted their beers in a salute. I couldn't actually remember if anyone besides Gabe had met Lorraine so I made some introductions and then Lorraine and I sat down in two free lawn chairs. "Beer?" Gabe offered.

"Soda for me, thanks," Lorraine replied. "A diet anything."

"Same here."

"Soda, is it?" Mojo marveled. "First he decides he's gonna be David now and then he stops drinking. Our friend has been stricken with a serious case of maturity."

"I haven't stopped drinking," I said, thinking about all those nights that the Captain had kept me company and wondering if they would find it ironic that I would refuse a beer but stay blitzed every night. "Just stopped drinking before lunch."

"I'll drink to that," Gabe said, taking a swig.

"We need to do something about that maturity crap," Whip said, "before our par-taying days crash and burn."

"I'll always want to party with you guys," I told them, though I seriously doubted it. They would always be my friends, but the joys of getting seriously trashed had faded.

Gabe dug two sodas out of the huge cooler, handed me a Fresca (of course) and Lorraine a diet Coke. "Maybe we should've gotten you some Doctor Peppers. A soda with a PhD. seems to be more your style these days, *Dave*."

I smiled but inside I just sighed. I nodded toward the parking area. "Who invited Parker?"

"We thought you did," Mojo said.

"Why would I invite him? He's no friend of mine."

"Not the way he tells it," Whip said.

"You're kidding," I frowned. "What's he been saying?"

"Nothing much," Whippet shrugged, "only he keeps trying to get all of us to come down to see you, have a little private party. He even suggested he could get us girls — Not that you need one," he added, giving Lorraine a wink.

"More de-dweebification?" Lorraine asked.

"What's that?" Whip asked.

"It just doesn't sound like old Parker. Where would he get girls — even *one* girl let alone plural girls?"

Mojo inclined his head toward one of the cabins. "Maybe the same place he found her." I looked toward where he indicated and I thought my eyes would just pop out of my head on those little springs like you see in cartoons. Parker — tanned, buff Parker with a definite six-pack — had just come out of one of the cabins with a gorgeous woman by his side. Mostly white, but with enough African-American blood to make her golden, a knock-out figure, long hair a shimmering light brown, wearing a thong bathing suit so small I could barely tell what color it was. (Turns out it was metallic, gold in fact, like her.) Parker had a wolfish grin on his face and with his arm around her, his hand regularly stroked and squeezed her right butt cheek. Not long ago we all would have been grinning vicariously ourselves at such a sight, maybe even hooting and hollering encouragement; now the gesture seemed weirdly obscene and we watched in silence.

Lorraine leaned over to me and whispered, "I feel strangely overdressed."

"How did Parker rate a woman like that?" Whippet asked no one in particular, voicing a question that buzzed around all our minds. "And for that matter, how did a guy like you get a girl like this," he added, eying Lorraine.

"I was just lucky. What's Parker's story?"

"He hasn't given us one," Mojo said. "He just offered to drive us down here, but Whippet and I wanted to come in my truck. Persnicky and D'Ante were interested in riding in Parker's hot RT, though, so they flipped for it and poor Persnicky and date—the redhead, her name's Mary Ann, like the Gilligan girl—lost so D'Ante and his new gal pal—Krystal—won the privilege."

"So where are your dates?" I asked.

"That's what I'd like to know," Mojo said. "How can any girl resist guys like us? They must have incredible fortitude not to give in to temptation like that."

"Or really good taste," I laughed.

"Maybe we should just wait for Parker to hook us up," Whippet grinned.

Parker spotted us then and came over, waving with the hand that wasn't attached to his new girlfriend's ass. "Well, if it isn't our man Dave and the fair Lorraine," he said. (That all of us didn't roll our eyes clean out of their sockets was a pure miracle.) He introduced the golden girl as Jade—well-named as it turned out because her eyes were that same cool pale green. "You going to have the gang out to the house now that we're all here together?" he asked me.

"I don't think so. The house isn't really fit for company. You know how bachelors are. Messy as all hell."

"As I recall you have a nice big field behind the house just begging to be used for setting off fireworks."

"I'm not about to get any illegal fireworks. I'm on probation, remember? That means I'm not supposed to get into any more trouble. I'll give the pyrotechnic duty over to one of the bully boys. Besides, fireworks will look better over the water."

"I didn't think you were so antisocial," Parker grinned, but it didn't seem like a real grin, you know? It was the kind done with the mouth while the eyes were AWOL in the mirth department.

"Just being careful," I shrugged. I wasn't sure I liked this new-and-improved Parker. Sure, he looked better, but his attitude was pushy if not downright belligerent. I couldn't help wondering what his problem was.

"So, Jade," Whippet said to the golden girl, "are there any more at home like you?"

"If you mean do I have sisters, no, but I do have friends," she said, turning those bottle-green eyes on my friend and practically making him melt into the lawn chair. Her voice was a husky-sexy purr, the kind of voice you were sure used to lure hapless sailors to their deaths on the river rocks. "Would you like to meet them?"

Now that was like asking a man who'd been dining on lawn grass for a month if he wanted a juicy burger with fries on the side.

"How about *two* friends?" Mojo asked and Jade smiled.

"Jade has lots of friends," Parker told us and the golden girl's smile widened.

"Let me make some calls," she said.

By then the smell of meat on the grill had started wafting in our direction making us all salivate. I was so used to soggy convenience store sandwiches for lunch that I felt I was getting a five-star gourmet meal. We got our paper plates and headed toward the grill, each of us opting for either a hamburger or a hotdog or — as in my case — one of each. Uncle Pete had also gotten some grocery store potato salad, macaroni salad, chips, baked beans, and a huge watermelon for later, along with a galvanized tub full of ice, soft drinks and beer galore. I was so hungry, I don't think I tasted the first few bites. By the time I had started on my second hot dog, another car pulled up next to Parker's yellow RT — a burgundy Corvette that looked just-off-the-showroom-floor perfect. We all gawped at it until we saw the girls who got out of it, and then we redirected our gawping to them.

"If those girls are for us, then I done died and gone to heaven," Mojo said and Whippet nodded, this close to drooling all over his tee-shirt. One was a tall, tanned blond, another looked Polynesian, a third was a stunning redhead. All three had long hair (Red's was curly) and all, remarkably, had to be double-Ds stuffed into tiny bikinis. The Island Trio wore matching sarongs wrapped around their tiny waists. We saw Parker grin at them and go over to greet them, taking their hands and kissing each of them in turn on the cheek in an oily, continental sort of gesture. I heard Lorraine sigh and though she had nothing to worry about with me, I imagine she felt the way I would have if I'd been plunked down in the middle of the Mr. Universe contest. Even Krystal and Mary Ann — who were decent looking gals in their own right, even if not eye-poppingly beautiful — seemed dismayed by the arrival of the trio.

"Guys," Parker said, bringing the three new girls over to us, "I want you to meet Amber—" He indicated the blond and I snorted making everyone look at me.

"Oh, let me guess. The redhead is Garnett and the other is an oriental Pearl, right?"

"Mai Lin, actually," Parker told us, scowling at me. "And Tonya."

I felt immediately stupid, but heck, if one is Jade and one is Amber—what was I supposed to think? The whole thing seemed incredibly weird to start with—and sort of contrived. It was strange enough to see one drop-dead gorgeous girl but four? What pageant did Parker raid, anyway?

"You feel like a little canoe trip?" I asked Lorraine as the girls made their choices among the single men.

"I can't remember when I've felt more like it," she said.

Since Gabe was too busy with Tonya to help us select a canoe, Uncle Pete just waved us over to the shore and told us to take our pick. I grabbed two paddles and after Lorraine clambered into the front of a sturdy green fiberglass, I pushed off and climbed in behind her.

Two miles down river I told her to start moving toward shore. I knew from previous trips with the guys that there was another fishcamp, Stogie Joe's, not far from the Waterin Hole. Near the tiny beach, Lorraine got out, and pulled our canoe onto the shore. "Why are we stopping? Don't tell me you're tired already."

"I'm really too full to paddle, but I wanted to get away from Uncle Pete's for a while."

Lorraine gave me a puzzled look but had no time to ask me why because a wiry, tanned woman with harshly bleached hair wearing a white visor with *Stogie Joe's* on it, came down to the canoe. She might have been in her twenties but life in the sun had given her a leathery, close-to-sixty look, and she had a thin "ladies' cigar" clamped between her teeth.

"Hep ya?" she asked us. She had on a white tank top—no bra, but she was small enough to get away with it—khaki shorts and well-worn work boots.

"Looking for a couple of cold drinks," I said. "You're Joe's daughter, aren't you?" I had seen her before during one of our trips.

"Yep," she said, though she didn't introduce herself. She could have been Stogie Jane for all I knew. Her father was a pal of Uncle Pete's but for all the years I'd spent at the fishcamp, I never did find out her name, nor what had happened to Mrs. Stogie.

"We just came down from the Waterin Hole," I told her.

"Didn't get very far, did ya?"

"No. It's hot as hell out there on the water."

She nodded. "Keep that up, gonna be a lobsta by mornin'. Plenty shade, drinks and snacks over at Pop's shack. Want me to tie ya up?"

"Please," I said. I took Lorraine's hand and we walked up to the snack bar, our soggy shoes making squelching noises with every step. The bar was thatched like a Seminole chickee and there were both bar stools in front of a counter and tables under another area to the left, likewise thatched. Behind the bar was a fat man—he wore what they called a wife-beater—a tank top tee-shirt—that strained to cover his belly. He had an unlit cigar clamped in his teeth. I greeted him by telling him I brought regards from Pete. It's a close-knit community. Everyone likes to do right by their neighbors. He gave us two diet Cokes gratis and we shot the breeze a few minutes—which was expected. Then Lorraine and I took our drinks and settled down at a table under the thatched roof, taking one as far from the bar as possible so that we could have some privacy and talk freely. There were two other couples having lunch; the real crowds would descend upon the area closer to dark when illegal fireworks were likely to light up the night sky.

"What's bothering you?" Lorraine asked me.

I just eyed her.

"Okay, having those girls just show up was a little weird, I admit."

"A *little* weird? I haven't seen women so perfect since I saw the movie 'The Stepford Wives.' They gave me the creeps."

"You find gorgeous women creepy?" Lorraine smirked.

"I find *those* gorgeous women creepy," I told her. "Don't you? Isn't there just something a little too strange about all of them just showing up like that? What are the chances that a knock-out like Jade is going to have three available knock-out friends just sitting at home, waiting to hang out with the likes of Mojo, Whippet and Gabe?" I took a sip of my cola. "Don't get me wrong, I love those guys, and I'd be glad for them to find some beautiful girls to hook up with, but— there's the matter of Parker. How does a dweeb like Parker Rodriguez—who for some odd reason doesn't really look like a dweeb so much any more—find even one girl like that, let alone a whole—flock all of a sudden?"

"They're attracted to his car? To his money?"

"But a dweeb with a car is still a dweeb. There are lots of rich guys out there who aren't dweebs." I took Lorraine's hand. "I wish I knew what he was up to because that sort of generosity just begs for repayment, don't you think?"

Lorraine's forehead had creased. "Do you think we'll ever be able to enjoy a day without wondering if something terrible is out there waiting to spoil it for us?" A sheen of tears had formed in her big brown eyes.

I pressed her hand against my lips and kissed it. "One day, I promise we will. For now, well, I guess we'll just have to be vigilant. You know," I added, "you probably wish you didn't have to deal with all this crap, but I'm glad I have you with me."

Lorraine squeezed my hand and gave me a smile though I could tell she was forcing it. "I'm glad I'm with you, too. Whatever you have to go through, I'll be there. I promise."

But it's an unfortunate fact of life that not all promises can be kept.

Casa de Almas (Day 53)
July 17_____

It was a day that pretty much started out like any other ordinary day, and you know when you hear someone say that that something really, really bad has happened, don't you? Because the really, really bad stuff doesn't ever come at the tail end of a day that started out crappy and got progressively worse. You never get any warning, do you? Not for the really bad shit.

You sure as hell don't.

The bad stuff always comes out of the blue, on one of those Plain Jane sort of days when all seems right (or sort of right) with the world.

Take 9/11 for instance. The sun was shining that day, people were going to work, going about their business, most of them minding their Ps and Qs, a nice early fall day. Not stormy, not rainy, not even cloudy. No smog, no traffic jams (at least, no more than usual), the stock market wasn't on the verge of crashing, no big business was about to go under costing people jobs, no big crime was going down—no major robbery taking place, no guy with a gun going postal—there wasn't any threat of war in the world (at least, no more than usual). So when the really, really bad shit came down and hit the fan that day—that very, very ordinary day—no one was prepared for it, not in the least.

Yes sir, it was a day pretty much like any other.

And then wham! The bad shit hit us all up the side of our collective heads, and all of a sudden out of the blue (like I said) a major landmark was in rubble and thousands of innocent people were dead or dying or injured.

So now, when I say that July 17th was a day that started out pretty much like any other, you know I'm about to tell you about some really bad shit that went down.

So I've warned you. Which is more than Fate or Destiny or Mother Nature ever does.

Lorraine had her usual early start at the hardware store, but I had to meet my probation officer—just a routine check-in—so I begged off from my community service at the Springs that morning to go report in. Lorraine offered to take off and drive me but I didn't want her getting into trouble with her Sweetheart Boss for doing that without *sufficient notice*, and besides it was a scant few miles to the courthouse in downtown Crawfordville from Bethel—the main reason I took the house in the first place, remember? All that outdoor work had made riding my bike a piece of cake. If I become a park ranger one day, I figured I would end up being so buff Lorraine wouldn't be able to stand keeping her hands off me. I sort of relished the idea of her lusting after me like that, if you want to know the truth (and I know you do!) I had planned to head to the Springs after my meeting so that I wouldn't lose the hours; Tuesdays I never worked at the diner as a rule, although, as I said a while back, just to stay away from the house I had been putting in extra hours as Carl needed me.

It seemed like a good plan: go to the courthouse, then hit the Springs, then see Lorraine after work. A great plan, actually.

Funny how good plans can go awry so damned easily.

My PO (that's *Probation Officer* for all you non-felons out there) had an impromptu staff meeting that morning so all of us waiting to check in had to cool our heels in the lobby about thirty minutes. I filled out the regular paperwork — reporting on the number of hours of community service I'd done, as well as where and how much I was working. The PO always calls to verify this information; I guess the legal system hopes to catch you in a big fat lie so they can find you in violation of probation and slap you with additional fines or more probation or maybe even serious jail time. The rest of the form was information I had already told them several times — you would think they'd have that in their computerized files by now, but no. Every time it's *name, soche number, residence*, blah, blah, blah. Maybe they think you will lie about all of that, make up an alias, a phony soche, whatever, who knows? Or maybe they just want to test probationers periodically to make sure we still had the ability to read and write.

Anyway when I finished that I just had to wait with the rest of the dolts who had managed to get themselves placed on probation. At least it was a comfort to know that I wasn't the only idiot in Wakulla County. In fact there were so many probationers, it was a wonder there were any people left in the county who weren't on probation. Multiply a gazillion people times the fifty bucks we all cough up every month for our upkeep and you realize that probation is big business. Little wonder why it's such a popular sentence with county judges. The only thing I still wonder about is what the legal system does with those fifty gazillion dollars it pulls in every month. (I bet it doesn't go toward prison reform, though.)

My PO was a middle-aged woman name Carol Childers who was pretty decent as court employees go. She seemed to understand that even something as lame as jaywalking probably could land you on probation and that being in the program didn't necessarily mean you were in the dregs of society. She treated us with respect and didn't go all hard-assed on us or anything (unless, I guess, you screwed up royally by shirking your community service or not having a job, especially if you were a parent owing child support). I know this because if you sit in the PO waiting room long enough eventually the conversation is bound to come around to the merits or short-comings of various POs and everyone seemed to agree that Carol Childers was okay.

An hour and fifteen minutes after I walked through the door I was called to Carol's office. (There were two guys ahead of me and one must've been a screw-up because he was in there longer than usual; probably Carol had had to go hard-assed with him, who knows?)

Anyway, I would be the second screw-up of Carol's morning, not that I meant to be. Mind you, I don't consider myself the sort who goes to meetings — especially ones involving the legal system — unprepared but maybe I should do some reconsidering.

Carol gave me a pained look when I had to confess that I had forgotten to bring my pay stubs as proof of my employment. Part of the reason I forgot, though, was because the stubs were on the desk in the loft at Casa de Almas and I hadn't set foot inside the house in more than two weeks. The last place on Earth I wanted to go was there, so maybe it was more like I conveniently forgot.

"I could get copies from my boss for next time," I assured her (not even sure that Carl kept copies!), but no, the legal system doesn't run well on making exceptions, although Carol allowed that I could bring them by later in the day and just leave them with the receptionist. Or fax them to her. (There must be a helluva lot of fax machines out there for people to assume that anyone can do that!) I promised I would pedal home and get them for her later that day. (I did mention that I had to use a bicycle as transportation and that it was especially hot out there on the road, but my play for sympathy didn't elicit an ounce of it. Carol is fair and respectful but she's firm on protocol.) Everything else, she told me, looked fine, I was making good progress on my community service hours, and I should just keep up the good work.

I promised her I would, and then repeated that I would get the stubs to her later that day. The last thing I wanted was to prolong my stay in Wakulla County! I really had intended on keeping my promise. Honest.

I had worked up a good sweat by the time I got to my driveway. Part of it was the heat of the day but another (and probably larger) part of it was dreading having to enter my little house of horrors. I wondered how fast I could run up the stairs, find and grab those pay stubs, and hightail it out of there before the beasties who lived there, frustrated by having no one to play their demonic little games with, reached out and tried to grab me. I envisioned myself running a gauntlet while being pursued by vicious pieces of furniture that had suddenly sprouted arms with claws and gigantic maws filled with spike-like fangs.

As I swung my bike into the dirt path to the house, I saw yet another surprise waiting for me.

That damned Top Banana yellow Daytona RT.

I could not imagine what Parker wanted but I was in no mood to deal with him (even if he could save me a trip to the courthouse and just drive me there in air-conditioned comfort). His habit of just showing up was really starting to bug me big time. This time, however, he was not alone. As I got closer, I saw Jade in the front seat, retying the straps of her halter dress and the way her boobs were wobbling it was obvious she had nothing on underneath. She looked up at me through the windshield and smirked and I got the feeling she was thinking about accidentally dropping one of the straps and giving me an eyeful. I pulled up next to the driver's side and Parker opened his window. Jade tugged at her skirt that apparently had been hiked up, making it obvious (probably on purpose) that the two of them had engaged in a quicky while waiting for me. Once the idea of such a wildly spontaneous sexual encounter would have amused me; today it made me feel slightly queasy. I think it was the idea of these particular two people rutting in my driveway that caused my discomfort. Jade seemed more like a highly paid prostitute than a girlfriend and Parker seemed to take way too much pleasure from his Lord-and-Master role by screwing her wherever and whenever he pleased.

I got off my bike and put down the kickstand. "Hey, Parker, what's up?" I asked, as I walked over to the car. I tried to avoid looking further at Jade who was raking her fingers through her long, disheveled hair but it wasn't easy to keep your eyes off of a woman like her especially when she was in more of a state of undress than she decently should be. She picked up a pair of lacy panties from the floorboard and held them up a minute before putting them in her purse; I pretended not to notice, but I suspect she knew I had. The smirk never left her face.

"We were just going to go to the store for some refreshments. I thought you were quite the party animal, but your cupboard seems pitifully bare for a bachelor man," Parker told me. His grin didn't falter once.

Most people when they smile at you cause you to smile back. Parker's just made me go cold inside. I think because the wider it got, the more insincere it seemed.

"You were in the house? How did you get in the house?"

"The door was unlocked."

The door could not have been unlocked. I would not have left it that way. Parker had broken into my house, or maybe he had a key (He had a key?) and that bothered me. A lot. But at that moment what bothered me more was his presumption that he could just come down here with his girlfriend and party with me whenever he wanted to.

"You were thinking of throwing a party for you and me and Jade?" I asked. Maybe some guys get off on having a ménage a trios but I wasn't one of them. I was so monogamous some guys would have probably thought me square as a cube, but that was okay by me. I was a one-woman man and especially a one woman at a time man.

"Now what sort of party would that be?" Parker asked and then giggled. The old Parker would have blushed beneath his tan but this new-and-improved Parker (well, new anyway — I'm not so sure about the improved part) didn't have the decency any more to do so. "That would be deliciously naughty," he said, reaching over to stroke Jade's golden thigh, "but another time perhaps. Something more festive this time, I think. One of those 'the more the merrier' sort of things. At least, that was the intention of the gang who wanted to show you how much they missed you. After all, we haven't seen you in two weeks. Ah," he said, glancing in his rear-view mirror. "Here come the girls."

I glanced over at the house just as Mai Lin and Amber were coming out. "Why were they in there?" I asked, annoyed with the liberties that Parker felt he could take with me. "They shouldn't be in there," I told him sternly.

"Oh, they're fine," Parker said, waving away my concern with a flick of his well-manicured hand. "You should've entertained more often, you know," he added, his grin finally dissipating as the beautiful Oriental woman climbed into the back seat behind Jade. Amber paused a moment before getting in behind Parker, smiled at me and touched my cheek. Her hand felt unnaturally warm. She ran her fingers down my chest and would've touched me more intimately had I not stepped back from her. She smiled, evidently finding my avoidance of her amusing, and got into the car. Parker himself was no longer amiable. He seemed, in fact, to get uglier by the minute.

"You had a good deal here," he told me, his face suddenly hard, "and what do you do? You waste it. You could've had a damned good time while you were here, but no, you had to be the little goody two-shoes, didn't you?"

"What are you talking about?"

"You always thought you were so much better than me, didn't you? You and your friends. So who do you think is going to get the last laugh now, Mr. Goody Two-Shoes? You and your friends can par-tay all you want all by yourselves now."

Parker started his car and raised the window, its tinting obscuring his face. For a moment I stood there, dumbfounded, until his last words reverberated in my brain.

You and your friends.

I had the sudden, sickening feeling that Parker and the girls had not come up here alone. Parker and Jade had come as a couple and Amber and Mai Lin —

Part of two other couples?

"No. Oh no!" was all I managed to gasp before I took off at a run toward the house.

Remember what I said before about there being a grief so profound it makes you think you've been hit with a two-by-four? That there was such a thing as a grief so deep and so hard that you can't be sure you'll get over it?

I was about to get whacked.

I flung open the door and let me tell you, not only is there a grief that hard and deep, but there's also such a thing as a horror that is beyond measure, something so big and so bad and so dreadful that it paralyzes you. A terror that hits you like two hundred watts of pure direct current. You know why they always talk about the deer in the headlights? Because to a deer, I guess headlights is about as deep and hard a fear as it ever encounters. The fear is so great, it can't move even with death barreling headlong toward it.

At that moment, I was that deer.

Mojo and Whippet were on the sofa.

What I should say is that what was left of Mojo and Whippet were there.

They (whoever *They* were) had left them their eyes, that was the worst thing, if you could even name a worse thing in that horrible mess. Mojo still had part of his lips, still open in a scream cut short, the tips of his ears, a bit of black bush that had been his hair. The tip of Whippet's greyhound nose still pointed above the gaping wound that was once his mouth. Part of me wanted to spring forward, grab them, rescue them, rip them away from the clutches of the demons that held them; the better part of me knew that that was no longer possible. There was nothing to grab on to, just a film of skin, a few ridges where bones had once been — a leg bone here, there an armbone; a cage of ribs; finger bones — some splayed, some clutching; a piece of hip, jutting; their clothes lying flat against the thin layer of their skin.

Their eyes looked at me with pleading terror, and knowing that they were still partly alive and conscious made this big horrible thing even bigger and more gruesome. Their eyes rolled wildly in what was left of their faces that, as I watched, kept melting like soft wax into the upholstery of the sofa where they had once sat as young men do, sprawling with a disjointed ease, waiting for their friend who would come too late. The sofa was not eating them; it was *absorbing* them. All of them—flesh and bone and worst of all, heart and soul.

I stood there, horrified, numb, shocked by helplessness and then became aware of the most god-awful sound, rising. Terrible in its inhuman wail, as if all the pain and terror and anguish of the world was summed up in one soul-wrenching shriek. I clamped my hands over my ears to shut it out, that dreadful keening that threatened to overwhelm me and drive me to my knees, quaking.

But I found I could not shut out that howl of pain and torment.

It came from inside of me.

Within me but clamoring to get out, bursting from lungs, throat, mouth as if my very soul were being ripped from me. I staggered back, shutting my eyes too late to miss the final melt of flesh and bone, the agonized eyes of my two dear friends sagging into the demon fabric.

And then they were gone. Just gone. As if they had never been at all.

I pressed my eyes more tightly shut, continued my backwards retreat, still screaming and unable to stop. Back, through the open front door. Back, to the porch steps.

(*Get away get away get away!*)

Hurrying. Careless in my haste.

My foot caught the edge of the top stair and I felt myself tumbling, falling, arms flailing now, and then I hit the ground, the air thrust violently from my lungs, my head hitting the hard pack of the driveway. For one second I saw stars.

Then the world melted into a weird sort of gray and it, too, was gone.

Trojan's Campsite
July 17 (Later)_____

I woke to the sound of voices, to a headache, and to the knowledge that I probably had just had the worst freakin' nightmare anyone on the planet has ever had. If I ever decide to make it into a book, watch out Stephen King! I will give you a run for your money right to the top of the *New York Times* best sellers' list!

Because my head was pounding—like a really, really bad hangover will give you, which was weird because I sure didn't remember having had a rollicking time with the Captain any time lately—I only cracked open my eyelids and saw that I was in a sea of green, as if I were lying on the bottom of the ocean looking up through the water. When I opened my eyes further, I saw that instead of being submerged in the sea, I was lying in the green light coming through the roof of Trojan's palatial tent. I called out to the voices in the room beyond my view. "Hello? Troj?"

A second later two familiar faces—Trojan's and Lorraine's—appeared through the flap that served as a door between the two rooms of Trojan's canvas home.

Lorraine's was creased with worry and it was she who was by my side in an instant. Maybe because she wasn't sure that the cot I lay on was sturdy enough for both of us (though it sure felt solid enough to me), she knelt beside me and stroked the tousled hair from my forehead. "David! Are you all right? I've been so worried!"

"I have a headache," I admitted.

Lorraine turned to Trojan with that I-told-you-so look that women get. "He should've gone to the emergency room."

"David doesn't need a hospital," Trojan replied. "Leastwise, I know that's the last place he'll want to be just now. At most he has a mild concussion though I doubt he hit his head hard enough for that. If he rests, he'll be all right."

"He was unconscious!" Lorraine protested.

"I think that came from him knocking the wind out of himself more than anything. His head isn't bleeding or anything. I checked."

"Why am I here?" I asked, growing peeved at being talked about instead of to. "How did I get here?"

"The house has a storage shed out back and I kept some gardening tools in there. Toted you over here to my tent in my old wheelbarrow. Good thing you already wore a rut between here and the house."

"Why did you need to bring me here? What happened?" Then, slowly, my memory began to clear. Not entirely, of course. Some things your brain simply doesn't want to remember and it'll fight you tooth and nail to keep you from dredging it up. But there was something. I knew it. Something really, really bad.

Trojan knew it too, knew I was on the verge of remembering something so awful it was likely to send me over the edge. "Missy," he said gently to Lorraine, "you think me and David could have some alone time for a little while?"

Lorraine looked from Trojan to me and replied, in a tone that suggested she felt a little betrayed by being excluded, "I thought we're in this together."

"We are," I told her. "She should stay," I told Trojan. As emphasis I reached out and groped for Lorraine's hand and when I found it, I entwined my fingers with hers. As far as I was concerned, it was already a matter of for better or for worse.

"She won't understand. No one can understand, unless they've seen it themselves. Unless they've lived through it."

"I'll do my best," she said, not angrily or anything, but firmly. She was determined to be a part of whatever shit was coming down and it made me love her all the more. At last Trojan nodded, retrieved two camp chairs from the main living area, and brought them back for himself and Lorraine. He sat close to me, not exactly edging her out, but somehow feeling I needed him near by.

"You asked me what happened," Trojan said. "What do you remember happened? Take your time. Your mind won't want to remember, I know, but you need to."

I tried to think back. I recalled Parker's yellow car, and his annoying visit, and how he was with three of the girls who had been at the Fourth of July bash at the Waterin Hole. I did not mention Parker's mini-orgy in my driveway or the seductiveness of Jade and her compadres.

(Some things your girlfriend really doesn't need to know, especially if they're irrelevant. Besides, I knew that Lorraine felt squirrelly enough as it was about those Stepford Girls.)

But then I remembered something more disturbing: how Parker had not been there with just the three girls, but how the girls had just been there as dates (or, more likely bait). How originally he must have been there with five other people—I had to swallow hard as I related this to Troj and Lorraine because the memories were coming back fast and furious, like a broken levee with a whole river full of water behind it, and part of me really, really, really did not want to remember. But then the memory was there, of the two of them who were my almost-like-brothers friends. Mojo and Whippet. I saw them again in my mind, sitting on that sofa that was evil incarnate. Tears flooded my eyes and Trojan knew then that I had remembered all of it. He reached over, taking my free hand in his and squeezing it hard. "Take it easy, son."

The vision of my dissolving friends, the way they had simply melted away, leaving for last their terrified eyes and the knowledge that no one—not even their best bud, David—could save them swirled around in my brain like a mad wind no matter how hard it fought to keep it out. "It didn't happen," I whispered, hearing the desperation in my voice. "It couldn't have happened. Things like that don't happen. It's impossible! It was just a bad dream!"

But the sad way that Trojan was looking at me told me that it had not been a nightmare at all. I moaned and shut my eyes hard as if that might banish the horrendous image (which, of course, it did not), and I felt my hot tears squeezing out from my eyelids and leaking down my cheeks and neck.

"What?" Lorraine asked. I could hear how desperately she wanted to know the source of my anguish. "What?" Trojan knew only because he had seen what I had seen, only for him it had been his beloved Linetta. As he said, some horrors cannot be told in words; they can only be understood by those who have lived through them.

"All in good time, missy," Trojan said, soothingly. "Your young man witnessed something no man should ever have to see. He just lost someone who was dear to his heart and he needs some time now."

"Someone dear to him? Who?"

"Mojo!" I gasped.

"Mojo?"

"And Whippet! Oh no! Oh God!" I sat up abruptly, no longer wanting these two good people clutching me, no longer wanting anyone touching me at all. I covered my face with my hands and wept, allowing myself whatever deep, wrenching sobs needed to escape from me in order to begin the slow, painful process of healing. Lorraine and Trojan, in their goodness, let me be.

When finally I had cried all that my heart and soul and eyes could stand, I wiped my face with the sheet that Trojan had put over me and heaved some deep breaths. I didn't look at anyone, but it was still good to know that they were both there.

"I know what you've been through, son," Trojan's soothingly sonorous voice told me, although I already knew this. "The same thing happened to my Nettie, and they made sure I was there to watch because that was my punishment, see? Like this was yours, for trying to defy them. They are pure evil and there are no bounds to their wickedness. They revel in the suffering of others, and though they need no excuse to inflict pain, I believe they are particularly amused when they have cause to mete out punishment."

"Mojo and Whippet—the guys from the July Fourth party—are—dead?" Lorraine asked, not me but Trojan. Her tone was incredulous as it naturally would be. You don't expect the young to die; you most especially don't expect anyone young who you know to die.

"Worse than dead," he replied sadly.

She didn't ask was what worse than dead but I think she already suspected. "The same as with his friends, Johnny and Theresa?"

Trojan nodded. "Only *They* didn't make David watch when the first two were taken. Making David watch what happened to his other friends—that was meant to be his punishment."

"Because he was staying on the porch and somehow broke the contract?"

"Because I wasn't good enough bait," I said. "Because I wouldn't *be* bait. Parker said it just before— 'You should've entertained more,' he said."

"That's right, son. You and I were bait. We were supposed to bring souls to the house for Them. I finally said *enough* and it cost me Linetta. When you said enough—"

"It cost me Mo and Whip," I said, feeling again a stab of pain. Because it wasn't just Mojo's and Whippet's loss that was so awful—horrible though it was—it was thinking about their families—mothers and fathers and grandparents and siblings. It was thinking of their potentials, their plans for the future—one to be a doctor, one a teacher—and our friendship that was supposed to have stretched out through the years until we were all a bunch of wrinkled, cackling old farts chugging down Captain Morgan and remembering the good old days when we were young and stupid and got busted for driving around drunk with a bucket of fried chicken. And the worst thought of all was about the hellish purgatory in which they were now undeservedly imprisoned.

Because of me.

Because of one stupid mistake, one reckless night, one thoughtless act, one wrong turn on the road of life. If only, if only, if only. The two saddest words in the world.

I threw myself back onto the cot and flung my arm over my eyes, trying to shut out the thoughts that kept knock, knock, knocking at my brain. "I'd like to be alone for a while," I said.

"Son...."

"David..."

Worried tones of voices from both of them. They meant well; I knew that. But at that moment I really didn't want either one of them there with me.

"Please. I'm not going to do anything stupid, anything *rash*, like they always say. Not going to off myself with a tent peg or drown myself in the port-a-potty. Just give me a while. By myself. Please."

I heard them leave, heard the tent flap that served as a door whisk open and fall shut, a tiny whisper of sound but enough to know that I was alone. I took my arm away from my eyes and saw that I wasn't quite alone. Squint had jumped onto the cot with me.

"You can go, too," I told him, and he answered by wiggling himself over onto his back, presenting his gray-and-white belly for me to rub. I gave him a little nudge. "Go away, Squint. Go hang with Lorraine."

The cat squinted at me and wriggled himself into an even more comfortable position.

"Go on, cat, go."

What was I thinking? Cats are not dogs. They do as they please, and right now it pleased Squint to keep me company.

"Have it your way," I sighed. I turned onto my side, pulling the covers up to my chin and soon began absently stroking the cat's fur after he had made a few more turns to find the most comfortable spot and pressed up against me. It was calming, to have that soft, warm little body curled there next to me. So the cat was smarter than me. No surprise there. My stupidity had already cost four people their lives.

The question now was, what next?

Worse than dead.

Trojan's words came back to hit me hard, making my gut feel as if someone had sucker-punched me as my already burning eyes tried to dredge up some more tears.

I wasn't a religious sort of guy, didn't go to church, didn't really believe in any one particular credo. I had always figured that most religions had most things right and also some things wrong, but ultimately all roads led to one place. Didn't much matter what route you took, even if you went way off the beaten path, most everyone (at least those who tried to do right by others) eventually arrived in the same spot. I did believe in an immortal spirit, in the fact that some part of us lives on after our bodies die. I got that—along with my thick dark hair that would never be best friends with a comb and my quirky sense of humor—from my maternal grandmother who I called Nonna (even though her real name was Elaine Azzari, before she married Mom's dad). She had been raised in a staunch Catholic household—with the communion and the Latin masses and the confession and the whole nine yards. But being Catholic never stopped her from developing her own eclectic view of how the world—the spiritual world—worked. To hear Nonna tell it (and I was probably her only confidante because I suspect most anyone else would have thought she was a raving lunatic) ghosts—spirits, souls, haints, whatever you wanted to call them—were as real as any living person, maybe more so. When we died, she said, our souls lived on, pretty much the way we lived here on earth except without any of the bad crap. Our souls were us, the essential us. (She never actually said she knew this from personal experience, but I always suspected that was the case, somehow.) She told me that sometimes they couldn't find their way to the light of God and these were very sad spirits—frightened, lost. Sad; sometimes angry. If she was right (and I didn't dare doubt Nonna's word) then my friends were, indeed, worse than dead. The house had taken their flesh but their souls were being held captive somewhere and not a good somewhere, either. Not in Nonna's heaven where there were beautiful houses with gardens and lawns you never had to mow; and where there were cool jobs to do where you were always creative, productive and appreciated; and where we'd be surrounded by all the people and pets we had ever loved. No, Mojo and Whippet were not there, but in a dark, ugly, evil place, separated forever from love and joy and hope. It would be some place where loneliness, pain and terror were your constant companions, and where there were beings that gorged themselves on your agony, stuffing their insatiable maws with every ounce of misery they could wring from you. These poor souls—my friends—weren't just lost, they were now the prisoners of beings so wicked that they faced an eternity of damnation and suffering. The thought sickened me but it did more than that.

It made me angry.

And that anger began to kindle a spark of resolve in my poor sucker-punched gut.

Just because I couldn't save their flesh-and-blood bodies didn't necessarily mean I couldn't save *them*.

I became aware of eyes on me and glancing down I saw that Squint was staring at me. He wasn't squinting now; his green eyes were wide, his pupils dilated. When our eyes locked he reached up a paw and touched my nose. Whether that meant it seemed that he understood my resolve and was urging me onward ("Atta boy, Dave, you go get 'em! Gird your loins, pull up your bootstraps, hi ho, Silver and all that!"). Of course, maybe he was trying to tell me I was the biggest fool whoever walked God's green earth, I didn't know for sure. But I suspected the former because, as Trojan said, this cat was no wimpy namby-pamby pussy, but there was no way to know for sure. There was only one thing I did know.

It didn't matter.

The new, improved David Fouraker's mind was made up, and no feline or human opinion was going to change it.

In the Woods
July 17 (Still Later)_____

I lay there as long as could until I started feeling
like I was imposing on Trojan's and Lorraine's good
nature. It wasn't fair of me to keep them sitting out there,
waiting for me to get a grip. I sat up abruptly, causing
Squint to jump off the cot, wiped my eyes and took a deep
breath. I would probably succumb to the blues later—
maybe even a crying jag or two—but right now I was
emotionally spent and ready to start planning my assault.
Funny how anger and a desire for vengeance can really
pull you out of the dumps. It focused you, gave you purpose. Maybe when it was all over (and provided I survived
which was sort of iffy at the moment) I would allow
myself to grieve for my lost friends, but at the moment, I
had more important things to do.

I got off the cot and opened the flap for Squint who
preceded me into the main room, tail held high, like a
squire announcing the arrival of his knight. Trojan and
Lorraine had been sitting at what served as his kitchen
table and both stood when I came in. Concern etched their
faces, so I tried to make myself smile. (At least I hope it

looked like a smile. It could have come out looking like a grimace or worse for all I knew.)

"Take a walk with me?" I asked Lorraine, who nodded. I took her hand and made for the main tent flap, but before we passed through it, I turned toward Trojan. "I'll see you soon," I told him, hoping my emphasis would clue him that I planned to be back shortly.

"Take it easy, son," he said, which didn't tell me whether he got my drift or not, although I felt I could be reasonably sure he would stick around. (If you don't have a car, where can you go?) He and I had some heavy duty parlaying to do.

I walked in the general direction of the house but was in no hurry to reach it. The closer we got, the slower I went until we stopped well before we reached the end of the scrub bushes that marked the edge of the property. Lorraine turned to me, thinking she knew why I had stopped — and she was partly right. I didn't want to see the house that had robbed me of my two closest friends — but as I said, she was only partly right. She wasn't going to like hearing my real reason, which was to have to alone time in order to have a heavy-duty conversation. I guess she read something in my face other than my revulsion for the house, though, because the worried creases on her face deepened.

"What's wrong, David?"

I could have hemmed and hawed and beaten around the bush — or whatever other clichés one could come up with for stalling — but I figured what I had to say was going to hurt her no matter how long I took to tell her, so I might as well just put it out there and get it over with.

"I need you to do something important for me," I said.

"Of course, sure. Anything."

"You're not going to like it, but I really need you to do this for me."

"So tell me, already."

I had to take a deep breath because, to be honest, I didn't like asking this of her, but I had to—for both our sakes. "I need you to stay away from me."

"What? Why?"

"Not forever," I told her, for the moment avoiding her questions. "Just until my contract is up. A measly four weeks. But when I say stay away, I mean really stay away. I don't want you even coming up into my driveway. And I'm not going to spend time in your apartment, either. We can see each other at the diner, but nothing more than that, and believe me, if I could think of an alternate route so you didn't even have to drive by this place, I would ask you to take it."

"We're in this together," she insisted.

"Not any more, we're not."

"Why not? What did I do?"

"It's not what you did, Lorraine, it's what could happen if you're anywhere near me."

"I don't understand. All I was doing was keeping you company on the porch."

"And we don't really know how safe that porch is, now do we?"

"No," she frowned, "but we've been okay so far."

"And until this afternoon, Mojo and Whippet were fine, too, and now they don't exist any more—at least not physically. Listen, Lorraine." I took her in my arms, wanting her to really, really listen, and I wanted her to look in my eyes and see how sincere I was about this. "I love you. I can't even remember right this minute if I've already told you that, or if I only said it to you in my mind, but that's the truth. I know I've known you about a month, which probably is a ridiculously short period of time to fall in love, but that's how it is. I love you. There is no one more important to me than you. The problem with that is—I'm not the only person who knows that."

"I don't understand."

"He, Eblis, probably knows, too, and at any rate, They know, those—things—whatever they are, demons, whatever, in the house. They know I love you. And loving you makes me very vulnerable, more defenseless than I can afford to be right this minute."

"Because—?"

"Because I defied them and they lured Mojo and Whippet here to punish me. Now there are only so many threats left that they can hold over my head. Sure, they could destroy strangers and that would make me feel awful, but if they really want to get to me, they'll use someone I really care about. That leaves my parents and you. They used Linetta to punish Trojan and they'll use you against me. Your being here makes me especially vulnerable. Knowing you're in potential danger gives them power over me, lets them control me, keeps me in line. That's why you have to stay away from here and me until this is over. And you have to be careful not to get tricked into coming here."

"What do you mean?"

"Parker lured Mo and Whip up here with those Stepford girls, whatever they are. He tricked them, you see? He's working with Eblis, I'm sure of it."

"Parker? The friend wannabe?"

I nodded. "He got way too cool too fast. Amazing car, new wardrobe, hot chick on his arm, hell, even his complexion cleared up. Things like that don't just happen over night. And when I saw him here with those three girls, it was so obvious that he was Eblis's henchman, I felt stupid not to have seen it sooner. He'll try anything to get you to come here—tell you I'm sick, or been hurt—that I need you. Don't listen to him, Lorraine. You have to ignore whatever he tells you, whatever anyone tells you. Unless— well, unless Trojan's cat comes to you with a message, it's bogus, you got that?"

There were tears standing in Lorraine's beautiful brown eyes and I hated that I put them there—although it's hard not to be glad someone cares so much about you.

"It's not fair," she whispered, looking away from me.

"I know."

"I mean, it's not fair that I should love and care so much about someone I've only known a few weeks. What's up with that, anyway?" She was making herself frown, making herself sound like a tough girl, but I knew she was all marshmallow inside and it was hard to keep from smiling just from the good feeling that gave me. It's an amazing thing to be loved, especially by someone like Lorraine. "It's supposed to take years, or at least a year, or several months, for god's sake, to feel this way. But then you come waltzing into town—"

"I didn't waltz. I wasn't even doing the box step," I said lightly and her mouth twitched as if she wanted to laugh and yet wasn't about to give into it.

"And all of a sudden I'm in love? Damn it! That's so not fair!"

I cupped her adorable, dimpled face—that was way too smooshed up right now with a frown—and turned it toward me, kissing her softly. "It'll be all right. I promise."

"You can't promise that," she said stubbornly.

"Well, I'm promising anyway. We're going to get through this, we're going to be together until we're just two old toothless farts rocking away on a porch some-where bragging about our great-grandchildren to what-ever schmo is unlucky enough to come by."

"I don't plan to lose my teeth," she grumbled, "and I don't think I ever want to sit on any porch ever again."

"Okay, riding around in our Ferrari, then," I said and her smile finally cracked, but just a little. It was more like a twitch, but it was better than nothing.

"You better get through this in one piece, David Fouraker," she said fiercely, tears streaming down her face. "Or I won't ever forgive you." She studied my face as if trying to read my thoughts. "You won't do anything stupid, will you?"

"Like stick my finger in a wall socket? Like ride my bike in the middle of the road?"

She frowned again. "You know what I mean. With Them."

"I'll give them a wide berth. Avoid them like the plague," I lied. I didn't like lying to her, but sometimes you have to lie to protect the ones who love you.

"Promise?" She peered at me a little too intently but I put on my dumb-and-innocent face.

"Of course," I answered lightly. If you don't actually say the word *promise*, is it still a promise? Is it still breakable? I didn't think the argument would hold up in a court of law, but it was good enough for me.

I kissed her again and she kissed me back, only we kept it light because to do otherwise would have made it seem too much like a goodbye and neither one of could have stood that. Lorraine turned away from me then and trudged through the last of the bushes to her car. I didn't watch her leave. I heard her start her engine, heard the tires crunching on gravel as the car turned toward the road, but I didn't watch. I couldn't. It would have been too much like seeing her ride off into the sunset. Alone. Forever. I turned back toward Trojan's camp and took out my cell phone. Two other people still made me vulnerable to Eblis and his nasty horde.

When my mother answered the phone, I kept my voice light, cheerful, like I was ten years old and calling her from summer camp. We chatted a few minutes. I told her I was incredibly busy but doing really, really well. Enjoyed being at the Springs, planned to go into the park service — which probably made her doubt that she was talking to the real me. Her child, with life goals? I knew that was a shocker — was just about done with my community service, blah blah blah. My point was to convince her that I was so busy and so immersed in my life at the moment that a visit from my parents was neither needed nor a particularly good idea. Ten minutes into the conversation I felt confident that they wouldn't get any ideas about paying me an impromptu call just for the fun of it—but there was always Sneaky Palmer and the Tricksters. I had to head them off at the pass, so to speak.

"Mom, there's one thing I should sort of warn you about," and as soon as those words were out of my mouth, I realized that one should never, ever use the word *warn* when they're taking to their mother. That sort of word sets off all sorts of alarm bells in the maternal ear. I would have to do some quick backtracking. "Well, not *warn*, exactly. See, there's a guy on my floor in the dorm named Parker who is an incredibly irritating practical joker and he's already conned Mojo and Whippet and some other friends. He's sort of into sick jokes—not that he's dangerous or anything—" I added quickly "—but he's annoying as hel--heck. He might call you and tell you that I've been in an accident or got sick or something stupid like that, just to make you and Dad run down here in a panic. Call me first, Mom, okay? Don't just pop down here. It's a long drive, and it'll be for nothing, okay?" I wanted to add *Do you really understand me, Mom?* but she just said, "Okay, honey," and then added, "My goodness, what an awful little creep."

"You have no idea."

"I hope your friends weren't too put out."

I winced. "No, Mom, it was just a royal pain in the a—in the patoot." I was about back at Trojan's campsite by then and decided to ring off. "Just pass the word on to Dad, okay?" Mom promised she would, still murmuring incredulity that anyone could be so crass. "I'll see you in August, okay?"

"Yes, honey, August."

I said goodbye as Trojan's tent came into view. It was time for David Fouraker, Demon Fighter, to have a parlay with the troops.

Yeah, I know, one other soldier does not a troop make, but sometimes you just have to take what you can get.

Trojan's Campsite
July 17 (Even Later Still)_____

"The way I see it, we have two main tasks," I said. Trojan and I were sitting across from each other at his camp table. It was a cool contraption that started off as something the size of a large suitcase and unfolded into an aluminum table with two attached benches. Trojan was probably the camper with the neatest stuff on the planet.

Trojan got up to get us a couple of RCs from his small refrigerator. "What do you mean *we*?" He set a can in front of me and eased himself back into his seat. Squint jumped up onto the table and sat there, looking from me to Trojan as if he wanted to be part of the conversation. "You know I can't go near that house," Trojan reminded me, "so I'm not about to be much help to you."

"I just need some back-up, some behind-the-scenes advice, that's all," I assured him. "And some information."

"I suppose I can handle that much," Trojan replied. "It's not that I don't want to help you, son, but while I was in that house, They got into me somehow. Not that you should worry about that," he added, seeing the shadow of concern waft across my face. "I can feel them pricking me once in a while, especially if I get too close to that house, but I can control them. I'm not going to go off the deep end and do something crazy. Don't mean to toot my own horn too loudly, but I'm not like Orin, Mike or Jessie. I think they already had bad seeds inside them before those things got a hold of them. I'm not perfect, but I have some sense of morality that doesn't appeal to Them. They're inside me, though. Like I said, I can feel them. You saw what they did to me a while back when I got too close to the house."

I remembered seeing Trojan struck with pain and his cat going crazy to break him away from the house's hold on him.

"Anyway, even though they're here," he tapped his chest, "I don't think they make me dangerous."

"I believe you," I said, not believing him entirely. I mean, I was sure he was sincere, but what did he really know about how far their powers could extend? What did either of us really know about them in general? "So as I was saying, I have two main tasks. Set the souls trapped in that house free and get rid of the house itself."

"You might just add achieve peace in the Middle East and solve global warming to that list," Trojan said, making a wry face.

"I'm not setting out to destroy evil in the world, Troj," I countered. "All I care about is that particular house and those people caught in it."

"I already told you, you can't destroy them or the house."

"Now wait, Troj, you don't know that for sure. You said that you can't destroy the house by setting fire to it, but that's about all you know for sure at this point." I popped the tab on my RC and took a swig. "Okay, first things first. The people — the souls — trapped in the house. You were able to free Linetta by setting fire to the chair that had —" I saw the image of Mojo and Whippet melting and didn't want to go there. "—taken her. So we know that's possible at least."

"The furniture won't burn inside the house."

"So we — I — take it out of the house."

Trojan shook his head, irritating me. The last thing I wanted at the moment was dealing with such a naysayer. "I was only allowed to take that chair because I traded it for the house. They let me have her, understand? What have you got to trade, son? Nothing, that's what."

"So I take the furniture out by force. Once it's out, it can be burned and they'll be free. Not alive physically, but at least free."

"And you think they're just going to stand by and let you do that? You couldn't do it fast enough. You got a lot of pieces to deal with — beds, a sofa, chairs. Eblis would be tearing down that driveway before you could get one stick out into the yard. You remember what happened the night they got upset about you camping out on the porch, right? They called him. He doesn't ignore a page like that."

I felt the scowl on my face deepening. "Troj, instead of being so damned negative, help me think of a way around that."

He sipped his cola and shrugged. "Just playing devil's advocate, son."

"That's a poor choice of words," I groused.

"You need to know the downside of what you're planning so you don't get tripped up by it later on. I admire you for wanting to take this on, son, but I want you to be realistic about what you're up against."

"I lived there, remember? I saw them take my friends. Believe me, I know what they can do. I'm not underestimating them."

Trojan tipped his can at me. "Just so you keep in mind how dangerous what you're proposing to do really is."

"I am, but there's got to be a way to keep Eblis away, at least long enough to liberate the furniture. Demons must be afraid of something, surely."

"Not sure garlic or crucifixes are much help outside of the movies."

"But there must be something," I insisted. "Anyway, I'm not going to let some roadblocks stop me, Troj. My grandmother, my Nonna, used to tell me that evil triumphs when good does nothing. That sounds sort of corny, I know, but that was my Nonna, and corny or not, I think she was right." I sighed. "I'll figure out some way to keep from getting interrupted. Let's move on to the house. You said we can't burn it down."

"That's right. Which is too bad, I know, because that would sure be killing two birds with one stone, wouldn't it?"

"There are more ways to destroy houses than to burn them down," I said.

"Yeah, well, we could sic an army of termites on it, maybe. Or just bide our time and let nature rot the wood."

"Be serious, Troj. I've been thinking about this. You were in the construction business. What would it take to get a building condemned?"

Trojan seemed to perk up a little at that, and peered at me over the rim of his RC can. "Major structural damage. Probably more than one person could inflict unless you're planning on renting a tank."

"Would you know who to call at City Hall to get the house condemned? Would they actually bring bulldozers and such out here and tear it down?"

"It would cost. They don't do it for nothing." He saw the disappointment in my eyes, knowing that poor college students usually didn't have more than a few bucks in their pockets at any one time. "'Course, I've got more money than an old man could ever use so if it comes to you needing to hit me up for a contribution, I guess I could oblige you. I also got some favors I could call in to get the job done, provided the damage was bad enough. You got any ideas on that?"

"Maybe. I need to do some research and here's where you can help me."

"If it's not near the house, I'm yours to command."

"I need a computer with internet access. Obviously I can't use the one at the house. And I'll need transportation. Do you think your daughter would lend you her car for the day?"

"A car and the computer in my old office," Trojan said.

"You still have your driver's license?"

"'Course I do. Not senile yet, son."

"I know, Troj," I smiled. "I just thought you might not have bothered keeping it since you no longer own a car."

"Still got to have ID." Trojan swigged his cola. "Listen, son, let's say you get that house reduced to rubble. Those things are still going to be in it. They're in the wood, in the substance of the house. You don't want to just end up recycling the evil."

"How about renting a backhoe and burying the pieces?"

Trojan thought a moment, then nodded. "You get it knocked down, it'll be my pleasure to see it put underground."

"Thanks, Troj." I stood up. "It's getting dark so I better get back before someone (or some thing) comes to check up on me."

Trojan saw me to the front door (flap, actually). "You be careful, son. You don't know for sure that you're free of those things either."

"What do you mean?"

"You slept in that house, on the bed upstairs, didn't you?"

"The sofa bed, yeah, and also once in a bed downstairs." I was a little slow, but I got his meaning. "You think they got inside of me somehow?" The idea that there was a demon seedling somewhere inside my body was more than creepy, it was borderline obscene. "I don't feel anything."

"They may not have bothered with you, but you can't know for sure. They had plenty of time to get to you. You can't be sure that they can't read your mind, especially if you're hanging out by the house."

"I have to stay at the house."

"I know that, but just try to think of something other than our little talk here. Think of that girl of yours, of the diner where you work, the Springs, anything but that. I know, I know," he said, shaking his head, "that's sort of like saying, don't think of a purple polar bear and all of a sudden that's all you can think of. But try to keep it out of your mind if you can. Don't let your guard down, not one second, you hear?"

I walked back to the house just as the sun was starting its downward slide into evening. I took the last few minutes of daylight to walk around the house and think about how one might go about doing "major structural damage" while avoiding the same sort of structural damage to oneself. The one advantage I might have was the fact that the house had wood floors and therefore was up on short pylons, leaving a crawlspace underneath that possibly could be vulnerable. As I made my way up the steps, though, I forced myself to think of Lorraine and Trojan and purple polar bears. I didn't think I would be able to sleep, but stress exhausts you. (It also doesn't hurt to keep a good supply of the Captain's special brew on hand, either). Though I heard *their* incessantly annoying whisperings and giggling, and from time to time some squirming beneath my mattress pad, after I had spent some quality time with the Captain, I quickly dozed off.

Crawfordville
(Wakulla County Seat)
July 20_____

Trojan and I waited outside his tent and watched the silver Chevy Tahoe bounce and jig its way up the rutted path to his campsite. The tall, golden brown woman who got out had an understated elegance. Crisp white shirt with rolled up sleeves, khaki slacks, flat shoes, a simple outfit with just enough gold jewelry to let you know she was the boss. Her dark hair was close cropped — a style only a black woman can pull off without looking like a guy — and yet she was attractive in an African princess sort of way. If I hadn't been expecting her, I would have known she was Trojan's daughter just by the shine in his eyes when he looked at her. I bet she reminded him of his Linetta.

"Hey, baby," he said to her, and introduced me as his neighbor. "This is my baby girl, Tasha."

She had a firm grip when she shook my hand. "Natasha Reynolds, and," she rolled her doe eyes at her father, "at 42, I'm hardly a baby girl, Dad."

"Well, you're *my* baby girl," Trojan smiled and when she released my hand, she went to her father and kissed his cheek.

When she stepped back she gave me a good once-over. "How are you Dad's neighbor? You renting that house?" The way she said it, *that house*, let you know in no uncertain terms that she had no fond memories of it though I'm sure she didn't know the half of it. Like how it had eaten her mother.

"Yes, ma'am, just for the summer."

She nodded. "You call me ma'am again and I'm going to have to slap you silly. It's Tasha. And why would any young man want to spend the summer in Bethel?"

"He's a college student," Trojan offered as if that explained it.

"Didn't know we had a college here in Wakulla County."

"No, ma'am—Tasha—I go to FSU but I'm working at the Springs. I plan to be a park ranger." It felt good to say that. Not only was I not lying to this nice lady but it made me feel I might actually have a future and a plan for living it, which I considered sort of iffy at the moment. Her scrutiny was a little unnerving—you could tell she was a no-nonsense sort of woman who was used to looking employees in the eye and judging their worth— but I must've passed her muster because at last she gave a nod.

"You said you needed the car, Dad?" she asked.

"Yeah, baby, I told David here that maybe I could help him run some errands."

"A college student without a car?" She gave me the eye again.

"It's in the shop. I had a little fender bender a while ago."

"He also needs to use a computer. I told him maybe he could use the one in the office, if that's okay with you."

"There's a computer in the house," Tasha said.

"It's not working," I lied. I liked it better when I could be up front with her. In fact, I hated lying, but I could hardly tell her the truth. You see, demons are online and they're interfering with my connection. Not only would she not loan a lunatic like that a car, she likely would call the nearest asylum and have them come pick me up armed with butterfly nets.

She looked at Trojan this time. I couldn't tell if she was buying all this — broken down car, broken down computer, a college student who willingly spent his summer in a podunk little town like Bethel — but she obviously trusted her father, so she just shrugged, gestured toward her Tahoe and said, "Well, get in."

Twenty minutes later Natasha pulled into the lot of Wakulla Wood and parked the Chevy SUV around back of a large two-story building — wooden, of course, and weathered a silvery grey. Trojan and I followed her upstairs where the administrative offices were housed. ("Some of the workshops are downstairs," Trojan explained to me, "although we've added a few more in separate buildings since I started.") A tall black man — also in a crisp white shirt with rolled-up sleeves — looked up from a desk when we came into the main office and rose.

Trojan introduced him as his son-in-law, Jefferson Reynolds and we shook hands.

"Talk to you a minute, Tash?" he asked. "You excuse us, Pop?"

"Sure thing, Jeff. Just letting the boy here use the computer for a few minutes."

"Have dinner with us Sunday, Pop," he added. "The kids have been complaining that they haven't seen their grandpa in a long time."

"Love to, thanks."

Jefferson Reynolds eyed me. "Bring your friend here, if you want to."

"'Appreciate it," Trojan said and I nodded politely, smiled and offered my thanks. It would be nice to think I would still be alive to have dinner on Sunday, but that was sort of iffy at this moment, too.

Natasha gave her father the keys to the Tahoe then went to confer with her husband about some glitch or something, while Trojan led me to one of the office computers which was already on and connected to the internet. There were three other workers upstairs who glanced at us but just nodded and smiled, saying, "Mornin' Mr. Barnes," to Trojan, and then went back to their tasks.

"Saw my grandkids just two weeks ago, but seems they like their old Grandpa," he told me as I sat before the keyboard.

"I bet they do. I'm fond of him myself."

Trojan clapped my shoulder affectionately. "You do what you got to do, son, and let me know when you're ready to go." I nodded and he ambled off to chat a minute or two with his former employees all of whom seemed genuinely glad to see him. I wondered if I would ever get a chance to be as good a man as Trojan Barnes. Wherever she was, I bet his Momma was proud.

I brought up Google and held my breath, just for a split second wondering whether any demons would choose to invade the monitor through the DSL. I admit I also was a little nervous about doing this particular search. What I was looking for was an encroachment on terrorist territory—decidedly subversive. After 9/11 there was no telling how much the feds were spying on us citizens. The Patriot Act gave them a lot of leeway. If they were tapping into random computers, the Barnes-Reynolds family would probably be screwed when someone found out what I'd been looking at, but what choice did I have? I needed information—stuff that likely would make me seem dangerous to the authorities—and though I didn't want to put anyone into harm's way (especially these nice people who were kind enough to help me) what could I do? I opened up a website, scanned it quickly to see that it told me what I needed to know, printed the pages, and quickly closed it, hoping I hadn't left an electronic trail. Just to be sure, I went into the system folder and deleted both the cookies and the content of the history file. Then I snatched up the pages and found Trojan visiting with one of the staff. He looked up when he saw me.

"You ready to go?"

"I am."

"Where to first?"

"Hardware store, but can we go to some place other than Bethel? I'd rather not shop too close to home."

"Fine with me."

I got into the passenger seat and Trojan climbed behind the wheel. "Where else besides the hardware store?"

"Wal-Mart, a gun store, and then to Medart."

"You want to try fighting these things in the house with a gun?"

"No, Troj, I know that's impossible. I just want some ammo."

"Well, you can get supplies for a gun at Wal-Mart, so that'll save a stop. What's in Medart?"

"First things first," I told him.

There was a Wal-Mart SuperCenter in Crawfordville which was en route to Medart, so that's where we headed. To pass the time, and because I figured Trojan would be curious about my ultimate plan and what we were shopping for, I read him some of what I had printed out. "I was thinking that a few pipe bombs might be in order to do structural damage without actually blowing the house to smithereens."

"I take it smithereens are something to be avoided?"

"I'm not sure, but I don't want to take any chances. You ever see that sequel to Night of the Living Dead? Something called Dawn of the Dead—no, I'm wrong, that took place in a shopping mall."

"Lordy," Trojan breathed, frowning.

"The one I'm thinking of was about punk rockers in a cemetery—well, it was a Living Dead something or other. Did you? Ever see it?"

"Sorry to say I missed that one," Trojan replied, not sounding the least bit regretful.

"Well, in this movie, the people fighting the brain-eating zombies decided to get rid of them by burning them at this crematorium, only the smoke went up the chimney and then it started raining and the chemicals that made the zombies in the first place rained down into the local cemetery, making a whole bunch more zombies. You see?"

"A real academy-award winner," Trojan grimaced.

"My point is that we have to be careful how we get rid of these things, because we don't want to make things worse."

"You think that if we do blow the house to smithereens something might get into the air?"

"I don't know, but it's possible, and I'm not taking any chances."

"What stops it from getting into the ground if it rains where we bury it?"

"Well, I do have an idea about that, too, but I'll explain that later, okay? The whole point right now is to keep anything from getting into the air where it would be more difficult to control."

"And you think you can do structural damage, qualifying the building for demolition, by using some pipe bombs?"

"I do."

"And you know how to make pipe bombs? They teach you this in college?"

"The internet is a treasure-trove of information. Sorry, that's what I needed the computer for, but I erased the trail—at least, I think I did."

"Lord," Trojan sighed.

"Listen to this. If it wasn't so damned serious, it would be funny. 'First a word of warning. Explosives are extremely dangerous devices, forget what you've seen in the movies.' Well, duh, no kidding, right?"

"There are stupid people out there, son."

"Yeah, I know, but listen to this disclaimer: 'If you venture into improvised explosives manufacture the chances are that you will lose your hands and other parts of your body no matter how good you think you are.' Other parts of your body. Ouch, huh?"

"You sure you want to try this?"

"What choice is there, Troj? You think of anything else?"

The old man sighed, but shrugged, shook his head, and kept driving. "So this article you downloaded tells you how to make one of these things?"

"Step by step. Weird, what they put on line these days, isn't it? Anyway, we'll need lengths of pipe—the article suggests three to eight inches long—and some gunpowder. I figure we can cut open some shotgun shells, you think? They'll be easiest to find. I mean, I don't have a clue where to find dynamite or TNT—not legally, anyway, and not by this weekend."

"Yeah, FedEx probably doesn't like delivering explosives."

"So does the plan make sense to you so far?"

"I guess so. Much as anything can make sense right now."

I nodded. Our conversation did have a surreal quality about it. Twenty minutes after leaving Wakulla

Wood Trojan pulled the car into the parking lot of Ace Hardware just south of Shadeville. You know that jingle about how Ace is the Place with the Helpful Hardware Man? Well, it's true, only in our case, the hardware man was a slender, red-haired woman with Casey on her name tag. In plumbing supplies, she found us short lengths of threaded pipe and pipe caps. I also bought six feet of thin braided rope. I didn't need that much to make the fuses, but I thought that getting only a foot of rope would seem too suspicious. From Ace, we went to Wal-Mart. I took a shopping cart and got one for Trojan as well. "We getting that much stuff here?" he asked, puzzled.

"Lots of heavy stuff," I told him. First off we went to the sporting goods section and put an ample supply of shotgun shells in our carts—virtually cleaned off the shelves—Trojan the whole time talking up a huge hunting trip with the guys and wondering aloud whether we were getting enough ammo for everyone. I knew he was just trying to keep a clerk within earshot from being suspicious about two guys buying enough gunpowder to have won the Battle of Yorktown, but I still had to consciously avoid rolling my eyes while listening to his musings. After the shells, I went to the toy section and got a medium-sized neon green and yellow Super Soaker water gun and then in the beverage section I loaded six five-gallon jugs of water. I also threw in a Bic lighter, a few emergency candles, and a five-gallon red plastic gas container.

"What's all the water for?" Trojan asked.

"Ammunition," I told him. "Or it will be when I get done with it."

"Lord, son, you must have one helluva plan. This is one crazy grocery list of yours."

As he helped me put our purchases onto the checkout counter, Trojan asked, "So where to now?"

"Now we go to Medart," I told him.

"And so what's in Medart?" he asked again.

"St. Elizabeth Ann Seton Parish," I said. "A Catholic church."

Medart, Florida
July 20, A Little Later_____

"So what's wrong with a Baptist church?"

My mind had been elsewhere, lulled into a kind of trance by the passing buildings and trees along the road to Medart, and Trojan's interjection almost startled me. "What?"

"A Baptist church. Why can't we just go to a Baptist church? Or any other church, for that matter?"

"Nothing. Nothing's wrong with a Baptist church. Why?"

"So why are we driving to a Catholic church in Medart?"

"Because St. Elizabeth Ann Seton Parish is the closest one around," I said.

"No, I mean why a Catholic church in particular? Won't any church do?"

I'd been thinking about this for a while so I had a ready answer. "The Catholic church has a long history of dealing with demons—more than any other religious sect, as far as I can tell. A lot of the sources cited on the demonology sites I'd searched on the web were connected to the

Catholic church. And consider this: in *The Exorcist*, who did they call when Linda Blair's head started spinning around?"

"A priest."

"Right. And when the folks in the Amityville house wanted to exorcise a demon, who did they call?"

"A priest."

"Right again."

"But those were movies, son," Trojan reminded me. "That Amityville business wasn't even true."

"I know, but if the Hollywood writers thought it was plausible for people plagued by demons to call a Catholic priest, they must base that on something, don't you think?"

"I suppose so." Trojan's tone suggested doubt.

"I'm sure they didn't just pull that out of the air. Besides, haven't you seen some of those paranormal TV shows, the ones that deal with demonic possession and stuff?"

"Nope, must've been on the same time as Judge Judy."

"Well, anyway, take my word for it. They always call in a Catholic priest. Never a Baptist minister, not a Lutheran pastor—a priest. Catholic. Not Episcopalian, even."

"But that's saying that people who end up with possessed houses or family members are always Catholics and we know that isn't true. I mean, look at me. I'm a Baptist. Not an every-Sunday-going-to-meetin' sort of Baptist, but close enough. Are you saying I should've found myself a priest in the yellow pages?" Trojan eyed me. "Sort of like you did, maybe?"

I frowned. "I found St. Elizabeth's on the 'net. Anyway, I need some sort of weapon against whatever is in that house and I can't think of anyone else to get it from but a priest. Even if I am reaching or flat-out wrong," I added feeling grumpy, "I'm doing the best I can. I'm not exactly an expert in demonology, you know."

Trojan reached over and patted my leg. "I know, son. I know."

A short time later we arrived at the church. I don't know about you, but I always expect a Catholic church to be something like Notre Dame, all flying buttresses and stained glass and towering steeples, not a little clapboard jobbie that looked like it had been plucked from Norman Rockwell's New England. Behind the main churchy looking building were two portable buildings, one an ordinary white double wide mobile home, the other also white but long with lots of windows and three doors each with a tiny landing and stairs. A brick-and-mortar sign that looked sturdier than either of those two buildings stood near the road. What appeared to be freshly painted on the front was

ST. ELIZABETH SEATON
CATHOLIC CHURCH

"They probably took it over from another church that was able to move into a larger facility," Trojan said. "Looks more Methodist or Presbyterian to me. Not that

that matters, I guess. Better than a storefront in a strip mall."

There was no formal parking lot, just an expanse of white gravel that crunched under our tires as Trojan parked the car. At the sound of our arrival, an older man wearing a straw hat, white shirt with rolled up sleeves, and pants with suspenders looked up from the small garden he had been tending. With one hand he took off his hat and wiped his forehead before planting it back on his head.

I got out of the car, putting on my most disarming smile (as a rule I don't look very threatening, but smiles go a long way if you're about to ask a huge favor). "Are you Father D'Arcy?" I asked.

"Me? No, I just hep out around here. Father Em was in the church, last I saw him. Go on in. Ain't locked."

I thanked him (with a fleeting thought of how sad a commentary it was on our modern society that many churches were locked even during the day) and Trojan and I made our way up the steps to the porch. (Narthex, my Nonna would have called it. Not like in a cathedral, of course — this was just a porch — but since it probably hadn't started life as a Catholic church, it couldn't be expected to be built like one.) Just inside the door at the head of the nave (See, Nonna imprinted me with all this stuff even though she didn't have a snowball's chance in hell of me being raised Catholic.) was the font of holy water. I had a brief urge to genuflect (as she had taken me to church a few times and that's what we always did) but resisted. The fact is, not only wasn't I a practicing Catholic, I pretty much wasn't a practicing anything—though if I lived to Monday I might reconsider my religious position.

A man dressed all in black except for his white collar (sort of casually, though, since his shirt was short-sleeved) was hard at work, polishing the brass railing in front of the altar where the faithful would kneel to receive communion. You could tell the part he had finished: it gleamed like new gold, and he was working furiously at the rest. I cleared my throat and made him start.

He wasn't much older than I was which surprised me. I'd never known a young priest. All of the ones at the church Nonna had sometimes taken me to had looked like they'd sat around the table at the Last Supper. This guy must've been fresh out of the seminary—which would explain why he had drawn a parish out in the boondocks of Medart, Florida. He pushed dark-rimmed glasses up the bridge of his nose with his index finger when he looked up. You could tell that his dark hair had been carefully combed that morning, but a lock had fallen onto his forehead with his cleaning efforts. "Father D'Arcy?" I ventured, although I knew he was. It was a relief to me to find him so young—maybe that would mean he'd be more open-minded when I presented him with my request.

He grinned and switched his cleaning rag from his right hand to his left so that he could offer me a hand to shake as he came to greet us. "I am. And you are?" He looked at the rag briefly before stuffing it into his pants pocket as I introduced myself and Trojan. "Sorry. Lots of chores to do around here and help is hard to find. I'm lucky to have Albert or I'd be out there mowing and pulling weeds." Albert, I guessed, was the old guy in the straw hat and suspenders. Father D'Arcy eyed Trojan with surprise when the name registered. "Did you say Trojan Barnes? *The* Trojan Barnes?" he asked making me marvel once again at how well-known my reclusive neighbor was in these parts. His name was a household word through the entire county.

"Just plain old Trojan nowadays, Father," Troj said.

Father D'Arcy nodded and smiled. "So, what can I do for you?" he asked me. The way he said it made me cringe a bit inside. He sounded so damned hopeful—like he thought I was a lost sheep searching for a new flock; he sounded so eager to extend the hospitality of his parish to a new member. I hated the idea of disappointing him, but it couldn't be helped.

I had rehearsed this speech a dozen times in our drive over to Medart—yet when the time came to deliver it, it turned to a handful of powdered cement in my mouth. Father D'Arcy watched me expectantly until I knew I just had to say something or he would start thinking I was deranged and that definitely would not be good given what I was about to tell him. "I need a favor," I said at last.

A small frown—not of anger or worry but more like puzzlement—formed on the priest's forehead. He jabbed at the nosepiece of his glasses again, resetting them on the bridge of his nose from where they had once again begun to slide. "All right," he said by way of giving me the go-ahead. "How can I help you?"

"It's not a huge favor," I told him.

"Okay, well, why don't we—why don't we go into my office—"

"I need some holy water," I said, putting it out on the table before things deteriorated into a counseling session.

"Holy water?" Father D'Arcy's frown deepened.

"Excuse me, Father," Trojan put in. "Just to give this whole thing a little perspective right off the bat. You've heard of me, right? So you must have a sense that I'm not a crackpot. Can't run a business successfully for a few decades and be nuts, now can you?"

"Ah—no—" The priest looked over at Trojan. "No, of course not."

"And I can vouch for this young fellow here. He's no crackpot, either. You may get tempted to think he is, but I'm telling you otherwise. And if he says he needs something, he needs it. Okay?"

"Okay," Father D'Arcy said, although his tone was uncertain. "What is this all about?"

"Here's the thing, Father," I said. "I'm living on a piece of property that's cursed. Big time."

"Cursed?"

"Can't think of any other way to put it. There are bad things living on it. Really *really* bad things. Evil things." I turned to Trojan. "Would you show him what they did to you?"

I had put Troj on the spot and I felt badly about that, but unless Father D'Arcy could be convinced that I was serious and not some lunatic who had just escaped from the asylum for the criminally insane in Chattahoochee, then there would be very little chance of getting the priest's help. And I needed his help.

Troj must have known this, too, because even though he sighed deeply, he unbuttoned his shirt, slipped it down past his shoulders and turned around, exposing the ugly webbing of scars that covered his back. The priest made a face. He was grossed out—and no priestly demeanor was going to cover that.

"What on earth happened to you? Were you burned?"

Trojan turned around, pulled up his shirt and rebuttoned it. "In a way. By hell fire. See, Father, where this young man is living—that used to be my house. You know I lost my wife, Linetta—do you?"

"I—heard some gossip—"

"Whatever you heard, what really happened was worse. The evil in that house got her. Got lots of other folks, to boot. Some of David's friends, too, not long ago." Trojan shrugged. "Now I'm not saying you have to believe us—but you do believe in the Devil, don't you, Father?"

"Yes, of course, but—"

"Well, if he isn't in that house, his minions are for sure."

"I—I'm sorry but I'm not equipped—authorized—to do an—an exorcism, if that's what you want. There are—strict rules, protocols—"

"No, nothing like that," I said quickly, hoping to reassure the priest who I could tell was becoming terribly agitated. Not that I blamed him. I saw him glance toward the door as if he was wondering how he might attract Albert's attention, or if whether he could just make a run for it and escape before the two of us could tackle him. "We're not dangerous," said, keeping my voice soft and calm so that hopefully I sounded rational. "We're not crazy. And we're not here to hurt you or anyone. I just need—"

"Holy water," he said and cleared his throat as if it had gone bone dry.

"I figure that will get rid of whatever's in the house," I told him, which wasn't the God's honest truth, but close enough.

"Well—I suppose—it wouldn't hurt to give you a vial—"

"No, not a vial, Father. Sorry, but I need more than that."

"How much do you need?" He blinked, pushed up his glasses. They slid more often now as perspiration broke out on his face.

I drew a deep breath. "Thirty gallons."

"Thirty—did you say thirty *gallons*?"

"Would that be a problem? Because I have the water out there in the car, in the trunk." I pulled the pages I had printed from the internet out of my pocket. Once again I made Father D'Arcy jump, as if he had expected me to pull out a gun instead of a wad of paper. I felt badly about that but plunged ahead. "I got this off of my Google search," I told him. "It says here that holy water can only be disposed of through the ground, and I promise you that's exactly what'll happen to it. I just want to put it in the ground around the property. I promise that we'll treat it with total reverence. But I need it. I really *really* need it. So I'm begging you, Father. If that's what it takes, I'll beg for it."

Father D'Arcy looked at Trojan, then at me, as if making a quick assessment. I could tell by his expression that he was considering my request as the best way to get rid of us. If you're confronted with lunatics, the best thing to do is humor them. So you give them a few gallons of holy water, so what? We were even supplying the water. Such a deal. "You just want me to bless the water?"

"That's it."

"What if you need more?"

"I won't need to bother you again. See what it says here." I showed him the page of information but he didn't look. Maybe he was afraid to take his eyes off us. "Although I guess you already know this, sorry. But it says you can replenish the water provided you add less water to the original than what you have left."

"They — they have all that on the internet, do they?"

"Amazing, huh?" I grinned but quickly sobered because I wasn't sure whether he was going to see a genuine smile or a wolfish leer. "I take it that if I go down a gallon, I can add a gallon to the remaining four in the jug and it'll be just as holy."

"Yes," the priest confirmed. He tried to draw his own mouth into a smile but it was pained. "Cool, huh?" he said lightly.

"So — what do you need, a book or something?"

"A book. Yes. From my office." He indicated a door just to the left behind him that I remembered led to the sacristy, the place where all the ritual stuff was stored.

"Okay," I said, knowing there was no way on earth we could let him go there alone and be given a chance to use a phone. I took a step to indicate that we were going with him. He wet his lips and nodded.

Inside the small room were books, a closet for vestments and the sacrarium—the special sink with a pipe that bypassed the sewer. Unlike an ordinary sink, it piped straight into the earth. Nonna told me it was used to preserve the dignity of sacred things that can no longer be used. For instance, the sacred vessels used in communion are rinsed there so that no particle of the consecrated Host or drop of the Precious Blood ends up in the sewer. After all, you can't have pieces of Jesus ending up in a septic tank. Father D'Arcy went to the shelf and pulled off a hefty brown leatherette book (easily an 800-pager) with a silver cross and the title "Book of Blessings" on the front. The priest cradled it in his arm and faced us. "Show me the water," he said.

When we got to the parking lot, Father D'Arcy beckoned to Albert who ambled over, once again pulling off his straw hat and wiping the sweat from his brow. "Why don't you take a break, Albert?" he said with a smile. "Can't have our master gardener collapsing from the heat, now can we?"

"I ain't bothered by it," Albert said, eying us.

"Well, indulge me and take a break anyway," the priest said lightly. "Good help is hard to find, you know."

Albert hesitated, but then shrugged and ambled toward the long white building toward the back of the church. When he was gone, Trojan popped open the back of the Tahoe, showing Father D'Arcy the six five-gallon bottles in the back.

"Holy water from Wal-Mart?" the priest asked. Without waiting for an answer, he opened the book of blessings. He placed his hand on one of the bottles and as he intoned the blessing, he touched each one in turn.

"I exorcise thee in the name of God the Father almighty, and in the name of Jesus Christ His Son, our Lord, and in the power of the Holy Ghost, that you may be able to put to flight all the power of the enemy, and be able to root out and supplant that enemy and his apostate angels; through the power of our Lord Jesus Christ, who will come to judge the living and the dead and the world by fire."

I glanced at Trojan who was watching the ritual intently. Father D'Arcy switched to Latin. "Deus, qui ad salutem humani generis maxima quæque sacramenta in aquarum substantia condidisti...."

I had no idea what he was saying, but it sounded impressive as hell. If I were a demon, I would be scared shitless by all those high-sounded words. Maybe that's why the Catholic Church used Latin for so long.

He then repeated the prayer in English, touching each bottle of water as he did so. " — pour down the power of your blessing into this element, prepared by many purifications."

He paused there. Of course the water had not been purified except by some factory operated by Wal-Mart, but the hesitation was only momentary. "May this your creation be a vessel of divine grace to dispel demons — "

(A pause again. I think maybe he had forgotten that some Catholic blessings did speak of demons and that he was a little surprised to see that term *demon* just pop up in his blessing like that.)

"—and sicknesses, so that everything that it is sprinkled on in the homes and buildings of the faithful will be rid of all unclean and harmful things." He took another breath and a quick look at me, but I just nodded. I had no idea that the ritual spoke so well to my need. I certainly was about to go up against unclean and harmful things.

"Let no pestilent spirit, no corrupting atmosphere, remain in those places: may all the schemes of the hidden enemy be dispelled. Let whatever might trouble the safety and peace of those who live here be put to flight by this water, so that health, gotten by calling Your holy name, may be made secure against all attacks. Through the Lord, amen."

Father D'Arcy stepped back and closed his book. He looked at me again and nodded his head. Trojan closed the hatch.

"Thanks, Father," I said. I would have offered my hand to shake but he clutched the book and didn't appear to want any more physical contact with me.

"God bless you and keep you, my son," the priest said, but then his boyish cheeks colored as if he realized how odd it sounded for someone maybe three or four years older than I was to be calling me *son*. But as for me, I was glad for his blessing. When you might only have a few days to live, it seemed like a good idea to take all the help you could get.

Trojan's Campsite
July 20, Much Later_____

"What are you doing here? Where have you been all day?"

It was a surprise to me to find Lorraine's car parked in front of Trojan's tent when we finally made it back to his campsite. (I thought she'd promised not to come around me!) I'd been so caught up with preparations for what I was coming to think of as the Big Showdown I hadn't even thought about Lorraine. And for me not to think about her — well, I guess that tells you where my mind was. "Carl just said you had taken the day off."

"Troj and I had to run some errands," I told her, making her frown. Even so, her disapproval made her dimples pop out and a part of me started to melt, just like it always did when I was face-to-face with adorable Lorraine. Only this time I couldn't afford to melt or waste time — even though that was a helluva way to think about being with her, as a waste of time.

"Errands? What kind of errands? I would've taken you."

"And leave Carl in the lurch?" I took her arm, a gesture that I hoped would convey to her the seriousness of what I was about to say. "Besides, weren't you sort supposed to keep your distance? I have to deal with those—those things in the house, Lorraine. I have to get rid of them. By myself. With Trojan's help," I added.

"What did you do? Pick up a few aerosol bottles of 'Demon-Rid' at Wal-Mart?"

I could understand her sarcasm—I'd hurt her by not including her, but how could I? The expression on my face must have touched her, though, because I saw her soften. "Don't shut me out, David. We're in this together, remember?"

"No, Lorraine. I've already told you, we can't be in this together. If I have to worry about you getting hurt, I won't be able to function, and I have to have my wits about me. Please—what I really need you to do is stay away from me until Tuesday."

"What happens on Tuesday?"

"It'll be over by Tuesday."

"Because—?"

"Because on Monday I'm having it out with whatever evil things are in that house. Not just me. Trojan and me together. We're going to destroy whatever's in there and set the souls of our friends free."

"You know how to do that?"

"I have a pretty good idea." I didn't say anything else even though I could tell that Lorraine was waiting for me to give her a detailed account of exactly how I planned to accomplish this monumental feat. After a minute of silence she figured I wasn't about to say more about and just sighed her frustration at being left out of the loop.

"Why Monday?" she asked, no doubt thinking that there was some special phase of the moon or that Mondays were especially good days for vanquishing demons or something.

I shrugged. I was lying to her, of course. My plan was to have The Big Showdown on Sunday, not Monday. But I knew her. I knew she would be tempted to sneak over to the house and help me. So I figured it would be best if she did her sneaking the day after everything had gone down. "Trojan and I have some preparations to make—we need another day to get ready. I don't want to put it off too long, though. God knows those things might get stronger over time. We figure we could be ready by Monday. Otherwise, there's no particular reason why Monday is better than any other day. The sooner the better, that's all."

Lorraine nodded and I was glad she had bought it. "Can't I help you prepare?"

"You can help me best by just staying away. If I can know for sure you're safe, that'll help me—emotionally, at least."

"I want to help, David," she said with that no-nonsense tone in her voice.

"I know, Lorraine. I know." I pulled her close, hugged her, kissed her softly. "Just say a prayer."

"Seriously?"

"Lorraine, if there are such evil things in this world, doesn't it stand to reason that there are godly things, too? I don't know the particulars of God and I suppose that doesn't matter. I don't know if He's one being or three beings or a hundred beings, whether He's a guy with a long white beard, or has six arms or is an animal spirit. I don't care if He's everywhere or housed inside a rock. I just know there has to be something, some Supreme Being out there. Because if there wasn't, then those evil things — that I know exist — would be controlling this world and making it into one big hell hole. The fact that they aren't, that Eblis is trying to get control instead of having control, tells me that something or someone is keeping them in their place — mostly. So yeah, say a prayer, and I'm going to believe that someone or something will hear it."

"Please, please be careful," she whispered in my ear.

"I'll see you on Tuesday," I told her. The odd thing is, she didn't ask me to promise her that.

I waved as she drove down the rutted path back to the highway.

"The plan is still to do this thing tomorrow, though, right?" Trojan asked me. I nodded and he gave me a half-smile. "I figured as much."

"Let's get the stuff out of the car and go over the plan."

After leaving St. Elizabeth's and poor Father D'Arcy, Trojan and I headed back to the offices of Wakulla Wood. While waiting for the last shift to knock off, we had an early dinner, then got into the workshop by 5:15. I few people were still around, putting in a little overtime, but they just acknowledged Trojan and went about their business.

Having a place to work that was stocked with the right equipment definitely made our task easier. We drilled tiny holes in half the caps, cut the fuses, opened every one of those shotgun shells, then soldered one cap onto each pipe. After inserting the fuses and filling the pipes with the gunpowder we'd liberated from the shells, we soldered on the remaining caps. Within two hours we'd assembled six devilishly simple, devilishly destructive pipe bombs. We stopped at a gas station and filled the gas cans, then headed for Trojan's campsite. On the way back I asked him about the plan for later. After the Big Showdown.

"You have the demolition team set up?"

Trojan nodded. "I told the fellow I know over in Building Regulations—Hake Hurley his name is—that it seemed to me the house was going to have to come down and he said he'd come look at it later in the week. I tell you, Hake was mighty puzzled how a new house like that could have gone to pot so quick, but I told him I'd had a problem with vandals and he seemed to buy it."

"And he's going to bury the rubble, right?"

"Right. He thought that was a tad weird, too, but I told him it would be cheaper than having it all hauled off. And Hake's all for saving money."

"And the blessing of the site?"

"My granddaughter's going to help me with that one. She likes all that witchy stuff. Told her we were going to be breaking a curse."

I nodded. At least everything seemed to be in place. Including the back-up in case something happened to me.

Of course, even the best plans always had glitches. Wondering about what glitch was going to come along to mess up ours made me silent for the rest of the ride.

After Lorraine left, I got the wheelbarrow Trojan now had stashed behind his tent and put three jugs of water into it. "Let's go," I said and I hefted the handles and maneuvered the barrow unsteadily through the scrub bushes. It was a good thing I'd already worn a rut with my feet; even so, the going wasn't easy. By the time we got to the house, I was huffing and puffing. At the edge of the property I put down the barrow and went to the shed behind Casa de Almas and retrieved two buckets. "What's up with those?" Trojan asked me as I brought them back to his campsite.

"Help me fill them with one of the jugs."

"The holy water?"

"Yeah, see, everything I've read on the internet about dealing with the paranormal says that you need to create a safe circle in which to work. We're going to draw a circle around the house with this water."

"But those demon things will be inside the circle," Trojan countered.

"That's true, but they won't be able to call for help, so to speak."

"You mean Eblis."

"Yes, and whoever or whatever he has working for him. We know that Parker's on his payroll, as well as those three girls and probably thousands of others for all we know. If we put a barrier between the house and the outside world, at least the cavalry won't be able to come in at the last minute."

"Good thinking. How'd you get to be so smart?"

"Educated at Google University."

Trojan and I filled the buckets, left the two other jugs in the wheelbarrow, and headed toward the house. "We better work fast. Just in case those things can sense what we're doing, I don't want Eblis showing up before we're done."

As we got to the closer to the house, my attention was drawn to Trojan who had stopped in his tracks. I saw him wince. "What's wrong? Is the house getting to you?"

"Just a twinge."

But I felt it was more than that. In my zeal to prepare for the Big Showdown, I'd forgotten that the house had a hold on Trojan and that it could hurt him. He tried to mask the pain it was inflicting on him, but I knew him too well to buy the old just a twinge routine. I nodded toward the buckets. "Think a little anointing might help?"

Trojan shrugged. "Can't hurt, I guess."

I scooped up a handful of the water from one of the buckets and splashed it on Trojan's face and chest. Now it was probably my imagination but it seemed to me that that cool water seemed to steam as it hit him. And yet—all I can say is that at the same time Trojan bared his teeth in a grimace. "Damn, it can hurt!"

"It hurts?" I asked, incredulous. After all, it was just water. Okay, so it was holy water, but that really was just water, wasn't it? I looked at my hand. My palm tingled in a weird way. Not really a painful feeling, but rather like a light electric current was playing over the skin.

Trojan gasped. "Like I ran—into a nest—of bees—"
Trojan gasped. He put down his bucket, leaned over and
braced himself with his hands on his knees.

"God, Troj—" I began, and put a hand on his
shoulder to steady him, but a few moments later he
straightened.

"It's okay—better now." He arched his back, his
face still contorted but easing. "Must be those things did
get inside me somehow. I was afraid of that." He huffed,
then blew out a final breath. "Well, one thing we've
learned. Doesn't seem as if they like that water."

I looked again at my hand. "I guess not." Was that
what that tingling meant? That a tiny piece of a demon had
wormed its way inside of me? Could it—would it—grow
there? Just lie dormant forever? Be destroyed when the
house—likely the source of its power—was destroyed? I
had no way of knowing so I wiped my hand on my jeans
and pushed the thought out of my mind for the time being.
No sense worrying about it. They were either in me or not
and there wasn't a damned thing I could do about it right
now.

"Let's not do that again, okay, son?" he said,
recovered. "I mean, I know you were trying to help, but
that definitely doesn't."

"Okay, I got it. Live and learn, huh? Sorry, Troj."

He waved his hand to let me know no apology was
necessary.

"Let's start right here. I'll circle around the back,
you do the front and we'll meet up at the other side. That
way we'll be sure to close the circle and we won't overlap.
Make sure you don't leave any gaps along the way, either.

For all we know, they could squeeze in through an opening as thin as a hair."

"They do say a whole heck of a lot of angels can dance on the head of a pin," Trojan said.

"Well, I don't want any more of those things dancing over here than are already at the party. Make the ground wet enough. Remember we can replenish the jugs provided we don't take the water levels down too low."

The buckets held about a gallon each. I decided I would add water before we refilled our buckets. I wanted to make sure Trojan had plenty of water to wet down the house once it was torn down and buried. (Well, I hoped we would have plenty of water for later on but I couldn't count on there being a *we* after tomorrow, now could I?)

Drawing the circle took close to an hour—mainly because we were being extra careful. When we finished, we both felt confident that the circle was unbroken. We made sure to step over it so we wouldn't mess it up, although our first dilemma appeared at that point.

"How will you know what to step over when the water dries?" Trojan asked.

We scrounged for a pair of rocks and marked a doorway in the circle, wetting them down so they would be part of the sacred spot. From now on, we would enter and exit the house's perimeter at that point.

"It's a pretty good-sized circle," Trojan observed.

"It's got to be. Lots of outdoors activities planned." I could tell that he was still experiencing discomfort— though whether from the demons inside him or the water, I didn't know. I jerked my head toward his campsite.

"I need to get the rest of the stuff, but why don't you go on and head back. I'm just going to refill that one water jug and store the three of them on the porch."

The sun was getting low and I knew I wouldn't have much time to collect the rest of our things and get back to the house before I was missed. Quickly I took a hose at the back of the house and refilled the jug we'd depleted, and then I hauled the three jugs of water onto the porch. After stowing them in a corner, I grabbed the wheelbarrow and headed toward Trojan's campsite, noting that the sun was getting low and burning the low clouds a fiery pink-orange. I paused for a few seconds just to marvel at its splendor.

The moment was not lost on me, you see.

We had reached the eve of the battle and I knew I might not get to see another sunset.

Casa de Almas
July 21 (aka the Big Showdown) Part I_____

I didn't think I'd sleep at all, and I certainly didn't sleep well, but for someone who might be on the verge of meeting the Grim Reaper at sunrise, I dosed surprisingly well. Maybe it's because the whole situation didn't seem quite real to me. I wondered as I lay there on the porch (and for once I hadn't invited the Captain to spend the night, knowing I needed to be as clear-headed the next morning as anyone ever needed to be) if soldiers felt as I did when they were on the eve of a big battle. Even though they knew they faced possible death, did they really believe they could die? For some reason youth gave you a feeling of invulnerability. If you were under 25, you were invincible, right? And yet there was the matter of Mojo and Whip. They hadn't been invincible, had they? Johnny and Tess, either. So what made me think I was any different?

Fact was, I was no different, yet I couldn't quite wrap my mind about the fact that I could actually die the next morning. Or worse.

When the sunrise woke me I didn't rise immediately but lay on my Wal-Mart mattress listening to the distant sounds of morning. Nothing alive willingly came near the house—no birds, no insects—but you could hear them in the distance, probably over where Trojan was camped. I guess I was trying to capture the last fragments of life—normal life—before all hell (literally) broke loose.

Only the crunch of gravel shook me out of my reverie. Turning my head, I peered through the porch railings and saw the silver Mercedes driving up, but stopping well short of the battle lines Trojan and I had drawn in the dirt. I took some deep breaths. Sort of would've preferred not to have started my morning with a visit from Harold Eblis but you got to deal the hand you're dealt, I guess, so as Eblis got out of his fancy car, I got off my mattress, picked up the water gun I had filled the night before, and walked down the steps to meet him. For a split second the image of Gary Cooper from *High Noon* crossed my mind—as he walked toward the gunslinger and stared down the barrel of that Colt 45. I hoped I had a bit of Cooper's cool bravado to throw at Eblis. One thing I noticed right off: Eblis did not cross the invisible line drawn in the dirt and I was heartened by that. (Of course he could've been playing me, too, for all I knew, but I tried not to think about that.)

"Mornin' Mr. Eblis," I said, as cordially as I could. I didn't want him to get one whiff of fear off me.

"What are you doing, David?" He spread his hands in supplication, a pained expression on his tanned face as if I had just become a major disappointment to him. "What on earth are you planning to do?" If he had added a *tsk tsk* at the end of that, it wouldn't have surprised me.

"A few housekeeping chores," I shrugged. "Gotta earn my keep, you know."

"Why do you resist us so?" he asked and his tone almost suggested that he was genuinely curious. "Your friend, Parker, has reaped tremendous rewards already and he's not a tenth as clever as you. You could go far in the organization."

"Sell my soul for a sexy babe and a hot car? No thanks."

"Such mumbo jumbo!" Eblis grinned and shook his head. "Oh, David, you are so terribly droll. 'Sell your soul,' indeed! Next you'll tell me that you think some fellow with a red cape, horns, a tail and cloven hooves will suddenly pop up and require you to sign your name on a contract in blood. This is the twenty-first century! Get with the times, David! He who you call Satan is just a businessman. That's all. It's just business."

"No offense, but I don't really like what you're selling."

"So what are you going to do?"

The fact that he was asking heartened me. It meant he couldn't read my mind and that was a great relief. Again, he could've just been playing me, but I didn't think he really would ask if he already knew the answer. "Take back what you had no right to take in the first place," I told him mildly.

He looked at me, and at the garish neon green and yellow water gun I held at my side, and grinned again.

"What's so funny?"

"Just the notion that you plan to go up against the so-called Prince of Darkness and his minions of evil beings with a—a toy!"

I raised it. "This is not a toy. This is a Master Blaster 3000," I told him and pulled the trigger. A jet of water shot from the barrel, striking him on the upper part of his chest and splashing against his cheek.

The grinning face dissolved in shock and pain as both the Guayabera shirt and the flesh underneath it began to sizzle and bubble, releasing a gout of oily black goop that gushed over the shirt's embroidery, soaking it. (I confess I stared with some disbelief that water could have inflicted so much damage!) One side of Eblis's mouth was eroding as I watched, so that his lips were skinned back from his teeth. He let out a howl of rage and agony, distorting his cool Mafioso features into a hideous mask. He clawed at the wounds I had inflicted, serving only to burn and blister his fingers when they touched the wet spots. He took a step toward me, his ruined hands clenched into fists, but he did not cross my barrier.

"You, you, little—*nothing!*" he snarled through ruined lips, mouth foaming, spraying spit and black goop. "You think you can go up against us? We will finish you, we will destroy you, and I personally will eat your soul!"

I raised the muzzle of my water gun and aimed it at his face. "But for the moment, I'm the one packing the Master Blaster 3000," I replied lightly.

Now don't think for a minute that I was (or thought I was) macho bravado Rambo or anything like that. I was about as scared (shitless, you might say) as I have ever been. The fact is, I was shivering inside like a

willow in a windstorm. It's just that I wasn't about to give
Eblis the satisfaction of seeing how badly he terrified me.
And now I knew for sure that he wasn't able to read minds
or he would've known that I had loaded my super soaker
with holy water (and known that he was scaring me
witless).

He glared at me, let about another unintelligible
roar of fury and frustration, but then reined in his wrath,
turned and stomped back to the Mercedes, his boot heels
pounding holes in the dirt with each irate step. "When I
come back, you will be so, so sorry, you stupid little boy!"
His voice was garbled, but his threat came through loud
and clear.

"Maybe," I called after him, "but right now, I'm not
the one with the hole in my chest." At that moment I
regretted not shooting him again and I wondered whether
my Master Blaster 3000 held enough water to just dissolve
him completely. I guessed not—that would have been way
too easy—but I probably should have given it a shot. (Bad
pun, I know.) The Mercedes' engine roared, spun its tires
as it shot backwards and slued around, then peeled out of
the driveway and went screaming back to the highway. I
watched it for a moment with a sense of disbelief. I pitied
the sheriff's deputy who pulled him over for speeding!

And then that feeling was immediately replaced
with a deep sense of dread. A man (or being) like Eblis
wasn't the sort to make idle threats. I couldn't even
imagine what he was planning to do to me, but I knew
when it happened, it would be bad. You've heard the term
frozen with fear? Well, I sure know what it means now. I

must've stood there several minutes just like that. Frozen with fear. And then a familiar voice snapped me out of it.

"You sure gave him what-for!"

I looked over toward the source of that voice with a mixture of joy, relief, and dismay. "You shouldn't be here, Troj," I said. "You know what this house can do to you."

"Of course I should be here," he replied, coming through our makeshift doorway and stepping over the line that was invisible to us but obviously all too visible to Eblis and his clan.

"But you know what the house…"

"Son, I'm not senile. I heard you the first time, and believe me, I know what the house can do to me. But I'm not feeling anything bad right this minute. Maybe that little baptism you performed on me gave me some immunity."

"It hurt you like hell."

"Oh, not much more than a tetanus shot. You know those things can smart like nobody's business but then they give you some protection."

"Well…." I began, not entirely convinced by that argument although I had to admit it had some logic to it.

"On top of that, you have to remember that I have friends trapped in there, too. And in a way, I'm responsible for them being there, so I'd like to help get them free, you understand?"

"Yeah, I guess if anyone should, it should be me."

"Exactly," he said with a curt nod, as if punctuating the end of that discussion.

"Okay," I relented. "But if I see so much as a twinge—"

Trojan gave me a grin. "Yeah, I know, you're the man right now, on account of you're packin' heat, aren't you, Mr. Master Blaster 3000?" I gave him a wry smile in return. "Besides," he added, "some of those pieces of furniture are heavy. You'll need help with them, especially the sofa and beds." Trojan stood there for a moment, hands on his hips, regarding the doorway with a creased brow. "Lord, I remember what a struggle the movers had with those things, getting them through the door. And I don't figure we have much time, do you?"

"No, but I'm planning on doing some quick and dirty remodeling." I handed him the super soaker water gun and went up to the porch. There I had stashed the long-handled axe which I now hefted. I looked back at Trojan, standing there like a sentry with his neon green and yellow squirt gun and grinned. "Oh, man, is this ever going to feel good."

First I opened the door and hit the hinges with the back of the axe head, knocking them loose. The door teetered and I pushed it out of my way, letting it fall with a hearty boom onto the porch. I didn't care if I was making enough noise to wake the dead (or the undead, or however you would refer to demons). I didn't delude myself into thinking that they didn't know that I was there and that I had some really bad intentions where they were concerned.

Working at the Springs had given my normally thin physique a hefty boost in the muscle department. Six months ago I would have struggled to lift that axe, let alone wield it with any force, but today, the combination of my more muscular frame and a psyche hell-bent on vengeance made it no more difficult than swinging a golf club. The sharp new blade bit into the door jamb, splintering the wood. Two more blows and a chunk fell to the porch floor. I attacked it with everything I had in me, and I have to admit, it felt good. Real good. I liked hitting back at something that had caused me so much pain, even if it was an inanimate (almost) object. After I had whacked off a good portion of the doorway, I paused to catch my breath and that's when I heard (or felt) the rumblings from the house. I couldn't really hear anything, not like words a person could understand, but it felt like concern. No, more than that. Distress? Dismay? A sense that something was going really wrong. Good. I was worrying them. I liked the idea of that. They probably wanted to believe I couldn't hurt them, but maybe they saw (or felt) what I'd done to Eblis and maybe, just maybe, they were a little scared that I might do the same to them. That gave me the boost to attack the other side of the door jamb and within minutes I had a hole in the house big enough to drive Eblis's Mercedes through.

From one of the jugs of holy water I filled both buckets. "Now what?" Trojan asked me, joining me on the porch. I studied his face for the slightest hint of discomfort but either there was none or he was doing one damned fine job of hiding it from me. I didn't have time to consider which it was; I just had to hope for the best.

"I don't think we want to be touching that furniture, do you? Not without giving it a little anointing."

Trojan nodded as he hefted one of the buckets. "Might work. Leastwise, it'll probably give us a few minutes of protection while we haul their asses out here."

Having sat a while untended, the house gave off a musty smell, which is pretty much how it goes in Florida. Turn off the A/C a day or two and never mind the Forces of Darkness. The damned mold will take over with a vengeance. Quickly I poured some of the water in my bucket over the arms and top of the sofa—the parts we were likely to touch in moving it. Immediately a sort of foul-smelling steam came off the fabric and a sound filled the air like screws scraping across a piece of metal. I can't be sure Trojan and I actually heard that sound; maybe we only felt it. But I can tell you we heard/felt it to our core. Was it pain? Rage? Maybe both, likely both.

"They're damned mad now," Trojan said.

Together we picked up the sofa and had it out in the yard in less than five minutes. My heart was pounding less from the exertion than from worrying about how much time we had before Eblis came back with reinforcements. Was Parker still human enough to cross the barrier we'd erected? Maybe not without pain, but probably so, and if Eblis ordered him to march in here and shoot me and Trojan dead, he would do it, too. Quickly I splashed one armchair and then the other, setting off more of that foul stench and horrid screeching that gave new meaning to setting your teeth on edge. My teeth were so far on the edge by now, it's a wonder they didn't go over the brink. We threw first one chair on top of the sofa, then got the second one and added it to the pile.

"Beds," Trojan reminded me of the two bedrooms downstairs.

I nodded. "At least the mattresses and box springs. The frames can get buried with the house."

Trojan took his bucket of water and doused the edges of the mattresses—by now the cacophony in the house was head-splitting—then he and I hauled first one mattress, then the other, then one box spring, then the other, out to the pile of living room furniture. My heart was racing with fear. There was no telling where Parker was or how long it would take him to get here. I hoped he was shacked up with his pseudo-girl Jade and had turned his cell phone off. (That was probably a major infraction of the rules of business, and Parker seemed all about following orders, but I hoped anyway. After all, it's not like he was the brightest bulb in the pack.)

"What's left? The sofa bed?"

"Yeah, and a recliner upstairs and I think that's it."

"That sofa bed'll be one mother to move," Trojan said, eying the stairs to the loft. He was pretty hearty for an old guy, but I could see that the exertion was taking its toll on him. That, or the house was starting to get to him. His face had started to resemble melted chocolate and he was grimacing pretty hard.

"Watch this," I said as I bounded up the stairs with a replenished bucket of water. (By then I should have been plodding upstairs, but my glands were working overtime and there was probably enough adrenalin in my system to fuel a train.) After dousing the sofa bed, I went to one end and shoved it to the head of the stairs. Upending it, I gave it one hard push and it began to topple down the steps, taking out a few of the posts on its way down, finally stopping three-quarters of the way to the ground floor. Trojan came up the last few steps to free it by jerking it back and forth a few times until it came loose from the posts. By then I had come down to the other side and helped him pick it up and take it outside with the rest of the furniture. I ran upstairs to get the recliner which I likewise shoved down the damaged stairs. "I think that's it," I said finally, giving Trojan another glance. He nodded. I could see that the exertion of our task had really worn him down by now. "You better take a break. I can handle things from here." Trojan was breathing hard, so he offered no protest, but sat down on the front lawn, resting his arms on his knees.

From the porch I got one of the five-gallon red plastic gas jugs and doused the pile of furniture we had created. "We're doing it, Troj," I said. "We're setting our friends free. Troj?" I expected some sign of exultation from Trojan and when I got none, I looked at him. No longer sitting, Trojan was sprawled on the lawn, one knee raised as if he had just fallen over from a sit. "Troj!" I dropped the gas can and flew to his side, throwing myself down on my knees in the dust. I grasped his shoulder and shook. "Troj!" It was a struggle for him to open his eyes and his lips were stretched back from his lips in a grimace of pain. His chest heaved as if he was having trouble breathing. "Oh my god oh my god!" I dug into my pocket and took out my cell phone, but before I could dial a single number, Trojan mustered every ounce of his strength and gripped my wrist. He peered at me with a fire burning in his eyes.

"Finish…it…" he said in a raspy whisper. "Finish it *now*. Coming…they're…."

I gave him a brief nod, but still took a moment to dial 9-1-1 on my phone. I didn't wait for an answer. I knew their GPS would kick in and they could triangulate to our position even if I didn't say a word. I put the cell phone down next to him and scrambled to my feet. "Hang on, Troj. Help's coming."

I took off at a run for the porch. Something inside of Trojan, in addition to attacking him, left him with the impression that someone (or something) was on its way to stop me and that it probably was close. Back on the porch, I grabbed up our box of six pipe bombs and two Bic lighters. (When you really really need a light, you make sure you have a back-up lighter! In the movies, the hero always only has one lighter and it never works. And cell phones are never charged, either. I wasn't about to make either of those mistakes.) I stuffed one lighter into my front pocket and hurried into the house (which, by now, was a major mess and would never earn the Good Housekeeping Seal of Approval, that's for sure).

In the living room, I took out pipe bomb number one, lit it and threw it into the kitchen. I immediately retreated to a far wall, covered my ears and braced myself. For a brief moment I had the fear that I had constructed them wrong, that the internet instructions had been bogus, written as a practical joke, or that I had read them wrong. But just as my confidence in my bomb-making skills was about to take a major nose-dive, a tremendous *KABOOM!* came from the back of the house, blowing a cloud of debris—a concoction of sink porcelain, wall tile, plaster and wood splinters, shards of china, pots, pans and other junk—into the living room. The house shook and not entirely from my pipe bomb. A great screeching howl of rage filled the air and assaulted my ears (even though I still had them firmly covered) sending prickles down my spine. The noise was so bone-rattling, so sharply metallic, that it made me cringe—but only for a moment.

As I stood there clutching my box, I quickly had to duck as the angry creatures in the house caused books to fly off their shelves, aimed at my head. A vase crashed into the wall behind me. Oh those things were *mad*, as in poltergeist mad, their evil energy setting up storms of fury like tornados in the living room. A lamp was caught up in the whirlwind, then flung at my head; a picture was ripped off the wall, and thrown at me, making me have to bob and weave. Ducking low and staying on the run, I dodged the flying junk, lit another pipe bomb and threw it into one of the back bedrooms, then lit the third and tossed it into other. The concussion of the double explosions threw me to the floor and I landed on my knee, sending a spike of agony up my leg that made me gasp. A corner of a picture frame stabbed my shoulder making me cry out in pain, then a book glanced off the back of my head, momentarily stunning me, but somehow I managed to scramble back to my feet. Quickly I darted toward the stairs, lit a fourth pipe bomb and lobbed it up into the loft. A moment later it exploded, showering me with debris. The force shot the desk chair through the upper railing, splintering the wood and launching it into the air along with pieces of the computer, end tables, lamps and a flurry of pages from destroyed books. The chair landed on the floor, barely missing me, and spun around several times as if a crazed ghostly secretary was playing with it. All of a sudden the cacophony stopped and the unexpected silence made me lurch. The chair squealed to a stop. My shoulder and knee throbbed and I felt a wave of dizziness wash over me. For a moment I wondered if the book hitting my head had given me a concussion, but it was more than just being dizzy. I was incredibly weak. Tired. Completely sapped. My arms and legs felt heavy, as if my entire body had suddenly been encased in quick-drying cement. I knew I should get out, throw the last two pipe bombs and get out, and I tried to do it, honest I did. I picked up number five, but all of a sudden, the little piece of pipe felt like it weighed fifty pounds and I dropped it on the floor. I saw the chair not two feet from me and I ached to sit down. Just for a minute. Just to catch my breath and stop my head from reeling. Just so I could get back out the door.

The second I did that, of course, I knew I had made a big mistake. I mean, you already know that I've made some real doozies in my life when it came to mistakes, but this was the grand high pooh-bah of mistakes. As soon as my rear end hit the seat I heard that annoying little giggling and a thousand sharp needle pricks assaulted my thighs, butt, back and shoulders as their nasty demonic tendrils pierced my clothes and flesh, securely fastening me to the chair. Within seconds I was their prisoner, and with no energy left within me, I had no hope of pulling away.

Casa de Almas
July 21 (aka the Big Showdown) Part II_____

I know what you're thinking right about now. What a moron! He sat down in that chair? Didn't he know what that *meant*? I hope the damned demons do eat him! The idiot deserves it!

A few words in my defense, please, because hey, we've been on a long trip here together and I don't want you to be disgusted with me *now*.

I don't think I did know what that meant when I sat down. They were in me, you see? They're why I got so bone-tired, so weighed-down-with-concrete weak all of a sudden. And when I saw that chair, I was so addled that they were able to make me see it as the most wonderful, most comfortable place anyone could ever want to put their weary butt. It was like showing a man dying of thirst in the desert a beautiful green oasis with a giant cool blue Dasani water jug smack dab in the middle of it. To tell you the truth, I think at that moment I literally was out of my mind—or, at least, they were in it and seriously crowding me.

Anyway, whatever you're thinking about me right about now, the thing is that they probably were going to eat me eventually. So for those of you who can't forgive me for my momentary stupidity, I guess you'll get your wish.

I told you in the beginning (if you can remember back that far) that *They* had left me my eyes for the purpose (I'm guessing) of seeing something not-so-good. Maybe they planned to let part of me continue to exist until Lorraine got here on Monday and then dissolve what was left of me before her eyes. My punishment for doing serious damage to *them* and to their head honcho Eblis would be to have to watch the horror on her face as I melted away to skin. Yeah, that would be just like them, wouldn't it? Make me suffer by watching her suffering.

Since I'm still thinking, (mostly grim thoughts, it's true) it's obvious that they also left me my brain for the time being (infected though it is at the moment). And an ear. I have at least one ear left. I know this because I hear a sound, a sound like a rumbling, like distant thunder, but I know it isn't that. It's too steady, too continuous. Thunder comes and goes. This just comes and comes and comes.

The sound isn't too close yet, but it sounds big. Something with an engine, yes. Nothing natural. Mechanical. Definitely a motor. Seems to have too much bass in it to be a car or even a pickup truck. But then maybe sound from the highway is amplified in here, in this hell hole in which I'm sitting, or maybe it's a convoy of logging trucks that just happen to be going by, or maybe my hearing was damaged by the pipe bombs going off. The only bad thing was that it was too early for the demolition team Trojan had lined up to take down the house. So did Eblis get some house-moving company to come in here on the spur of the moment to haul what's left of Casa de Almas to another location? Was that what I was hearing? Or were they just teasing me with some sound of their own making? (You know how much they like their fun!) There was no way to tell.

And then I remembered the pile of furniture, doused with gasoline but—unlit.

Now the fire would never be lit, the souls of our friends and loved ones would never be released. Eblis would probably clean it up, douse it with Febreze fabric refresher, and stick it back in Casa de Almas as soon as the house healed itself or someone came into to fix the damage I'd inflicted. All clean and smelling of spring flowers and ready to suck down some more souls into its insatiable maw.

My life would be over and there would be nothing to show for it. Not one damned good deed. Not even something as simple as lighting a match.

I felt a tear slide down my cheek.

A tear? Down my cheek?

So I was wrong about having been mostly absorbed as yet. I was held fast in the chair, that's true, but apparently I still had my eyes (and lids—I was wrong about that, too, because I was able to blink) and my ears and my brain— and my cheeks. I glanced down expecting to see just a slick of skin draped over the Naugahyde of the desk chair, but no! There were still legs with muscles and bones there, and arms, too, with hands and fingers—glued to the chair, yes, but still there. And if they were there, then likely I still had a chest, an abdomen—and all my other body parts.

But what good was still being intact if I was held fast as if I had been superglued to the bonded leather upholstery and had no chance of escape? I had no physical strength whatsoever and even my will seemed sapped, as if they were tapping into my soul and robbing me of my desire to live.

Where was the ambulance that was supposed to rescue Trojan? I didn't know how much time had passed—maybe not enough to get a rescue team over here from Crawfordville. When they got here, would he be able to tell them of my peril inside the house? In time to rescue me, as well? Maybe yes, maybe no, but right now I was thinking—likely *no*. At the first howl of the sirens, the demons would suck me into the chair like soda through a straw. One good slurp and it would be goodbye David Fouraker.

It was then, when I was in what my father would have called a deep blue funk—some term from back in the dark ages of the '60s—contemplating my imminent demise by being sucked into the maw of the Prince of Darkness—that I saw him.

I don't know how long he'd been there—probably not long since my rampage through Casa de Almas had not ended more than a short time before—though you tend not to notice a ten-pound fur ball when bombs are exploding and poltergeists are throwing everything including the kitchen sink at you. But I saw him now. And he seemed a lot bigger than the two sacks of sugar he added up to. Maybe that was because his fur had bristled out turning him into a feline porcupine, or maybe because I was seeing him through the eyes of my captors and to them he seemed larger than life. I knew they feared him. I didn't know why they feared him, but I knew They did. Maybe because they knew they couldn't control him. At any rate, there he was, a one-cat cavalry unit.

Squint.

Like I said, at that moment he didn't look a whole lot like the old Squint who hung around Trojan's campsite. His eyes were full of green fire and he seemed enormous, some supernatural catlike creature with only the barest resemblance to the family pet. His lips were peeled back from his sharp cat teeth and the inside of his mouth was blood red. He alternately hissed and growled, and eyed me in a very unsettling way.

In two leaps he was on me. Needle-sharp claws raked my cheek leaving behind four bleeding, burning gouges that made me gasp. He bit down on my shoulder, then my upper arm, all the while digging those white-hot claws into my flesh until I let out a scream of such agony at first I didn't even realize it was me that had made such an ungodly sound. My adrenal gland must have wrung out the last drop of flight hormone, because the weakness that had imprisoned me dissolved just long enough for me to wrench myself from the chair in a desperate attempt to flee my tormentor. Squint jumped to the floor and out of my way.

Suddenly my backside from my shoulders to my knees screamed with a pain so intense I thought I might black out until my old pal Squint bit me again on my ankle and jolted me back to my senses. The fact is, I was on fire.

Not literally on fire, but that's how I felt. As if someone
had just given me a blast with a flame thrower. On top of
that, I could feel something warm and wet oozing down
my back. I staggered toward the door and freedom, only
then looking down first at my left arm then the right, and
seeing the blood that dripped from my fingers.

Ironic, isn't it? Escape the Forces of Darkness only
to bleed to death on the front porch.

How I made it across the room and out the
smashed doorway I don't know. I didn't bother with the
last two pipe bombs. The house was in shambles—enough
for any demolition team to deem it unsafe for habitation
unless Eblis rescued it before they could reduce it to
rubble. Whatever happened in that regard was out of my
control so I shoved worrying about it aside. One or the
other would get there first and that was a matter of Fate or
Destiny or God's Will or whatever. My concern now was,
and had to be, the unlit pyre of furniture in the yard.

That, and Trojan.

Trojan lay where I had left him, one knee cocked.
He was ashen, the melted chocolate of his face having
given way to the way chocolate looks when you've had it
in the refrigerator too long. I looked at him, then at the pile
of furniture.

Furniture. Trojan.

Help was on the way for Trojan (or so I hoped) and
there was no one else who was going to set fire to the pile
of sofas, chairs and bedding but me. I couldn't do anything
for Trojan but hold his hand and whisper words of
comfort, and I knew what he would want me to do. (And
it wasn't that.) I staggered down the porch steps, each foot-

step agonizingly slow, and excruciatingly painful. My sneakers scraped the floorboards while my hips, knees and thighs screamed like banshees. The barest movement (and you have to move a lot to get down stairs and cross a yard) caused waves of agony to wash over me and it was a struggle to remain conscious. (I think Squint must have known that because he kept doing figure eights around me, monitoring my state of consciousness and being ready to sink his teeth into my ankle again should it even appear as if I was on the verge of passing out.)

A few pages from the ruined books in Trojan's old library had blown out into the yard. With great effort I bent and retrieved two of the sheets, rolling and crushing them into a crude torch that became smeared with my blood. I managed to dig my spare Bic lighter out of my front pocket despite the fact that it also was slick with my blood. (The other one had been lost somewhere in the house.) My blood seemed to be everywhere; even the air had taken on a sweet metallic smell. I lit the torch, hobbled to the pile, and when the pages were burning brightly, I threw it, trying to ignore the stabbing pain in my shoulder as I did so. Immediately I sank down onto my knees, and as the gasoline ignited, sending a bright bloom of fire twenty feet into the air, I collapsed, falling face down in the dust.

Somehow, with great effort, I managed to turn my head. Partly that was to keep from suffocating with a snootful of Wakulla County dirt (as it was, there was grit in my mouth, nose and eyes), but mostly it was because I wanted to watch the pyre burn.

The heat from the bonfire washed over me like a fiery tsunami and my eyes burned and watered from the flames and the smoke. Maybe I was too close to the fire for safety, but I was in no condition to move. At that point, even crawling would have been out of the question. Besides, the heat felt cleansing. Great gouts of black smoke began to boil from the pyre and if my 9-1-1 call hadn't roused the rescue squad, that would surely do it. I bet they could see that column of thick oily smoke for twenty miles. From somewhere in the distance I thought I heard sirens, but nothing could wrench my attention from watching that pile of furniture burn to cinders.

And as I watched, I saw something I swear was not a hallucination.

First, a great white light seemed to part the sky. It was so bright, you'd think it should be blinding, but there was no discomfort in looking at it. To the contrary, it seemed to radiate peace. (That sounds sappy, I know, but that's how it was.) I knew then that I must be dying, for it seemed very much like that amazing white light those who'd had near-death experiences had witnessed, and I don't think I could've seen it had I not been so close to death myself. For a moment I felt sorry about dying — leaving behind my adorable Lorraine who I'd hoped to build a life with, my friend Trojan, my parents. But the sorrow was very brief and dissolved in the glow of that beautiful light. And then I saw them. No, not *Them*... the *Others*.

Thin tendrils of the purest white smoke threaded out from beneath the heavy black layer and began to waft skyward where they finally disappeared into the light. With the sun fully up, I would not have seen them at all were it not for the inky backdrop, but I swear they were there. And it wasn't just a matter of seeing them, I could feel them, too. Insubstantial as they were, what seemed to radiate from them was a feeling of pure joy and love.

How many were there?

I think I counted eight.

In my heart, I knew what they were. Who they were. The Lost Ones.

You believe me, right? You know, too—right?

I watched until the last of them had gone, then I closed my eyes and gave myself over to the darkness without regrets.

Former Site of Casa de Almas
October 19
What You'd Call the Epilogue_____

To say I felt uneasy about pulling my truck into the driveway of that house after all the shit that had gone down there would be the understatement of the decade. But there was unfinished business that had to be taken care of and there wasn't anyone else to do it—not rightfully so, anyway. I had to finish what I'd started, just to make sure it was done right. And I wasn't alone, so there was that.

Yeah, you read the date right. *October.* So right about now you're wondering what happened to August and September, right? It's only natural to want closure, to want to see the last ends tied up and all. Okay, I guess I owe you that for sticking around so long, so here's what happened after the Big Showdown.

First of all, I can't tell you a damned thing (firsthand, leastwise) about what happened between July 21 and August 12 because I don't know. Everything I know about those three weeks or so was related to me. The first thing I remember after the Big Showdown was seeing a face that looked like a human version of Uga, the bulldog mascot from the University of Georgia, peering down at me. I also remember saying (though I didn't mean to say it out loud) "So I *did* die, only I went to hell, right?" That's not the sort of thing you want to say to a nurse, to a person who has the authority to wield hypodermic needles, even if she is plug ugly. I swear from that day on she took a helluva lot of pleasure out of administering shots to me. After that I was surrounded by more friendly faces. It seems that my parents and Lorraine bonded while I was floating somewhere in la-la land and Mom (bless her for this) insisted that Lorraine be the first one to go in and visit me when I regained consciousness. There's no better medicine than seeing the adorable face of your girl and I guess Mom knew that.

Lorraine told me that I had been so badly injured that I'd been Lifeflighted to Shands Hospital in Gainesville. The doctors were afraid that the pain of my injuries literally would kill me so they made the decision to put me into a drug-induced coma until I had healed enough to tolerate it. I didn't know a person really could die of pain, but apparently it's so stressful on a body that you can — and there's only so much morphine a body can tolerate. So when I woke up on August 12, it was a planned wake-up call.

I had lost a lot of blood and a lot of skin and it took a number of surgeries to sew me back together. My entire backside was going to look like a patchwork quilt (made by a really lousy seamstress) ala Trojan. I probably could have opted for more surgeries to make me prettier but when I talked it over with Lorraine, she convinced me to leave things as they were.

"I never was one get a kick out of looking at a man's butt," she told me. "And I plan to interact mostly with your front side." The scars would be ugly but if she didn't care, well, I wasn't out to win any beauty contests.

"How's Trojan?" I asked her and the cloud that came into her eyes spoke volumes. "No," I said—the only thing I could say. "Oh, no."

"I'm sorry, David," she said, taking my hand. Her beautiful eyes got teary.

Since I had been unable to go to the funeral, Lorraine went to represent both of us. She said that half of Wakulla County and a whole lot of folks from as far away as the Carolinas had turned out for Trojan's send-off and I was glad that his family had the comfort of knowing that their patriarch had been so well loved.

As for me, although I felt sad over the loss of my friend, two things kept me from being entirely despondent. One, I had first-hand knowledge that our souls survive after death so I knew Trojan was out there, somewhere, and probably in even better shape than I was at the moment. And two, I knew that he was with his beloved Linetta. (And maybe also with the friends he had helped set free that day.) Believe me, nothing's more comforting than knowing that death isn't the end, that there's no kerplunk bye-bye so-long all gone about it.

"And Squint?" I asked her. "Is he okay?"

Lorraine smiled at that question and wiped her eyes. "The Reynolds family—that's Trojan's daughter—was going to take him, even though they have two cats already, but when I went to their home after the service, Squint was all over me like he wanted to be with me. Or us. They asked me if I wanted him and I said yes. I figured you'd be okay with that, though why he was so—so clingy—I don't know."

"I'm glad you have him," I said and meant it. He would keep Lorraine safe.

That was all the news I got that day because I was still a little out of it and Mom and Dad wanted a turn to see their boy, so it wasn't until August 13 that Lorraine was able to fill me in on more of what I'd missed.

First of all, Denny was able to go back to work at **Alice's Eats** and though he was a little skittish about working the grill, after a day or two Carl managed to convince him that what had happened to him was just a fluke that couldn't happen again. The gal, Kathy, who had filled in for Denny really didn't care for cooking and was happy to take on Lorraine's waitressing duties. That left them without a bus boy (me) but the Tressels (Martha and Hubert—remember them from way back at the beginning of my story?) who owned the grocery store next door had a nephew looking for a job and he wasn't too choosy. So I expect everything worked out okay at the diner.

Dad was able to give me news about my legal situation which obviously had been put on hold what with me being nearly skinned alive and all. The judge decided that my community service sentence could be fulfilled with time served so I didn't need to worry about going back to the Springs. (I think my doctor convinced the judge that a guy who has been sewn back together and needs physical therapy isn't a good candidate for doing hard physical labor.) Ranger Zeke had been sorry to see me go, but had written me a great letter of recommendation and said he expected me to earn my ranger hat one day.

The judge also moved my probation to Lake County so I could recuperate at my parents' house once I was released from the hospital. While I was still laid up Mom, Dad and Lorraine met with my dean at FSU and arranged for me to finish my coursework on line so that I could graduate at the end of winter semester. What a team! Oh, yeah, and I got my truck back (Dad forgave my loan for the impound fees and all) and I was deemed eligible for a hardship license until my regular one was no longer suspended.

Of course the disappearances of Mojo, Whip, Johnny and Tess were never resolved; those cases went cold as a witch's you-know-what and unfortunately that's how they would stay. I hated that their families would never know what happened to them; believe me when I tell you how bad I felt about that. But I didn't feel like I could tell anyone the truth without getting some serious time in the asylum. They did eventually locate Johnny's car some-where out in Arizona. I suspect Eblis and his cronies hot-wired it and stuck it out there just to make everyone who cared about Johnny and the others crazy. Evil loves mental torture like that.

Now all that is sort of mundane crap but I figured you'd want to know, so there it is. The really juicy stuff involves Parker.

Apparently I wasn't totally out of it when para-medics arrived the day of the Big Showdown. (Actually, EMTs made up only a small portion of the responders who rushed to the scene that day. The fire department, the county sheriff's department and an ambulance crew swarmed all over the place and I bet they had a helluva a time trying to figure out what happened there, what with me half skinned, the house with gaping holes where bombs had gone off, a raging bonfire, and a old black man lying dead on the lawn. I guess there are times when it's good to be unconscious!)

Lorraine told me that before I was loaded onto a stretcher, I said, "Parker" to one of the EMTs. I don't know why I said that. Maybe I had glimpsed his car coming down the driveway just before I collapsed and just don't remember, or maybe he was just in my mind as the one person Eblis could send to try and stop me. I don't know for sure. But you can believe that the Wakulla County law enforcers definitely wanted a name on which to pin all that mayhem so when I said "Parker" they were all over him like Tar Baby was all over Br'er Rabbit. It didn't take long for them to track down who he was, although where he was was another matter. When he heard that sheriff's deputies were looking for him, Parker apparently tried to get out of Dodge with his gal pal and ended up crashing his beautiful bright yellow car into a pine tree along Route 98 down by the coast. Lorraine handed me the newspaper article on Parker and the crash and that was what was really interesting.

A photo of Parker that accompanied the story — taken the day of the accident — showed him back to the way he had been at the beginning of the summer before Eblis had given him a make-over: greasy blond hair, glasses, acne blooming all over his cheeks, chin and throat.

The photo showed him with his "companion," a middle-aged, flabby hooker named Jade with stringy hair, sporting fishnet stockings, a miniskirt and makeup that looked like it had been applied to her face with a trowel. The car was a mess—almost unrecognizable as the gorgeous hot rod he'd been tooling around North Florida in—and a deputy was quoted as saying, "An old rust bucket like that had no business even being on the road."

Apparently one of the balding tires had blown out, throwing the vehicle into a tailspin that ended up with it crashing nose first into the tree. Jade had only been banged up, but Parker had broken his right leg in three places, no doubt in part because he had used it to apply the brakes (that could have failed, who knows?) It was obvious that all the perks Parker had earned working for Eblis had been suddenly revoked because of his inability to stop my rampage (and losing all those souls on top of it). Well, that's business for you.

Although Parker had the opportunity to be involved in the mayhem at the house, he didn't have much of a motive and there was no way to say whether he had the means, so while he remained a person of interest and was questioned by deputies who visited him in the hospital, he was never arrested. I suspect the loss of his job with Eblis (and consequently having no money, a fucked up complexion, no car, no girlfriend, and a permanent limp) was probably punishment enough.

At the end of August they released me from the hospital and I went to begin my recuperation in Lake City with my parents while Lorraine started classes as a veterinary assistant down in Gainesville. (We were an hour apart—not a bad commute until I healed up enough to join her.) Then at the beginning of September I received a letter (on impressively formal cream-colored stationery) from Copeland, Reed & Marley, Attorneys at Law, requesting my presence at the reading of Trojan Barnes's will on Friday, October 19 at two in the afternoon down in Wakulla County.

On the morning of that day, Lorraine picked me up from my parents' house and we drove together to the attorneys' offices. Natasha and Jefferson were already there when we arrived and after greetings they wanted to know how I—and we—were doing.

"Recovering, though I still have a little trouble sitting for long periods of time," I told her. "You never realize how much you count on your butt until part of it goes missing." Suddenly I felt like an awkward schoolboy called on to deliver a lecture. "So—why exactly am I here?" I asked Trojan's daughter.

"Well, obviously Dad remembered you in his will."

"I don't see why he'd do a thing like that. I feel very weird about this."

She touched my arm and smiled. "Well, don't. My Dad was about as sound of mind as they come, and if he put you in his will, then he believed you should be there. Jeff and I have no problem with that."

One of the trio of lawyers came in—I learned through introductions that he was Mr. Marley—and got right down to business. "Basically, Mr. Fouraker," he began, "for your part in this, Mr. Barnes left you his tent, the contents of said tent, and the seventy-four acres that it's sitting on."

I was astounded. "I—that's not right. That land belongs to his family." I turned to Natasha and Jeff. "I want you to take it. I want to give it to you." (Now I confess I wasn't being entirely altruistic because there was no way on earth I would want to spend any more time in Wakulla County than I had to, so the idea of owning property there was ridiculous. On the other hand, I did believe the land belonged in the Barnes-Reynolds family.)

Natasha raised her hand to cut me off. "I won't hear of it. Dad wanted you to have it. However," she added, eying me and Lorraine and giving us a knowing look, "I suspect you two might one day be needing a nest egg, so how about if we buy it from you? We'll give you a fair price."

I hesitated, but looked over at Lorraine who nodded and smiled. "Okay," I told Natasha. "It's a deal, provided you make it a fair price to you."

"That land is loaded with prime timber," Jeff told me. "We can easily get back our investment and then some."

So that's what we did. And after we left the lawyers' offices, Lorraine and I went over to Trojan's campsite. It gave me pause to stand there and see the tent I knew to be empty. I expected him to be sitting there in his camp chair, sipping on his RC and offering me a cola from his ever-present cooler. Today there was no Trojan, no pop of the soda can's tab; just the sound of insects buzzing, birds twitting, a good breeze kicking through the pines and making the front flap of the tent slap against the poles. There was a severe emptiness there that lay heavily on my heart.

"You sure you want to do this?" Lorraine asked.

"No," I replied, taking a deep breath. "But it has to be done."

I told Natasha that I would like to have the tent and the camp chairs (and the solar panels that drove all that stuff were pretty cool, too), and a few pieces of other furniture, but that I wanted the rest of Trojan's personal belongings to go to her family—especially to his grand-children. Lorraine and I offered to go and pack up all the stuff and deliver it to Wakulla Wood, an offer that Natasha gratefully accepted. I think it would've been hard for her (even more than for me) to confront what had been her father's home for the past few years.

Everything that Trojan owned was easily boxed up or folded up and stowed in the bed of my truck. The empty space left after everything was packed up gave me another pang in my already sore heart and I was glad to get out of there. After we dropped off Trojan's personal belongings and said goodbye to Natasha and Jeff, we left Wakulla Wood for good with a tent, camp chairs, beds, a table, some solar panels—and three five-gallon jugs of holy water.

Lorraine and I spent the night with Gabe and Uncle Pete at the Waterin Hole and the next morning over a pancake breakfast at a local Huddle House I asked Lorraine to marry me. (I chose this day especially because it was "The Sweetest Day" --a little-known holiday that was founded around 1922 in Cleveland, Ohio by a local candy company employee and is always celebrated on the third Saturday of October. Didn't know that, did you?

Well, now you do.) Oh yeah— she said yes. As if you didn't know she would, right?

After breakfast we had one more stop to make before we could leave Wakulla County behind us forever.

So that brings us to October 20 which is where I started this wrap-up, with us driving down the dirt path to where Casa de Almas used to stand. No, Eblis didn't get the movers to come in and collect what was left of it. True to his word, Trojan had gotten the demolition guys out there right on time. (How they handled all the legal paperwork, I don't know, and frankly I don't care. I imagine Eblis's boss didn't fight the idea of tearing down the house too vigorously. They probably owned real estate all over the world—what did they care about one little insignificant building?)

Where once the house stood was now a mound of earth—a damned good sized one, too. I saw Lorraine hug herself as if she were suddenly cold. I didn't blame her. Just the site alone could give you the willies. "I'm glad it's gone," she said, then turned to me. "So what are we doing here? Is this what you call closure?"

"We have to make sure it's completely destroyed."

"All I see is dirt. How much more destroyed can it get?"

"It's *under* the dirt. They buried the evil but it's still there and I want to make sure it can't get out."

"How?"

"Help me with the water."

"We're going to drown them? With fifteen gallons of water?"

"Ten. I want to save one jug. And we're not drowning them. We're going to neutralize them. Trojan and his granddaughter were going to do it but—well, you know— Watch your step, now."

"I don't think I can trip over a mound that big," she told me with a tight smile that popped her adorable dimples.

We took buckets and filled them with water from one of the jugs. I then gave her the same instructions I had given Trojan when we'd drawn the protective circle around the house. Just as we started, I saw her bend over and I knew what she was going to do—pick up a piece of wood from the house from the ground—and I wanted to stop her but it was like slow-motion, like a dream where you want to call out a warning, want to scream at someone to stop, just *STOP* but the words stick in your throat and you can't make a sound. But just as quickly, just as she grasped the stick of wood, I found my voice.

"Don't touch that!"

Startled, Lorraine dropped it, a small piece of white wood that once had been part of the siding, no doubt. "Ouch," she frowned, examining her finger.

"What? What?" I went to her, looked at her hand, expected to see a piece bitten out of it (although no one says *Ouch* when part of their hand is missing! I know how stupid that sounds!)

"Nothing. A splinter." And she went to pull it out with her teeth (Why would she do that? To get a better grip?)

Scaring her now big time, I grasped her wrist and pushed her hand into the bucket of water. She yelped, this time out of pain not alarm, and pulled her hand out. Where the splinter had been was a caustic little bubble, as if a drop of acid had fallen on her skin. I took her wrist again, again forced her hand back into the bucket. This time she didn't cry out, and when she took out her hand, the bubble was gone, washed away.

"What the hell—?" You didn't hear Lorraine curse often, but when you did, you could be sure she was really, really upset.

"They're in the wood, Lorraine. That's why we're doing this. That's not just water. It's holy water."

"They sell holy water at Wal-Mart in five-gallon jugs?"

I sighed, but explained to her about Father D'Arcy and how I'd managed to wound Eblis with my super soaker and how Trojan and I had kept his henchmen (or man) away with our circle. After that she was full of enthusiasm for soaking those sons of bitches, and as we poured the water over the mound the ground began to roll and writhe and boil, as if a thousand enraged snakes—and not garters, either but big ugly suckers, like anacondas— were buried beneath us. We had to widen our stance to keep from being knocked down. "Be careful! Be careful!" I yelled at her, which was stupid because of course she was being careful (obviously you didn't want your butt to end up on top of ground that was moving like that), only that's what you said to someone you loved, just as a matter of course, isn't it? At once a yellowish mist began to pour from the ground, and the clamor of a hundred angry, non-human voices assaulted our ears making us screw up our faces against the attack of pure, evil noise; and then the most god-awful stench you can imagine—like sulfur and shit and vomit and decay all rolled into one terrible rotten bouquet—rose up around us making our stomachs lurch and our eyes burn.

"I'm going to be sick," Lorraine said, but she wasn't. We both just held our breaths as best we could and kept pouring the water until both jugs were empty and the ground ceased to roll, the violent, furious sounds finally died away, and the foul-smelling vapors were dispersed on the breeze.

"They're gone," I told her. "I can feel it. They're gone."

"Good riddance. And what's the last jug for?" she asked.

"Insurance."

See, I could feel that the demons in the ground were gone, but I wasn't sure why I could feel them gone. I didn't know if I had just become sensitive to them, or whether they had kindred spirits inside of me reacting to their brethren being destroyed. There might not be the seeds of evil inside me, dormant. But then again, there might be.

I was never a boy scout and I sure never would be one, but one thing I'd learned through this ordeal: it paid to be prepared.

About the Author

G.M.S. Altman has lived in Tallahassee since 1969, in Florida since 1955, is married (23 years) and has one son, Eric, 20, a tattoo artist. Altman was a 1973 graduate of Florida State University, and though a staunch Seminole, is eternally grateful to the University of Florida's Veterinary Hospital for saving Gauge, one of the Altman canines, who happily continues to sail on the Altman Ark along with another dog, two cats, two birds, two fish, and two turtles. Altman spends a well-deserved retirement endlessly writing, writing, writing.

www.ingramcontent.com/pod-product-compliance
Lightning Source LLC
Chambersburg PA
CBHW031926280626
47169CB00017BA/93